MAGE-GIFT

The ordinary young woman with the graceful white horse was—not ordinary at all. She *was* the bearer of an untrained, but major Mage-Gift; one so powerful it sheathed her in a closely wrapped, sparkling aura in his Mage-Sight, that briefly touched everyone around her with exploratory fingers she was apparently unaware of. Quenten was astonished, and surprised she hadn't caused problems with it before this. *Surely* she must have Seen power-flows, energy-levels, even the nodes that he could See, but could not use. Surely she had wondered what they were, and how could she not have been tempted to try and manipulate them? Then he recalled something; these Heralds, one and all, had mind-magic and were trained in it. If they didn't know what Mage-Talent was—it could, possibly, be mistaken for something like Sight. And if she was told that this was just another way of viewing things, that she could not actually affect them, she might not have caused any trouble.

They have no idea how close they came. If she had ever been tempted to touch something. . . .

One thing was certain; it wasn't a question of whether she could be trained or not; she *had* to be trained.

Now the question was, by whom?

WINDS OF FATE

WINDS OF FATE

Book One of The Mage Winds

MERCEDES LACKEY

DAW BOOKS, INC.

DONALD A. WOLLHEIM, FOUNDER

375 Hudson Street, New York, NY 10014

ELIZABETH R. WOLLHEIM
SHEILA E. GILBERT
PUBLISHERS

For color prints of Jody Lee's paintings, please contact:
The Cerridwen Enterprise
P.O. Box 10161
Kansas City, MO 64111
Phone: 1-800-825-1281

Interior Illustrations and maps by Larry Dixon.

All the black & white interior illustrations
in this book are available as 11″ × 14″ prints
either in a signed, open edition singly, or in
a signed and numbered portfolio from

FIREBIRD ARTS & MUSIC, INC.
P.O. Box 14785
Portland, OR 97214-9998
Phone: 1-800-752-0494

Time Line by Pat Tobin.

DAW Book Collectors No. 861

DAW Books are distributed by Penguin U.S.A.

First Paperback Printing, July 1992

7   8   9

DAW TRADEMARK REGISTERED
U.S. PAT. OFF. AND FOREIGN COUNTRIES
—MARCA REGISTRADA
HECHO EN U.S.A.

PRINTED IN THE U.S.A.

Dedicated to
the memory of
Donald A. Wollheim
A gentleman and a scholar

OFFICIAL TIMELINE FOR THE

by Mercedes Lackey

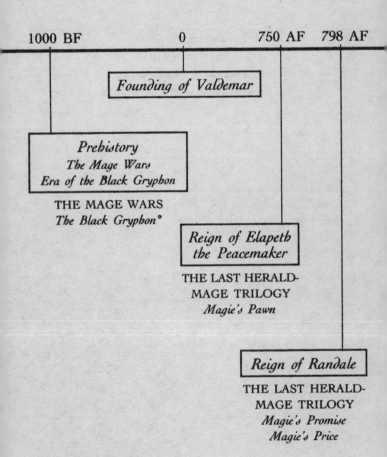

1000 BF   0   750 AF   798 AF

Founding of Valdemar

Prehistory
The Mage Wars
Era of the Black Gryphon

THE MAGE WARS
The Black Gryphon°

Reign of Elapeth
the Peacemaker

THE LAST HERALD-
MAGE TRILOGY
Magic's Pawn

Reign of Randale

THE LAST HERALD-
MAGE TRILOGY
Magic's Promise
Magic's Price

BF—Before the Founding
AF After the Founding
° Upcoming from DAW Books in hardcover

HERALDS OF VALDEMAR SERIES

Sequence of events by Valdemar reckoning

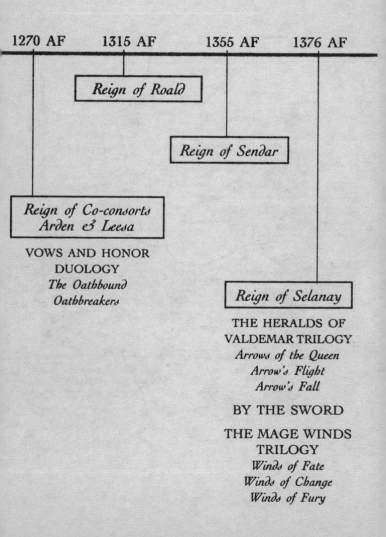

1270 AF   1315 AF   1355 AF   1376 AF

Reign of Roald

Reign of Sendar

Reign of Co-consorts
Arden & Leesa

VOWS AND HONOR
DUOLOGY
The Oathbound
Oathbreakers

Reign of Selanay

THE HERALDS OF
VALDEMAR TRILOGY
Arrows of the Queen
Arrow's Flight
Arrow's Fall

BY THE SWORD

THE MAGE WINDS
TRILOGY
Winds of Fate
Winds of Change
Winds of Fury

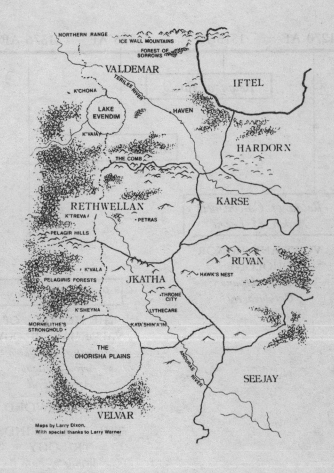

NORTHERN RANGE
ICE WALL MOUNTAINS
FOREST OF SORROWS

VALDEMAR

IFTEL

TERILEE RIVER

K'CHONA

LAKE EVENDIM

HAVEN

K'VAIA

HARDORN

THE COMB

RETHWELLAN

KARSE

K'TREVA

PETRAS

PELAGIR HILLS

RUVAN

K'VALA

HAWK'S NEST

PELAGIRIS FORESTS

JKATHA

THRONE CITY

LYTHECARE

K'SHEYNA

MORNELITHE'S STRONGHOLD

KATA'SHIN'A'IN

THE DHORISHA PLAINS

ANDURAS RIVER

SEEJAY

VELVAR

Maps by Larry Dixon.
With special thanks to Larry Warner

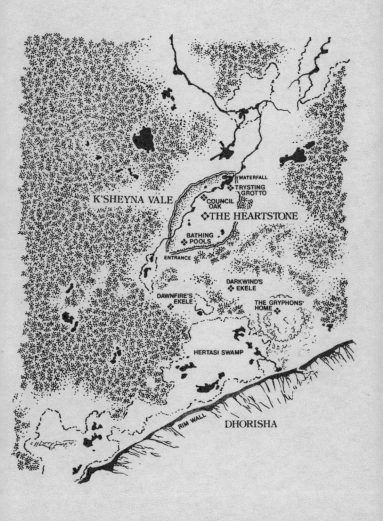

WATERFALL
TRYSTING
GROTTO

K'SHEYNA VALE

COUNCIL
OAK

◆ THE HEARTSTONE

BATHING
POOLS

ENTRANCE

DARKWIND'S
EKELE

DAWNFIRE'S
EKELE

THE GRYPHONS'
HOME

HERTASI SWAMP

RIM WALL   DHORISHA

Prologue

The Legend:

Long ago, in the days of the first King, for whom the Kingdom of Valdemar is named, it came to the King that he was growing old. Now Valdemar had led his people out of the hands of a tyrannical monarch and had no wish to see them fall again into the hands of tyranny. He knew that his son and Heir was a worthy, honest man—but what of his son's sons, and theirs?

He longed for a way to determine who would be a worthy successor to the throne, so that Valdemar the kingdom need never become less free than it was at that moment.

So he went into the fields and gardens beside the Palace, alone, and wrought what was half a prayer and half a spell, begging all benign Powers for their aid in this desire of his.

And as the last rays of the sun died from the sky, there was a mighty wind, and a shaking of the ground, and out of the grove of trees before him came a being like unto a white horse. And it spoke into his mind—

Then came a second, and a third, and before Valdemar could think to question why these came, his own son and his chief herald came to the place as if they had been called. And these two beings spoke into their minds, also, saying "I Choose you." So did the king know then that these Companions would choose only worthy folk to bear them company, for all their lives—and that these folk would be the instrument of justice and honor for all of the Kingdom from this moment. So did he name those Chosen by Companions to be Heralds, for only one could be a Monarch, and only one could be the Heir, but all could aspire to be a Herald. And he had made for them clothing of white, like the coats of their Companions, so that all might know them at a distance, or in a crowd; and he decreed then that only a Herald could be the Heir or the Monarch. And he decreed that there should be one Herald always to advise and serve and befriend the Monarch, so that his decisions be tempered with another view, and that Herald was to be called the Monarch's Own.

So it was. And so Valdemar has prospered. The Heralds increased, and the Monarch's justice spread.

The Chronicles:

In the first year of Herald Talia's investiture as full Queen's Own, Prince Ancar of Hardorn slew his father and all his father's men in a bloody and successful attempt to take the throne. He slew also Herald Kris who was there as ambassador on behalf of Queen Selenay, and imprisoned and tortured Herald Talia who was with him. She was rescued, out of all expectations, by the power of Herald Dirk, the young Heir Elspeth, and all the Companions together. Such a thing had never been known before, that the Companions would all add their strength to the Heralds to accomplish a task.

Ancar then made a trial of the strength of Valdemar, using both magic and his private army, but he was thrown back.

Some two years later, he made trial of the borders again. This time he was beaten back by the combined forces of the mercenary Company the Skybolts, under Captain Kerowyn; the armies of Valdemar; and the army of Rethwellan under Lord-Martial Prince Daren, who had come in answer to a promise of aid long forgotten. In the heat of the battle, the Prince and the Captain lost their horses and were both Chosen—and the Prince and Queen were taken with a lifebonding, a circumstance that both pleased and disturbed many.

Our ancient enemy, Karse, remains quiet, for Karse is beset with internal troubles. Ancar makes incursions on the Border from time to time; nothing but feints, however. So it has been to this day, some seven years from the last battle, when the events occurred that I now relate. . . .

Herald-Chronicler Myste

Elspeth

Chapter One

ELSPETH

"But—" Elspeth protested weakly. The empty salle echoed back her words faintly. She stared at Herald Kerowyn and tried to make some sense of what she'd just been ordered to do. *Repair armor? Why should I repair armor? I don't even know the first thing about repairing armor! And what does that have to do with anything?* She sat down, her arms sagging beneath the weight of a set of worn-out leather practice armor, a set long past its useful lifespan, and smelling faintly of sweat, leather-oil, and dust. "But I—"

"You know leatherwork, don't you?" Kerowyn asked, her generous mouth twitching as if she were trying not to laugh. Elspeth squirmed uncomfortably on the wooden bench, feeling very much like a tiny brown mouse facing a bored cat.

"Yes, but—"

"You've seen me and Alberich repair armor before, haven't you?" the mercenary-captain-turned-Herald continued with patient logic, arms folded across her chest. Elspeth looked from Kerowyn's weather-tanned face to the dust motes dancing in the sunlight to the whitewashed walls of the salle in hope of finding an answer.

She was unable to come up with one. She'd been put

directly under Kerowyn's command this week, in lieu of the "usual" duties of a Herald. Those "usual" duties—riding circuit on a Sector, acting as lawbringer, occasional judge, paramilitary advisor, and general troubleshooter—brought a Herald into areas of significant risk—risk the Council was not willing to take with the Heir to the Throne.

So her assigned duty at the moment consisted of doing whatever Herald Kerowyn told her to do. She'd assumed her tasks would be things like acting as an assistant trainer, perhaps. Learning command tactics. Perhaps even acting as liaison between Kerowyn's mercenary Company and the Council.

Especially since the Council members still weren't certain what to do with a mercenary Captain who was also a Herald.

These were all things she knew how to do—or at least make a start on. After all, those were the kinds of things Heralds were supposed to do. They were *not* supposed to be repairing armor.

"Yes, but—" she repeated weakly, not knowing what else to say.

"You don't happen to think you're *too good* to repair armor. . . ." Kerowyn's tone held a certain silky menace that told Elspeth that *someone* had given Herald Kerowyn chapter and verse on the ill-tempered Royal Brat. Of course, the Brat was a phase she had long ago outgrown, but some people couldn't seem to forget that stage of her life.

"No!" she said hastily. "But—"

"But *why* do I want you to repair armor—especially when it's someone else's job?" Kerowyn unbent enough to smile and shifted her weight to her right foot. "Let's play 'just suppose' for a moment. Let's suppose you are—for some reason—out in the back of beyond. Not even alone. We could have a situation like the one that brought me up here in the first place—where you're with a fighting force, maybe even in command, but there *aren't any* armorers around." She gestured at the pile of leather in Elspeth's arms. "Your gear gets damaged, and there's nobody free to fix it. What are you going to do, wear something with a weak spot and hope nobody notices?

Hope you can find somebody to fix it before the next engagement?''

"Did *you* ever have to fix your own gear?" Elspeth countered. She had *so* been looking forward to a free afternoon.

"I assume you mean after I made Captain?" The Herald laughed out loud, displaying a fine set of strong, white teeth. "My dear child, the Skybolts were so badly off that first year that I helped *make* armor. And arrows and lances and even some horse-gear. No, dear, you aren't going to wiggle out of this one. Leather armor isn't that hard to repair; merely time-consuming. So I suggest you get to it. As for how, you take apart everything that doesn't look solid and replace it." The former—and current—Captain of "Kerowyn's Skybolts" nodded her blonde head emphatically and turned away toward the heap of practice armor that had been tossed into the "needs repair" pile.

Resigned to the situation, Elspeth watched Kero toss her blonde braid over her shoulder, thought of her own dull brown hair, and sighed a little enviously. *If I weren't the Heir, nobody would ever pay any attention to my looks. Mother is gorgeous, the twins are adorable, my stepfather is the handsomest man at Court—and I'm the little brown sparrow. Why couldn't I have been born looking like her?*

Kerowyn was certainly an amazing person. Lithe, strong, and with a face even her critics had to call "striking," she would have had dozens of suitors if it hadn't been for the fact that she and Herald Eldan discouraged even the most persistent with their devotion to one another. The Captain had been blessed with a head of hair as bright as new-minted gold and thick as a horse's tail. And despite the fact that she was literally old enough to be Elspeth's mother, it showed no sign of graying. Whatever Kerowyn's past life had been like, it had left no outward marks on her. And from the stories Kero had told over the past few years, she'd been through enough to gray the hair of four women.

For that matter, her present was just as hectic, and it hadn't left that much of a mark on her. She juggled two dedications, Herald and mercenary Captain, either one of which would have been a full-time career for anyone else.

And there are plenty of folk who think she should stick to one or the other. . . . Elspeth smiled to herself. Those were the same folk who were mightily annoyed that the Herald Captain wouldn't wear Whites unless it was ordered by the Queen herself. She compromised—if one could call it that—by wearing the same kind of dark gray leathers the Weaponsmaster favored. And the Queen smiled and held her peace. Like Alberich, Kerowyn was a law unto herself.

"Besides, you have all the resources of the armory at your disposal," Kerowyn said over her shoulder, as she hefted another corselet in need of repair—this one of metal scale, a mending task Elspeth didn't even want to *think* about. "You wouldn't have that in the field. Be grateful I don't demand that you fix it with what folks carry in their field kits."

Elspeth bit back a retort and spread the shirt out over the bench she was sitting on, giving the armor the kind of careful scrutiny she imagined Kero must have.

Well, it isn't as bad as I thought, she decided, after a second examination proved that some of the worst places had already been repaired. Evidently the Captain had taken *that* much pity on her. . . .

She bent to her task, determined to make as good a job of it as Kerowyn would.

Her determination did not last more than a few moments.

Someone distracted her as soon as she turned her attention to a tricky bit of stitchery that had to be picked out without ruining the leather. A whisper of air was all that warned her of the attacker's rush—but that was all the warning she needed. What Weaponsmaster Alberich had not pounded into her, the Herald Captain was making certain she learned, and in quick-time, too. And Kerowyn was a past master of the unconventional.

:Gwena!: she screamed mentally, as she acted on what had become reflex. She tumbled off her bench, hit the hard wooden floor with her shoulder, and rolled. She came up on the balls of her feet, poised and ready, the tiny knife she'd been using to cut the stitches still in

her hand. Her heart pounded, but from battle-readiness, not fear.

She found herself facing someone who had recovered just as rapidly as she had; he stood in a near-identical pose on the opposite side of the bench, and she sized him up quickly. Taller and heavier than she, an anonymous male, in nondescript clothing, his face wrapped in a scarf and head covered with a tight hood, so that all she could see were his wary eyes.

A thousand fleeting thoughts passed through her mind in that moment of analysis. Uppermost was a second mental scream for help to her Companion Gwena. Hard on the heels of that was the sudden question: *Why doesn't Kero do anything?* She glanced out of the corner of her eye. The Captain stood with arms crossed, watching both of them, no discernible expression on her handsome face.

The obvious answer was implied by the question. *Because she was expecting this.*

And because Kerowyn was a Herald and her Companion Sayvil would never permit her to betray another, and further, because Elspeth's own Companion Gwena was not beating down the doors of the salle to get in and help her stand off this attacker, it followed that the "assassin" was nothing of the sort.

Her heart slowed a little, and she dared a mental touch. Nothing: her assailant was shielded. Which meant he knew how to guard his thoughts, which only another Mindspeaker could do.

And a closer look at the bright brown eyes, and the additional clue of a curl of black hair showing outside the assailant's hood gave her all the information she needed to identify him.

"Skif," she said flatly, relaxing a little.

:*Good girl,*: came the voice in her mind. :*I told Sayvil you'd figure this out before it got anywhere, but she didn't believe me.*:

She shifted her gaze over to Kerowyn, though without taking Skif out of her line of sight. "This was a setup, wasn't it?" she asked the older woman. "You never really intended for me to fix that armor."

Kero shrugged, not at all discomfited. "Hell, yes, I did. And tomorrow, you *will*. But I also intended for you to figure out that you *could,*" she temporized as Skif relaxed minutely. "That's a good thing for you to know if you're ever in the situation I described. If you don't know you *can* do something, it doesn't occur to you as an option. But don't relax," her voice sharpened as Skif started to come out of his crouch and Elspeth followed suit. "Just because you've identified him, that doesn't mean that the rest of the exercise is canceled. Take it up where you left off."

"With this?" Elspeth looked doubtfully at the tiny knife in her hand.

"With that—and anything else you can get your hands on. There're hundreds of things you can use in here, including that bench." Kerowyn frowned slightly. "Anything can be a weapon, child. It's time you learned to improvise."

Kerowyn did not have to outline the reasons for that statement; even if the current interkingdom situation had been full of light and harmony, there would always be the risk of someone with a grudge or grievance—or even a simple lunatic—who would be willing to risk his life to assassinate the next in line to the throne of Valdemar.

And with at least two enemies on the borders, Hardorn and Karse, the political situation was far from harmonious.

Still—*Anything can be a weapon? What on earth is she talking about?*

But she didn't have time to question the statement in detail. Elspeth went back on guard just in time to dodge Skif's rush for her.

She sidestepped him and reversed the knife, not wanting to really hurt him, and feinted for his eyes with the wooden hilt. He recognized the feint for what it was and ignored it, coming in to grapple with her. So far he hadn't produced any weapons of his own.

So his "orders" must be to capture rather than to kill. That makes my job easier and his harder. . . .

Relatively easier. Skif had learned his hand-to-hand skills in the rough world of Haven's slums. Even the capital of Valdemar was prone to the twin problems of crime and poverty, and young Skif had been the godchild of both. Orphaned early, he had apprenticed himself to a thieving uncle, and when *that* worthy was caught, set up shop on his own. Probably only being Chosen had saved him from hanging like his uncle—or death at the hands of a competitor, like his mother.

His "style" was a mixture of disciplines—a kind of catch-all, "anything that works," devious, dirty, and deadly. The Queen's Own Herald, Talia, had learned quite a bit from him, but no one had ever thought to have him teach Elspeth as well. At least—not that. He *had* taught her knife throwing, which had saved her life and Talia's, but even Queen Selenay had been horrified a few short years ago at the notion of her Heir learning street-fighting. Elspeth had begged but to no avail.

Many things had changed in those few years. Among them, the arrival of Kerowyn, who had sent one of her commandos to prove to Selenay that she and her daughter needed the kind of protection only instruction in the lowest forms of fighting could provide. Alberich undertook the Queen's instruction; Kero and Skif got Elspeth's. The lessons were frequently painful.

Dirk's taught me a thing or two since the last lesson—she told herself as she circled him warily, testing her footing as she watched his eyes. *—and I bet neither of them knows that.*

She sensed the pile of armor behind her, and tried to remember what was topmost. Was it something she could throw over his head to temporarily blind him?

"Pick up the pace, boy," Kerowyn said. "Take some chances. You only have a few more moments before she either calls for help herself with Mindspeech, or her Companion brings the cavalry."

Skif lunged just as she made a grab for the nearest piece of junk, a leather gambeson. He waited until she moved, then struck like a coiled snake. He caught her in the act of bending over sideways and tackled her, both of them flying over the pile and landing in a heap on the other side of it. Her knife went skidding across the floor as her cheek hit the gritty floor, all the breath knocked out of her.

She writhed in his grip and grabbed the edge of his hood and tried to pull it down over his eyes, but it was too tightly wrapped. She struggled to get her knee up into his stomach, clawed at the wrappings around his head with no effect, and kicked ineffectually at the back of his legs. He simply pinned her with his greater weight, and slapped the side of her head at the same time, calling out "Disable!"

Damn. She obediently went limp. He scrambled to his feet, heaved her up like a sack of grain, slung her over his shoulder and started for the door. She watched the floor and his boots, and wondered what her Companion was supposed to be doing while the "assassin" was carrying her off.

:Not that way,: Gwena said calmly in her mind, right on cue. *:I've got the front door blocked, and Sayvil has the rear. The only way out is by way of the roof.:*

"No good, Skif," Elspeth said to his belt. "The Companions have you boxed in."

"Well, then I'll have to abort and follow my secondary orders," he replied, "Sorry, little kitten, you're dead."

He put her down on her feet, and she dusted herself off. "Crap," she said sourly. "I could do better than that. I wish I'd had my knives." She couldn't resist a resentful glance at Kero, who had made her take them off when she entered the salle.

"Well," Kero told her. "You didn't do as badly as I had expected. But I told you to get rid of those little toys of yours for a reason. They aren't a secret anymore; *everybody* knows you carry them in arm-sheaths. And you've begun to depend on them; you passed up at least a half dozen potential weapons."

Elspeth's heart sank as Skif nodded to confirm Kerowyn's assessment. "Like what?" she demanded. She didn't—quite—growl. It was ironic that a room devoted to weaponswork should be so barren of weaponry. There was *nothing* in the room; at least, nothing that could be used against an enemy. The salle's sanded wooden floor stood empty of everything but the bench she sat on and the pile of discarded armor. There were a few implements for mending the armor that she'd brought in from the back room. There were no windows that she could reach; they were all set in the walls near the edge of the ceiling. Even the walls were bare of practice weapons, just the empty racks along one wall and the expensive—but necessary—mirrors on the other.

"The bench," Skif said promptly. "You were within range to kick it into my path."

"You should have grabbed that leather corselet when you went off the bench," Kero added.

"Any of the mirrors—break one and you've got a pile of razor shards."

"The sunlight—maneuver him so that it's in his eyes."

"The mirrors again; distract me with my own reflection."

"The leather-needles—"

"The pot of leather-oil—"

"Your belt—"

"All right!" Elspeth cried, plopping down heavily on the bench, defeated by their logic. "What's the point?"

"Something that you can learn, but I can't teach in simple lessons," Kerowyn told her soberly. "An attitude. A state of awareness, one where you size everyone up as a potential enemy, and everything as a potential weapon. And I mean *everyone* and *everything*. From the stranger walking toward you, to your mother—from the halberd on the wall to your underwear."

"I can't live like that," she protested. "Nobody can." But at Kero's raised eyebrow, she added doubtfully, "Can they?"

Kero shrugged. "Personally, I think no royalty can afford to live *without* an outlook like that. And I've managed, for most of my life."

"So have I," Skif seconded. "It doesn't have to poison you or your life, just make you more aware of things going on around you."

"That's why we've started the program here," Kerowyn finished. "A salle is a pretty empty room even with repair stuff scattered all over it; that makes your job easier. Now," she fixed Elspeth with a stern blue-green eye, "before you leave, you're going to figure out one way everything in here could be used against an assailant."

Elspeth sighed, bade farewell to her free afternoon, and began pummeling her brain for answers.

Eventually Kero left for other tasks, putting Skif in charge of the lesson. Elspeth breathed a little easier when she was gone; Skif was nowhere near the taskmaster that Kerowyn could be when the mood was on her. Heraldic trainees at the Collegium used to complain of Alberich's lessons; now they moaned about Kerowyn's as well, and it was an open question as to which of the two was considered the worst. Elspeth had once heard a young girl complain that it was bad enough that the Weaponsmaster refused to grow old and retire, but now he'd cursed them with a female double and it wasn't *fair!*

But then again, she had thought at the time, *what is?*

Skif grilled her for a little longer, then took pity on her, and turned the lesson from one on "attitude" to simply a rough-and-tumble knife-fighting lesson. Elspeth found the latter much easier on the nerves, if not on the body. Skif might be inclined to go easy on her when it came to the abstract "lessons," but when it came to the physical he could be as remorseless as any of the instructors when he chose.

Finally, when both were tired enough that they were missing elementary moves, he called a halt.

In fact, she thought wearily, as he waved her off guard and stepped off the salle floor, *I doubt I could be a match for a novice right now.*

"That's . . . enough," he panted, throwing himself down on the floor beside the bench, as she slumped down on the seat and then sprawled along the length of it, shoving the forgotten leather armor to the floor. The angle of the sunlight coming in through the high clerestory windows had changed; there was no longer a broad patch of sunlight on the floor. It was starting to climb up the whitewashed wall. Not yet dinnertime, but certainly late afternoon.

"I have to get back to drilling the little ones in a bit," he continued. "Besides, if I spend too much more time in your unchaperoned company, the rumors are going to start again, and I don't feel like dealing with them."

Elspeth grimaced and wiped sweat from her forehead with the back of her hand. The last time rumors had started about a romance between her and Skif, she'd had to placate half the Council, and endure the knowing looks of half the Heralds. She wasn't sure which group was worse.

Now I know how Mother and Stepfather felt when they were my age. Every time someone gets interested—or interesting—most of the time they're frightened off by the matchmakers. You'd think people would have more important things to worry about.

But it was too bad poor Skif had to pay the price of *her* rank. There ought to be something she could do about that, but right now her weary mind was not supplying the answer.

"I'll see you later, then," she said instead. "I've got a few things of my own I'd like to do before dinner—if you're satisfied with my progress, that is."

"You're getting there," he told her, getting up with an effort, his sweat-damp hair curled even tighter. "I was making more mistakes than you were, toward the end. What's the closest weapon to your right hand?"

"The bench I'm on," she replied without thinking. "I roll off it and kick it in your direction."

"I was thinking of the shears on the floor there, but that'll do," he said with a tired chuckle. "See you at dinner?"

"Not tonight. There's some delegation from Rethwellan here to see Father. That means all meals with the Court until they're gone." She levered herself up on her elbows and smiled apologetically. "I guess they won't believe I'm not plotting against the rest of the family unless they see us all together."

Skif was too polite to say anything, but they both knew why that suspicion of treason might occur to a delegation from Rethwellan. Elspeth's blood-father, a prince of Rethwellan, *had* plotted to overthrow his own wife and consort, Queen Selenay—and in the end, had attempted to assassinate her himself.

Not the best way to handle foreign relations. . . .

As it happened, though, no one in Rethwellan had any idea he might attempt such a thing—certainly there was no one in the royal family who had backed him. In fact, there been no love lost between him and his two brothers, and there had been no repercussions from Rethwellan at the news that he had not survived that assassination attempt. The Queen quietly accepted King Faramentha's horrified apologies and disclaimers, and there the matter had rested for many years.

But then war and the redemption of a promise made to Selenay's grandfather had brought one of those brothers, Prince Daren, to the aid of the Queen of Valdemar, and the unexpected result of that first meeting had been not only love, but a lifebonding. Rethwellan lost its Lord-

Martial, and Valdemar gained a co-ruler, for Daren, like Kerowyn, had been Chosen, literally on the battlefield.

Whether the bedding had followed or preceded the wedding was moot; the result had been twins, nine months to the day after the ceremony.

Which left the titular Heir, Elspeth, with two unexpected rivals for her position. Elspeth, whose father had tried to murder the Queen and steal her throne. . . . And there were the inevitable whispers of "bad blood."

King Faram, the current king of Rethwellan and brother to both her father and stepfather, held no such doubts about her, but occasionally some of his advisors required a reminder that treason was not a heritable trait. Elspeth slipped out of her musings and stretched protesting muscles.

"I wish—" she began, and stopped.

"You wish what, kitten?" Skif prompted.

"Never mind," she said, dragging herself to her feet. "It doesn't matter. I'll catch up with you tomorrow, after Council. Assuming Kerowyn doesn't have me mucking out the stables or something equally virtuous and valuable."

He chuckled and left the salle, leaving her alone with her thoughts.

She cleaned up the scattered equipment from their lesson while the sweat of her exertion cooled and dried, and took herself out before her erstwhile mentor could return and find her "idle."

A warm summer wind whipped her hair out of its knot at the back of her neck, and dried her sweat-soaked shirt as she left the salle door. She made a hasty check for possible watchers, trotted around the side of the salle, and didn't slow until she reached the edge of the formal gardens and the relative shelter of the tall hedges. The path she took, from the formal garden and the maze to the herb and kitchen gardens of the Palace, was one normally used only by the Palace's husbandmen. It ran along the back of a row of hedges that concealed a line of storage buildings and potting sheds. She wasn't surprised that there was no one on it, since there was nothing to recommend it but its relative isolation, a commodity in short supply at the Palace/Collegium complex.

Not the sort of route that anyone would expect to find

her taking. Nor was her destination what anyone who
didn't know her well would expect. It was a simple potting shed, a nondescript little building distinguished from
its fellows only by the stovepipe, a stone kiln, and the
small, glazed window high up on one side. And even
then, there was no reason to assume it was special; the
kiln had been there for years, and had been used to fire
terra-cotta pots for seedlings and winter herbs.

Which made it all the more valuable to Elspeth.

She opened the door and closed it behind her with a
feeling of having dropped a tremendous weight from her
shoulders. This unprepossessing kingdom was hers, and
hers alone, by unspoken agreement. So long as she did
not neglect her duties, no one would bother her here, not
unless the situation were direst emergency.

A tiny enough kingdom; one bench in the middle with
a stool beside it, one sink and hand pump, one potter's
wheel, boxes of clay ready for working, shelves, and a
stove to heat the place in the winter and double as a small
bisque-firing kiln in the rear. But not one implement here
reminded her of the Heir or the Heir's duties. This was
the one place where Elspeth could be just Elspeth, and
nothing more. A proper kingdom as far as she was concerned; she'd been having second thoughts about ruling
anything larger for some time now.

Up on the highest shelf were the finished products—
which was to say the ones, to her critical eye, worth
keeping—of her own two hands. They began with her
first perfectly thrown pots and bowls, ranged through
more complicated projects, and ended with some of the
results of her current efforts—poured-slip pieces cast
from molds that had in turn been made from her own
work.

The twins were going through a competitive stage at
the moment—and any time one of them got something,
the other had to have something just like it. But different.

If Kris got a toy horse, *Lyra* had to have a toy horse—
same size, shape, length of tail, and equipage. But if
Kris' horse was chestnut, hers had to be bay, dapple-
gray, or roan. If he got a toy fort, *she* had to have a toy
village; same size, number of buildings, number of toy
inhabitants as his fort. And so on. The only thing they

agreed on was toy Companions; they had to be twins, like the twins themselves.

Not that they need "toy" Companions, Elspeth thought with amusement. *They have the real thing following them around by the nose every time Mother takes them with her into the Field. No doubts there about whether or not they'll be Chosen!*

In fact, Gwena had remarked more than once that the only question involved would be *which* Companion did the Choosing. There were apparently a number in the running. *:Mark my words,:* she'd said with amusement. *:There are going to be fights over this in a couple of years.:*

But that made gift giving both harder and easier. Trying to find—or make—absolutely identical presents in differing colors had been driving Elspeth (and everyone else) to distraction. They were able to pick out the most amazing discrepancies and turn them into points of contention over whose present was "better." Finally, though, she'd hit on the notion of making a mold and copying a successful piece. Her first effort had been a pair of dragon-lamps, or rather, night-lights; comical, roly-poly fellows who gently burned lamp-oil at a wick in their open mouths. Those had been such a hit that Elspeth had decided to try dolls, specifically, dolls that looked as much like the twins themselves as she—who was not exactly a portrait sculptor—could manage.

It's a good thing that they're in that vague sort of "child-shaped" stage, she thought wryly, as she surveyed the row of greenware heads waiting to be cleaned of mold-marks and sorted for discards. *I doubt if I could produce anything more detailed than that.*

Well, dressing the completed dolls in miniatures of the twins' favorite outfits would take care of the rest. And providing the appropriate accessories, of course. She would have to appeal for help on that. To Talia for the outfits, since she could probably bribe the Queen's Own with an offer of another doll for Talia's son Jemmie; her plain-sewing was as good as many of the seamstresses attached to the Palace staff, though her embroidery was still "enough to make a cat laugh," as she put it. To Keren for the rest. Lyra was in a horse-crazy phase at the moment, a bit young for that, perhaps, but the twins—

and Jemmie—were precocious in most areas. Kris had gone mad for the Guard; half the time, when asked, he would assert that he wanted to be a Guard-Captain when he grew up (which usually made any nearby Companions snort). Tiny swords and miniature riding boots were a little out of Elspeth's line, but perhaps Keren or Sherrill, Keren's lifemate, could arrive at a solution.

The first three heads weren't worth bothering with; bubbles in the slip had flawed the castings badly enough to crack when they were fired. The fourth was perfect; the fifth, possible, and the sixth—

The arrangement of the window and door in the shed made it a regrettable necessity that she sit with her back to the door. That being the case, she had left the hinges unoiled. It simply was not possible to open the door, however carefully, without at least some noise, however slight.

She froze as she heard the faintest of telltale squeaks from behind her, then continued examining the head as if she had heard nothing. A lightning-quick mental probe behind her revealed that it was Skif—again—at the door. This time his thoughts were unguarded. He assumed that she had already put this afternoon's lessons out of her mind, a little tired and careless, here in the heart of the Palace grounds.

Not a chance, friend, she thought. And as he slipped through the door, she shifted her weight off the stool she had been using, and hooked one foot around one of the legs.

At a moment when he was poised and unbalanced, she pulled the stool over, whirled, and kicked it under his feet, all with a single motion.

He was hardly expecting opposition, much less that he would be on the defensive. He lost his balance as his feet got tangled up with the stool and couldn't recover. He fell over backward with a crash of splintering wood as her stool went with him, landing ingloriously on his rear. She stood over him, shaking her head, as he blinked up at her and grinned feebly.

"Uh—"

"Ever heard of knocking?" she asked. She picked up her stool without offering him a hand and made a face. He'd broken two of the bottom rungs and loosened all four of the legs, and it had not been that sturdy to begin with.

"You owe me a new chair," she said, annoyed all out of proportion to the value of the stool. "That wasn't just a dirty trick, Skif, that was dangerous. You could have broken some of my best pieces, too."

"Almost broke some of mine," he grumbled. "You aren't going to get an apology, if that's what you're looking for. You knew very well we'd be springing these surprise attacks on you."

But not in the one place I can relax, she thought, seething with resentment. *Not in the only place I can get away from everything and everyone.*

"You still owe me, lout," she said stubbornly, righting the stool and rocking it to check how wobbly it was going to be. She sat on it and folded her arms, making no attempt to disguise how put out she was. "You still could have broken something. I don't ask for much, Skif, and I give up a lot. I think it's only fair to be off-limits when I'm out here."

He didn't say, *Will an attacker go along with that?* and he didn't give her a lecture, which mollified her a little. Instead, he grinned ingenuously and pulled himself up from the floor, dusting off his white uniform once he reached his feet. "I really have to congratulate you," he said. "You did a lot better than I expected. I deliberately came after you when I knew you were tired and likely to be careless."

"I know," she said crisply, and watched his bushy eyebrows rise as he realized what that meant. First, that she'd detected him soon enough to make a mental test of him, and second that she'd gone ahead and read his thoughts when she knew who it was. The second was a trifle unethical; Heralds were not supposed to read other's thoughts without them being aware of the fact. But if he was going to violate her precious bit of privacy, she was going to pay him back for it. *Let him wonder how much else I read while I was peeking and sweat about it a little.*

"Oh." He certainly knew better than to chide her for that breach of privacy at this point. "I'll see you later, I guess."

"You'd better have a new stool with you," she said,

as he backed hastily out the door, only now aware that she was still clutching the much-abused doll's head. She looked at it as soon as he was out of sight. Whatever shape it had been in before this, it was ruined now. She disgustedly tossed it into the discard bucket beside her bench.

It wasn't until she had a half dozen usable heads lined up on the bench in front of her, and had smashed the rejects, that she felt as if her temper was any cooler. Cleaning them was a dull but exacting task, precisely what she wanted at the moment. She didn't want to see or talk to anyone until her foul mood was gone.

So when she felt the stirring of air behind her that meant the door had cracked open again, she was not at all amused.

I'm going to kill him.

She readied a mental bolt, designed to hit him as if she had shouted in his ear—when her preliminary Mind-touch told her something completely unexpected. This was not Skif—or Kerowyn, or anyone else she knew.

And she ducked instinctively as something shot past, overhead, and landed with a solid *thunk* point-first in the wall above the bench.

A hunting knife, ordinary and untraceable. It quivered as she stared up at it, momentarily stunned. Then her training took over before the other could react to the fact that he had missed.

She kicked the stool at him as she rolled under the bench and came up on the other side. He kicked it out of the way, slammed the door shut behind him, and dropped the bar; a few heartbeats later, the door shuddered as Gwena hit it with her hooves.

Now I wish this place wasn't quite so sturdy—

The stranger turned with another knife in his hands. Gwena shrieked and renewed her attack on the door. He ignored the pounding and came straight for Elspeth.

With her lesson so fresh in her mind, she flung the first thing that came to hand at him—the half-cleaned doll's head. It didn't do any damage, but it made a hollow popping sound which distracted him enough so that she could get clear of the bench, get to where he'd kicked the stool, and snatch it up. Using it as a combination of shield and lance, she rushed him, trying to pin him against the abused door with the legs.

But the battering the stool had taken had weakened the legs too much to hold; his single blow broke the legs from the seat and left her holding a useless piece of flat board. Or almost useless; she threw it at his head, forcing him to duck, and giving her a chance to grab something else as Gwena's hooves hit the door again.

That ''something else'' proved to be one of her better pots, a lovely, graceful, two-handled vase. But she sacrificed it without a second thought, snatching it off the shelf and smashing it against the wall of the shed, leaving her with a razor-sharp shard. A knife-edge, with a handle to control it.

She took the initiative, as he started at the crash of shattering crockery, and threw herself at *him*.

He wasn't expecting that either, and she caught him completely off guard. He tried to grapple with her, and she let him, sacrificing her own mobility for one chance to get in with that bit of pottery in her right hand.

He grabbed her, but it was too late to stop her. Before he realized what she meant to do with that bit of crockery, she slashed it across his throat, cutting it from ear to ear, as Gwena's hooves hit the door and it shattered inward.

''Are you going to be all right?'' Kerowyn asked, as she wiped Elspeth's forehead with a cold, damp cloth. Elspeth finally finished retching and licked her lips, tasting salt and bile, before she nodded shakily.

''I think so,'' she replied, closing her eyes and leaning back against the outer wall of the shed. The others had arrived to find her on her hands and knees in the grass, covered in blood—not her own—with Gwena standing over her protectively as she emptied her stomach into the bushes.

Her stomach still felt queasy, as if she might have another bout at any moment. No matter that she had seen death before—had even killed her share of the enemy in the last war with Hardorn—she'd taken down Lord Orthallen with her own two hands and one of Skif's throwing knives.

That wasn't close, not this close. I was dropping arrows

into people from a distance. I threw a knife from across the room. Not like this, where he bled all over me and looked up at me and—

Her stomach heaved again, and she quelled the thoughts. "Who was he?" she asked, wiping her mouth with the back of her hand, trying to get her mind on something else. "How did he find out where I was? And how did he get past the guards?"

"I don't know the answers to your second and third questions," Kero replied, as Elspeth closed her eyes and concentrated on the coolness against her forehead. "But I can tell you the answer to the first. There's a spider-web brand on his palm. He's one of the followers of the Cold God. They hire themselves out as assassins, and they're very expensive because they don't care if they get caught. He was either providing a legacy for a family, or doing penance for some terrible sin. If you hadn't killed him, he'd have killed himself." Kero dropped the cloth and sat back on her heels, and Elspeth opened her eyes and gaped at the older Herald, her nausea forgotten.

"I've never heard of anything like that!" she exclaimed.

Kero nodded. "Not too many people have; the Cold One's advocates come from farther south than anyone I know has been except Geyr. He's the one who told me about them, after the last try at your mother, and told me what to look for. Said that if Ancar really got desperate and knew how to contact them, he might try hiring one of the Cold Blades." She frowned. "I didn't take the threat seriously, and I should have—and believe me, it won't happen again. Frankly, you were lucky—they usually aren't that careless. And there is nothing, *nothing*, more dangerous than a suicidal fanatic."

"But—how did he get in here, in the gardens?" she asked, bewildered. "How could he? We have guards everywhere!"

Kero frowned even harder. "If Geyr's to be believed, by m–m–m–m–magic," she said, forcing the word out around the compulsion that seemed to overtake all Heralds when discussing anything but the mental Gifts and the Truth-Spell. "There're m–mages among the Cold Ones that give them a kind of invisibility. My grandmother could do it—make people think that when they looked at her, they were actually seeing someone they knew and trusted and expected to be there. Works with the mind, like Mindspeech, but it's set up with a spell. Dangerous stuff—and now the guards are going to have to double-check everyone they think they know. There're going to be some unhappy folks, unless I miss my guess. . . ."

He either underestimated me, or he was inexperienced, she thought soberly, as Kero left her to talk quietly with some of the Guard who were dealing with the body. *And—I don't think we're ever going to find out how Ancar found him because I have the funny feeling that he used magic.*

She shivered and stood up, her knees shaking. Her Whites were ruined—not that she'd ever want to wear *this* set again. Magic again. Whatever had protected Valdemar in the past, it was not proof against Ancar anymore.

Chapter Two

DARKWIND

Darkwind k'Sheyna balanced his bondbird Vree on his shoulder, and peered out across the sea of grass below him with a touch of—regret? Envy? A little of both, perhaps. From where he stood, the earth dropped in a steep cliff more than a hundred man-lengths to the floor of the Dhorisha Plains—a formidable barrier to those who meant the Shin'a'in and their land any ill. It took knowledge *and* skill to find the paths down into the Plains, and from there, intruders were visible above the waist-high grass for furlongs.

His bondbird lifted narrow, pointed wings a little in the warm, grass-scented updraft that followed the cliff. *:Prey,:* Vree's thought answered his own, framed in the simple terms of the bondbird's understanding. Not so much a thought as a flood of images; tree-hares, mice, quail, rabbits, all of them from the viewpoint of the forestgyre as they would appear just before the talons struck.

Prey, indeed. Any would-be hunter attempting to penetrate the Plains without magic aid would find himself quickly turned hunted. The land itself would fight him; he would be visible to even a child, he would never guess the locations of seeps and springs, and without landmarks that *he* would understand, that intruder would become disoriented in the expanse of grass and gently rolling hills. The guardians of the Plains, and the scouts that patrolled the border, had half their work done for them by the Plains themselves.

Darkwind sighed and turned away, back to his own cool, silent forest. No such help for him—other than the fact that the eastern edge of k'Sheyna territory bordered the Plains. But to the south and west lay forest, league upon league of it, and all of it dangerous.

:Sick,: complained Vree. Darkwind agreed with him. Magic contaminated those lands, a place Outlanders called the "Pelagir Hills" with no notion of just how much territory fell under that description. Magic flowed wild and twisted through the earth, a magic that warped and shaped everything that grew there—sometimes for the better, but more often for the worse.

Darkwind took Vree onto his wrist, the finger-long talons biting into the leather of his gauntlet as Vree steadied himself, and launched him into the trees to scout ahead. The forestgyre took to the air gladly; unlike his bondmate, Vree enjoyed the scouting forays. Hunting was no challenge to a bondbird, and there was only so much for Vree to do within the confines of k'Sheyna Vale's safe territory. Scouting and guarding were what Vree had been bred for, and he was never happier than when flying ahead of Darkwind on patrol.

Darkwind didn't mind the scouting so much, even if the k'Sheyna scouts *were* spread frighteningly thin—after all, he *was* a *vayshe'druvon*. Guard, scout, protector, he was all of those.

It's the magic, he told himself—not for the first time. *If it wasn't for the magic—*

Every time he encountered some threat to k'Sheyna that used magic or was born of it, and had to find some way *other* than magic to counter that threat, it scorched him to the soul. And worse was his father's attitude when he returned—scorn for the mage who would abandon his power, and a stubborn refusal to understand why Darkwind had done so. . . .

If I could go back in time and kill those fools that set this loose in the world, I would do so, and murder them all with my bare hands, he thought savagely. His anger at those long-dead ancestors remained, as he chose a tree to climb, looking for one he had not used before.

A massive goldenoak was his choice this time; he slipped hand-spikes out of his belt without conscious thought, and pulled the fingerless, backless leather gloves on over his palms. The tiny spikes set into the leather wouldn't penetrate the bark of the tree enough to leave places for fungus or insects to lodge, but it would give him a little more traction on the trunk. As would the *shakras*-hide soles of his thin leather boots.

In moments he was up in the branches. The game-trail along the edge of the territory lay below him. When two-legged intruders penetrated k'Sheyna, most of the time they sought trails like this one.

When scouts patrolled, it was often up here, where the trails could be seen, but where the scouts themselves were invisible.

He shaded his eyes and chose a route through the next three forest giants by means of intersecting limbs, stowing his climbing-spikes and removing his double-ended climbing tool from the sheath on his back. Then he picked his way through the foliage, walking as surefootedly on the broad, swaying branch as if he were on the ground, pulling another branch closer with the hook end of his tool and hopping from his goldenoak to the limb of a massive candle-pine just as the branch began to bow beneath his weight. He followed the new branch in to the trunk, then back out again to another conifer, this time stowing the tool long enough to leap for the branch above him and swing himself up onto it.

As he chose his next route, his thoughts turned back to that wild magic, as they always did. *What it has done to the land, to us, is unforgivable. What it could do is worse.*

Never mind that the Tayledras tamed that magic, cleansed the places it had turned awry, made them safe for people and animals alike to live there. Not that there weren't both there now—but they often found their offspring changed into something they did not recognize.

But that isn't our real task. Our real task is more dangerous. And my father has forgotten it ever existed, in his obsessions with power and Power.

Darkwind looked back at the treeless sky where the

Plains began. The Shin'a'in had no such problems. But then, the Shin'a'in had little to do with magic. *Odd to think we were one, once.*

Very odd, for all that there was no mistaking the fact that Tayledras features and Shin'a'in were mirrors of each other. The *Kaled'a'in,* they had been the most trusted allies of a mage whose name had been lost over the ages. The Tayledras remembered him only as "The Mage of Silence," and if the Shin'a'in had recorded his true name in their knotted tapestries, they had never bothered to tell anyone in the Tayledras Clans.

Father forgets that the real duty of the Hawkbrothers is to heal the land of the scars caused by that war of magics, even as the Goddess has healed the Plains.

He often felt more kinship with his Shin'a'in "cousins" these days than he did with his real kin. *The Lady gave them the more dangerous task, truth to tell,* he admitted grudgingly. He looked back again, but this time he shuddered. The Hawkbrothers cleansed—but the Shin'a'in guarded. And what they guarded—

Somewhere out there, buried beneath grass and soil, are the weapons that caused all this. And not all of them require an Adept to use them.

Only the Shin'a'in stood guardian between those hidden weapons and the rest of the world.

I don't envy them that duty.

:Men,: Vree sounded the alert, and followed it with a vocal alarm-call. Darkwind froze against the tree trunk for a moment, and touched Vree's mind long enough to see through the bondbird's eyes.

He clutched the trunk, fingernails digging into the bark. Direct contact with the forestgyre's mind was always disorienting. His perspective was skewed—first at seeing the strangers from above, as they peered up through the branches in automatic response to Vree's scream, the faces curiously flat and alien. Then came the dizzying spiral of Vree's flight that made the faces below seem to spin. As always, the strangeness was what kept him aware that it was the forestgyre's eyes he was using and not his own—the heightened sharpness of everything red, and the colors Vree saw that human eyes could not.

He was a passive traveler in Vree's mind, not an active controller. It was a measure of the bond and Vree's trust that the forestgyre would let him take control on occasion, but Darkwind took care never to abuse that trust. In general it was better just to observe—as he found yet again. Vree spotted one of the strangers raising what was probably a weapon, and kited up into the thick branches before Darkwind had registered more than the bare movement of an arm.

Darkwind released his link with Vree, and his hold on the trunk at the same time, running along the flat branch and using his tool as a balance-aid, and leaping to the next tree limb a heartbeat later. In his first days with Vree it had taken him a long time to recover from a link—

—and some never did, especially the first time. Caught up in the intoxication of the flight and the kill, they never detached themselves. And unless someone else discovered them, they could be lost forever that way—their bodies lying in a kind of coma, while their minds slowly merged with that of the bird, diminishing as they merged, until there was nothing left of what they were.

That had never happened in Darkwind's lifetime by accident, although there had been one scout, when he was a child, who had a lightning-struck tree crush him beneath its trunk. He had been far from a Healer, and had deliberately merged himself with his bird, never to return to the crippled and dying wreck of his body. He remained with k'Sheyna within his bird's mind, slowly fading, until at last the bird vanished one day, never to return.

Slower death, but death all the same. Darkwind thought pragmatically, climbing a pine trunk by hooking the stub of a broken branch above him to ascend to a crossover branch. He preferred to avoid such a nonchoice altogether.

He slowed as he neared the strangers, and dropped to all fours, stalking like a slim tree-cat along the branch and taking care not to rustle the leaves. Not that it would have mattered to the intruders, who called to each other and laughed as if they had no idea that they were being observed, or that they were in forbidden territory.

His jaw tightened. *They are about to find out differently. And they're damned lucky that it's me who found them. There are plenty of others—including Father—who would feather them with arrows or make ashes of them without waiting to find out if they're ignorant, stupid, or true hostiles. Not that they'll ever know enough to appreciate the difference, since I'm going to throw them out.*

There were seven of them, however, and only one of him, and he had not survived this long as a scout by being incautious. First he called to Vree, for his Mindspeech was not strong enough to reach to the two nearest scouts.

:Call alert,: he said shortly. Vree knew what that meant. He'd contact the birds of the two scouts nearest, and they, in turn, would summon their bondmates. If Darkwind didn't need their help, he would let them know through Vree, and they would turn back. But if he *did* need them, they were already on the way.

He followed the intruders for several furlongs as they blundered along the game trail, their clumsiness frightening all the creatures within a league of them into frozen silence, leaving behind them a visible trail in the scuffed vegetation, and an invisible one in the resinous tang of crushed pine needles and their own human scent. Two of the men bore no visible weapons; the rest were armed and armored.

Vree's scorn, as sour and acidic as an unripe berry, tempted him to laughter. *:Cubs,:* the bird sent, unprompted, images of bumbling young bears and tangle-footed wolf pups.

Well, this was getting him nowhere. Nothing that the intruders had said or done gave him any idea of their intent. With a sigh, he decided that there was no choice in the matter. He was going to have to confront them.

Decision made, he worked his way up ahead of them, climbed down out of the branches, restored his climbing-tool to his back, limbered his bow, and waited for them to catch up to him.

They practically blundered into him; the one in the lead saw him first; an ordinary enough fellow, his brown leather armor marking him as a fighter rather than a forester. He shouted in surprise and quite literally jumped, even though Darkwind had not moved. Of course, Darkwind's own intricately dyed scouting gear and hair dyed a mottled brown made a near-perfect camouflage, but he wasn't *that* invisible.

Citymen, Darkwind groaned to himself. *I ought to just let the ice-drakes do my job for me. . . .*

Except that there were no ice-drakes in k'Sheyna territory, nor anything else large and deadly enough to eliminate them. Except the gryphons or the firebirds—but that might well be what brought them here in the first place. Darkwind did not intend to have either his friends or his charges wind up as some fool hunter's trophies.

Instinctively, they closed ranks against him. He spoke before the strangers recovered from their startlement; using the trade-tongue that the Shin'a'in favored in their dealings with Outlanders. "You are trespassing on k'Sheyna lands," he said, curtly. *A bluff, but I doubt they'll know how thin we're spread. And let them wonder if they'd have been taken by Tayledras, or something else.* "You must leave the way you came. Now."

They certainly couldn't miss the bow in his hands, his hooked climbing-staff on his back, or the steely menace in his voice. One of them started to object; the man next to him hushed him quickly. The fellow in the lead narrowed his eyes and frowned, looking him up and down as if measuring him.

"There's only one," the objector whispered, obviously unaware of how keen Tayledras hearing was; his silencer cut him off with "Only one we can *see,* you fool. Let me handle this."

The man stepped forward, moving up beside Leather Armor. "Your pardon, my lord," he said, with false geniality. "We didn't know, how could we? There are no signposts, no border guards—"

"Tayledras have no need of signs," Darkwind interrupted coldly. "And I am a guard. I am telling you to leave. Your lives will be at hazard, else."

Did that sound as stupid as I think it did? Or did I convince them that they don't dare chance that I may not be as formidable as I'm pretending to be?

"I shall not permit you to pass," he warned, as they continued to hesitate.

The Objector plucked at Speaker's sleeve; Leather Armor frowned and turned his head to listen to the others' whispered conference without taking his eyes off Darkwind. This time they spoke too softly even for him to hear, and when they turned back to face him, Speaker wore a broad, bright—and empty—smile.

Damn. They've seen through me. I look like a lad, and I didn't feather one of them before I stopped them. My mistake.

"Of course we'll leave, my lord," he said with hollow good humor. "And we're very sorry to have trespassed."

Darkwind said nothing. Speaker waited for a response, got none, and shrugged.

"Very well, then, gentlemen," he said and gestured back down the path. "Shall we?"

They turned, as if to go—

I've seen this before. They somehow know—or guess— there's only one of me right now. They think they're going to catch me off-guard. Idiots. He alerted Vree with a touch, dropped, and rolled into the brush at the side of the trail. They were making so much noise they didn't even hear him move.

They turned back, weapons in hand, and were very surprised to see that he wasn't where they expected him to be. Before they managed to locate him, he had popped up out of the brush, and the one Darkwind had mentally tagged as "Speaker" was down with an arrow in his throat.

He dropped back into the cover of the bushes as Vree dove at the unprotected head of one of the men in the rear of the party, the one who had been making all the objections. The man shrieked with feminine shrillness and clapped both hands to his scalp as Vree rose into the branches with bloody talons.

That's one down and one hit. I think that takes out anyone who might be a mage.

It didn't look as if the rest of this was going to be that easy, though. Leather Armor was barking orders in a language Darkwind didn't recognize, but as the rest of the men of the party took to cover and began flanking him, Darkwind had a fairly good idea what those orders were.

Do they want a live Hawkbrother, or a dead border guard? The question had very real significance. If the former, he could probably take them all himself; they would have to be careful, and he wouldn't. But if the latter, he was going to have his hands full.

His answer came a few moments later, as an arrow whistled past his ear, and no rebuke from Leather Armor followed. *A dead border guard, then. Damn. My luck is simply not in today. . . .*

There were at least two men with bows that he recalled, and he was not about to send Vree flying into an arrow. He told the forestgyre to stay up in the branches and worked himself farther back into the bushes.

That proved to be a definite tactical error. Within moments, he discovered that he had been flanked.

Just my luck to get a party with an experienced commander. Now he had the choice of trying to get to thicker cover, or taking on one of the men nearest him.

Thicker cover won't stop an arrow. That decided him. He put aside his bow, and slid his climbing-staff out of the sheath at his back.

He rose from cover with a bloodcurdling shriek not unlike Vree's, the staff a blur of motion in his hands. The man nearest him fell back with an oath, but it was too late. He had misjudged the length of the staff, and the wicked climbing-hook at the end of it, designed to catch and hold on tree bark, caved in half his face and lodged in his eye socket.

Darkwind jerked the hook free and dropped, as another man belatedly aimed an arrow at him. It went wild, and Darkwind took to cover again.

That leaves four.

:Brothers come,: Vree said. And, hopefully, added, :Vree hunt?:

:No, dammit, featherhead, stay up there!:

:?: Vree replied.

Darkwind swore at himself. *Got too complicated for him again.* He thought emphatically, :Arrows!:

:!: replied Vree, just as rustling in the dry leaves told Darkwind that he was being stalked.

He Mindtouched cautiously, ready to pull back in an instant if it proved that the stalker had any mind-powers.

Ordinary, unGifted—but this one was Leather Armor. Darkwind knew he wasn't going to take *him* by surprise with a yell and a hooked stick.

He worked his way backward, wondering where the other two guards that Vree had called for him were. His Mindspeech wasn't strong enough to hear them unless they were very near, but Vree and the other bondbirds of the scouts patrolling nearby were in constant contact. Vree was trained to serve as a relay point—if there was anything to relay.

The rustling stopped, and Darkwind froze so that he did not give himself away. They remained where they were, he and Leather Armor, for what seemed like hours. Finally, just when Darkwind's leg had started to cramp, Leather Armor moved again.

Meanwhile, Darkwind had an idea. *:Vree, play wounded bird. Find a man with no arrows, and take him to the brothers.:* It was an old trick in the wild, but it just might work against citybred folk. After a moment, Darkwind heard Vree's distress call, faint with distance, and growing fainter. The rustling stopped for a moment; someone cursed softly, then the rustling began again.

That's four.

Darkwind moved again, but the cramp in his leg made him a just a little clumsy, and he overbalanced. He caught himself before he fell, but his outstretched hands brushed by a thick branch and it bent, shaking enough to rustle the leaves, and betraying his location.

Damn!

No hope for it now, he half-rose and sprinted for the shelter of a rock pile, pounding feet and crackling brush not far behind him. The woods were too thick here to afford a good shot; it was going to be hand-to-hand if Leather Armor overtook him.

Ill luck struck again; just as he reached the rocks, something shot at ankle-height out of the shadows. He leapt but couldn't quite avoid the tangle-cord. It caught one foot, and he tumbled forward. He tucked and rolled as he went down, but when he came back up, he found himself staring at the point of a sword.

Behind the sword stood Leather Armor, frowning furiously. A few moments later, panting up behind him, came the man with the bloody, furrowed scalp.

"No spindly runt is going to tell us where we can go," sneered Leather Armor. "One little brat to play guardman, hmm? So much for your big bad Hawkbrothers, milor—"

Two screams from out in the woods interrupted him, and both their heads turned for a fraction of a heartbeat. Just long enough for Darkwind to reach the kill-blade he had hidden in his boot—and Vree to begin his stoop.

"What made you think I was alone?" he said, mildly. Leather Armor's head snapped back around, giving Darkwind a clear shot at his eye. A quick flick of the wrist, and the knife left his hand and went straight to the mark, just as Vree struck the second man from behind, his talons aimed for the neck and shoulders, knocking the mage to the ground with the force of the blow. As Darkwind's victim toppled over, Vree's talons pierced the back of his target's neck, and he bit through the spine, the powerful beak able to separate even a deer's back-bone at need. It was over in moments.

Vree flapped his wings and screamed in triumph, and Darkwind licked the blood away from his lip; he had bitten it when he fell. The taste was flat and sweet, gritty with forest loam.

He rose slowly and brushed himself off, waiting for Vree to calm down a little before trying to deal with him. Like all raptors, the bondbirds were most dangerous just after a kill, when their blood still coursed hot with excitement, and they had forgotten everything but the chase and strike.

When Darkwind's own heart had settled, he turned, and called Vree back to the glove. The bondbird mantled and screamed objection at him, still hot with his hunting-rage, but when Darkwind Mindtouched him—carefully, for at this stage it was easy to be pulled into the raptor's mind—he calmed. Darkwind held out his arm and slapped the glove again, and this time Vree returned to his bond-mate, launching himself from the body with a powerful shove of his legs, and landing heavily on Darkwind's gauntlet. The wicked talons that had so easily pierced a man's neck closed gently on the scout's leather-covered wrist.

Darkwind pointedly ignored the second body, Vree's victim, and stooped over the first corpse to retrieve his knife, Vree flapping his wings a little to keep his balance. Admittedly, it was no uglier a death than the one *he* had just delivered, but it was easy to forget that the Tayledras-bred forestgyres, largest of all the bondbirds other than the eagles, were easily a match for many wild tiercel eagles in size, and fully capable of killing men.

And when Vree did just that—sometimes the realization of just what kind of a born killer he carried around on his wrist and shoulder every day came as a little shock.

At least he doesn't try to eat them, Darkwind thought with a grimace. In fact, Vree was even now fastidiously cleaning his talons, his thoughts full of distaste for the flavor of the blood on them.

The bird looked up, suddenly. Darkwind tensed for a moment, but *:Brothers come,:* the bird said and went back to cleaning his talons.

Even to Darkwind's experienced eyes it seemed as if a man-shaped piece of the forest had detached itself and was walking toward him when Firestorm first came into view. The sight gave him a renewed appreciation for the effectiveness of the scouts' camouflage.

He'd heard somewhere that one of the Outlanders' superstitions about the Tayledras was that they were really all mirror-copies of the same person.

I suppose it might look that way to strangers. . . .

The scouts all dressed so identically in the field that they might well have been wearing uniforms; close-fitting tunic and trews of a supple weave and of a mottled, layer-dyed green, gray, and brown. There were individual differences in the patterns, as distinct as individual fingerprints to the knowledgeable, but to an Outlander the outfits probably looked identical. And their hair *was* identical, except for length. Hair color among the Hawkbrothers was a uniform white; living in the Vales, surrounded by magic, hair bleached to white and eyes to silver-blue by the time a Tayledras was in his early twenties—sooner, if he was a mage. The scouts dyed their hair a mottled brown to match their surroundings—the rest of the Clan left theirs white.

I suppose Outlanders have reason to think us identical.

Firestorm's bondbird was nowhere in sight, but as the younger scout came into the clearing, Kreel dove down out of the treetops to land on Firestorm's casually outstretched arm. Kreel was a different breed from Vree; smaller, and with the broad wings of a hawk, rather than the rakish, pointed wings of the falcon. Neither bird had bleached out yet; since Darkwind no longer used his magic powers, and Firestorm never had been a mage, it would be years before either bird became a *ti'aeva'leshy'a,* a "forest spirit," one of the snow-white "ghost birds," with markings in faint blue-gray.

Too bad, in a way. The white ones frighten the life out of Outlanders who see them. We could use that edge, Vree and I. If this lot had seen him *first, they might not have chanced taking me on.*

Vree's natural coloration was *partially* white already. His white breast sported brown barring; the same pattern as the underside of his wings. His back and the upper face of his wings were still brown, with a faint black barring. Kreel was half Vree's size, with a solid blue-gray back and a reddish-brown, barred breast. Kreel's red eyes had begun to fade to pink; Vree's eyes had already faded to light gray from his adolescent color of ice-blue.

"I got one of the bastards, Skydance got one, and Skydance's Raan got the third," Firestorm said, ruffling the breast-feathers of his cooperihawk. He shook his head in admiration at the gyre on Darkwind's wrist, as Vree fastidiously preened the blood from his breast-feathers. "Makes me wish I'd bonded to a gyre, sometimes. This little one is faster than anyone would believe, but she can't take down a man."

"A bird doesn't have to be able to take a man down to take one out," Darkwind reminded him. "Kreel does all right. *You're* too damned bloodthirsty."

Firestorm just chuckled, reached into his game-pouch, and fed Kreel a tidbit. Vree clucked and shifted his weight from one foot to the other, in an anxious reminder that *he* was owed a reward as well.

Darkwind scratched the top of Vree's head, then reached into his own game-pouch for a rabbit quarter. Vree tore into the offering happily. "Funny, isn't it," Firestorm observed, "We can shape them all we like, make them as intelligent as we can and still have flight-worthy birds, but we can't change their essential nature. They're still predators to the core. Who were those fools?"

"I don't know." Darkwind frowned. "I listened to them for a while, but I didn't learn anything. I think there were two mages and the rest were fighters to guard them, but that's only a guess. I don't know what they wanted, other than the usual." Flies were beginning to gather around the fallen bodies, and he moved out of the way a little. "Dive in, steal the treasures of the mysterious Hawkbrothers, and try to get out intact. Greedy bastards."

"They never learn, do they?" Firestorm grimaced.

"No," Darkwind agreed soberly. "They never do."

Something about the tone of his voice made Firestorm look at him sharply. "Are you all right?" he said. "If you got hurt but you're trying to go all noble on me, forget it. If you're not in shape for it, we can take over your share for the rest of the day, or I can send back for some help."

Darkwind shook his head, and tossed his hair out of his eyes. "I'm all right; I'm just tired of the whole situation we're in. We shouldn't *be* out here alone; we should be patrolling in threes, at least, on every section. K'Sheyna is in trouble, and anyone with any sense knows it. Most of our mages won't leave the Vale, and the best of our fighters are out of reach. I don't know why the Council won't ask the other Clans for help, or even the Shin'a'in—"

Firestorm shrugged indifferently. "We haven't had anything hit the border that we couldn't handle, even shorthanded," he replied. "After all, we *had* cleaned this area out, that's why the children and minor mages and half the fighters were gone when—"

He broke off, flushing. "I'm sorry—I forgot you were there when—"

"When the Heartstone fractured," Darkwind finished for him, his voice flat and utterly without expression. *I'm not surprised he doesn't remember.* Darkwind had been "Songwind" then, a proud young mage with snow-white hair and a peacock wardrobe—

Not Darkwind, who refused to use any magic but shielding, who never wore anything but scout gear and wouldn't use the formidable powers of magic he still could control—if he chose—not even to save himself.

He was—*had been*—Adept-rank, in fact—and strong enough at nineteen to be one of the Heartstone anchors. . . .

Not that it mattered. He watched Vree tear off strips of rabbit and gulp them down, fur and all. "I don't know if you ever knew this," he said conversationally, not wanting Firestorm to think he was upset about the reminder of his past. "I watched the building of the Gate to send them all off."

Firestorm tilted his head to one side. "Why *did* they send everyone off? I wasn't paying any attention—it was my first Vale-move."

"We always do that," Darkwind said, as Vree got down to the bones and began cleaning every scrap of flesh from them he could find. "It's part of the safety measures, sending those not directly involved in moving the power or guarding those who are to the new Vale-site, where they'd be safe in case something happened."

"Which it did." Firestorm sighed. "I guess it's a good thing. The gods only know where they are now. Somewhere west."

Somewhere west. Too far to travel, when over half of them were children.

"And not an Adept able to build a Gate back to us in the lot of them." Darkwind scowled. "Now that *was* a mistake. And it was bad tactics. Half of the Adepts should have been with them, and *I* don't know why the Council ordered them all to stay until the Heartstone was drained and the power moved."

Firestorm relaxed marginally, and scratched Kreel with his free hand. "Nobody ever tells us about these things. Darkwind, why haven't we built a new Gate and brought them back?"

A damned good question. Darkwind's lips compressed. "Father says that what's left of the Heartstone is too unstable to leave, too dangerous to build a Gate near, and much too dangerous to have children exposed to."

Firestorm raised an eloquent eyebrow. "You don't believe him?"

"I don't know what to believe." Darkwind stared off into the distance, over Firestorm's shoulder, into the shadows beneath the trees. "I probably shouldn't be telling you this, even. That kind of information is only supposed to be discussed by the Council or among mages. There's another thing; Father was acting oddly even before the disaster—he hasn't been quite himself since he was caught in that forest fire. Or that's the way it seems to me, but nobody else seems to have noticed anything wrong."

"Well, I haven't, at least not any more than with the rest of the Council." Firestorm laughed, sarcastically. "Old men, too damned proud to ask for help from outside, and too feeble to fix things themselves. Which is probably why *I'm* not on the Council; I've said that in public a few too many times."

The scout tossed his hawk up into the air and turned to go. Kreel darted up into the trees ahead, and all the birds went silent as he took to the air. Everything that flew knew the shape of a cooperihawk; nothing on wings was safe from a hungry one. And no bird would ever take a chance on a cooperi being sated. "If you're all right to finish, I'll get back to my section. Do we bother to clean up, or leave it for the scavengers?"

"Leave it," Darkwind told him. "Maybe a few bones lying around will discourage others."

"Maybe." The younger man laughed. "Or maybe we should start leaving heads on stakes at the borders."

With that macabre suggestion, the scout followed his bird into the forest, moving in silence, blending into the foliage within moments. Vree had finished his rabbit, dropping the polished bones, and Darkwind launched him into the air as well, so that they could resume their interrupted patrol.

He'd meant what he told Firestorm, every bitter word of it. *I hardly know Father anymore. He used to be creative, flexible; he used to have no trouble admitting when he was wrong. Now he's the worst of the lot. Every time another Clan sends someone to see if we need help, he sends them away. How can we not need help? We've got an unstable Heartstone, we don't have enough scouts to patrol a border that we had to pull back in the first place. Our children are gone and we can't get them back—and we don't dare leave. And he's pretending we can handle it.*

That was part of the reason he spent so little time in the Vale anymore; the place was too silent, too empty. Tayledras children were seldom as noisy as Outlander children, but they made their presence—and their absence—felt.

The once-lively Vale seemed dead without them.

And another part of the reason he avoided the Vale was his father. The fewer opportunities there were for confrontations with the old man, the better Darkwind liked it.

He would have to go in at the end of his patrol, though, and he wrinkled his nose in distaste at what he would have to endure. This invasion would have to be reported. And as always, the Council would want to know why he hadn't handled things differently, why he hadn't blasted the intruders or shot them all when he first saw them. And because he was an Elder, the questions would be more pointed.

I didn't kill them because they could have been perfectly innocent, dammit!

And Starblade would want to know why he hadn't used magic.

And as always, Darkwind would be unable to give him an answer that would satisfy him.

"Because I don't want to" isn't good enough. He wants to know why I don't want to.

Darkwind pulled his climbing-staff out of the sheath, and hooked a limb, hauling himself up into the tree and trying not to wince as he discovered new bruises.

He wants to know why. He says. But he won't accept my reasons because Adept Starblade couldn't possibly have a son who gave up magic for the life of a Scout. Even when the magic killed his mother in front of his eyes. Even when the magic ruined his life. Even when he's seen, over and over, that magic isn't an answer, it's a tool, and any tool can be done without.

He looked out over the forest floor and briefly touched Vree's mind. All was quiet. Even the birds, frightened into silence by the noise of the fight and the appearance of the cooperihawk, were singing again.

Well, he'd better start learning to change again, Darkwind decided, *because I've had enough. I'm taking this incident to the Council as usual, but this time I'm going to make an issue of it. And I don't care if he doesn't like what he's going to hear; we can't keep on like this indefinitely.*

And if he wants a fight, he's going to get one.

Chapter Three

ELSPETH

Elspeth bit her lip until it bled to keep herself from losing her temper. Queen Selenay, normally serene in the face of any crisis, had reacted to the attack on her eldest child with atypical hysteria.

Well, I'd call it hysteria, anyway.

Elspeth had barely gotten clean and changed when the summons arrived from her mother—accompanied by a bodyguard of two. As a harbinger of what was to come, that bodyguard put Elspeth's hackles up immediately. The sight of Selenay, standing beside the old wooden desk in her private apartments, white to the lips and with jaws and hands clenched, did nothing to make her daughter feel any better.

And so far, Selenay's impassioned tirade had not reassured her Heir either. It seemed that the Queen's answer to the problem was to restrict Elspeth's movements to the Palace complex, and to assign her a day-and-night guard of not less than two at all times.

And that, as far as Elspeth was concerned, was totally unacceptable.

But she couldn't get a word in until her mother stopped pacing up and down the breadth of her private office and finally calmed down enough to sit and listen instead of talking. It helped that Talia, though she was privy to this not-quite-argument Elspeth was having with Selenay, was staying discreetly in the background, and so far hadn't said a word, one way or the other.

I think if she sided with Mother, I'd have hysterics.

"I can't believe you're taking this so—so—casually!" Selenay finally concluded tightly, her hands shaking visibly even though she held them clenched together on the desktop, white as a marble carving.

"I'm not taking it 'casually,' Mother," Elspeth replied, hoping the anger she thought she had under control did not show. "I'm certainly not regarding this incident as some kind of a bad joke. But I am *not* going to let fear rule my life." She paused for a moment, waiting for another tirade to begin. When Selenay didn't say anything, she continued, trying to sound as firm and adult as possible. "No bodyguards, Mother. No one following me everywhere. And I am *not* going to live behind the Palace walls like some kind of cloistered novitiate."

"You're almost *killed,* and you say *that?* I—"

"*Mother,*" Elspeth interrupted. "Every other ruler lives with that same threat constantly. We've been spoiled in Valdemar—mages have never been able to get past our borders, and the Heraldic Gifts—especially the Queen's Own's Gifts—have always made sure that we knew who the assassins were before they had a chance to strike. So—now that isn't necessarily true anymore. *I* am not going to restrict my movements with a night-and-day guard just because of a single incident. And, frankly, I'm not going to lose any sleep over it."

Selenay paled and seemed at a loss for words.

"That doesn't mean I'm going to be careless," she added, "I'm going to take every precaution Kerowyn advises. I'm not foolhardy or stupid—but I am not going to live in fear, either."

Finally Talia spoke up. "There really isn't that much more danger than there always was," she said mildly. "We've just been a lot more careless than the monarchs were in—say—Vanyel's day. We *have* been spoiled; we thought we were immune to danger, that magic had somehow gone away. The fact is, we didn't learn from the last two wars. We have to do more—much more—

than we have in finding ways to counter this threat. Or should I say, in rediscovering them—''

Now that's odd. No one seems to have any trouble discussing magic when it's in the past—the stories of Vanyel's time, for instance. It's only when we're talking about it happening now—and here, inside Valdemar—that the restriction seems to hold.

But before she pursued that train of thought, she had to come up with some convincing arguments first. ''Mother, I'm a Herald first, and your Heir second. The fact is, I can't do *my* job with somebody hovering over me all the time.'' When Selenay looked blank, Elspeth sighed. ''I'm still on duty to the city courts, remember? And on detached duty with Kerowyn. What if she wants me to go work with the Skybolts for a while? What would your allies say if I went over there with a set of bodyguards at my back? They'd say you don't even trust your own people, that's what.''

Not to mention what a pair of hulking brutes at my back is going to do to my love-life, she thought unhappily. *There wasn't a lot there to begin with, but I can't even imagine trying to have a romantic encounter with half the Guard breathing down my neck.*

:You could always try confining your pursuits to your bodyguards,: Gwena suggested teasingly.

:Oh, thanks. That's a wonderful idea. I'll take it under advisement,: she replied, trying to keep her level of sarcasm down to something acceptable.

''To suddenly start trailing bodyguards around isn't going to do much for my accessibility, Mother,'' she continued, thinking quickly. ''People come to the Heir when they are afraid, for one reason or another, to come to the Monarch—and you *know* that's been true for hundreds of years. If there's something you want done, but don't want the open authority of the Crown behind it, you give it to me. Talia is your double in authority—*she* can't do that. I'm your unfettered hand, and now you want to shackle me. It just won't work, anyone could tell you that. It not only cuts down *my* effectiveness, it cuts down on yours.''

:Good girl; that's the way to win your argument. I agree with you, by the way. Bodyguards are not a solu-

tion. Not unless those bodyguards were also Heralds, and we have no Heralds to spare.:

Elspeth felt a little more relaxed and confident with Gwena's support. *:Thanks. At least I'm not just being boneheaded and stubborn about this.:*

:Oh, you are being boneheaded and stubborn,: her Companion replied cheerfully. *:But it's for the right reasons, and there's nothing wrong with a little stubbornness for the correct cause.:*

Elspeth could hear the gentle good humor in Gwena's mind-voice and couldn't take offense, though for a moment she was sorely tempted.

Selenay did not look convinced by the argument, however.

"I can't see that it's worth the risk—" she began. Talia interrupted her.

"Elspeth's right, I'm afraid," she said, in her quiet, clear voice. "It *is* worth the risk. When Elspeth goes out, off the Palace grounds, you could assign her a discreet guard, but other than that I think that extra care on everyone's part will serve the same purpose. If Kero is right, simply having the guards question anyone they see who doesn't seem to be acting normally will prevent another incident like the last one."

Selenay's jaw tightened in a way Elspeth knew only too well. "You think I'm overreacting, don't you?"

Yes, Elspeth replied—mentally. And kept a very tight shield over the thought.

"No," Talia said, and smiled. "You're just acting the way any mother would. I know if it were Jemmie—let's just say I'd have him hidden away with some family— say, a retired Guardsman-turned-farmer—so far out in the country that no one could counterfeit a native and *any* stranger would cause a stir."

"Maybe—" Selenay's expression turned speculative, and Elspeth started to interrupt the thought she *knew* was going through her mother's mind.

Talia did it for her. "That won't work for Elspeth, I'm afraid. She's too old to hide that way, even if she would put up with being sent off like an exile. However—her uncle's court is very well protected. . . ."

Not too bad an idea, Elspeth had to admit, *even if it doesn't feel right.*

"That's a thought," Selenay acknowledged. "I don't know; I'll have to think about it."

"So long as you aren't planning on putting me under armed guard, like the Crown Jewels," Elspeth said, in a little better humor.

"Not at the moment," her mother admitted.

"All right, then." She ran a hand over her hair and smiled a little. "I can put up with one guard in the city; we probably should have had one anyway. If I'm not safe on the Palace grounds, after Kero gives the Guards one of her famous lectures, I won't be safe anywhere. I should know, I got one myself today. Two, in fact. As soon as she figured I was all right, she gave me a point-by-point critique on my performance."

Talia chuckled, and Selenay relaxed a little. "I can just see Kero doing that, too," Talia said. "She doesn't ever let up. She's like Alberich. The more tired you are, the more she seems to push you."

"I know, believe me. Uh—on that subject, sort of— would there be any problem if I had a tray in my room?" she asked, drooping just a little—not enough to resurrect Selenay's hysteria, but enough to look convincingly tired. "I don't think I can handle Uncle's delegation right now. . . ."

"After this afternoon, I doubt anyone would expect you to," the Queen replied, sympathetically. "I'll make your apologies, and hopefully, after this afternoon, the current batch of rumors will be put to rest for a while."

"And I'll see that someone sends a tray up," Talia offered. "With honeycakes," she added, giving Elspeth a quick wink.

Elspeth managed to keep from giving herself away, and stayed in character. "Thanks," she sighed, throwing both of them grateful looks. "If anyone wants me, I'll be in the bathing room, under hot water. And frankly, right now all you need to worry about is whether or not I drown in the bathtub. All I want is a hot bath and a book, dinner, and bed."

She made a hasty exit before she betrayed herself. After all, it was partially the truth. She really *was* tired; her afternoon's double-workout had seen to that even before the attack. She really *did* want a hot bath and a tray in her room.

But she had no intention of going to bed early. There was too much to think about.

A candlemark later, wrapped in a warm robe and nibbling on a honeycake as she gazed out into the dusk-filled gardens, she still hadn't come to any conclusions of her own.

Things just felt wrong; she was restless and unhappy, and she wasn't certain why. The restrictions Selenay had wanted to place on her movements had merely heightened those feelings, which had been there all along.

It's almost as if there was something I should be doing, she decided, as the blue dusk deepened and shrouded the paths below in shadows. *As if somewhere I have the key to all this, if I can just find it.*

One thing she was certain of: this would not be the last time Ancar attempted an assassination, or something of the sort. He wanted Valdemar, and he was not going to give up trying to annex it. There was no way he could expand eastward; the Aurinalean Empire was old and strong enough to flatten him if he attacked any of its kingdoms. North was Iftel—strange, isolationist Iftel—guarded by a deity. He could not move against them; not unless he wanted a smoking hole where his army had been. South was Karse, and if rumor was true, he was already making moves in that direction. But Karse had been at war with Valdemar and Rethwellan for generations, and they were quite prepared to take him on as well. Taking Valdemar would give him protection on the north, a western border he would not need to guard, and another place from which to attack Karse. Besides doubling his acquisitions.

He probably assumed that if the rightful rulers and their Heirs died, it would leave the country in a state of chaos and an easy target for takeover.

He might not be ready for another war now—but he would be, given time and the chance to rebuild his forces.

So no matter what, there's going to be another war, she thought, shoving the rest of her dinner aside, uneaten. *I know it, Kero knows it, Stepfather knows it—Mother knows it, and won't admit it.*

She turned away from the window and rested her back against the sill. She'd had a fair number of discussions with Kero and Prince-Consort Daren on this very subject. Her *stepfather* didn't treat her like a child.

Then again, her stepfather hadn't ever seen her until she was adult and in her full Whites. It was an old proverb that a person was *always* a child to his parents . . . but it was war she should really be worrying about, not how to make her mother realize that she was an adult and capable of living her own life. The two problems were entwined, but not related. And the personal problems could wait.

The next try Ancar makes is going to involve magic, I know it is—combative magic, war-magic, the kind they use south of Rethwellan. The kind the Skybolts are used to seeing. Kero says so, and I think she's right. She can talk about real magic, and I can . . . and that might be a clue to what I need to be doing right there.

For Valdemar was not ready to cope with magic, especially not within its borders. For all the efforts to prepare the populace, for all the research that was *supposed* to have been done in the archives, very little had actually been accomplished. Yes, the ballads of Vanyel's time and earlier had been revived, but there was very much a feeling of "but it can't happen now" in the people Elspeth had talked to. And she wasn't the only one to have come to that conclusion. Kero had said much the same thing. The Captain was worried.

Elspeth licked her bitten lip, and thought hard. *Kero's told me a lot of stories she hasn't even told Mother. Some of the things the Skybolts had to deal with—and those were just minor magics.*

"Most of the time the major magics don't get used," she'd said more than once. That was because the major mages tended to cancel one another out. Adept-class mages tended to be in teaching, or in some otherwise less-hazardous aspect of their profession.

Most mages, Adept-class or not, were unwilling to risk themselves in all-out mage-duels for the sake of a mere employer. Most employers were reluctant to antagonize them.

But when the ruler himself was a mage, or backed by one—a powerful mage, at that—the rules changed. Mages could be coerced, like anyone else; or blackmailed, or bribed, if the offer was high enough. There was already evidence of coercion, magical and otherwise; outright control, like the men of his armies. And where there was a power broker, there were always those who wanted power above all else and were willing to pay any price to get it.

So Valdemar wasn't protected anymore because there was someone willing to pay the price of breaking the protections.

Or bending them. . . .

All right; when the Border-protection has failed, what's been the common denominator? She rubbed her temple, as she tried to think of what those failures had in common.

It didn't keep Hulda out—but she didn't work any magic while she was here. It didn't keep some of Ancar's spells out, but they were cast across *the Border. It didn't keep that assassin out—but the spell must surely have been cast on him when he was with Ancar. And it didn't keep Need out, but Need hasn't done a blessed thing— openly—since Kero got here.*

So; as long as there wasn't any *active* magic-casting within the borders, the protections they had relied on weren't working anymore.

Or else there were now mages who were stronger than the protections, so long as they worked from outside.

And, without a doubt, Ancar had figured that out, too.

Furthermore, no matter how powerful the protections were, unless they were caused by some deity or other— which Elspeth very much doubted—they could be broken altogether, instead of merely circumvented.

And when—not if, but *when*—Ancar accomplished that, they were going to be as helpless as a mouse beneath the talons of a predator.

As if to underscore that, Elspeth heard the call of an owl, somewhere out in the gardens.

Someone was going to have to find a mage—preferably a very powerful mage, one who wouldn't suffer from whatever had kept the Skybolts' mages out—and bring him to Valdemar.

That was going to take a lot of money, persuasion, or both. The first they had—or could get. The second just required the right person. Someone who was experienced in diplomacy and negotiation.

Or, failing being able to bring someone in, a Herald was going to have to learn magic herself.

That's it, she decided. *That's what I need to do—find a mage and bring him in. I'm the perfect instrument for the job. Or learn magic; Kero says there are some things—according to her grandmother—that just need a trained will. I've certainly got that.*

And as for where to find a mage—I think I know just the place to start.

This time Elspeth called the meeting, at breakfast, in her mother's suite. She hoped to catch her in a malleable mood—which she often was in the early morning. Not that Elspeth enjoyed being up that early; on the whole, she preferred never to have to view the sunrise.

But for a good cause, she'd sacrifice a bit of sleep.

She stated her case as clearly and logically as possible, before Selenay had finished her muffins, but after she'd had her first two cups of tea. She'd thought about her presentation very carefully; why someone had to go chasing mages, and why that someone had to be her. Then she sat back and waited for her answer.

She has to agree. There's no other choice for us.

"No," Selenay stated flatly. "It's not possible."

For a moment she was taken aback, but she rallied her defenses, thought quickly and plowed gamely onward. "Mother, I don't see where there's any choice," Elspeth replied, just as firmly as her mother. "I've told you the facts. Kero backs up my guesses about what's likely to happen, and she's the best tactician we have. And Alberich backs *her* up. The three of us have talked this over a lot."

"I don't—" Selenay fell strangely silent, looking troubled and very doubtful. Elspeth followed up her advantage. *I can't give her a chance to say anything. Look at her hands, she's clutching things again. It's conflict between being a mother and the ruler. I think I can convince the Council, but I have to convince her before I convince the Council.*

"We can't do this on our own anymore; we have to have help. We *have* to have a mage—'Adept-class,' is what Kero says. Someone who can work around whatever it is that keeps active mages out. We have to find someone like that who is willing not only to help us but to teach Heralds if he can.''

"I don't see why—" Selenay began. "We've managed all right until now. Why can't the Gifts provide an adequate defense? They've worked so far.''

"Mother, believe me, there hasn't been a real trial of them,'' Elspeth countered. "I've listened to Kero's stories, and frankly they won't hold against a real effort by *several* mages. I'll tell you what, I suspect that *we* have people capable of becoming mages. The Chronicles all talk about a 'Mage-Gift' just as if it were something like—oh, Firestarting; rare, but not unusual. *I* don't think it's been lost. *I* think that we've just forgotten how to tell what it is, and how to train it. But to do that, we need a mage. A good one. And Kero says that all the good teachers are Adept-class.''

"Even if all that is true,'' Selenay said, after a long silence, her hands clenched around her mug. "Why should you be the one to go?''

"Well, for one thing, I've got Crown powers. When I find a mage we can trust, I can offer him anything reasonable—and I know what's reasonable; Kero's briefed me on hiring mages. For another—I'm not indispensable. You have two more heirs, and if you want to know the truth, I'm not certain I *should* wear the crown.'' She smiled ruefully. "I take shortcuts a little too often to make the Council comfortable.''

Selenay returned the smile reluctantly, but it faded just as quickly as it came.

Elspeth shrugged. "The truth of the matter is that the twins are probably going to be better rulers than I would. The Council can't object to letting me go, with two more candidates for the throne still here. I'm a full Herald, I know what we need, Kero can probably give me contacts, and I have Crown authority. I'm the best—absolutely best—person for the job.''

Selenay started to say something—Elspeth waited for the rebuke—but it never came. It was almost as if something had interrupted her before she could say anything. *Odd.*

But she followed up on her advantage.

"Let me give you another reason. You wanted me safe, right? You can put forty layers of guards on the twins and they won't mind, but you know very well that *I* won't put up with it. On the other hand, if you send me to Uncle Faram, Ancar won't know where to find me at first—and when he finds out, he won't risk a try for me in Rethwellan. Uncle has a larger army, *he* has mages, and I don't think even Ancar would risk all-out war with him.'' She firmed her jaw and raised her head stubbornly. ''Besides, I won't be there for long, I'll be looking for Kero's old mage Quenten. He has a school, she says, and if anybody can find us mages, I should think he would. When I'm there, I'll be surrounded by mages. I couldn't *possibly* be safer than that.''

Selenay finally sighed and unclenched her hands. ''There must be something wrong with that logic, but I can't figure out what it is,'' she said, her brow furrowed with an unhappy frown.

Elspeth turned a look of appeal on Talia, who bit her lip and looked very uncomfortable. *As if part of her wants to side with me, and part of her doesn't.*

''I just don't like it,'' Selenay said, finally. ''You're far too vulnerable. Even traveling through Valdemar, I wouldn't feel comfortable unless you had a full company of troops with you. Traveling across the Comb is nearly as dangerous in summer as winter—there are thunderstorms, wild beasts—and the only decent pass is too close to Karse for *my* comfort.'' She shook her head. ''No, I can't allow it. Bringing in a mage—that's not a bad idea. I think you're right about that much. But the person I send won't be you.''

Selenay's chin came up and her voice took on a steely quality that Elspeth knew only too well. There was no arguing with her mother in *this* mood.

She *could* appeal to her stepfather and Alberich. Kero was already on her side.

But not now.

And it might take weeks, even months, to get Selenay to change her mind. By then it would be fall or winter, and she would have another excuse to keep Elspeth at home—the weather. And perhaps by then it would be too late.

She closed her eyes for a moment. The odd pressure inside her, now that she had a goal in mind and a task that really needed to be done, was already uncomfortable. Any delay would make it intolerable.

She had to go—*had* to. And she couldn't. She wanted to scream, argue, cry, anything.

But just a single word at this point would ensure that she would *never* win Selenay's permission. And without that permission, there was no point in going to the Council; they would never override the Queen on this.

If I just ran off and did it—

No, that wouldn't work, either.

She had to have Crown and Council authority to make this mission a success, and running off on her own was not going to win her either.

So instead of bursting out, as she really wanted to, she simply clamped her mouth shut.

She got up, leaving her breakfast untasted, bowed stiffly, and took herself out of the room altogether.

She managed to keep her temper as far as her rooms—where she slammed the door shut behind her, and yanked open the closet so hard she nearly took the door off the hinges. The handle *did* come loose in her hand, and she flung it across the room without a single word, grabbing a set of old clothes from the back of the closet, pulling off her uniform and throwing it in a heap on the floor, and pulling on the new clothing with no care whatsoever.

She heard several stitches pop as she pulled the shirt over her head and ignored them.

:Kitten?: Gwena said, tentatively. *:Dearest, don't be too discouraged. Things can change, sometimes in a heartbeat. There are events occurring out on the borders that none of us know about yet—one of those may force your mother to change her mind.:*

:Don't patronize me,: Elspeth snarled. *:I'm past the age when you can tell me that everything will be all right. We have trouble, and no one wants to admit it or let me do my part in meeting it. So leave me alone, all right? Let me cool down my own way.:*

:Oh—: Gwena replied, very much taken aback by the barely-suppressed rage in Elspeth's Mind-voice. Then she remained silent though Elspeth sensed her watchful presence in the back of her mind.

She ignored it; leaving her rooms with another slamming of doors and heading defiantly out to the gardens and her pottery shed.

No one even tried to stop her. Several people looked curiously at her as she stormed past, but no one spoke.

Most of the evidence of the assassination attempt was gone, along with the remains of those pieces that were smashed in the struggle. The floor had been swept clean—much, much cleaner than Elspeth ever kept it.

No, it was more than that. There was a new stool beside the bench where the old one had stood, there was a new door in place of the shattered one. Her old stove had been replaced with a new kiln and a new stove, her shelves had been replaced with stronger ones, the walls had been scoured, the floor scrubbed, and the place had been tidied up with meticulous precision.

Elspeth stared around with a sense of affront.

Bad enough that she'd been attacked here—but someone had taken it upon himself to ''improve'' the place.

Her sanctuary had been violated. With good intent, but violated, just the same. It wasn't hers anymore. . . .

But it was all she had.

Resolutely, she squared her shoulders, went to one of the waiting boxes of raw clay, and cut herself a generous chunk—quite enough to make another two-handled vase.

Better than the last one.

And she set about grimly wedging the helpless hunk of clay into submission.

Stubborn, unreasoning woman, she fumed, punching the defenseless clay as hard as she could, flattening it to a finger-wide sheet on the smooth slate top of the bench.

A lot like her daughter, whispered her conscience.

So what? she answered it. *I can see sense when I have to, whatever it costs me. She won't even consider what this could mean if I succeed—or what it* will *mean if I'm not allowed to try. I don't even know if she'll send someone else—she might decide not to. She might even forget.*

Her conscience persisted as she rolled the sheet of clay up into a cylinder and flattened the cylinder into a sphere. *You've never been a mother, so how can you know what letting you go would cost her? You heard Talia—if it were her son that was in jeopardy, she'd be just as irrational, and she is the most sensible person you know. And be-*

*sides, you aren't the only one who could take this mission
on and make a success out of it.*

Oh, no? she snarled at her conscience, picking the ball
of clay up, and throwing it down on the slate, over and
over again. *Who else is there?*

Kerowyn, for one, her conscience replied too promptly.
*After all, her uncle—if he's still alive—is a White Winds
Adept. And Quenten used to be one of the Skybolts'
mages. She has the same contacts she would be giving
you. Surely one of them could be persuaded to help.*

And if not? she challenged.

*If not—there're King Faram's court mages. They aren't
exactly apprentices, and they've already proved they'll
work for hire by being in his employ. And Kero is Daren
and Faram's very good friend. She could probably even
persuade Faram to part with one or more of his mages,
if they are willing to come up here.*

But I'm their relative, she countered. *That should be
twice as effective.*

Her conscience had no counter to that, but she had no
answer for it, either. So she *wasn't* the only person who
could go—so what? She was still the best choice, if not
the only one, if only Selenay would admit it.

The clay was ready—but she wasn't. She continued to
pound her temper out on it as she sought reasons why
Kerowyn could not be spared to go in her place.

She's the Captain of the Skybolts—

*Who are in Valdemar's employ. And she has perfectly
adequate stand-ins.*

*She doesn't have Crown authority, in case she has to
negotiate with someone besides the people she knows.*

Well, there's always a writ.

She's too old.

That sounded like a stupid excuse even to Elspeth. *Too
old, sure. She can beat me nineteen falls out of twenty.
Not even close, girl.*

She doesn't know what we need.

Now that might be a good reason. The needs of a mercenary Captain and the needs of a country like Valdemar
were vastly different. A Company might be able to use
someone who didn't necessarily fit their profile. Valdemar was going to need someone very special.

For one thing, he's going to need a pretty good set of

ethics. He'll have to be able to get along with people. He'll have to know when not to use his power. And most especially, he'll have to be someone who would never, ever, abuse either his power or position.

In other words, he would, for all intents and purposes, be as much like a Herald as possible.

And ideally, really, he would be Chosen as soon as Elspeth returned to Valdemar with him. That would be perfect.

But that would make him the first Herald-Mage since Vanyel. . . .

She shook off the haze of speculation. What mattered was that Kero—*if* she went—was all too likely to bring back someone who was picked with a Captain's eye, rather than a Herald's. And that could be a major mistake.

She might well take the best of a dubious lot, without looking any further. She could get someone who had managed to conceal his motives. She could even get someone in alliance with Ancar, who had not only managed to conceal his motives, but his intentions.

Kero was smart, but she hadn't been a Herald for very long. She still took some folks aback by her attitudes. That was amusing inside Valdemar, but in a situation where Valdemar's well-being depended on her attitudes— a difference of opinion could be dangerous.

And there was always the possibility that she would pick someone who was not strong enough to pass the borders. Then what?

Would she simply conclude that this mage-hunting was a waste of time, and return?

Elspeth wouldn't—but she wasn't sure that the same would be true of Kero.

This may be one case where my stubborn streak is an advantage. I won't give in until I have someone. Kero might. And if she winds up having to go outside of Rethwellan—I think her reputation as a mercenary might be held against her. There might be mages with active morals who would feel that working with a mercenary, former or no, wasn't ethical, no matter how worthy the cause.

Kero had worked all of her life to keep her emotions

out of her negotiations. That lack of obvious passion might work against her in a case like this.

But Elspeth might be convincing enough. . . .

I have all the reasons and counters I need, she thought, grimly kneading her clay. *Now if only someone would be willing to listen to them.*

Darkwind

Chapter Four

DARKWIND

"So, you have encountered another situation," Starblade k'Sheyna said coldly as he regarded his son without blinking. The *ekele* was too low on the tree trunk to sway, but the branches surrounding it moved in a gentle wind. Darkwind tried not to shift position in any way that might be interpreted as showing his discomfort. It was difficult to remain cool beneath that measuring, inscrutable gaze. Starblade's bondbird, a huge, hawk-sized crow, gazed at him with the same, impassive expression as its bondmate. It might have been a stone bird, or a shadow made into flesh and feathers.

What ever happened to the Father I knew? He's gone as thoroughly as Songwind.

"Let me see if I understand this correctly. You were on patrol along the border. Your bondbird located invaders. There were some seven intruders, two of whom *may* have been mages, the rest of whom *may* simply have been in their employ." Sun poured through the leaves, beyond the open windows, engulfing them in a dappled silence.

"Yes, Elder," Darkwind replied, just as impersonally. *Perhaps if I give him a little taste of his own attitude. . . .*

Starblade inclined his head a little, in mocking acknowledgment of the imitation, and the tiny multicolored crystals braided into his waist-length, snow-white hair sang softly as he moved, echoing the wind chimes strung in each window. "But you are not *sure.*"

"No, Elder." Darkwind knew very well what Starblade was up to and did not rise to the bait. *He wants me to get angry, and I won't. That would be an acknowledgment of weakness and lack of control.*

"Why not?" Starblade persisted, narrowing his ice-blue eyes to mere slits. "What was it that you did to try and determine what they were?"

As if he didn't know what would be the proper procedure. "I followed them for some distance, before I judged they had ventured too far into k'Sheyna territory. Nothing in their conversation gave me any clues as to their identity, Elder," Darkwind replied, holding his temper in check.

There was no real reason for this interview. They had already been over this several times; once before the entire Council, once with the other three Elders, in detail, and now, for the second time, with his father alone. The Council had heard his story without allowing him to confront them over the situation of being so shorthanded on the border. *That,* they had assigned to Starblade, as the most senior Adept, and presumably the one who could make a decision about the situation. *Perhaps he is supposed to conjure up something,* Darkwind thought bitterly.

Which meant he had to go over this as many times as Starblade wanted in order to get his point made. "I listened carefully to the conversation, what there was of it. The armed men treated the unarmed men with a certain amount of deference, but there was no outward sign that they were not—say—adventurous traders. I thought they might be mages because they were unarmed, so I moved to neutralize them first."

"You did not spellcast to determine if any of them were using magic of any kind?" Starblade settled back in his green-cushioned chair. In contrast to his son's camouflage outfit, his own elaborate clothing made him look like an exotic, silver-crested, blue-plumaged bird perched in the shrubbery.

"No, sir," Darkwind replied, allowing a hint of effrontery to carry into his voice. "I did not."

"And why not?" Starblade asked softly. "You have the power, after all."

"Because I do not choose to use that power, Father," Darkwind said, holding in his temper with an effort. "You know that. As you know my reasons."

"As I know your excuses," Starblade snapped. "They are not *reasons*. You put k'Sheyna in jeopardy because you refuse to use your abilities."

"I did no such thing. I *kept* k'Sheyna from jeopardy because I destroyed the interlopers when they would not turn back," Darkwind interrupted. "I did so *without* the foolish use of magic, which might have attracted more trouble, that close to the border. Despite being shorthanded, I did so with the limited resources at my disposal."

"Without magic."

"*Without* magic," Darkwind repeated. "*Because* it was not needed, and *because* other things might have been attracted that it would not have been possible to combat, with *only three* guards and their birds within range to stand against the threat." He glared at his father. "If you are so insistent on having mages on the border, Father, perhaps you would care to join us for some of our patrols."

And we can lead you about by the hand.

They could not have been more of a contrast, he and Starblade. The mage wore his waist-length, silver hair braided with crystals, feathers, and rainbow beads. His costume, of peacock-blue spider-silk, cut and decorated elaborately, was impressive and impractical in the extreme. Darkwind, when he was not in his scout clothing, tended to wear brown or gray, cut closely to his body, high-collared and mostly without ornament; his hair was barely shoulder-length.

Most of the mages dressed the way Starblade did, though some made concessions to camouflage by wearing white in the winter and leaf-colors in the rest of the year, garments that could blend in with the woods after a fashion. Not that long ago, he had looked like the rest of them.

This is growing tedious.

"Father, we have been over this any number of times. I did my duty; I rid k'Sheyna of the interlopers. The *point* is not that I did or did not get rid of them using magic. The *point* is that we are chronically shorthanded. We shouldn't be here at all, Father. More than half of k'Sheyna is—elsewhere. What's wrong with us? Why haven't we *done* something about this situation?"

"That is none of your concern," Starblade began coldly, drawing himself up and staring at his son in astonishment.

"It *is* my concern," Darkwind interrupted. "I'm on the Council, too. I *am* the representative of the scouts. I'm one of the Clan Elders now, which you seem to have forgotten. And as the scouts' representative, I would like to know exactly what we are doing to drain the Heartstone, or stabilize it, and rejoin the rest of our Clan." He drew himself up to match his father's pose, and looked challengingly into Starblade's eyes.

Starblade met the challenging gaze impassively. "That is the business of the mages. If you wish to have a say in the matter—" he smiled, "—you may take up your powers again. *Then* you may join the mages and have your words heeded."

Darkwind felt himself flushing with anger, despite his earlier resolutions. "What I choose to do with my powers has nothing to do with the matter. Those of us who are not mages have a right to determine k'Sheyna's future as well." He paused a moment, and added, "*That* is the tradition, after all—that every voice in a Clan has some say in the running of the Clan."

Starblade looked past his son's shoulder for a moment and took a long, slow breath. "What you choose to do with your powers is precisely at issue here." He lowered his eyes to meet Darkwind's again, and there was an anger to match his son's in his gaze. "You are risking the lives of your scouts by your refusal to use your magic. Your abilities are *required* on our boundaries, and yet you will not use them. And I *do not* accept why you refuse."

Darkwind closed his eyes, but he could not block the memories.

* * *

The Heartstone, a great crystal-laced boulder taller than he, pulsing with all the life and power of the Vale. Its surface glowed with intricate warm red and golden tracings, as the inner circle of Adepts continued to drain the excess mage-energy from the land about them, to empty the nodes and the power-lines so that there was nothing left that could be used to harm.

That was how the Tayledras left a place; concentrating all the realigned power of the area in their Heartstone; then draining the Heartstone and channeling most of its awesome energy into a new one, at the site of their new Vale.

Power crackled and seethed, pouring into the stone, as Darkwind held to his position, anchoring the West— outside the circle of Adepts that contained his mother and father. The shunting off of the great stone's energy was a dangerous task and required many protectors and guides from outside the main circle; he was an important part of the linkage. Songwind k'Sheyna was the youngest Adept of his Clan ever to take such a task and quite conscious of the responsibilities involved.

There was no warning, no unsettling current of unclean energy. Just—a brightening of the stone, more intense than the last, and a disorienting sensation like lightning striking—

Hell opened in front of him. A blaze of incandescent white, power that scorched him to the soul. Silhouetted against the hellfires, his mother—

"I don't trust my so-called 'abilities,' Father," he said slowly, shaking off the too-vivid memories. "No one knows why the Heartstone fractured, and the power broke loose."

Was it his imagination, or did his father start a little?

"I was the youngest Adept there," he persisted. "I was the only one who had never participated in moving a Heartstone's power before. What if it was something *I* did, and everything I do magically is forever flawed that way? I will not take that chance, Father, not when what is *left* of our Clan is at stake."

Starblade would not look into his son's eyes, but his voice was implacable. He gazed down at his hand as if he had never seen it before, examining the long fingers as he spoke. "I have told you, many times, it was nothing you did or did not do. It . . . it had *nothing* to do with you."

"Can you be certain of that?" He shook his head and started to stand up. "Father, I know exactly what my abilities are with my hands, my senses. I can't count on my magic—"

Starblade looked up, and his expression had changed to one of scorn. ". . . If you have no confidence in yourself," the Elder finished. "Your magic is flawed only if you choose to believe it is so. Songwind was not that—fearful. I remember and loved Songwind. He saw his power as a source of pride, and our Clan was proud of him for it. Our children and old ones are gone from us now, and you have refused those powers to defend what is left of us here. I have little respect for you for that, Darkwind."

The heat of Darkwind's anger cooled to ice, as he felt the blood draining from his face. The golden sunlight drifting through the windows and making patterns upon the white wooden floor suddenly lost all its warmth. "The Starblade who is my Elder is not the Father I remember either," he replied. "Perhaps a change of name is in order for you, as well. Iceblade, perhaps—or Brokenblade, for you seem to have lost both your courage and your compassion." He stood, while Starblade gaped at him in startled surprise. "You are unwilling to face the fact that circumstances have changed. I think that you are terrified to face that change. I don't know—I only know that you seem to think that we who work without magic are not worth aiding. If you see no reason to help the scouts, Father, then we must take what help we can get—even to calling on the *hertasi*, the *dyheli*, and the others of the Hills whose well-being you scorn in your arrogance."

He started to turn, and had taken one step toward the door, when Starblade's voice stopped him.

"Arrogance?" the Elder said, as coolly as if Darkwind had not said anything at all. "An interesting choice of words from you. Songwind was the youngest Adept in the Clan—but it has occurred to me of late that perhaps that distinction was not enough for you."

Darkwind turned back to his father reluctantly. "What

is that supposed to mean?'' he asked, the words forced
from him unwillingly.

"Songwind was only an Adept. Darkwind is on the
Council—is, in fact, an Elder.'' Starblade shrugged.
"That was an opportunity that would not have been given
to Songwind for some time—but with the scouts so shorthanded, and poor, newly-bereft Darkwind so eager to
join them—and so—charismatic—''

"If you are suggesting that I have left magic solely for
the sake of another kind of power—'' Darkwind could
feel himself going red, then white, with anger. He struggled to control his temper; an outburst now would win
him nothing.

"I am suggesting nothing,'' Starblade replied
smoothly. "I am only saying that the appearance is
there.''

A hundred retorts went through Darkwind's mind, but
he made none of them. Instead, he strove for and regained at least an appearance of calm.

"If that were, indeed, the case, Elder,'' he said quietly, but with just a hint of the rage that he held tightly
bottled within, "it seems to me that I would already have
been acting on those ambitions. I should have been moving to consolidate that power, and to manipulate both the
non-mages and the weaker mages. As you are well aware,
I have been doing no such thing. I have simply been
doing the work assigned to me—like any other scout.
Like any *responsible* leader. I never sought the position
of leader or Elder, it was pressed upon me; I would never
have used personal attraction to get them.''

Starblade smiled, tightly. "I merely suggest, Darkwind, that if you returned to magic you would be forced
to give up that position. In fact, in light of the fact that
you are out of practice, you might be asked to return to
the position of student rather than Adept. And that perhaps—unconsciously—you are reluctant to return to the
position of commanded, having been commander.''

"You have hinted that before, Elder,'' Darkwind answered him grimly. "And the suggestion was just as re-
pellent the first time as it is now. I think I know myself
very well now, and there is no such reluctance on my
part for *that* ridiculous reason. If there were anyone else

within the scouts who wanted the position, I would give it to him—or her—and gladly.''

And if we were a less civilized people, those words would be cause for a challenge.

''I have said that I do not know this thing you have become, Darkwind—'' Starblade began.

Darkwind cut him off abruptly with an angry gesture. ''Indeed, Elder,'' he replied, turning on his heel and tossing his last words over his shoulder as he left the outer room of Starblade's *ekele*. ''You do not know me at all, if you think that little of me.''

It was not—quite—the kind of exit he would have liked. There was no door to slam, only a *hertasi*-made curtain of strung seeds—and it was difficult, if not impossible, to effectively stamp his feet the few steps it took to reach the ladder, without sounding like a child in a temper.

Which is how he wants me to feel, after all.

And if he rushed angrily down the ladder, even so short a distance as he needed with his father's tree-dwelling, he risked taking some stupid injury like a sprain or a broken limb. Starblade's *ekele* was hardly more than a few man-heights from the floor of the Vale, and had several rooms, like a bracelet of beads around the trunk of the huge tree it was built onto. The access leading to it was more like a steep staircase than a ladder.

So it was quite impossible to descend in any way that would underscore his mood without playing to his father's gloating.

He settled for vaulting off of the last few feet of it, as if he could not bear to endure Starblade's ''hospitality'' a moment more. He landed as lightly and silently as only a woods-scout could, and walked away from the *ekele* without looking back, his purposeful steps taking him on a path that would lead him out of the Vale altogether.

He knew that he was by no means as calm as he looked, but he was succeeding in this much at least. He was working off some of his anger as he pushed his way through the exotic, semitropical undergrowth that shadowed and sometimes hid the path. The plants themselves were typical of any Tayledras Vale, but the state of rank overgrowth was not.

The Hawkbrothers always chose some kind of valley for their Clansites, something that could be ''roofed over'' magically, and shielded from above and on all sides, so that the climate within could be controlled, and undesirable creatures warded off. Then, if there were no hot springs there already, the mages would *create* them—and force-grow broad trees to make them large enough to hold several *ekele*.

The result was always junglelike, and the careful placement of paths to allow for the maximum amount of cover and privacy for all the inhabitants gave a Vale the feeling of being uninhabited even when crowded with a full Clan and all the *hertasi* that served them.

It appeared uninhabited to the outsider. To a Tayledras, there was always the undercurrent of little sounds and life-feelings that told him where everyone was, a comforting life-song that bound the Clan together.

But there was no such song here, in k'Sheyna Vale. Instead of a rich harmony, with under-melodies and counterpoint, the music halted, limped, within a broken consort. *Hertasi* made up most of the life-sparks about Darkwind, as the little lizard-folk went about their business and that of the Clan, cleaning and mending and preparing food. And that was not right.

Further, there were no child-feelings anywhere about. Only adults, and a mere handful of those, compared to the number a full Clan should muster.

Any Tayledras would know there is something wrong, something out of balance, just by entering the Vale.

Silence; Tayledras that were not mages undertook all the skilled jobs that *hertasi* could not manage—besides the scouts, there should have been artisans, musicians, crafters. All those activities made *their* own little undercurrent of noises, and that, too, was absent. The rustle of leaves, the dripping of water, the whisper of the passing of the shy *hertasi*, sounds that he would never have noticed seemed too loud in the empty Vale.

Then there were the little signs of neglect; *ekele* empty and untenanted, going to pieces, so that *hertasi* were constantly removing debris, and trying to get rid of things before they fell. Springs were littered with fallen leaves. Vegetation grew unchecked, untrimmed, or dying out as rare plants that had required careful nurturing went untended.

It all contributed to the general feeling of desolation—

but there was an underlying sense of pain, as well. And that was because not all of the *ekele* stood empty by choice.

Half the Clan had moved to the new Vale, it was true, and were now out of reach until a new Gate could be built to them. There were no mages strong enough in the far-away, exiled half of the Clan to build that Gate, and not even the most desperate would choose to take children and frail elders on a trek across the dangerous territory that lay between them. But k'Sheyna-that-remained was at a quarter of its strength, not a half. And most of those were not Adepts. The circle of Adepts that had been charged with draining and moving the Heartstone had been the strongest the Clan could muster; they had taken the full force of the disaster.

Fully half of those that had remained behind—most of the Adepts—had died in the catastrophe that claimed Darkwind's mother. Many of those that were left were still in something of a state of shock, and, like Darkwind himself, trying to cope with the unprecedented loss of so many mates, friends, and children. The silence left by their absence gnawed at the subconscious of mage and scout alike.

Only a few went to Darkwind's extreme, and changed their use-name, but he was not completely alone in his reaction. To change a use-name meant that, for all intents and purposes, the "person" described by that name was "dead."

That was why "Songwind" became "Darkwind." When he had recovered from his burns and lacerations, he repudiated magic altogether. Then, when that move brought him into conflict with his father, he moved out of the family *ekele,* and took up life on his own, with the scouts and craftsmen who were left.

Another mage, Starfire, became Nightfire, and became obsessed with the remains of the Heartstone, studying it every waking moment, trying to determine the cause of the disaster.

And the most traumatized mage of all, Moonwing, became Silence.

I could have been like Silence, he thought, beating a branch aside with unnecessary force. *I could have retreated into myself, and become a hermit. I could have stopped speaking except mind-to-mind. I could be broad-casting my pain to anyone who dared touch my thoughts. I didn't do that; I'm doing something useful.*

But that, evidently, was not enough for Starblade.

He'll have me as a mage, or not at all. Darkwind scowled at the trail before him, frightening a passing *hertasi* into taking another route. *He should look to the Clan; there are more important problems than the fact that I will not use magic.*

The physical wounds had mended, but the emotional and mental injuries were still with k'Sheyna, and they were not healing well.

But then, those that could have taken care of such deep-seated problems had all perished themselves.

There was no one skilled enough, for instance, to enter Silence's mind and Heal her—

Heal Silence? There's no one even skilled enough to Heal me. . . .

There should have been help coming from other Clans—

There can only be only one reason why there isn't, he thought, and not for the first time. *The Elders' pride. They will not admit that we failed so badly, or that we need help at all.*

Fools. Fools and blind.

In the first few weeks after the disaster, there had been messengers from other Clans. That much he knew for a fact; the rest was a guess, for he had been delirious from brain-fever and the pain of his burns. He had been in no position to make any pleas, but the visitors did not stay long, in any case. He had no doubt that they had been rebuffed. Now no visitors—or offers of help—came at all.

Darkwind reached the edge of the Vale, where the shield met the outside world. The boundary line was quite clear; within the Vale grew a riot of flowers and plants with enormous, tropical leaves, all of it surrounding individual trees that reached higher than the cliffs beside them, trees with trunks as large as houses. Flowers bloomed and plants flourished no matter the season. Outside the Vale—one scant finger-length from the shield— it was pine forest, with the usual sparse undergrowth. And if Darkwind looked closely enough, he could see a kind of shimmer where the one ended and the other began.

Of course, if he cared to use Mage-Sight on that barrier—which he did not—that shimmer was a curtain of pure energy, tuned only to allow wildlife, the Hawkbrothers, their allies, and select individuals across.

He paused before crossing that invisible border, and looked reluctantly at a stand of enormous bandar-plants. Behind those plants lay a hot spring, one of many that supplied the heat and moisture the plants required . . . and provided places of refreshment as well.

Gods above, I could use a soak . . . it's been a long day, and there is still more ahead of me.

Well, perhaps a short pause would not hurt anything.

He slipped between two of the plants and shed his clothing quickly, leaving it in a pile on the smooth stones bordering the spring.

This was not one of the larger springs, nor one of the more popular. It was too close to the edge of the Vale and the shield, and the reminder of the Real World outside their little sheltered Vale made many of the remaining mages too uneasy to use it.

While the scouts, who were more than a little uneasy *within* the heart of the Vale, in close proximity to the shattered, but still empowered and dangerous Heartstone, did not much care to use the larger, carefully sculptured springs there, with their pools for washing as well as pools for soaking away aches—or disporting.

Hertasi did their best to keep all the little pockets of hot, bubbling water free of fallen leaves and other debris, but they had too many other duties to attend to. This particular spring had not been attended to in some time and ran sluggishly, the surface covered with fallen vegetation. Darkwind tossed a half dozen huge leaves out to the side, and scooped out quite a bit of debris at the bottom before the spring bubbled up freely again.

Then he relaxed back into the smooth stone of the seats built into the sides, created by magically sculpting the rock before the water had been called here.

As the warm water soaked away his aches and bruises and relaxed too-taut muscles, he closed his eyes and, for once, tried to remember back to those dark and chaotic days immediately following the catastrophe.

Did we know then how bad the area was outside our own borders? He didn't think so; it seemed to him that no one had paid any attention to the lands outside the purview of the Clan, and to be fair, they had their hands full with the territory they had undertaken to cleanse.

We definitely had enough to do—and whatever was out there tended to leave us alone while we were strong. There was no reason to think that it was any worse than our own lands.

It was only after they had cleaned up their own areas, and were preparing to move, that they realized that the blight they faced on their southern border was at least as pervasive as the one they had just dealt with. And was, perhaps, more dangerous than the area to the west that they had chosen as the new Vale-site.

Why hadn't they seen the blight? Well, it might have been because there had been a clear zone between the two, a zone that disguised the true nature of what lay beyond. It was only after the disaster, when creatures from across that clear zone swarmed over the wreckage of the Vale, that anyone realized just how tainted that area was.

Now, of course, they could not deal with it, could not clean it out, and could not eliminate it.

There's at least one Adept in there, Darkwind thought, clenching his jaw involuntarily. *It was his constant "attentions" after the accident that forced us to pull back our borders in the first place.*

And now that there were no more offers of help from the other Clans, they could not ask for one of the others to lend aid. They could not even push the unseen enemies back, not without help.

I'd try to contact the other Clans myself, but I would have to do so by magic means. I don't know where the other territories are, and Father isn't about to give me a map.

And using magic would only have attracted more unwelcome attentions. He had seen all too often how blatant use of magics brought a wave of attackers from the Outside. The one mage who had been willing to work with the scouts had fallen victim, he suspected, to just that.

He was certainly overwhelmed before we could reach

him. And I know there were not that many Misborn there before.

He suspected that the Adept watched for magic-use, and turned his creatures loose when he saw it. So long as k'Sheyna confined themselves and their magic to their Vale, he seemed content to pursue his own plans, only pressing them occasionally, rather than sending an army against them.

There may be more than one Adept out there, but somehow I don't think so. Dark Adepts don't share power willingly.

So far, they had been able to beat all attempts to penetrate the new boundaries. So far, they had not lost more than a handful of scouts, and a mage or two.

And right now, we seem to be operating under an uneasy truce, as if he had decided we were too weak to threaten him, but too strong to be worth moving against. At least nothing major has come out of there for about a year. And there haven't been any attacks from Outlanders that I can prove originated from there.

Nothing had made any attempt at the creatures k'Sheyna protected, either. So far the *hertasi* enclaves remained untouched, the *dyheli* herds had not been preyed upon. The firebirds had fled the area though—and that bothered him.

And there were no human villages within k'Sheyna territory anymore. Crops had failed, wells dried up, traders ceased to come; only a handful of hunters and a religious hermit or two stayed behind.

No overt attacks for a year. But who knows what that means, he thought pessimistically. *We have a weak and unstable Clan facing a nebulous enemy, and our options grow fewer with every passing day.*

Starblade's answer to their troubles was simple: more magic. More mages. Everyone who had a spark of Mage-Gift should train it, and use it in their defense, while the handful of *real* mages worked to find an answer to their unstable Heartstone. Magic was the answer to every problem.

But how many times have I seen that using magic attracts problems? Hundreds. And what happens when we attract something we can't handle?

No, more magic was *not* the answer. Not to Dark-wind's way of thinking.

What we should do is appeal for help to one of the other Clans; we need Adepts who can drain the old Heartstone or stabilize it and take over this Vale for us. Then we can build a Gate and rejoin the rest. So what if they can't Gate in to us? That doesn't matter; and while we wait for the Heartstone to be made safe, we can defend ourselves with stealth, with cleverness.

He had to force his shoulder muscles to relax again, and sank a little deeper into the hot water. *In fact, that's what we should be doing about this Adept. We should find some way of luring him out into the open, maybe by "playing dead." Then we should neutralize him—but the one thing he wouldn't be expecting is a physical assault.*

He nodded to himself, the pieces finally falling together for him. *That Adept wants something—the power in the Heartstone, probably. He has to be watching constantly for magic power in use, and sending things against us only when he sees it. He really hasn't made an all-out assault against us because he's clever. He knows it would cost him less to take us by attrition than by full force.*

And right now, he's hoping to lull us into forgetting that he's out there.

He tightened his jaw, thinking about how Starblade kept dismissing the importance of the scouts, and the threats on the borders. *Right. He just might, too.*

That brought up another thought. *I wonder if he sent those intruders to test us? It could be. And not using magic told him—what?*

That we don't have mages to spare, probably. He should have a pretty good idea of how weak we really are at this point.

But what if I can use that against him? What if I can lure him out into the open, and find out who and what he is?

What if I could destroy him—or at least convince him that we're too strong, still, to be worth the trial?

He shook his head at his own ambitions. *Certainly. And what if I could grow wings and fly out of here for help? The one is as likely as the other.*

Best to stick to what he *knew* he could accomplish.

He looked up through the leafy canopy above him; not

long until sunset, and that meant he had better get back to his own *ekele*. The day-scouts would be waiting to report, the night-scouts to be briefed. And Vree would be waiting for his dinner, for that bit of rabbit earlier was hardly enough to satisfy him.

Reluctantly, he pulled himself out of the spring, dried himself with his shirt, and pulled on the rest of his clothing.

If I can see what needs taking care of, then it's my job to take care of it. My duties won't wait—whether or not Father approves.

Chapter Five

ELSPETH

Elspeth stood on guard, trembling with exhaustion, with the last of the dulled practice swords in her hands. The Captain went off-guard and nodded. "Right," Kerowyn said, just a hint of satisfaction in her voice. "Let's go through it again."

Did I hear satisfaction? Approval? Gods, maybe all the bruises are worth it after all.

Elspeth shook sweat out of her eyes, picked up the scattered practice blades with hands that still tingled from Kero's disarms, and distributed them randomly around the perimeter of the circle. It was kind of funny, really. This was the one and only time she had ever been *ordered* to just drop weapons carelessly, leaving them exactly where they fell.

This had been another one of Kero's little exercises in "attitude." Today had been entirely defensive; she had not been permitted to strike a single blow.

And she'd had one of the most strenuous workouts she'd ever had in her life.

The exercise was simple; Kero disarmed her, and she would try to get to another weapon—by whatever means possible—before Kero could corner her. Hence the rough circle of weaponry scattered around the salle.

Her setup—such as it was—completed, she stood in the middle of the circle, sword in hand, and waited for Kero to disarm her.

Kero went into "ready" stance, and Elspeth matched her.

Here it comes— Her heart beat a little faster, and her mouth dried. No matter that it was "just" a practice. With Kerowyn or Alberich, nothing was ever "just" a practice. When they delivered killing blows, they left bruises, as a reminder of what could have happened.

The Captain came in slowly this time; Kero feinted and fenced with her for a few moments, forcing her to move away from her original position. Then, when Elspeth was not expecting it, the Captain bound her blade and sent it flying out of her hand.

She didn't waste a moment; the instant she lost the blade, she dove to one side, rolled, and came up with another in her hand; a shortsword, this time. Without thinking, she shifted her grip until the balance was right.

This time Kero rushed her before she had a chance to settle herself, catching her off-guard while she was still finding the balance for the blade.

Crap!

She back-pedaled but not fast enough; Kero got to her and literally swatted the blade out of her hand.

She did the unexpected—as Kero had been *trying* to get her to do. She rushed the Captain, barehanded, shouldering past her and springing for the next sword on the floor.

This time, she didn't even get a chance to get her hands on it. Kero beat her to the spot and kicked it away before she reached it.

She dove after another, sliding belly-down across the wooden floor; she got it and started to roll over—but Kero was on top of her, and swatted that one out of her hands, too.

This one fell short, and Elspeth made a short dive and grabbed it again; her hand tingled, and she had trouble feeling her fingers, but she got it all the same, just as Kero reached her and cut down.

This time she didn't lose it. This time she managed to hold onto the hilt long enough to counter Kero's first three attempts at disarming her—even though her grip was an entirely unorthodox, two-handed one, and she never managed to return a blow.

"That's enough," Kero said, stepping back and wiping the sweat from her forehead with the back of her hand. Elspeth simply collapsed where she lay for a moment, spread-eagled on the floor. She blinked several times to clear her eyes, and rolled over onto her side. And when Kero offered her a hand to help her up, she took it without shame.

"Not bad," the Captain said, as she started to pick up the scattered swords. "Not bad at all." Elspeth cast her a startled glance. "Oh, I mean it," the Captain grinned. "You were exhausted, your hands were numb—and you still *always* managed to get a weapon in your hands before I could close with you. Good job, kitten."

And this is the person Alberich *says is better than he is.* For a moment Elspeth truly did not know what to say in reply. Finally, she managed to think of something that wouldn't get her into trouble. "Do you think I could have kept myself alive for a little while longer?" she asked.

"At least until help came—and if Gwena couldn't get to you in time to help, you'd be in deeper compost than *anyone* could be expected to get out of," Kero told her, as she got the remainder of the practice blades and took them over to the wall to rack them. "And that is all anyone can ask for."

Someone cleared his throat conspicuously, and Skif emerged from the shadowed entry of the door leading to the outside of the salle. "Excuse me, Captain," he said meekly, "but if you're through with Elspeth, the Circle and Council want to talk to her."

"Now?" Kero asked, her eyebrows arching.

Dear gods, now what? Elspeth wondered. Skif looked very odd, and unusually subdued.

"Well, yes, sort of," he replied, uncomfortably. "I mean, they're meeting now, with the Queen, and they really wanted to talk with her now."

"Well, they can just give her a moment to sluice herself off," Kero replied firmly. "There's no sense in making her show up looking like a shambles."

:Kitten,: she Mindspoke, in private-mode, *:There's a set of my Whites and a kind of wash area in my office; you'll fit my uniform closely enough. I know from expe-*

rience that it's easier facing an official situation if you feel as if you look presentable.:

:Thanks,: Elspeth replied gratefully, surprised a little at the Mindspeech. Kero seldom used it, except with Eldan and her Companion, having had to conceal the fact that she had the Gift for most of her life. She was almost as flattered by Kero's use of it with her as by the Captain's earlier compliments.

Elspeth darted into the Weaponsmaster's office before Skif had a chance to stop her; there was, indeed, a pump and a deep basin in a little room in the back behind a screen, and a stack of thick towels beside it. The basin was deep enough for her to duck her head under water, and she did so. The water, fresh from the pump, was cold enough to make her yip, but it revived her considerably. She was toweling off her hair when the promised set of Whites appeared over the screen.

She scrambled into them, and discovered, as Kero had promised, they were a close fit.

I didn't think Kero had a set of Whites—I thought she'd convinced everybody she was never going to wear them. Well, there are times when she plays the uniform game with everyone else. Not often, but I've seen her do it. I suppose if she absolutely has to show up as a formal Herald, this is as good a place to keep her Whites as any.

They were a little loose across the shoulders and tight in the chest, but no one was likely to notice. And she realized, as she wound her wet hair into a knot at the back of her neck, that she *did* feel a little more confident.

Skif was still waiting for her when she trotted out of the office, and he didn't look *too* impatient. "Let's go," she said; he just nodded, and fell into step beside her. The two left the building side-by-side, setting a brisk pace toward the Palace.

She glanced at him in open inquiry, but he avoided her eyes. *Dear gods. What is it I'm supposed to have done?* she wondered. *Is this over that argument I had with Mother about recruiting mages?* She tightened her jaw stubbornly. *If it is—I'm not backing down. I'm right, I know I'm right.*

Why would they take her to task about that, though? What was the problem? It wasn't as if she was espousing open revolt against the Crown. . . .

On the other hand, she'd been pressuring Selenay to allow *her* to do the mage-hunting. That might well be the problem. Some of the Councilors considered her to be impetuous, and sometimes hotheaded. *Maybe they figure I intend to go riding out of here anyway, with or without permission.*

Now *that* was a stupid idea, if that's what they were thinking. *Not that I hadn't considered it . . . if I could get Gwena to go along with it.*

But I didn't think about it for more than a couple of heartbeats. Really, it was a stupid idea. The only way I could get a decent mage to go along with this, would be if I had official blessing—and how would I have gotten that by running off on my own?

But while she had been thinking about that, would anyone have "eavesdropped" on her? She didn't think so.

But if they had—

She stifled a slow wave of hot anger. No use in getting angry over something that might not have happened.

But if it has—someone is going to pay.

They kept her cooling her heels for some time before finally letting her into the Council Chamber. Skif left her at the door and disappeared, leaving her no one to question, and being kept there did not help her smoldering temper any.

But after she had waited, impatiently, for what seemed like hours, she heard footsteps coming down the hall leading to the Council Chamber. She turned to see the rest of the Council approaching—and at that point the door to the Council Chamber opened, and they *all* filed in to take their places. Elspeth no longer felt quite so annoyed at being dragged off to see the Circle, then left in the hall.

Though it would have been nice if someone had bothered to tell her they were waiting for the other Council members to arrive.

She took her seat with the rest, casting covert glances at the faces of those Councilors who were also in the Heraldic Circle: Teren, who had taken Elcarth's place as Dean of the Collegium; the Seneschal's Herald, Kyril; the Lord Marshal's Herald, Griffon; the Queen's Own Herald, Talia; Selenay; and Prince Daren. Their expressions didn't tell her much; their faces were tightly controlled. That, in itself, was something; it meant they were worried. And since there was a White-clad Herald with the silver-arrow insignia of the Special Messenger sitting on the extra chair reserved for guests and petitioners, chances were slim that the Circle and Council were going to take Elspeth to task for her notions.

She relaxed and sat back a little into the familiar bulk of her Council seat. *So this is just Council business after all.* If the others hadn't looked so serious, she'd have chuckled at herself. *See, Elspeth, the world* doesn't *revolve around you!*

Selenay rose when the others had settled themselves. "This messenger arrived from the Eastern Border earlier this afternoon, from Shallan, one of Herald-Captain Kerowyn's lieutenants. She had ordered this messenger to come to me, first, before reporting to his Captain."

Elspeth stifled a smile. *There's one in the eye for anyone who still wonders where Kero's loyalties lie. Or the Skybolts', for that matter.*

"Since the Circle was in session, and since I understood that his message was fairly urgent, I had him brought here. After hearing what his message was, I decided to call an emergency Council meeting." She nodded at the messenger as she sat down. "Herald Selwin, the floor is yours."

The messenger cleared his throat—though not self-consciously, Elspeth noted—and stood. "I think most of you know that the Eastern Border is considered a sensitive enough area for messengers to be posted at garrisons full time. My current post is the town garrisoned by Kerowyn's Skybolts. Now, what you probably don't know is that the Skybolts have—with the Queen's knowledge and permission—been engaging in some—ah—covert activities."

He flushed a little, and Elspeth raised a surprised eyebrow. Some of the other Councilors muttered a little, and one of them stood up; Lady Kester, speaker for the West. "Just what do you mean by 'covert' activities?" she asked sharply, looking a great deal like a horse who is about to refuse a jump.

"Well—" Herald Selwin glanced at the Queen, who shook her head imperceptibly. "Some of them—I can't talk about. I'm sure you'll understand—the Queen and the Consort both know every move, but it's very much a situation where the fewer who know, the better.''

''I trust the situation that brought you here is something you *can* talk about,'' the woman said dryly.

''Uh—yes, of course.'' Selwin quickly regained his aplomb. ''We've been smuggling; people and information out of Hardorn, and—uh—supplies in. One of the people we just smuggled out was not just one of Ancar's farmers who has been pressed too far; this was an escaping prisoner.''

We? Huh, that means Selwin's involved, too. He's not just a messenger. Elspeth glanced around the table; from the looks of speculation, she suspected that this had not come entirely as a surprise.

''This wasn't an ordinary prisoner, either,'' Selwin continued. ''He had been one of the under-secretaries in Ancar's officer corps.'' This time murmurs of surprise met the statement. ''He held the same position under Ancar's father, and the reason he was never replaced, like so many *were*, is that he is so ordinary as to be invisible. He says—and we've Truth-Spelled him, so we believe him—that he didn't know what was going on until recently.''

Elspeth was very skeptical of *that* statement, until Selwin finished describing the former prisoner. Then she could believe it. Lieutenant Rojer Klinseinem was exactly the kind of focused, obsessive individual their own Seneschal and Lord Marshal prayed to see come into their secretarial corps. His life was in his accounting books; he never left his office except to eat and sleep, and he truly never thought about what those figures he toted up daily meant.

Until Ancar's excesses among his people began to affect even him. He found officers and court officials he had known all his life vanishing without a trace. He discovered friends, neighbors, even children in the street avoiding him when he wore his uniform. Then he noted some odd discrepancies in his accounts. One of his duties was to take care of the prison accounts. The number of prisoners in the cells had gone up, substantially, but the amount of money allotted for their maintenance had *not* increased in the corresponding amounts. Furthermore, the names of those imprisoned changed, sometimes weekly. For all his shortsightedness, he was an ethical man, and all these things worried him, so he decided to investigate them himself, an investigation that led him eventually to the prisons and the barracks rooms, then the king's own dungeons.

What he discovered horrified him. Then one of the king's sorcerers caught him.

He'd had the sense to keep his mouth shut about most of what he'd learned, and because he was so completely ordinary, with no record of ever thinking for himself, he was actually put under house arrest until he could be questioned by someone they called the "Truth-finder General." He didn't wait to discover who or what that was; he got out a back window, stole a horse, and fled toward Valdemar.

He remembered the old days, the days of friendship with Valdemar and its Queen, and he was no longer inclined to believe the official stories about the cause of the hostilities between Valdemar and Hardorn. He fled toward a hoped-for sanctuary with the hounds on his heels.

"I won't go into all the details," Selwin said, "You can question him yourself when we bring him here. Right now he's not up to much traveling."

Elspeth nodded, grimly. Nothing Rojer said would surprise her, not after some of Kero's stories—and not after what had happened to Talia.

"What's important at the moment is that he learned where the prisoners were vanishing to. They're being used as sacrifices in blood-rites—and there are more of them dying every week. Ancar is bringing in mages, *lots* of mages, and those he is not buying outright or coercing, he's making alliances with. Rojer says that Ancar's long-range plans include another major war with Valdemar, and this one is going to include those mages as a major part, rather than in a support capacity. The one that caught him boasts that not even a god would be able to hold defenses against all the mages Ancar is gathering."

Now the muttering around the Council table grew louder, and there were distinct undertones of alarm.

"That's not all," Selwin said, over the voices. The Councilors quieted, and some looked at him with real fear in their eyes. "Right after we got Rojer out, there was an attack on the Skybolts' garrison town. A magical attack, and *it* got across the Border. Past the protections."

"Why?" asked the Lord Patriarch—Father Ricard, who had replaced elderly Father Aldon. At the same time, the Lord Marshal asked "How?"

"Why should be fairly obvious," Prince Daren said, the first time he'd spoken since the meeting began. "They knew we had Rojer, and they felt what he had to tell us was important enough to try to silence him."

Selwin nodded. "Precisely, Your Highness," he replied. "As for 'how,' I presume the mage managed to overcome the Border-protections somehow. I saw the attack. At first, I thought it was some kind of mist, and I didn't think it looked all that dangerous. But Lieutenant Shallan said the Skybolts had seen this sort of thing before, and got us all evacuated; she said they had something to take care of it, but it would only work at a distance. The 'mist' turned out to be a swarm of tiny insects, no bigger than gnats, but poisonous enough to drop a man. And they were guided, there's no doubt of that. They came out of a kind of hole in the sky." He shook his head. "I really can't properly describe it. But the hole appeared near the outskirts of town, *inside* the Valdemar Border."

"These insects," the Seneschal asked, "are they gone now?"

"Not gone, my lord," Selwin replied. "Dead. The Skybolts, as I said, have seen this kind of weapon before. They evacuated the town, then used small catapults to lob pots of burning herbs into the streets. The insects were killed so completely that there were none to follow us, and few to return when the hole in the sky reopened."

He sat down again when no one else had any more questions. Prince Daren stood up in his place. "This is not going to be the last attempt, my lords and ladies," he said grimly. "I think we can count ourselves fortunate that it *was* the Skybolts who encountered this first. If it had not been—if it had been a regular garrison—they would have died to a man, and we would never have known what it was that killed them."

Prince Daren sat down and took his wife's hand; Selenay looked very pale.

"I must admit," she said, "that I doubted when Kerowyn and my daughter swore that Ancar would find a way to penetrate our Border with magic. I was wrong."

Selenay looked over at Elspeth, and bit her lip. "My daughter also proposed a solution that I rejected out of hand; she suggested that Valdemar seek out magical allies as well, and find some mage who was strong enough to pass our borders to help us from within, and perhaps even teach new mages. She suggested that, since the Chronicles all speak of a 'Mage-Gift,' that there may still be Heralds carrying that Gift. She thinks that Gift has simply gone unrecognized and untaught because there was no one to teach it. She also suggested that *she* be the one to leave Valdemar, find such a mage, and bring him—or her—back to us."

Silence met her words as the Councilors turned looks of doubt toward Elspeth's end of the table. She did her best to look as mature and competent—and confident—as any of them could have wished. She was very glad now that Kero had insisted she wash and change before the meeting. She doubted she would have been able to convince any of them looking like a disheveled hoyden.

"May I speak?" she asked. At Selenay's nod, *she* stood up.

"Always speak to the Council from a standing position, kitten." Kero had tutored her a few weeks ago, after watching one of the sessions from the visitor's seat. The Council had wanted a report on what the Skybolts had been assigned to—and now Elspeth knew why Kero had been fairly reticent.

But what the Council didn't realize was that Kero had learned more about them than they had from her. The Captain had made careful assessments of the Council and their reactions to Elspeth, and had some fairly shrewd observations to make afterward.

"Always speak to them from a standing position. That will put your head higher than theirs, and give you an emotional advantage. Put your hands on the table, and lean forward a little. Showing your hands tells their guts that you have nothing to hide, leaning says that you are comfortable with your power, and leaning forward tells

them that you are earnest. Never raise your voice; in fact, if you can, speak a little lower than usual. That tells their guts that you're not just an emotional female. But if you feel passionately about something, choose your words carefully, and put some punch behind them.''

Talia and Selenay did all these things, but they did them without thinking, without knowing the reasons why they worked. Talia analyzed the audience through her Gift of Empathy, and adjusted herself accordingly, all without ever thinking about it. Selenay had been trained by her father—who may have known why his advice worked, but didn't bother to explain it to his daughter. Kerowyn, on the other hand, had to fight her way up to the top in a predominantly male profession—and she was a superb tactician in any arena. She knew how to deal with authority figures, and *why* the tactics she used worked.

Elspeth tried to keep all her advice in mind as she began.

"Herald-Captain Kerowyn and I have had several conversations about this eventuality," she said, quietly. "That in itself is unusual, because until now, it seems as if it has been very difficult even to *speak* about magic within the bounds of our realm, especially for Heralds. Please think back, think about what has happened every time in the past that you've spoken about magic in this Council Room—you've gone outside these walls, and gradually forgotten all about it, haven't you?"

She looked around, and got slow nods from most of the Councilors. "Somehow, as urgent as the threat seemed to be, it became less urgent once the immediate danger was over, didn't it? It did for me, too, until I met Kerowyn. I suspect that 'forgetting' may be a symptom of whatever it is that has protected us until now. But now—if you'll notice, we're speaking about magic, all of us, and I don't think we're going to forget about it outside the room. And I am terribly afraid that this is a symptom of something else—a symptom of the fact that this protection is weakening."

A swift intake of breath was the only sound that broke the silence following her words, but she couldn't tell who it was that had gasped. She glanced around the horseshoe-shaped table. Several of the Councilors were nodding, though not happily. She continued.

"I don't think we have a choice; I believe we *must* find a mage or mages to help us. I have several reasons why I think that the person who goes to look for one should be me." She paused again, waiting for opposition, but she didn't see anyone leaping to his—or her—feet to object. "A Herald *must* be the person we send to find us a mage—or mages. That is because only a Herald is likely to be able to weigh the motives of those we consider, and find a person of sufficient ethics to do us any good. As to my qualifications, first of all, my rank is such that I'm not likely to encounter anyone who doubts my ability to negotiate. Now, Talia *is* the Queen's Own, but she also has a small child. I think it would be unreasonable to ask her to leave him for an indefinite length of time. And there is a very sinister reason for her to avoid taking him with her; if someone captured her child, Jemmie could be held to be used against her."

Emphatic nods around the table gave her confidence to continue. "As you know, Ancar has made an assassination attempt on me. I think he will find it harder—as Kero would say—to hit a moving target. There may be other Heralds who have sufficient rank to be able to negotiate, but of all of them, only Kero and I seem to be able to even *speak* of magic clearly, much less assess the capabilities of a mage. And Kero was a mercenary—frankly, the kind of mage we are looking for may hold that against her." She spread her hands and shrugged. "The answer seems obvious to me. And if I may be so blunt as to say so, I *am* expendable. Mother has the twins, either of whom can easily succeed me as Heir."

She sat down carefully, and then the uproar began.

Elspeth had a pounding headache before it was over, and the arguments went on long past dinnertime and well into the night. Servants were sent out for cold meat, cheese, and other provisions, then called in again to light the lamps. Because of the nature of the arguments, young Heraldic trainees in their final year were brought in to serve at the table, and keep a steady supply of tea and other nonintoxicating drinks on hand. This was not the longest Council session on record, but it was certainly right up with the record holders.

And Elspeth was right in the middle of it all. Half the time, the Councilors went at her like a horde of interrogators, shouting questions, each one trying to make himself heard over the rest. The rest of the time, they acted as if she weren't even there, arguing about her and her competence at the tops of their lungs. Talia spared her a sympathetic glance or two, but she had her own hands full.

And besides, this was Elspeth's fight. It was up to her to win it; no one else was as convinced of her mission as she was. And her mother was still dead set against it.

So she fought by herself, grimly determined that she *would* win, no matter how long it took.

She did notice something odd, however. Every time it looked as though one of the Heralds would say something against her decision—he or she would freeze for a moment, sometimes in mid-sentence, and then fall silent.

Heralds often did that when their Companions were speaking to them, but Elspeth had never seen it happen so many times—or so abruptly. It was almost as if the Companions were arguing on her behalf, against their Chosens' better judgment. Elspeth even caught her mother in that momentary "listening" pose.

Shortly before midnight, the Council was finally in reluctant agreement. Elspeth could go; in fact, *must* go. She had succeeded, she and Selwin, in persuading everyone of the urgency of the situation. She had persuaded even her mother that she was the only person with the right combination of talents and credentials to successfully carry it off.

However, her route and ultimate destination would be watched over, at least inside Valdemar, and she would not go alone.

"You can't possibly go without an escort," the Lord Marshal said firmly. "I would say—twenty armed at the least."

"Thirty," said the Seneschal, over her squawk of outrage. "No less than that."

"Absolutely," Lady Cathan of the Guilds seconded. "Anything less would be inappropriate."

I'm trying to track down mages, she thought in exasperation. *I'm trying to find people who are notoriously shy, and they want me to bring an entire army with me?*

But she didn't say that; instead, she waited while the Councilors argued about the size of her escort, building it up until it *did* resemble a small army, then entered into the affray again when she thought she had a chance of being heard over the din.

"Impossible," she said, clearly. All heads turned in her direction. "Absolutely impossible," she repeated, just as firmly. "You're asking me to haul an entire armed force along with me. I'm trying to make speed—and I doubt if you could find fifty fighters with beasts able to keep up with a Companion even among the Skybolts. I may have to leave Rethwellan, and the presence of a troop like that could greatly offend the rulers of other countries that I might find myself in. But most importantly of all, insofar as my movements remaining a secret from Ancar, you might just as well post him a message every day telling him where I'm going, because that's how visible I'd be with that many armed fighters around me."

That brought all the arguments to a dead silence. The Lord Marshal actually looked sheepish.

"Now," she continued reasonably, "if you really *want* to make a big, fat target out of me, I wish you'd tell me. There are easier ways to get rid of me."

"Oh, come now," replied Lord Palinor, the Seneschal, wearing a superior expression that made her want to bite something. "Surely that's an exaggeration."

"Is it?" she asked raising one eyebrow, but otherwise keeping her expression sweetly innocent. "You just heard a description of something that could have destroyed an entire garrison—a weapon Ancar deployed inside our borders, and without having to come within sight of Valdemar. *Protected* Valdemar. What's likely to happen if he knows my every movement outside our borders?" She chuckled dryly. "Kind of negates the benefit of being a moving target, I'd say."

Silence for a moment, while they thought that one over. "Well," said Prince Daren. "What do *you* want to do?"

"My preference is to go alone," she admitted. "Basically, I'm safest if no one else knows where I am."

But the Prince shook his handsome head. "No," he said, with a touch of regret. "If it were anyone else, that wouldn't be a problem—but not you. You may think you're expendable, but you're still the Heir right now. You can't go running off the face of the earth all alone. And there is one argument that applies to Talia that also applies to you. If *you* were taken, you could be used as a hostage as well.''

Elspeth sighed, but nodded in agreement. ''That's true, Stepfather. I admit that I hadn't thought too much of that—but frankly, between Gwena and myself, I don't think we could be taken by anything but a small army.''

''There's always treachery,'' Daren said firmly. ''You'll have to take at least one other person with you. And personally, I would suggest a Herald.''

''Someone responsible, capable—'' said Father Ricard.

''Crafty and clever,'' said Talia.

''Fine,'' she agreed—and then, before they could engage in a till-dawn debate on exactly who she could take with her, said, ''But it's going to be Skif, or no one. There is no one in the entire Heraldic Circle who is better suited to watching my back.''

She expected an explosion of argument; after all, given the fuss there had been over the rumors started simply by being in Skif's company, the Councilors should, one and all, roundly denounce such a notion.

And after they argued themselves into exhaustion, she just might be able to talk the Council into letting her have her own way and going out alone.

''Fine,'' Selenay said, instantly. ''Skif is perfect. He's everything we could ask; responsible, capable, clever, crafty—''

Lord Palinor laughed. ''Aye, and tricky, the young devil. Ancar wouldn't catch *him* napping, I'd wager.''

And while Elspeth gawked, caught entirely flat-footed with surprise, every single one of the Councilors agreed to the choice she would have bet money they thought unsuitable. Before she quite realized what was happening, they approved her authority as negotiator for the Crown, approved her escort, and closed the session.

And began filing out, heading straight for their beds, while she stared at them, dumbfounded. Talia even patted her on the shoulder as she left, whispering, ''Good choice, kitten. I think it was the only thing that could have convinced them.''

Finally she was alone in the Council Chamber, sitting back in her seat, staring at the guttering candles, still wondering what on earth had happened.

And wondering just who, exactly, had been outmaneuvered.

Chapter Six

DARKWIND

Council meetings. Endless dithering about nothing, while we guardians dance with death out there on the border. And no help for us, either. If I could get anyone else to do this, I'd give up the Council seat in a heartbeat.

Darkwind pushed aside a tangle of vines covered with blue, trumpet-shaped flowers and restrained himself from pulling the whole curtain of vegetation down in a fit of anger. It had been days—weeks—since his confrontations with his father and the Council, demanding that they *do* something about the situation of the Clan, of the scouts, and what had they done?

Nothing. Or rather, they had "taken it under advisement." They would "weigh all the possible options." They were "studying the problem."

They're sitting on their backsides, afraid to do anything, that's what's really going on. Father won't let them act because he's afraid of what it will do to the Heartstone. And they still won't go outside k'Sheyna for help.

Not that he had really expected anything else after the way Starblade had treated him. Really, when it came to anything important, especially where magic was concerned, the entire Council spoke with Starblade's words.

I'll have to start considering those other plans of

Dawnfire's, using the hertasi and some of the others. They've left us no choice; if we're going to guard them effectively, we'll have to use whatever allies we have.

And he didn't particularly care if pulling the *hertasi* away from their other duties left some of those jobs undone. So what if the Vale got a little more overgrown? It didn't look to him as if it would make much difference. And maybe if some of the Elders had to suffer a little, if their *ekele* went unrepaired and their gardens untended because the *hertasi* were out helping keep their Vale safer—well, maybe then they'd notice that there was something wrong with their little world. And maybe they'd decide that it might be a good idea to try and fix what was wrong.

I hope. But I'm not going to count on anything like sense out of them.

He took the shortest possible route to the pass out of the Vale, cutting down long-neglected paths until he reached the boundary and the shield-wall. As he burst through a stand of wildly overgrown, flowering bushes, he saw Vree waiting for him in a tree growing just outside the mage-barrier. The gyre preferred not to enter the Vale itself if he could help it; many of the other bondbirds demonstrated Vree's distaste for the Vale proper, and tried to stay outside of the shield. Darkwind wasn't sure if it was because they shared their bondmates' dislike of magic, or sensed the problems with the Heartstone. One thing was certain, he *knew* that aversion dated back to the disaster, and not before.

He just wished *he* could avoid the Vale as well.

The place made him uneasy, for all its luxury. Here, near the edge, it wasn't so bad. The flora were tropical and wildly luxuriant, but it was nothing that couldn't be found in a glassed-over hothouse. But the closer he came to the damaged Heartstone, the stranger the plants became—and the odder he felt; slightly disoriented, off-balance, lethargic. As if something was sapping his energy, clouding his thoughts.

And it's not my imagination, either, he thought stubbornly. *If Vree and the other birds don't like the Vale, that should tell us all something. No matter what Father claims. What would he know, anyway? His bondbird is that damned crow—hardly bred out of the wild line, and it might as well be a metal simulacrum for all the intelligence it shows. It does what he tells it to, it doesn't talk to the other birds at all, and most of the time it sits on its perch in the corner of the* ekele, *like some kind of art object.*

He passed through the barrier—a brief tingling on the surface of his skin—and emerged into the real world again. Already he felt lighter, freer, and it seemed to him as he walked out on the path taking deep breaths of the pine-scented air, that even his footfalls were more confident. No cloying flower-scents, no heavy humidity— just an honest summer breeze. No one to answer to, out here. No one questioning his judgment unless it really needed to be called into question.

:Vree!: He Mindcalled the gyre, suddenly anxious to feel the bird's familiar weight on his shoulder. Vree obliged him by sweeping down out of the top of the nearest pine, landing on his leather-covered wrist with a thunder of pinions, and stepping happily from there to his favorite perch, on the padded shoulder of Darkwind's jacket.

:Don't like Vale,: the falcon complained. *:Too hot, too empty, feels bad. Don't like crow, stupid crow. Don't go back.:*

He Sent agreement tinged with regret. *:I have to, featherhead. But you don't have to go in if you don't want to. And I don't have to go back for a while.:*

The bird crooned a little, and preened a beakful of Darkwind's hair, as the scout laughed softly. Feeling considerably more cheerful now that he was outside the Vale and wouldn't have to face another Council meeting for days, Darkwind returned the bird's affectionate caress, scratching the breast and working his fingers up to the headfeathers. Vree made a happy chuckling sound, and bent to have his head scratched a little more.

"Sybarite," Darkwind said, laughing.

:Feels good,: the bird agreed. *:Scratch:*

:Report, featherhead,: he told the gyre, *:Or no more scratches.:*

Vree actually heaved a sigh, and reluctantly complied. The bondbirds had some limited abilities at relaying and reporting messages; while Darkwind was in the Vale, he depended on Vree to keep in contact with the rest of the scouts under his command. Vree had messages from most of the scouts; all those who had not reported in person before Darkwind went to the Council meeting this afternoon.

Most of the messages were simple enough, even by Vree's standards: "Nothing to report," "All quiet," "All is well." A normal enough day; he'd been half expecting that something disastrous would happen while he was out of touch, but it seemed that all the scouts had things well in hand.

All except for the handful of scouts who shared the southern boundary with him.

Those sent back messages that there were problems. Three of them said that they had turned their watch over to the night-scouts and would meet him at his *ekele*, to make their reports in person. Vree could not imitate the emotional overtones of those Mind-sent messages, relayed through their birds to Vree, but the terse quality did not auger well.

He swore silently to himself; the last time he'd had to take reports in person, he and the rest of the scouts had faced a week-long incursion of magically-twisted creatures that ultimately cost them two scouts and the only mage who had deigned to work with them.

That had been shortly after he'd joined the scouts, and before they made him their spokesperson. He could only hope that if this was the situation they faced again, they were sufficiently aware of the problems *now* to deal with it without more losses.

:Home?: Vree asked hopefully when he'd finished listening to the last of those messages.

:Yes,: he confirmed, to the bird's delight. *:Meet me there.:* He let Vree hop back down to his wrist and tossed the heavy gyre into the air; Vree pushed off and flapped upward, driving himself up through the branches with thunderous wing-claps. Darkwind waited until he had disappeared, then started off through the forest at a trot— *not* on one of the usual paths, but on a game-trail—heading for his *ekele*.

He never took the same route twice; he never approached his *ekele* the same way. While he ran, as silently as only a Tayledras scout could, he kept his mind as well as his other senses open, constantly on the alert for traces of thought that were out of the ordinary, for the scent of something odd, for a color or texture where it didn't belong, or movement, or the sound of a footfall in the forest beyond him.

Other scouts had not been that cautious. Rainwind hadn't; he'd been ambushed halfway between the Vale and his *ekele* after a long soak in one of the springs. He'd been lucky; his bondbird had spotted one of the ambushers first, so he had only had to deal with one enemy. The creatures had not sported the kind of poisoned fangs and claws so many others had and he'd escaped with only a permanent limp from a lacerated thigh.

Others had not been so fortunate; they had been just as careless, and had paid for it with limbs or lives.

That was the cost of living outside the Vale. No single Tayledras could hope to shield more than his *ekele*, even if he were an Adept-class mage. Since most of the scouts *weren't,* they paid the price of freedom in personal safety.

But anyone who lived out here felt it was worth that cost.

There were too many other things that were bad about living in the Vale these days; it was good to have a little distance from the Heartstone, and space between themselves and the mages.

The run stirred up his blood, and made him feel a little readier to face whatever trouble was coming. He Felt the presence of the other scouts long before they knew he was there. Out of courtesy, they had not climbed to his *ekele* while he was not in it; instead, they waited below, patiently, while Vree perched above, impatiently.

:Hungry,: Vree complained, as soon as his keen eyes spotted Darkwind approaching. The three scouts waiting caught the edge of the Mind-sent plaint, and he Felt their attention turning toward him, little brushes of thought, as they each tested for him and found him with their individual Gifts.

They waited until he came into view, though, before tendering some very subdued greetings. And not the usual *"zhai'helleva,"* either; Winterlight and Stormcloud only raised their hands in a kind of sketchy salute, and Dawnfire tendered him a feather-light mental caress, a promise of things to come, but also carrying overtones of deep concern.

This did not indicate good news at all.

He signaled to Vree, who swooped down and landed on one of the lower branches. Although he could not see the bird, hidden as he was by growth, he knew what Vree was up to. The gyre sidled along the branch to the trunk, and pulled a strap on the hook holding his rope ladder out of reach. The ladder dropped down to the ground with a clattering of wooden rungs; Darkwind motioned the others to precede him, and followed after with the strap that was attached to the end of the ladder tucked into his belt.

The others were far above him on the ladder; he had to go slowly, as he was bringing the end of it up with him. They were already hidden in the branches when he was only halfway up. His *ekele*, like those of the other scouts, was actually more elaborate than any of those inside the Vale. It had to be; it had to withstand winter winds and summer downpours, snow and hail, and the occasional "visit" from some of the distinctly hostile creatures from the Outlands.

At last, after penetrating the growth of the first boughs, he reached the place where the ladder-release was fastened to the bark of the trunk. He hooked the end of the ladder back in place, and followed his guests up through the trapdoor in the floor of the first chamber of the *ekele*.

The tree holding his home was an amazing forest giant, but it was nothing like the trees that supported a half-dozen *ekele* apiece, back in the Vale. Like them, though, it was a huge conifer, with a girth more than ten men could span with outstretched arms, and an arrow-straight trunk that towered without a single branching up for several man-heights above the forest floor. The first branches concealed his ladder; his *ekele* began, well sheltered, another man-height above that.

He pulled himself up onto the floor, closed and locked the trapdoor, then went to the glazed window of the first chamber, unlocked the latch at the side, and held it open for Vree. The forestgyre dove through it in a rush, landing on his outstretched arm, then hopped to his shoulder. Darkwind shut the window and relatched it, then turned to climb the stairs to join his guests.

The entire *ekele* was built of light, strong wood, stained on the outside to resemble the bark of the tree, but polished to a warm gold within. The first chamber was nothing more than a single, barren room, meant to buffer the effects of the wind coming up from below; there were all-weather coats hung on pegs on the wall, some climbing-tools and weapons, but that was all. The other scouts had already gone ahead of him, following a staircase built into the side of the trunk, a stair that spiraled up to the next chamber.

Each chamber was built upon the one below it, in a snailshell-like spiral pattern, using the huge branches as supports for the floor. The next chamber was one commonly used for the gathering of friends; it was considerably larger than the entrance chamber, and covered an arc fully one-third of the circumference of the trunk. Heated in winter by a clever ceramic stove that he also used for cooking, it supplied warm air to the two chambers above it. One of those was a sleeping room, the other, a storeroom and study. To bathe, he had to descend to the ground. As soon as his head and shoulders had cleared the doorsill—if one could rightly call an entrance that was placed in the floor a "door"—Vree hopped off his shoulder and bounced sideways toward his perch, in the ungainly sidling motion of any raptor on the ground. The floor and wall-mounted perch was a permanent fixture of the room, placed in the corner, where it could be braced against two of the walls, and near one of the windows. Vree leapt up onto it, roused his feathers, and yawned, waiting for his dinner.

Aside from the perch and the stove, the only other permanent features of the room were the low platforms affixed to the floor. Those platforms, upholstered in flat cushions, now hosted the three scouts: Winterlight, Stormcloud, and Dawnfire.

Three of the best. If they have problems, it's not from incompetence.

Winterlight was the oldest of all of them; he had held the position of Council-speaker and Elder but had given it to Darkwind with grateful relief when the others suggested him.

Now I know why he gave it up. I'd gladly give it back.

He seldom dyed his hair; longer than his waist, he generally kept the snow-white fall in a single braid as thick as his own wrist. Winterlight was actually Starblade's elder by several years but was of such a solitary nature that he had lived outside the Vale for most of his life. He was also unusual in that he flew two bondbirds; a snow-eagle, Lyer, by day; a tuft-eared owl, Huur, by night. Both birds had mated, and although the mates had not bonded to the scout, they provided extra security for Winterlight's *ekele*, nesting near each other in a rare show of interspecies tolerance, for given the chance, owls and eagles would readily hunt and even kill one another. Huur and Lyer's offspring had been in high demand as bondbirds.

Had been—but the reduced population and the absolute dearth of children meant that this year's crop of nestlings would probably go unbonded, and fly off to some other Clan to seek mates. Unless one of the scouts chose to bond to a second bird, or lost his bird before the eyases fledged and became passagers. Darkwind had briefly toyed with the notion of bonding to an owlet, but Vree had displayed a great deal of jealousy at the idea, and he had discarded it, albeit regretfully.

Stormcloud might have been a mage, but as a child his Gift was not deemed "enough" by Starblade and the other Adepts, and now he refused to enter training at all. His argument, using their own words against them in a direct quote, was "It's better to have a first-quality scout than a second-class mage."

And I don't blame you, old friend. No matter what Father says about "ingratitude and insolence." I'd have said and done the same as you.

He was Darkwind's oldest and best friend, their friendship dating back to when they were both barely able to walk. His features differed from the aquiline Tayledras norm considerably, with a round chin and a snubbed nose. He alone among k'Sheyna cut his hair short, with a stiff, jaylike crest. He flew a white raven, Krawn, that was as loquacious as Starblade's crow was silent. Krawn was easily the brightest of all the corbies flown in k'Sheyna, and very fond of practical jokes, as was Stormcloud. It was a measure of how serious the situation among the scouts was that neither Krawn nor his bondmate had played any of their famous jokes for months.

Dawnfire flew a red-shouldered hawk, Kyrr, a bird as

graceful—and as sought-after for mating—as her bond-mate. Dawnfire cast Darkwind a look full of promise as he entered the room, and he marveled that he, of all the scouts, had captured her fancy. She typified the opposite end of the extreme from Stormcloud; in her the aquiline Tayledras features had been refined to the point that she resembled the elfin *tervardi,* the lovely flightless bird-people she often worked with. That was her strongest Gift; she Mindspoke the nonhuman races with an ease the others could only envy, and communicated equally well with animals of all sorts. Her hair, now bound tightly into three braids, was as long as Winterlight's when she let it down. An errant beam of light reflected from the snow-goose lanterns touched her head, giving her an air of the unearthly as Darkwind watched her.

That light was provided during the day by four windows, all of which could be opened, that were glazed with a flexible substance as clear as the finest glass, but nearly impossible to break. Tayledras artisans created it; how, Darkwind had no idea, but it was as impervious to wind and weather as it was to breakage. By night, the light came from Darkwind's single concession to magic; mage-lights captured in the lanterns, that began glowing as dusk fell, and increased their pure light as the external sunlight faded.

Darkwind dug into his game-pouch as soon as his feet touched the floor of the room; Vree had waited long enough. He came up with a half rabbit; a light meal by Vree's standards, but enough to hold him until the discussion was over. Vree looked up at him with an expression of inquiry when presented with the rabbit. :?: the bird said, reminding Darkwind of his hunger.

:More, later,: he promised the bird. :I have a duck waiting for you.:

Vree chirped a happy acknowledgment, and began tearing the meat from the bones, gulping it down as fast as he could. One thing the bondbirds were not, and that was dainty eaters.

"So," he said, leaving Vree to his snack, and sitting cross-legged on one of the couches. "What's the problem?"

"The barrier-zone," said Winterlight succinctly, his hands resting palm-down on his knees, a deceptively tranquil pose. "We've got some real problems on the south. Things moving in, things and people, and we don't like the look of either. They're coming in from that bad patch of Outland, and it looks like they're settling. They're making dens, lairs, and fortified homes. I don't like it, Darkwind; it's got a bad feel to it, these creatures aren't overtly evil, but they make the back of my neck crawl. They're *inside* the old k'Sheyna boundaries now, and not just in the old 'barren' zone. You know how one bird will 'crowd' another, getting closer and closer until the other one either has to peck back or be forced off a perch? That's what it feels like they're doing to us."

"I've got the same," Stormcloud told him, wearing a slight frown. "And I've got enough Mage-Gift to read some other things as well. There's a new node that's being established just off my area, and a lot of ley-lines have been diverted to feed it. There's a new line going off that node, too—and it's feeding straight into Outland territory, into one of the places we *know* that Adept has made his own. It's bad, Darkwind, it's feeding him a lot of power, and anyone that can divert lines is damned good. He's pulled some of the lines away from us completely. And I've caught him trying to read the Vale for power, too. I think he might be planning to use one of the lines to tap into the Vale itself."

Darkwind frowned. "This is a new tactic for him, isn't it? He's never stolen power before that I can recall."

"Exactly," Stormcloud said, and bit his lip. "I don't like it, Darkwind. And I like it even less that our own mages haven't sensed him doing anything. Unless that was what this meeting you had to attend was all about—?"

Darkwind shook his head. "No. At least, that wasn't on the agenda. So unless they're keeping it from me— and they could be, I'll admit—they haven't noticed either the new node or the diversion of the ley-lines."

Winterlight snorted his contempt. "You could probably start a mage-war out here and they'd never notice inside the Vale. They're lost in their own little dream of what-was-once. Even if they were alert, the Heartstone just blanks out everything that's not in there with them."

Darkwind's frown deepened a trifle; that was *not* the way it was supposed to be. The Heartstone was supposed to sensitize the mages to what was going on with energies outside the Vale, not destroy or bury their sensitivity. But he realized that Winterlight was right; that was another of the side effects he disliked about being inside the Vale. When he was within the shield-area, it was as if he had been cut off from the energy-flows outside.

No one had said anything about that, not even right after the Heartstone shattered—which meant either that the effect was new, another developing side effect of living next to the broken stone—

—or it's been that way since the disaster, and nobody noticed. Which is just as bad.

Dawnfire had been silent up until now; he turned toward her and raised an eyebrow.

"Well," she said, with a frown that matched his own, "Stormcloud is the one who knows energies, and Winterlight's Huur is absolutely the best at spying. So I'll just say that I think the same things have been happening in my area, but I'd like someone to check to be sure. What I have that they don't is a network of allied species acting as my informants—*hertasi, dyheli, tervardi,* and a few humans who aren't fond of civilization. Most of the humans are a little crazy, but they're sharp enough when it comes to noticing what's going on around them."

Darkwind nodded; Dawnfire was the one who had suggested taking volunteers among the nonhumans in the first place, and she had proved the idea was viable by establishing a network outside the k'Sheyna boundaries.

"Well, some of my informants are missing," she said, some of her distress coming through despite her best efforts to control it. "And when I sent someone to try and find them, there was nothing. They haven't just disappeared, they've gone without a trace. That wouldn't be too hard to do with *dyheli,* but *hertasi* have real homes—they actually build furnishings for their caves and hollow trees—and *tervardi* build *ekele,* and even those are gone. It's as if they never existed at all."

"Gone?" Darkwind repeated. "How could anyone make a tree vanish?"

Dawnfire shook her head. "I don't know—though the trees themselves don't vanish, just the hollows and *ekele.* But the caves *do* vanish; there's solid earth and rock where the cave used to be. At least, that's what my bird tells me.''

Winterlight frowned. "Could that be illusion?"

"It could," she acknowledged with a nod. "Kyrr can't tell illusion from the real thing, and she's not particularly sensitive to magic. I wasn't about to ask her to test it. But my *tervardi* and *hertasi* aren't mages, either, so they wouldn't have used illusion to conceal their homes. Something took them, then covered its tracks by making it look as if there had never been anything living there.''

"Who, why, and how?" Stormcloud asked succinctly.

"There *is* an Adept out there—"

"But again, this isn't like anything he's ever done before," said Winterlight.

"That we know of," Darkwind added. "He might have decided to change his tactics. And it might not be him—or her—at all. It might be another Adept entirely. 'Why' is another good question; why take them at all, and why try to make it look as if they never existed?"

"To confuse us?" Stormcloud asked facetiously. "And make us think we're crazy?"

"Why not?" was Dawnfire's unexpected reply as she sat straight up, with a look of keen speculation on her face. "He has to know how badly the Heartstone has been affecting us. If we were only in sporadic contact with those particular creatures, erasing their very existence *might* make us uneasy about our own sanity.''

Winterlight nodded, slowly, as if what she had said had struck a note with him, too. "A good point. But the question is, what are we going to do about it?"

"About losing neutral territory—there's not much we *can* do," Darkwind sighed. "We could make things uncomfortable for the things moving in, I suppose; uncomfortable enough that they might move back without our having to force a confrontation we haven't the manpower to meet.''

"Like some really nasty practical jokes?" For the first time in the meeting, Stormcloud's eyes lit up. "Krawn and I could take care of that. Now that it's summer, there are a *lot* of things we can do to make them miserable, as long as we have your permission." He grinned evilly. "I know where there are some *lovely* fire-wasp nests. And Krawn can bring in absolute swarms of other corbies.

They aren't going to be able to leave anything outside without having it stolen or fouled.''

"Do it," Darkwind told him. "And don't stretch yourself too thin, but if you can extend your reach into Dawnfire's and Winterlight's areas, do so."

"I can," Stormcloud replied, with barely concealed glee. "The thing about tricks is that they're more effective if they're sporadic and unpredictable. Krawn is going to love this.''

"What about the power-theft?" asked Winterlight anxiously. "We can't do anything about that—as well try to bail water with a basket—but surely someone should."

"I'll tell the mages," Darkwind said, "But I can't promise anything. They might seal off the leaks, they might not. There's no predicting them these days."

"And my missing creatures?" Dawnfire was giving him that look of pleading he found so hard to resist, but there wasn't anything he could do that would satisfy her.

"They'll have to stay missing," he said, and held up his hand to forestall a protest. "I know, I know, it's not right, but we haven't enough guardians to spare to send even one into the neutral territory to find out what happened to them and protect the rest."

"If your gryphon friends were the ones missing," she said, her eyes sparking with momentary anger, "would you still be saying that?"

"Yes, I would," he replied. "*If* they had nested outside our boundaries. And even then, well, anything Treyvan and Hydona couldn't take care of themselves, I rather doubt *we* could handle. But I promise this much; if you and Kyrr can catch our predator in the act, we'll see what can be done to save whoever he's after. And if we can catch him in the act, we may have a chance at figuring out a defense for the rest of your friends."

Dawnfire obviously didn't like the answer, but she knew as well as he did that it was the only one he could give her.

"Anything else?" he asked, stifling a yawn, and casting a look at the windows. The sky beyond the branches was a glorious scarlet; they had spoken until sunset, and if the others were to get back to their *ekele* before dark, they'd have to leave soon. "I'm going to have to get out on patrol before dawn to make up for stealing a couple of hours of Amberwing's time so I could go to the blamed meeting. So I've got a short night ahead of me."

"I think we've covered everything," Winterlight said, after a moment of silence. "I'll catch up with the others, and let them know what we've decided."

He got up from the couch, and started down the stairs. Stormcloud followed him, then paused at the top of the stairs just long enough for a slow wink.

Dawnfire glanced at the windows, at the heavy branches standing out blackly against the fire of the sunset. "Are you really that tired?" she asked. She didn't get up from the couch.

"Not if you're going to stay a while," he replied, with a slow smile.

"You haven't taken back your feather," she said, somehow gliding into his arms before he was aware she had moved. "And I certainly don't want mine back. Of course I'll stay a while."

The scent of her, overlaid with the musky trace of her bird, was as intoxicating as *tran*-dust, and the soft lips she offered to him made his blood heat to near-boiling. He lost himself in her, their two minds meeting and melding, adding to the sensuality of the embrace. Her hands caressed the small of his back and slid down over his hips; his right was buried in her hair at the nape of her neck, his left crushed her to him.

He had just enough wit to remember he still had to pull up his ladder.

So did she, fortunately. "Go secure the door. The sunset, if I recall correctly, is incredible from upstairs."

She pushed him away; he moved down the stairs in a dream. The trapdoor was still unlatched; he brought the ladder up, rung by rung, and rehung it, latched down the trapdoor, and keyed the mage-light to a dim blue.

Then he ran up the two flights of stairs to the sleeping room.

She was waiting, clothed only in her loosened hair, curled like a white vixen on the dark furs of his bedspread, her hair flowing free and trailing behind her like a frozen waterfall.

She turned a little at his footfall, and smiled at him, holding out her hand—and they didn't see a great deal of the sunset.

* * *

:Brother comes, fast,: said Vree. Then, with an overtone of surprise, *:Very fast.:*

Vree's alert interrupted what had been an otherwise completely dull and uneventful patrol along the dry streambed that formed part of the k'Sheyna border. It hadn't always been dry—in fact, a week ago, there had been a stream here. Evidently not only ley-lines were being diverted.

Darkwind had not been overly worried when he discovered the condition of the stream; the diversion could easily have had perfectly natural causes. It could have gone dry for a dozen reasons, including the "helpful" work of beavers. But it was one more thing to investigate. . . .

That was when Vree's call alerted him. Before Darkwind had a chance to wonder just what that "fast" meant, he heard the pounding of hooves from up-trail. A moment later, a *dyheli* stag plunged over the embankment above him, coming to a halt in a clatter of cleft hooves, and a shower of sand and gravel. The graceful, antelope-like creature was panting, his flanks covered with sweat, his mane sodden with it. As Dawnfire slid from his back, he tossed his golden head with its three spiraling horns and Mindspoke Darkwind directly.

:Cannot run more—help my brothers—:

Then he plunged back into the brush, staggering a little from exhaustion, as Darkwind turned toward his rider.

"What—"

"There's a *dyheli* bachelor herd just outside the boundaries," she said, her words tumbling over each other with her urgency. "They're trapped in a pocket valley, one they can't climb out of. I don't know what chased them in there, or even if they just went in there last night figuring it was a good place to defend in the dark—but they've been trapped, and they're going mad with fear—"

"Whoa." He stopped the torrent of speech by placing his hand over her lips for a moment. "Take it slowly. What's holding them there?"

"It's—it's like a fog bank," and it fills the outer end of the valley," she replied, her voice strained, "Only it's bluish, and anything that goes into it doesn't come out alive. Darkwind, we have to get them out of there!''

"You say they're outside the borders?" he persisted.

She nodded, her enormous, pale-silver eyes fixed on his.

"I—" he hesitated, presented with the pleading in her expression. *I shouldn't. It's outside, it could be a diversion to get several of us out there—it could be an attempt to ambush us—*

But her eyes persuaded him against his better judgment. "I—all right, *ashke*. I'll come look at the situation. But I can't promise anything."

It took them a while to reach the spot, even with the assistance of two more *dyheli* from a breeding herd inside k'Sheyna borders. By the time they reached the valley, the situation had worsened. The fog had crowded all the young *dyheli* bucks into the back of the valley, and they milled around the tiny space in a state of complete, unthinking panic. Trampling everything beneath their churning hooves, with horns tossing, their squeals of desperation reached to Darkwind's perch on the hill above them.

He studied the situation, his heart sinking. The sides of the valley—it was really a steep cup among the hills, with a spring at the bottom—were rocky, and far too steep to bring the *dyheli* up, even if they'd been calm. In their current state of panic, it was impossible.

The fog was mage-born, that much he could tell, easily. But the mage himself was not here. There was no one to attack, and no way to counter such a nebulous menace. Even calling up a wind—if he could have done so—would not have dispersed the evil cloud.

It roiled beneath him, a leprous blue-white, thick and oily, too murky to see into. Twice now, he'd seen young bucks overcome with fear and madness, try to break through into the clear air beyond. They had never come out on the other side.

"We have to do something!" Dawnfire pleaded. He hesitated a moment, then gave her the bad news.

"There isn't anything we can do," he said, closing his mental shields against the tide of fear and despair from below. The *dyheli* were so panicked now that they weren't even capable of thinking. "Maybe the rain tonight will disperse it in time to save them."

"*No!*" she shouted, careless of what might overhear her. "No, we can't leave them! I'm a guardian, they're my responsibility, I *won't* leave them!"

"Dawnfire—" he took her shoulders and shook them. "There isn't anything we can do, don't you understand that? They're too panicked to get harnesses on and haul them up—even if we had enough people here to try! And I *won't* call in all the scouts from their patrols. It's bad enough that I left mine! Don't you see, this could easily be a diversion, to clear the way for something else to come in over the border while it's unguarded!"

She stared at him, aghast, for a long moment. Then, "You *coward!*" she spat. "You won't even try! You don't care if they die, you don't care what happens to anyone or anything, all you care about is yourself! You won't even use your magic to save them!"

As the envenomed words flew, Darkwind kept a tenuous grip on his temper by reminding himself of how young Dawnfire was. *She's only seventeen,* he told himself. *She lives and breathes being a guardian, and she doesn't understand how to lose. She was barely assigned her duties when the Heartstone blew. She doesn't mean what she's saying. . . .*

But as her words grew more and more hurtful and heated in response to his cool silence, he finally had enough. His temper snapped like a dry twig, and he stopped the torrent of abuse with a mental "slap."

And as she stood, silent and stunned, he folded his arms across his chest and stared at her until she dropped her eyes.

"You say you are a guardian. Well, you pledged an oath to obey *me,* your commander, and abide by my decisions. Have you suddenly turned into a little child, regressed to the age of ten, when sworn oaths mean only 'until I'm tired of playing'? No?" He studied her a moment more, as she went from red to white and back again. "In that case, I suggest you calm yourself and return to your assigned patrol. *If* you comport yourself well and *if* you can keep yourself under control, I will consider leaving you there, rather than reassigning you elsewhere. Is that understood?''

''Yes, Elder,'' she replied, in a voice that sounded stifled.

''Very well,'' he said. ''Go, then.''

Chapter Seven

ELSPETH

"Elspeth?"

Despite the anxious tone of Skif's voice, Elspeth didn't look up from her book. "What?" she said, absently, more to respond and let Skif know she'd heard him than a real reply. She was deep in what was apparently a first-hand description of the moments before Vanyel's final battle.

It was then that we saw how the valley walls had been cut away, to widen the passage, and the floor of the vale had been smoothed into a roadway broad enough for a column of four. And all this, said Vanyel, was done by magic. I knew not what to think at that moment.

"Elspeth, don't you think we should be getting out of here?" Skif persisted. "On the road, I mean." She looked up from her page, and into Skif's anxious brown eyes. There was no one else to overhear them; they were the only ones in the library archives, where the oldest Chronicles were stored.

Sunlight damaged books, so the archive chamber was a windowless room in the center of the library. Smoke and soot damaged them as well, so all lighting was provided by smokeless lanterns burning the finest of lamp oil, constructed to extinguish immediately if they tipped

over. No other form of lighting was permitted—certainly
not candles. Elspeth realized, as she looked into Skif's
anxiety-shadowed face, that she didn't know what time
it was. If any of the Collegium bells had rung, she hadn't
noticed them.

Her stomach growled in answer to the half-formed
question, telling her that it was past lunchtime, if nothing
else.

She rubbed her eyes; she'd been so absorbed in her
reading that she hadn't noticed the passage of time.
"Why?" she asked, simply. "What's your hurry?"

He grimaced, then shrugged. "I don't like the idea of
riding off south with just the two of us, but since you
seem so set on it—I keep thinking your getting the Council to agree was too easy. They didn't *argue* enough."

"Not argue enough?" she replied, making a sour face.
"I beg to differ. *You* weren't there. They argued plenty,
believe me. I thought they'd never stop till they all fell
over from old age."

"But not enough," he persisted. "It should have taken
weeks to get them to agree to your plan. Instead—it took
less than a day. That doesn't make any sense, at least,
not to me. I keep thinking they're going to change their
minds at any minute. So I want to know why we aren't
getting out of here before they get a chance to."

"They won't change their minds," she said, briefly,
wishing he'd let her get back to her researches. "Gwena
says so."

"What does a Companion have to do with the Council
changing its mind?" he demanded.

That's what I would like to know, she thought. *Gwena's
playing coy every time I ask.* "I don't know, but ask
yours. I bet she says the same thing."

"Huh." His eyes unfocused for a moment as he Mindspoke his little mare; then, "I'll be damned," he replied. "You're right. But I still don't see why we aren't
getting on the road; everything we need is packed except
for your personal gear. I should think you'd be so impatient to get out of here that *I* would be the one holding
us back."

She shrugged. "Let's just say that I'm getting ready.
What I'm doing in here is as important as the packing
you've been doing."

"Oh?" He shaded the word in a way that kept it from sounding insulting, which it could easily have done.

"It's no secret," she said, gesturing at the piles of books around her. "I'm researching magic in the old Chronicles; magic, and Herald-Mages, what they could do, and so forth. So I know what to look for and what we need."

If he noticed that some of those Chronicles were of a later day than Vanyel's time, he didn't mention it. "I suppose that makes sense," he acknowledged. "Just remember, the Council could change their decision any time, no matter what Gwena says."

"I'll keep that in mind," she replied, turning her attention back to her page. After a moment, Skif took the hint; she heard him slip out of his chair, and leave the room.

But her mind wasn't on the words in front of her. Instead, she gave thought to how much Skif's observations mirrored her own.

This *was* too easy. There was no reason why the Queen should have agreed to this, much less the Circle and Council. The excuse of the magical attack on Bolton, the Skybolts' deeded border town, was just that; an excuse. She had checked back through the Chronicles of the past several years, and she had uncovered at least five other instances of magical attacks on Border villages, all of which looked to her as if they showed a weakening of the Border-protections. The records indicated no such panic reaction as she'd seen in the Council Chamber; rather, that there was a fairly standard way of responding. A team of Heralds and Healers would be sent to the site, the people would be aided and removed to somewhere safer, if that was their choice, then the incident was filed and forgotten.

Farther back than that had been Talia's encounter with Ancar, that had signaled the beginning of the conflicts with Hardorn. There had been long discussions about what to do, how to handle the attacks of mages; Elspeth remembered that perfectly well. And there *had* been some progress; the Collegium made a concerted effort, checking the Chronicles following Vanyel's time, to determine how Heralds without the Mage-Gift could counter magical attacks. Some solutions had been found, the appropriate people were briefed and trained—

And that was all. The knowledge was part of the schooling in Gifts now, but there was no particular emphasis placed on it. Not the way there should have been, especially following Ancar's second attempt at conquest.

File and forget.

For that matter, there was even some evidence that Karse had been using magic, under the guise of "priestly powers." No one had *ever* followed up on that, not even when Kero had made a point of reminding the Council of it.

There had to be another reason for letting her go on this "quest." Especially since there were overtones in the Council meetings she attended of "the Brat is getting her way." It would have been obvious to anyone with half a mind and one ear that now that the initial excitement was over, they regretted giving her their permission to leave, even to as safe a destination as Bolthaven, deep in the heart of her uncle's peaceful kingdom.

Even the Heralds on the Council gave her the unmistakable feeling that they were *not* happy about this little excursion, and they'd gladly use any excuse to take their permission back.

But they didn't. Gwena had said repeatedly that they wouldn't. There was something going on that they weren't talking about. And it didn't take a genius to figure out that, whatever it was, the Companions, *en masse*, were hock-deep in it.

And did it have something to do with her growing resistance to this compulsion to forget magic, to avoid even thinking about it?

Once her suspicions were aroused, Elspeth had decided that, before she ran off into unknown territory, she was going to do a little research on the Herald-Mages. Not just to find out their strengths and weaknesses, nor to discover just what the limits and gradations of the "Mage-Gift" were, but to see just how extensive the apparent prohibition against magic was; how deeply rooted, and how long it had been going on.

And what she had learned was quite, quite fascinating. It dated from Vanyel's time, all right—but not exactly.

To be precise, it dated from the time that Bard Stefen, then an old and solitary man, vanished without a trace.

In the Forest of Sorrows.

At least, that was Elspeth's guess. He was supposed to be in the company of some other young, unspecified Herald, on a kind of pilgrimage to the place where Vanyel died. He never arrived at his destination, yet no one reported his death. Granted, he had not yet achieved the kind of legendary status he had in Elspeth's time, but still, he *was* a prominent Bard, the author of hundreds of songs, epic rhymed tales and ballads, and the hero of a few of them himself. He was Vanyel's lifebonded lover, the last one to see him alive, and Vanyel *did* have the status of legend. *Someone* would have said something if he had died—at the very least, there should have been an impressive Bardic funeral.

No mention, no funeral. He simply dropped out of sight.

Nor was that all; even if he had vanished, someone *should* have noticed that he disappeared; surely searches should have been made for him. But no one did notice, nor did anyone look for him.

He simply vanished without a trace, and no one paid any notice. And that—possibly even that precise moment—was when it became impossible to talk about magic, except in the historical sense. That was when the Chronicles stopped mentioning it; when songs stopped being written about it.

When encounters with it outside the borders of Valdemar—or, occasionally, just inside those borders—were forgotten within weeks.

Fortunately those encounters were usually benign, as when ambassadors from Valdemar would see the mages in the Court of Rethwellan performing feats to amuse, or ambassadors from outside of Valdemar would mention magic, and some of the things their kingdoms' mages could do. The Chronicler of the time would dutifully note it down—then promptly forget about it. So would the members of the Council—and the Heralds.

Did they attribute all of that to boasting and travelers' tales? Now I wonder if, when other people read the Chronicles over, do their eyes just skip across the relevant words as if they weren't even there?

It wouldn't surprise her. Elspeth herself had noticed whole pages seeming to blur in front of her eyes, so that she had to make a concerted effort to read every word. She had initially ascribed the effect to fatigue and the labor of reading the archaic script and faded inks, but now she wasn't so sure. It had gotten easier, the more she had read, but she wondered what would happen if she stopped reading for a while, then came back to it.

She had even found a report from Selenay's grandfather, back when he was plain old "Herald Roald," and the Heir, about his encounter with Kero's grandmother Kethry and *her* partner.

Tarma shena Tale'sedrin, a Shin'a'in Kal'enedral, sworn to the service of her Goddess, was plainly some kind of a priest. In fact, much to Roald's surprise, she had achieved a physical manifestation of her Goddess right before his eyes. Never having seen a Goddess, he was rather impressed.

So would I be!

He'd described the manifestation; the impossibly lovely young Shin'a'in woman, clothed as one of her own Swordsworn—but with strange eyes with neither pupil nor white; just the impression of an endless field of stars.

Brrr. I would probably have passed out.

He and Tarma had become quite firm friends after that; Roald's Companion approved of both the priest and her Goddess, which Roald had found vastly amusing. But if Tarma was a powerful priest, Kethry was just as clearly a talented and powerful mage. Roald had quite a bit to say about her; it was evident that he was quite smitten with her, and if it hadn't been for the fact that she was obviously just as smitten with the Rethwellan archivist they had rescued, he hinted that he might well have considered a try in that direction.

A superb tactician, however, he knew a hopeless situation when he saw one and wisely did not pursue his interest any further.

It was Roald's account of Kethry's magical abilities that interested Elspeth. It was in this account that she got a clearer idea of the differences between Journeyman class and Master, of Master and Adept. That alone was useful, since it proved to her that what Valdemar needed was indeed an Adept, more than one, if at all possible. Certainly a teacher. There was no reason why the Mage-Gift should have vanished from the population of Valdemar, when it was clearly present elsewhere.

Roald did not have a great deal to say about Kethry's magical sword, "Need," other than the fact that it was magical, with unspecified powers, and would only help women. So at that point in time, the song "Threes" had not migrated up to Valdemar, or Roald would have made certain to mention it.

Interesting about songs. . . .

As evidence of just how strong that magic-prohibition had been, Elspeth had come across another fascinating bit of information in the Bardic Chronicles, which were also stored here. The song "Kerowyn's Ride" had preceded the arrival of the real Kerowyn by several years—ascribed to "anonymous." Which it wasn't; several times visiting Bards had attempted to set the Valdemaran record straight. Each time the attribution was duly noted, then the very next time the song was listed in a Court performance, it was ascribed to "anonymous."

It was the habit of Master Bards, particularly the teachers, to write short dissertations on the meaning and derivation of popular songs to be used as teaching materials. Out of curiosity, Elspeth had made a point of looking up the file on "Kerowyn's Ride."

At that point, it would have strained the credulity of even a dunce to believe that there was nothing working to suppress the knowledge of magic—for even *after* the arrival of the real Kerowyn, Master Bards were writing essays that claimed it was an allegorical piece wherein the Goddess-as-Crone passed her power to the Goddess-as-Maiden at Spring Solstice. She found several other papers stating that it described an actual event that had taken place hundreds of years ago, as evidenced by this or that style.

That was quite enough to get Elspeth digging into more of the Bardic Chronicles, and that was when she discovered corroborating evidence for her theory that something was suppressing the very idea of magic.

Despite the fact that there had been a concerted effort to get the songs about Herald-Mages and magical conflicts back into the common repertory, despite the fact that this was Bardic Collegium's top priority—and despite the fact that perfectly awful, maudlin songs like the unkillable "My Lady's Eyes" stayed popular—the "magic" songs *could not be kept in repertory.* Audiences grew bored, or wandered away; Bards *forgot the lyrics,* or found themselves singing lyrics to another song entirely. When given a list of possible songs for various occasions, a Seneschal or Master of the Revels would inexplicably choose any song but the ones describing magic.

Only those songs that did not specifically mention magic, or those where the powers described could as easily be ascribed to a traditional Gift, stayed in popular repertory. Songs like the "Sun and Shadow" ballads, or the "Windrider" cycle, songs that were hundreds of years older than the Vanyel songs and written in archaic language, were well known—was it because not once was there a reference to a specific spell, only vague terms like "power" and "curses?"

Furthermore, Elspeth herself had heard the "problem" songs being sung, not once, but fairly often, and with a great deal of acclaim and success. So it wasn't that there was anything wrong with the songs themselves. It *had* to be because of their content. And was it possible that the reason the songs had been successful was that they were sung in the presence of many Heralds? For that seemed to be the common factor. It was when they had been sung with no Heralds present at all that the worst failures occurred.

She had learned several other things from the Chronicles of Vanyel's time—things which had no direct bearing on her present mission, but which explained a great deal.

For instance: there had been something called "The Web," which demanded the energy and attention of four Herald-Mages. Those four apparently had been somehow tied to one-quarter of Valdemar each, and were alerted to anything threatening the Kingdom by the reaction of the spell. The problem was, by the end of Queen Elspeth the Second's reign, there were not enough Herald-Mages to cover the four quarters . . . not and deal with enemies, too.

That was when Vanyel altered the spell, tying *all* Heralds into this "Web," so that when danger threatened, *everyone* would know. Before that, it was only chance that a ForeSeer would bend his will to a particular time and place to see that something would be a problem. After, it was *guaranteed*; ForeSeers would see the danger, and would know exactly what Gifts or actions were required to counter it. Heralds with those Gifts would find themselves in the saddle and heading for the spot whether or not they had been summoned. The Chronicles were not clear about how he had done this, only that it definitely worked, and there was a great deal of relief knowing that the Kingdom no longer depended on having four powerful Herald-Mages to act as guardians.

Vanyel had done something else at that time, though whether or not it was part of the alterations to this "Web" or not, the Chronicles were unclear. He had summoned—something. Or rather, he had summoned *things*. Having called them, he did something to them or with them, somehow gave them the job of watching for mages and alerting Herald-Mages to their presence in Valdemar.

What happened when there weren't any more Herald-Mages? she wondered. *Did they just keep watching, or what? Have they been trying to alert Heralds, or not?*

At least this accounted for something Kero had said, about why Quenten and the rest of the Skybolts' mages couldn't stay inside Valdemar. "He said it felt like there was someone watching him all the time," she'd told Elspeth. "Like there was someone just behind his shoulder, staring at him. Waking or sleeping. Said it just about drove him crazy."

That certainly made a good enough reason for Elspeth; she didn't think *she* would want to stick around anywhere that she felt eyes on her all the time.

Unless, of course, she was a truly powerful mage, one able to shield herself against just about anything. One that knew she was so much the superior of other mages that she felt totally confident in her ability to hide from the enemy.

Like Hulda, maybe? We still don't know everything she can do. We've been assuming she was just Ancar's teacher and attributing all his success to Ancar himself. . . . But what if it's really Hulda, letting him think he's in control, while she is really the power and the mind behind his actions?

Again, that would explain a great deal, particularly

Ancar's obsession with eliminating Talia, Selenay, and Elspeth.

It could be he simply hated suffering defeat at the hands of women.

But it also could be Hulda, egging him on. If he felt somehow shamed at being defeated by females, she could be playing on that shame, making him obsessive about it. After all, *she* had very little to lose. If Ancar was goaded into defeating Valdemar, she won. And if he lost, or was killed during the conflict—she would be there to inherit his kingdom and pick up the pieces. And Hulda would never repeat his mistakes. . . .

It all made hideous sense, a good explanation of otherwise inexplicable behavior. And Elspeth didn't like the explanation one bit. Ancar as an enemy was bad enough. But the idea of an enemy like Hulda who had been plotting for decades—

It was enough to send a chill down the toughest of spines. It was more than enough to give Elspeth nightmares for three nights running.

Elspeth closed the book she'd been reading, fighting down a queasy sensation in her stomach.

She had just finished reading the passages in the Chronicles about Tylendel, Vanyel's first lover; his repudiation and his suicide. It didn't make for easy reading; it had been written, not by the Chronicler of the time, but by a non-Herald, a Healer, who had been a friend of Tylendel's mentor. Evidently the Heralds had all been affected so strongly by this incident that they were unable to write about it.

But that was not why she was fighting uneasy feelings.

Tylendel—at seventeen—had evidently been able to construct something called a "Gate" or a "Gate Spell," which enabled him to literally span distances it would take a Companion days or even weeks to cross.

Her blood ran cold at the idea, and even though the author had hinted that the mage who used this spell had to know precisely where he was going, that fact was no comfort. Hulda had been to Valdemar—and it would not be very difficult to insert other agents into Valdemar simply to learn appropriate destinations.

What if Ancar were to control this spell? What if he

were able to get it past the protections? There would be no stopping him; he would be able to place agents anywhere he chose.

In fact—Hulda had been in the Palace. For years. There was probably very little she *didn't* know about the Palace.

She could place an agent in the Queen's very bedroom, if she chose, and all the guards in the world would make no difference.

That might even be how that assassin got onto the Palace grounds. She shuddered. *I think I'm going to have nightmares again. . . .*

This had not been an easy day for reading. Elspeth was just as disturbed by the Chronicle she had completed before this one, the one describing Vanyel's last battle.

The Herald-Mage had commanded tremendous power; so tremendous that the author had made an offhand comment to the effect that he could have leveled Haven if he so chose. Granted, Haven was a smaller city then than it was now, but—the power to level a city?

It simply didn't seem possible, destruction on that kind of scale seemed absurd on the face of it. Yet for the writer, such power seemed to be taken for granted.

At first reading, she had been skeptical of such claims; Chroniclers had been known to indulge in hyperbole before this. She had assumed that the descriptions were the embroideries of a "frustrated Bard," a Chronicler's version of poetic license. But on the second reading she had discovered the signature at the end, modestly tucked away in small, neat handwriting that matched the rest of the Chronicle, but not anything else in the book.

Bard Stefen, for Herald-Chronicler Kyndri.

Now there was no reason for Stefen to have invented outrageous powers for his lifebonded. There was *every* reason for him to have been absolutely factual in his account. He was not a would-be Bard, like many of the Chroniclers; he *was* a Bard, with all the opportunity to play with words that he wanted, outside of the Chronicles. And everything else in those Chronicles had been simple, direct, without exaggeration.

So it followed that Herald Vanyel *had* that power, that ability. The ability to level a city.

And if Vanyel had commanded that kind of power,

there was no reason to suppose that Ancar could not ally himself to a mage with that same power, sooner or later. There probably weren't many with that kind of ability, but if there was one with the same kind of lust for conquest that drove Ancar, the King of Hardorn would eventually find him.

Elspeth sat for a moment with her head in her hands, overwhelmed by a feeling of helplessness. How could Valdemar possibly stand against the power of a mage like that?

By finding another like him, she finally decided. *If there is one, there have to be more. And surely not all of them will find Ancar's offers attractive. And that's exactly what I'm going to have to do.*

She shook back her hair, and pushed her chair away from the book-laden table. She was a little surprised by the bulk of her scattered notes; she'd been so engrossed she hadn't noticed just how much she'd been writing down.

All right, she decided. *I've learned all I can from books. Now it's time to get out there and see how much of it applies to current reality.*

She collected her notes into a neat stack, and shoved them into a notebook. Then she rose, stretched, and picked up the books, restoring them to their proper places on the shelves. Finally, though, she had to admit to herself that she wasn't being considerate of the librarians, she was putting off the moment of departure.

She squared her shoulders, lifted her head, and walked out of the archives with a firm step—showing a confidence she did not feel.

Not that it really mattered. This was her plan, and she was, by the gods, going to see it through. And the first step on that road was to go find Skif and tell him it was time to leave; that she had everything she needed.

If nothing else, she told herself wryly, *Skif will be ready. Even if I'm not sure I am.*

Skif *was* ready; he had wisely refrained from repeating just how ready he was, but he was so visibly impatient that she decided to get on the road immediately, instead of waiting for morning. She headed back to her room at a trot, to throw her personal things into packs, while he had the Companions saddled and loaded with saddle-bags. It was, after all, only a little after noon. They could conceivably make quite a bit of progress before they had to stop for the night.

From the look on his face, that was exactly what Skif intended.

She intercepted a young page and sent him around with farewell messages for everyone except her mother and Talia; those farewells she would make in person.

Mother would never forgive me if I just sent a note, she thought ruefully, as she stuffed clothing into a pack. *Not that I wouldn't mind just slipping out of here. She's bound to raise a fuss. . . .*

Selenay still was not resigned to the situation; Elspeth was as sure of that as she was of her own name. She had been so involved in her researches that she hadn't spent much time in her mother's company, but the few times she had, she'd been treated to long, reproachful looks. Selenay hadn't said anything, but Elspeth would have been perfectly happy to avoid any chance of another motherly confrontation.

She fully intended to plead the need for a hasty departure, putting the blame on Skif and his impatience if she had to. *If I can just get this over quickly—*

Just as she thought that, someone tapped on her door. She started, her heart pounding for a moment, then winced as she forced herself to relax. She hadn't realized just how keyed up she was.

A second tap sounded a little impatient. *Don't tell me; Mother's already found out that I'm leaving!*

"Come in," she called, with a certain resignation. But to her surprise, it wasn't Selenay who answered the invitation, it was Kero.

A second surprise: the Herald-Captain was carrying a sword; Need to be precise. Not *wearing* it, but carrying it; the blade was sheathed in a brand new scabbard, with an equally new sword-belt, both of blue-gray leather. And before she had a chance to say anything, Kero thrust the sword—sheath, belt, and all—into her hands.

"Here," she said gruffly, her voice just a little hoarse, as if she was keeping back emotions of some kind. "You're going to need this. No pun intended."

Her hands left the sheath reluctantly, and it seemed to

Elspeth as if she was wistful—unwillingly so—at parting with the blade.

For her part, Elspeth was so dumbfounded she felt like the village idiot, unable to think at all coherently. *I'm going to what—she's giving me—that's* Need, *it's magic, she can't mean me to have it! Why—what—*

"But—" was all she could say; anything else came out as a sputter. "But—why?"

"Why?" Kero shrugged with an indifference that was obviously feigned. "Right after you and I met, Need spoke for you. I couldn't do without her, not right then, and she hasn't said anything since, but there's never been any doubt in *my* mind that you're the one she was supposed to go to."

"Go to?" Elspeth repeated, dazedly. Now that the blade was in her hands, she felt—something. An odd feeling. A slight disorientation, as if there was someone trying such a delicate mental probe on her that it was at the very edge of her ability to sense it. It was a little like when she'd been Chosen, only not nearly as strong.

"It's something like being Chosen, I suppose," Kero said, echoing her thought. "She picks the one she wants to be passed to. Better that than just getting picked up at random, or so I'd guess, though women are the only ones that can use her. Grandmother got her from an old female merc when she left her mage-school; she gave Need to me, and now I'm giving her to you. You'd have gotten her from me in any case eventually, but since you're going out past the borders, I think it would be a good idea if you take her with you."

Suddenly, the blade seemed doubly heavy.

"You mean the sword talks to you?" Elspeth replied vaguely, trying to sort out surprise, the odd touches at the back of her mind, and just a touch of apprehension.

"Not exactly talks, no," Kero chuckled. "Though let me warn you now, she is going to try and exert a lot of pressure on you to do what *she* wants—which is to rescue women in trouble. Don't give in to her more than you have to. She'll try two things—she'll either try to take over your body, *or* she'll give you a headache like you've never had in your life. You can block it and her out; I learned to eventually, and I should think with all the training you've had in the Gifts you should be able to manage just fine. After all, when I faced her down, I was only half-trained at best. Whatever you do, don't give in to her, or you'll set a bad precedent, as bad as giving a troublesome falcon its own way. She manipulated my grandmother, but I never let her manipulate me if I could help it.''

Elspeth regarded the gift dubiously. ''If she's that much trouble—''

''Oh, she's worth it,'' Kero said, with a rueful chuckle. ''Especially for somebody like you or me, somebody who doesn't know beans about magic. For one thing, she'll Heal you of practically any injury, even on the battlefield in the middle of a fight. That alone is worth every bit of bother she ever gave me. But for the rest of her abilities, if you're a swordswinger, she'll protect you against magic—and I mean, real protection, as good as any Adept I've ever seen. I had some encounters with some mages of Ancar's that I haven't talked about—there wasn't anything any of them threw at me that she couldn't deflect.'' Kero chuckled.''Gave them quite a surprise, too.''

''But your grandmother was a mage,'' Elspeth said.

''Right. If you're a mage, she protects you, too—but she doesn't do anything for you magically.''

''She takes over your body and makes you a good fighter?'' Elspeth supplied.

''Right! But she doesn't do anything for a fighter in the way of fighting ability.''

''I think I remember something about your grandmother being a fighter in some of the songs, only I knew you said she was a mage,'' Elspeth said, looking down at the blade in her hands with a touch of awe. ''I never could figure out how the confusion happened. From everything I've read, becoming a mage takes up so much of your time you couldn't possibly learn to fight well.''

Kero shrugged. ''Yes and no. It really depends on how much you want to curtail your social life. If you want to be a celibate, you could learn to be both.''

Huh. Like Vanyel. . . .

''Anyway, Need makes you a swordmaster if you're a mage, protects you from magic if you're a fighter. And if you aren't either—''

''Like in 'Kerowyn's Ride'?'' Elspeth asked, with a sly smile.

Kero groaned. "Yes, gods help me, like in that damned song. If you aren't either, she takes over and makes you both. *Her* way, though, which tends to make you almost as big a target as one of your 'Here I am, shoot me' uniforms."

Elspeth chuckled; Kero was, as usual, *not* wearing Whites. Then she sobered. "But you said I can fight the compulsion, right?"

Kero nodded. "I did it. It takes a little determination, if you don't know what you're doing, but it can be done. I had to threaten to drop the damned thing down the nearest well. And I've already told it that you'll do the same if it gives you too much trouble."

Seeing Elspeth's hesitation, she added, "If you don't want it, don't draw it—it can't force you to take it, you know. If you don't draw it, it won't have any kind of hold on you."

Elspeth wasn't entirely sure of that—not after the tentative touches in the back of her mind, but she *was* certain that the hold the blade had on her could be fought. If she chose to. If Kero could, so could she.

Carefully, she weighed all the factors in her mind. This was not going to be a decision to make lightly.

She'll have a hold on me—but she'll protect me from things I not only don't understand, but might not detect until it's too late. And the Healing—that's damned important. If I'm hurt, I may not be able to get to a Healer, but I won't have to if I have her.

Not such a bad trade, really. And since Elspeth had already been Chosen, perhaps the hold would be that much less. Gwena would surely help fight it; she could be very possessive when she wanted to be.

Another good reason to take the blade suddenly occurred to her. One that Kero might not have thought of. *If I* don't *find a mage—I'm a woman, and Mother's a woman. How well would this magic sword work against Ancar, I wonder?*

Given that scenario, how could she *not*, in good conscience, accept the blade?

Without hesitation, she pulled Need from her sheath.

For a moment, nothing at all happened.

Then—

Time stopped; a humming, somehow joyful, gleeful,

filled the back of her head. *It is just like being Chosen,* she thought absently, as the blade glowed for a moment, the fire coalescing into script, runes that writhed, then settled into something she could actually read.

Woman's Need calls me, as Woman's Need made me, she read, as her eyes watered from the fiery light. *Her Need will I answer, as my Maker bade me.*

The runes writhed again—then faded, the moment she had the sense of them. The hum in the back of her mind stilled, and Time hiccupped, then resumed its stately progress.

"What the hell was that supposed to mean?" she demanded, as soon as she could speak again.

Kero shrugged. "Damned if I know," she admitted. "Only the gods know her history now. Grandmother said that's what happens when she gets into the hands she wants. But that, my dear, is the first time she's roused since I brought her inside the borders of Valdemar."

Elspeth slid the blade gingerly into her sheath.

Her. I doubt I'll ever call her "it" again. . . .

"What happens when I take her outside Valdemar?" she asked with trepidation. There had been such a feeling of power when Need had responded to her—a feeling of controlled strength, held back, the way a mastiff would handle a newborn chick.

And I'm not sure I like feeling like a newborn chick!

"I don't know," Kero admitted. "She hasn't been outside Valdemar for a long time. Whatever happens, you're going to require her, of that much I'm certain."

"But what about you?" Elspeth was forced by her own conscience to ask. "Where does that leave you?"

Kero laughed. "The same as before; I haven't *ever* depended on her to bail me out of a tough spot. And to tell you the truth, I don't think I'm going to be seeing anything worth being protected against."

"And I am." Elspeth made that a statement.

"I'd bet on it." Kero nodded, soberly. "I'll tell you this much; while she's given me trouble in the past, she's always been worth the having. I may not have depended on her, but she's bailed me out of things I could never have gotten myself out of alone. I feel a lot better knowing you have her."

"I—" Elspeth stopped, at a loss for words. "Kero, 'thanks' just doesn't seem adequate. . . ."

"Oh, don't thank me, thank her," Kero grinned. "She picked you, after all."

"I'm thanking you anyway." Elspeth hugged her, sword and all, then bade her a reluctant farewell. It was hard saying good-bye; a lot harder than she thought it would be. She stood with the sheathed sword in her hands for a long time after Kero was gone.

Finally Elspeth buckled the swordbelt over her tunic, and wriggled a little to settle Need's weight. Once in place, the sword felt right; most swords took some getting used to, they all weighed differently, their balance on the hip or in the hand was different.

But most swords aren't magic.

The thought was *un*settling; this was the stuff of which ballads and stories were made, and although Elspeth had daydreamed herself into a heroine when she was a child, she'd given up those daydreams once she achieved her Whites.

I thought I had, anyway.

That made for another unsettling thought, though; stories all had endings—and she was beginning to feel as if the ending to this one was already written.

As if she had no choice in where she was going, or how she was going to get there; as if everyone knew what her goal was except her.

"Destiny" was one word she had always hated—and now it looked as if it was the one word that applied to her.

And she didn't like the feeling one bit.

Treyvan & Hydona

Chapter Eight

DARKWIND

:*Stupid,*: said Vree, with profound disapproval.

Darkwind's stomach lurched as Vree made another swooping dive—not *quite* a stoop—skimming through the pocket valley that held the trapped *dyheli* bucks.

There were times when the gyre's viewpoint was a little—unsettling.

The gyre wheeled above the *dyheli* herd, just above the highest level of the mist, giving Darkwind the loan of his keener eyes and the advantage of wings and height. :*Stupid, stupid. We should go.*:

Not that Darkwind needed a bird, even a bondbird, to tell him that. The gentle *dyheli* huddled together in an exhausted, witless knot, too spent by panic to do anything sensible.

Through the gyre's eyes he looked for anything that might pass as a track out of the valley—and found nothing. The spring dropped from a height five times that of the *dyheli* to the valley floor, down a sheer rock face. The other two sides of the valley were just as sheer, and sandstone to boot.

Nothing short of a miracle was going to get them out of there.

Vree's right. We should go. I can't risk all of k'Sheyna

for the sake of a dozen dyheli. *I made pledges, I have greater responsibilities.*

So why was he here, lying under the cover of a bush, just above the mist-choked passage out of the dead-end valley, searching through his bondbird's eyes for a way out for the tiny herd? Why was he wasting his time, leaving his section of the border unpatrolled, tearing up his insides with his own helplessness?

Because I'm stupid.

One of the bucks raised a sweat-streaked head to utter a heartbreaking cry of despair. His gut twisted a little more.

And because I can't stand to see them suffering like that. They're fellow creatures, as intelligent as we are. They looked to Dawnfire for protection and help, even if they did range outside our boundaries. They acted as her eyes and ears out here. I can't just abandon them now.

Which was, no doubt, exactly the way Dawnfire felt. There was no difference in what he was doing now, and what she wanted to do.

Except that I'm a little older, a little more experienced. But just as headstrong and stupid.

The mist—whatever it was—rose and fell with an uneasy, wavelike motion, and wherever it lapped up on the rock wall, it left brown and withered vegetation when it receded. And it took quite a bit to kill those tough little rock-plants. So the mist was deadly to the touch as well as deadly to breathe. There was no point in trying to calm the *dyheli* enough to get them to hold their breath and make a dash for freedom . . . they'd never survive being in the mist for as long as it would take them to blunder through.

As if to underscore that observation, the mist lapped a little higher just below his hiding place. A wisp of it eddied up, and he got a faint whiff of something that burned his mouth and throat and made his eyes water. He coughed it out as the mist ebbed again.

Poisonous and caustic. First, burns to madden them further, then the poison. They're horribly susceptible to poisons; they'd probably get fatal doses just through skin contact, through the area of the burn.

No, no hope there.

He rubbed his eyes to clear them, and sent Vree to

perch in the tree over his head. Another of the *dyheli* called mournfully, and the cry cut into his heart. He knuckled his eyes again, blinking through burning eyes, but still could see no way out of the trap.

Even the spring-fed waterfall was not big enough to do more than provide a little water spray and a musical trickle down the rocks. There was no shelter for even one of the *dyheli* behind it.

I can't bear this, he decided, finally. *All I could do is shoot them and give them a painless death, or leave them, and hope that whatever this poison is, it disperses on its own—or maybe won't be able to get past the mist that the waterfall is throwing.*

Two choices, both bad, the second promising a worse death than the first. His heart smoldered with frustration and anger, and he swore and pounded his fist white on the rock-hard dirt, then wiped the blood off his skinned knuckles. *No! Dammit, it's not fair, they* depended *on Tayledras to protect them! There has to be someth—*

He looked back into the valley, at the tugging of an invisible current, a stirring in the fabrics of power, the rest of his thought forgotten.

A sudden shrilling along his nerves, an etching of ice down his backbone, that was what warned him of magic—magic that he knew, intimately, though he no longer danced to its piping—the movements of energies nearby, and working swiftly.

His fingers moved, silently, in unconscious response. He swung his head a little, trying to pinpoint the source.

There—

The mist below him stirred.

The hair on the back of his neck and arms stood on end, and he found himself on his feet on the floor of the valley before the wall of mist, with no memory of standing, much less climbing down. It didn't matter; magic coiled and sprang from a point somewhere before him, purposeful, and guided.

Striking against the mage-born wall of poison.

The mist writhed as it was attacked, stubbornly resisting. Magic, a single spell, fought the mist, trying to force it to disperse. The mist fought back with magic and protections of its own. It curdled, thickened, compacted against the sides and floor of the valley, flowing a little farther toward the *dyheli*.

The spell changed; power speared through the mist, cutting it, lancelike. A clear spot appeared, a kind of tunnel in the cloud. The mist fought again, but not as successfully this time.

Darkwind *felt* it all, felt the conflicting energies in his nerves and bones. He didn't have to watch the silent battle, he followed it accurately within himself—the spell-wielder forcing the mist away, the mist curling back into the emptying corridor, being forced away, and oozing back in again. He reached out a hand, involuntarily, to wield power that he had forsaken—

Then pulled his hand back, the conflict within him as silent and devastating as the conflict below him.

But before he could resolve his own battle, the balance of power below him shifted. The magic-wielder won; the mist parted, held firmly away from a clear tunnel down the middle of the valley, with only the thinnest of wisps seeping in.

But he could feel the strain, the pressure of the mist on the walls of that tunnel, threatening to collapse it at any moment.

It can't hold for long!

But again, before he could move, the balance shifted. The ground trembled under his feet, and for a moment he thought it was another effect of the battle of mist and magic being fought in front of his very eyes. But no—something dark loomed through the enshrouding mist, something that tossed and made the ground shake.

The *dyheli!*

Now he dared a thought, a Mindspoken call.

It didn't matter that someone or something might overhear; they had been started, or spooked, but without direction, they might hesitate, fatally. *:Brothers—hooved brothers! Come, quickly, before the escape-way closes!:*

There was no answer except the shaking of the ground. But the darkness within the mist began to resolve into tossing heads and churning legs—and a moment later, the *dyheli* bucks pounded into sight, a foam of sweat dripping from their flanks, coughing as the fumes hit their lungs. And behind them—something else.

Something that ran on two legs, not four.

It collapsed, just barely within the reach of the mist. And as it collapsed, so did the tunnel of clear air.

He did not even stop to think; he simply acted.

He took a lungful of clean air and plunged into the edge of the roiling, angry mist. His eyes burned and watered, his skin was afire. He could hardly see through the tears, only enough to reach that prone figure, seize one arm, and help it to its feet.

He half-dragged, half-carried it out, aware of it only as lighter than he, and shorter, and still alive, for it tried feebly to help him. There was no telling if it was human or not; here in the borderland between k'Sheyna and the Pelagirs, that was not something to take for granted. But it had saved the *dyheli,* and that was enough to earn it, in turn, aid.

The mist reached greedily for them; he reached clear air at the edge of it; sucked in a lungful, felt his burden do the same. Both of them shuddered with racking coughs as a wisp of mist reached their throats.

He stumbled into safety at the same moment that the other collapsed completely, nearly carrying Darkwind to the ground with him.

Him?

At that moment, Darkwind realized that this was no male. And as he half-suspected, not human either.

:Run!: Vree screamed from overhead, with mind and voice, and Darkwind glanced behind to see the mist licking forward again, reaching for them, turning darker as if with anger.

From somewhere he found the strength to pick her up, heave her over his shoulder, and stumble away at a clumsy run.

He ran until exhaustion forced him to stop before he dropped the girl, fell on his face, or both. Vree scouted for him, as he slowed to a weary walk, muscles burning, side aching. He figured he must have run, all out, for furlongs at least; he was well out of sensing range of the evil mist, if that still existed and had not been dissipated. That was all that mattered. By the time he came to a halt, in the lee of a fallen tree, he was sweating as heavily as the *dyheli* bucks.

He knelt and eased his burden down into the grass

beside the bark-stripped trunk of the tree, and didn't bother to get up. He sat right down beside her, his legs without any strength at all, propping himself against the tree with his back against the trunk.

For a long time he just sat there, his forehead against his bent knees, wrists crossed over his ankles, every muscle weak from the long run, relying on Vree to alert him if anything dangerous came along. Sweat cooled and dried, his back and scalp itched, but he was too tired to scratch them. He was only aware of his burning muscles, his aching lungs, the pain in his side.

After a while, other things began to penetrate to his consciousness as his legs stopped trembling and the pain in his side and lungs ebbed. Birds called and chattered all around, a good sign, since they would have been silent if there had been anything about to disturb them.

He began to think again, slowly. His mind, dull with fatigue, was nevertheless alert enough to encompass this much; as a nonhuman *and* an Outlander, she was not going to be welcome in k'Sheyna. She was not, as he recalled from the brief glimpse he'd had before he had to pick up and run with her, a member of any of the nonhuman races k'Sheyna had contact with. And unknown meant "suspect" in the danger-ridden lands beyond the borders of the Vale.

Now what am I going to do with her? he wondered, exhaustion warring with the need to make a quick decision. *I'd better take a closer look at her. We aren't inside the Vale yet. If she isn't badly hurt, maybe I can just leave her here, keep an eye on her until she comes around, then make sure she takes herself off, away from the Vale.*

He raised his head and turned his attention to his silent companion—still unconscious, he saw. As he turned her over to examine her, everything about her set off ripples of aversion.

Not only was she nonhuman, she was only-too-obviously one of the so-called "Changechildren" from the Pelagirs, creatures modified from either human or animal bases—at their own whims, frequently, if the base was human; or that of their creators if they were modified from animals. It was what the Tayledras had done with the bondbirds, and what they had done to horses on behalf of the Shin'a'in, taken to an extreme. An extreme that many Tayledras found bordering on the obscene—perhaps because of the kinds of modifications that had been done at the time of the Mage Wars. It was one thing to modify; it was quite another to force extreme changes for no good reason, be the base human or animal.

His experienced eye told him which it was; there was only so much that could be done with an animal base. You couldn't grant equal intelligence with humans to an animal, except over the course of many generations. It had taken the *hertasi* many generations to attain enough intelligence for a rare mage to appear among their ranks, and that event itself had been centuries ago. *Human base, modified to cat. . . .*

Even unconscious, she oozed sexual attraction, which made him both doubly uneasy and pitying. That attraction—it was a common modification, based on smell and the stimulation of deep, instinctual drives in the onlooker. Whether he decided ultimately on pity or revulsion would depend on whether she'd had it done to her, or done it herself. If herself—

Already he felt a deep, smoldering anger at the idea. *I may pitch her back into the damned mist.*

Those who modified themselves for sexual attractiveness were generally doing so with intent to use themselves and their bodies as a weapon. And not an honest one, either.

On the other hand, if she'd had it done *to* her—it was likely with the intent of her master to use her as a kind of sexual pet. That was as revolting to Darkwind as the first, but it was not a revulsion centered on the girl.

For the rest, the overall impression was of a cat, or something catlike. Her hair was a dark, deep sable, and rather short, with a subtle dappled effect in the direct sunlight, like his own dyed hair-camouflage. Her face was triangular, with very little chin; her ears, pointed, with furlike tufts on the ends. Her eyebrows swept upward, her eyes were slanted upward, and when he pulled an eyelid open to see if she really *was* conscious, he was unsurprised to see that her golden-yellow eyes had slit pupils. Which were dilated in shock; her stunned condition was real.

She wore the absolute minimum for modesty; a scanty

tunic of cream-colored leather, and skin-tight breeches
that laced up the side, showing a long line of dark golden-
brown flesh beneath. Not practical garb for woods running.

Even unconscious, she lay with a boneless grace that
echoed the cat theme, and her retractile fingernails were
filed to sharp points, like a cat's claws.

Whatever she had been, she was not even as human
now as the Tayledras. The changes had been made to her
from birth; possibly even before. In fact, in view of the
extensiveness of the changes, it was increasingly unlikely
that she'd done them to herself. *Unless she was born in
one of the contaminated areas, the poison twisted her in
this direction, and she decided to continue the shift.*

She was barefoot, but the tough soles of her feet convinced him that she had spent most of her life without
wearing foot coverings. Again, not practical for woods
running, which argued that she had run away from something or someone.

Then he saw the patterns of old and new bruises over
much of her body, as if someone had been beating her
on a regular basis. Nothing to mar the pert perfection of
her face—but everywhere else, she was marked with the
signs of frequent blows. The darkness of her skin had
hidden it from him at first, but she was covered with the
greenish-yellow of old, healing bruises, and the purple-
black of fresh ones. Some of them, on her arms, were as
big as the palm of his hand. He could only wonder, sickened, about the parts of her hidden under her clothing.
The evidence was mounting in her favor.

She was thin—*too* thin, with bones showing starkly, as
if she never had quite enough to eat.

Darkwind sat back on his heels, no longer certain what
to think. The Changechild was a bundle of contradic-
tions. If she was, as she seemed, the escaped chattel of
an Adept-level mage, how was it she had commanded the
power to free the *dyheli* herd? No mage would have permitted a "pet" to carry the Mage-Gift, much less learn
how to use it.

But if she was an enemy, why did she bear the marks
of beatings and semistarvation? And why had she freed
the herd in the first place?

She represented a puzzle he did not have enough information to solve.

I have to give her the benefit of the doubt, he decided, after pondering the question for a moment. *She did save the* dyheli. *Whatever else she is, or is not, will have to wait. But I can't make a decision until I know what she is.* He thought a moment more. *I have to see that she stays safe until she wakes. I do owe her that much, at the very least—and I owe her the protection of a place to recover afterward.*

At a guess, she hadn't breathed enough of the poison to have put a healthy creature into the unconscious stupor she lingered in. But she had not been healthy, and she had depleted her resources considerably in fighting that evil mist. She was *not* Adept-level; that much was obvious. She was not even a Master; no Master would have exhausted herself in fighting the mist directly. A Master would have transmuted the mist into something else; an Adept would have broken the spell creating it and holding it there. Both would have involved very powerful and difficult spells and would have alerted every mage within two days' ride that there was another mage plying his powers. That was what Darkwind would have done—before he swore that nothing would ever induce him to wield magic energies again. Before it became too dangerous for him to draw the attentions of other Adepts to the depleted and disrupted Clan of k'Sheyna.

She had not—probably could not—either break or change the spell. She could only fight it. That meant she was Journeyman at best, and that the energy to create the tunnel of safety had come directly from her. It was what made Journeymen so hard to track; since the only disturbances in the energy-flows of mage-energies were those within themselves, they couldn't be detected unless one was very nearby. And, thank the fourfold Goddess, that was what had kept her magics from attracting anything else. Probably he had been the only creature close enough to detect her meddling.

But that was also what limited a Journeyman's abilities to affect other magic, and limited his magical "arsenal" as well. When the energy was gone, the mage was exhausted, sometimes to the point of catatonia depending on how far he wanted to push himself, and there was no more until he was rested.

That was what brought the Changechild to this pass; depleting herself, on top of her poor physical condition, then taking one whiff too many of the poison mist. She might be a long time in recovering.

But Darkwind could not, in all conscience, leave her where she was. It wasn't safe, and he could not spare anyone to protect her. And even if it was safe, she might not recover without help; he didn't know enough of Healing to tell.

He rested his chin on his knee and thought.

I need someplace and someone willing to watch her and keep her out of mischief. But I can't take her into the Vale; Father would slit her throat just for looking the way she does. I need a neutral safe-haven, temporarily— and then I need a lot of good advice.

He knew where to find the second; it was coming up with the first that was difficult.

Finally with a tentative plan in mind, he hefted her over his shoulder again—with a stern admonition to his body to *behave* in her proximity, as her sexual attraction redoubled once he was close to her.

His body was not interested in listening.

Finally, in desperation, he shielded—everything. And thought of the least arousing things he could manage— scrubbing the mews, boiling hides, and finally, cleaning his privy. That monthly ordeal of privy-scrubbing was the only thing that ever made him regret his decision to move out of the Vale. . . .

The last worked; and with a sigh of relief, he headed off to the nearest source of aid he could think of.

:Vree!: he called.

The bondbird dove out of the branches of a nearby tree; he felt the gyre's interest at his burden, but it was purely curiosity. The Changechild—thank the stars—was of the wrong species to affect Vree.

If she'd been tervardi, *though—she'd have gotten to both of us. And I don't think Vree's as good at self-control as I am. I would truly have had a situation at that point.*

:Where?: the bondbird replied, with the inflection that meant "Where are we going?"

:The hertasi, *Vree,:* he Mindspoke back. *:The ones on the edge of k'Sheyna. This-one hurt-sleeps.:*

:Good.: Vree's Mind-voice was full of satisfaction; the *hertasi* liked bondbirds and always had tidbits to share with them. He could care less about Darkwind's burden; only that she *was* a burden, and Darkwind was hindered in his movements. *:I guard.:*

Which meant that he would stay within warning distance just ahead of Darkwind, alert at all times, instead of giving in to momentary distractions.

Unlike his bondmate. . . .

Latrines, he thought firmly. *Cleaning out latrines.*

Nera looked up at Darkwind—it was hard for the diminutive *hertasi* to do anything other than "look up" at a human—his expressive eyes full of questions.

:And what if she wakes?: the lizard Mindspoke. He turned his head slightly, and the scales of the subtle diamond pattern on his forehead shifted from metallic brown to a dark gold like old bronze. Nera was the Elder of the *hertasi* enclave and an old friend; Darkwind had brought his burden—and problem—straight to Nera's doorstep. Let the mages discount the *hertasi* if they chose, or ignore them, thinking them no more than children in their understanding and suited only to servants' work. Darkwind knew better.

:I don't think she will,: Darkwind told him honestly. *:At least not until I'm back. I risked a probe, and she is very deeply exhausted. I expect her to sleep for a day or more.:*

Nera considered that, his eyes straying to the paddies below, where his people worked their fields of rice. The *hertasi* settlement itself was in the hillside above a marsh, carefully hollowed out "holes" shored with timbers; with walls, floors and ceilings finished with water-smoothed stone set into cement, and furnished well, if simply. The swamp was their own domain, one in which their size was not a handicap. They grew rice and bred frogs, hunted and fished there. They knew the swamp better than any of the Tayledras.

That had made it easy for Darkwind to persuade the others to include them within the bounds of the k'Sheyna territory. The marsh itself was a formidable defense, and the *hertasi* seldom required any aid. A border section guarded by a treacherous swamp full of clever *hertasi* was something even the most stubborn mage would find a practical resource.

Though they knew how to use their half-size bows and arrows perfectly well, and even the youngest were trained with their wicked little sickle-shaped daggers and fish-spears, the *hertasi* preferred, when given the choice, to let their home do their fighting for them. Enemies, for the most part, would start out chasing a helpless-looking old lizard-man, only to find themselves suddenly chest-deep and sinking in quicksand or mire.

The *hertasi* were fond of referring to these unwelcome intruders as "fertilizer."

Nera was still giving him that inquisitive look. Dark-wind groaned, inwardly. There were some definite draw-backs to a friendship dating back to childhood. Old Nera could read him better than his own father.

Thank the gods for that.

The Changechild's attraction didn't work on Nera, any more than it did on Vree—but Darkwind had the feeling that the *hertasi* knew very well the effect it was having on the scout. And he was undoubtedly giving Darkwind that *look* because he assumed the attraction was affecting his thinking as well as—other things.

Darkwind sighed. :*All right,*: he said, finally. :*If she wakes and gives you trouble, she's fair game for fertilizer. Does that suit you?*:

Nera nodded, and his flexible mouth turned up at the corners in an approximation of a human smile. :*Good. I just wanted to be certain that your mind was still working as well as the rest of you.*:

Darkwind winced. Nera was so small it was easy to forget that the *hertasi* was actually older than his father, and was just as inclined to remind him of his relative youth. And *hertasi*, who only came into season once a year, enjoyed teasing their human friends about their sus-ceptibility to their own passions.

It didn't help that this time Nera's arrow hit awfully near the mark.

:*I'm still chief scout,*: he reminded the lizard. :*Any-thing that comes out of the Pelagirs is suspect—and if it's helpless and attractive, it's that much more suspect.*:

:Excellent.: Nera bobbed his muzzle in a quick nod. *:Then give my best to the Winged Ones. Follow the blue-flag flowers; we changed the safe path since last you were here.:*

With that tacit approval, Darkwind again shifted his burden to the ground, this time laying her on a stuffed grass-mat just inside Nera's doorway. When he turned, the *hertasi* Elder had already rejoined his fellows, and was knee-deep in muddy water, weeding the rice. He might be old, but he had not lost any of his speed. That was how the *hertasi*, normally shy, managed to stay out of sight so much of the time in the Vale; they still retained the darting speed of that long-ago reptilian ancestor.

Darkwind pushed aside the bead curtain that served as a door during the day, shaded his eyes, and looked beyond the paddies for the first of the blue-flag flowers. The *hertasi* periodically changed the safe ways through the swamp, marking them with whatever flowering plants were blooming at the time, or with evergreen plants in the winter. After a moment he spotted what he was looking for, and made his way, dry-shod, along the raised paths separating the rice paddies.

Dry-shod only for the moment. When he reached the end of the cultivated fields, he pulled off his boots, meant mostly for protection against the stones and brambles of the dryland, fastened them to his belt, and substituted a pair of woven rush sandals he kept with Nera.

Rolling up the cuffs of his breeches well above his knees, he waded into the muddy water, trying not to think of what might be lurking under it. The *hertasi* assured him that the plants they rooted along the paths kept away leeches, special fish they released along the safe paths would eat any that weren't repelled by the plants, and that he himself would frighten away any poisonous water snakes, if he splashed loudly enough, but he could never quite bring himself to believe that. It was very hard to read *hertasi* even when someone knew them well, and it was all too like their sense of humor to have told him these things to try and lull him into complacency.

He could have gone around, of course, but this was the shortest way to get to the other side of the swamp, where the marsh drained off down the side of the crater-wall into the Dhorisha Plains. The swamp, barely within k'Sheyna lands, ended at the ruins he sought—and when he had apportioned out the borders, he had made sure that both were within his patrolling area.

One advantage of being in charge; I could assign myself whatever piece I wanted. Dawnfire gets the part facing on the hills that hold her friends, and I get the area that holds mine. Seems fair enough to me.

Normally he didn't have to get there by wading through the swamp. This was *not* the route he chose if he had a choice.

The water was warm, unpleasantly so, for so was the heavy, humid air. A thousand scents came to his nostrils, most of them foul; rotting plants, stale water, the odor of fish. He looked back after a while, but the *hertasi* settlement had completely vanished in waving swamp-plants that stood higher than his head. He thought he felt something slither past his leg, and shuddered, pausing a moment for whatever it was to go by.

Or bite me. Whichever comes first.

But it didn't bite him, and if there had been something there, it didn't touch him again. He waded on, watching for the telltale, pale blue of the tiny, odorless flowers on their long stems, poking up among the reeds. As long as he kept them in sight, he would be on the path the *hertasi* had built of stone and sand amid the mud of the swamp. There were always two plants, one marking each side of the path. The idea was to stop between each pair and look for the next; while the path itself twisted among the reeds and muck, it was a straight line from one pair of plants to the next. And there were false trails laid; it wasn't a good idea to break away from the set path and take what looked like a more direct route, or a drier one; the direct route generally ended in a bog, and the "dry" one *always* ended in a patch of quicksand or a sinkhole.

Once again he was sweating like a panicked *dyheli*, and that attracted other denizens of the swamp. Below the water all might be peaceful, but the *hertasi* could do nothing about the insects above. Darkwind had rubbed himself with pungent weeds to enhance his race's natural resistance to insects, but blackflies still buzzed about his eyes, and several nameless, nearly invisible fliers had already feasted on his arms by the time he reached dry land again.

There was no warning; the ruins simply began, and the marsh ended. Darkwind suspected that the marsh had once been a large lake, possibly artificial, and the ruins marked a small settlement or trading village, or even a guard post, built on its shore. If whatever cataclysm had created the Plains had *not* altered the flow of watercourses hereabouts, he would have been very surprised— and after that, it would have been logical for the lake to silt up and become a swamp. He climbed up on the stones at the edge of the swamp, slapping at persistent insects, vowing silently to take the long way around on his return.

He looked up to make sure of Vree, and found the bondbird soaring overhead, effortlessly, in the cloud-dotted sky.

Not for the first time, he wished for wings of his own.

:And what would you do with them, little one?: asked a humor-filled mind-voice. *:How would you hide and creep, and come unseen upon your enemies, hmm?:*

:The same way you do, you old myth,: he replied. *:From above.:*

:Good answer,: replied Treyvan, and the gryphon dove down out of the sun, to land gracefully on a toppled menhir in a thunderous flurry of backwinging, driving up the dust around him and forcing Darkwind to protect his eyes with his hand until the gryphon had alighted.

"Sssso, what brings you to our humble abode?" Treyvan asked genially, somehow managing to do what the *tervardi* could not, and force human speech from his massive beak.

"I need advice, and maybe help," Darkwind told him, feeling as small as the *hertasi* as he looked up at the perching gryphon. Those hand-claws, for instance, were half again as wide and long as his own strong hands, and their tips were sheathed in talons as sharp and black as obsidian. Treyvan jumped down from the stone, and his claws clenched and released reflexively as the gryphon changed its position before him, absentmindedly digging inch-deep furrows into the packed earth.

"Advissse we will alwayss have forrr you, feather-lesssss sson. Advissse you will take? That iss up to you,"

Treyvan smiled, gold-tinged crest raising a little in mirth. "Help we will alwaysss give if we can, wanted orrr not."

Darkwind smiled, and stepped forward to grasp the leading edge of the great gryphon's folded wing, and leaned in to run a hand through the spicy-scented neck feathers, seemingly unending in their depth. "Thank you. Where is Hydona?"

"Ssssearrrching for nessst-lining, I would guess." Treyvan let a trace of his pride show through, fluffing his chest feathers and raising his tailtip.

"So soon? When . . . when will you make the flight?"

"Sssoon, sssoon. You will be able to telllll. . . ." Treyvan chuckled at Darkwind's blush, then half-closed his eyes, and Darkwind felt the wing-muscles under his hand relax.

It was easy—very easy—to fall under the hypnotic aura of the gryphon, a state of dreamy relaxation brought on by the feel of the soft, silky feathers, the faintly sweet scent, the deep-rumble of Treyvan's faint purr. It was the gryphon himself who broke the spell.

"You have need of usss, Darrrkwind," he reminded the scout. The muscles in the wing retensed, and he stood, wings tucked to his side under panels of feathers. "Let usss go to Hydonaaa."

He turned and paced regally on a path winding deeper into the ruins. Darkwind had to hurry to keep up with his companion's ground-eating strides.

The gryphons had arrived here, in these ruins, literally out of the sky one day, when Darkwind was seven or eight. He'd claimed these ruins—then, well within the safe boundaries of k'Sheyna territory—as his own solitary playground. There *was* magic here, a half-dozen leylines and a node, but the mages had decreed it safe; tame and unlikely to cause any problems. It was a good place to play, and imagine mysteries to be solved, monsters to conquer, magics to learn.

Watching Treyvan's switching tail, he recalled that day vividly.

He had rounded a corner, the Great Mage investigating possibly dangerous territory and about to encounter a Fearsome Monster, when he encountered a *real* one.

He had literally walked into Treyvan, who had been watching his antics with some amusement, he later learned. All *he* knew at the time was that he had turned a corner to find himself face-to-face with—

Legs. Very large legs, ending in very, very large claws. His stunned gaze had traveled upward; up the furry legs, to the transition between fur and feathers, to the feather-covered neck, to the beak.

The very, very, *very* large, sharp, and wickedly hooked beak.

The beak had opened; it seemed as large as a cave.

"Grrr," Treyvan had said.

Darkwind had turned into a small whirlwind of rapidly pumping arms and legs, heading for the safe-haven of the Vale, and certain, with the surety of a terrified eight-year-old, that he was not going to make it.

Somehow he had; somehow he escaped being pounced on and eaten whole. He had burst into the *ekele,* babbling of monsters, hundreds, thousands of them, in the ruins. Since he had never been known to lie, his mother and father had set up the alarm, and a small army of fighters and mages had descended on a very surprised—and slightly contrite—pair of gryphons.

Fortunately for all concerned, gryphons were on the list of "friendly, though we have never seen one" creatures all Tayledras learned of some time in their teens. Treyvan apologized, and explained that he and Hydona were an advance party, intending to discover if these lands were safe to live and breed in. They offered their help in guarding k'Sheyna in return for the use of the ruins as a nesting ground. The Elders had readily agreed; help as large and formidable as the gryphons was never to be disdained. A bargain was struck, and the party returned home.

But all Darkwind knew was that he was huddling in his parent's *ekele,* his knife clutched in his hand, waiting to find out if the monsters were descending on his home.

Until his parents returned: unbattered, unbloody, perfectly calm.

And when he'd demanded to know what had happened, his father had ruffled his hair, chuckled, and said, "I think you have a new friend—and he wants to apologize for frightening you."

Treyvan *had* apologized, and that had begun the happiest period of his life; when everything was magical and wondrous, and he had a pair of gryphons to play with.

He hadn't realized it at the time, but it hadn't entirely been play. Treyvan and Hydona had taught him a great deal of what he knew about scouting and fighting, playing "monster" for him as they later would for their fledglings, teaching him all about dangers he had not yet seen and how to meet them.

Now he knew, though he had not then, that they had chosen the ruins deliberately, for the magic-sources that lay below them. Magic energies were beneficial for gryphon nestlings, giving them an early source of power, for gryphons were mages, too. A different kind of mage than the Tayledras, or other humans; they were instinctive mages, "earth-mages," Hydona said, using the powers about them deftly and subtly for defense and in their mating flights, for without a specific spell, a mating would not be fertile.

That was what Treyvan had meant by "you will know;" when he and Hydona flew to mate for their second clutch, any mage nearby would know very well that a spell with sexual potency was being woven.

The last time they'd risen, he'd been fourteen, and just discovering the wonders of Girls. Fortunately he had been alone, and there had been no Girls within reach. . . .

The offspring of that mating were six or seven years old now, fledged, but not flying yet, and still sub-adult. *Pretty little things*, he thought to himself, with a chuckle, though the term "little" was relative. They were bigger and stronger than he was. At fourteen he'd already acquired Vree, and the appearance of the gryphlets hadn't appalled him the way it might have. Vree had looked *much* scrawnier and—well—awful, right out of the egg. Lytha and Jerven were born alive, and with a reasonable set of fluff-feathers and fur—and Treyvan hadn't let him see them until their second or third day, when their eyes were open and they didn't look quite so unfinished.

The gryphons' nest was very like an *ekele*, but on the ground, presumably to keep the flightless gryphlets from breaking their necks. The pair had created quite an impressive shelter from stone blocks, cleverly woven vegetation, and carefully fitted logs.

As Darkwind neared it, he realized that it was bigger than it had been; it wasn't until he got close enough to measure it by eye that the difference was apparent. From without it looked almost like a tent made of stone and thatch, with a roof quite thick enough to keep out any kind of weather; it looked very much as if the gryphons had dismantled and rebuilt it, keeping the same shape with an increase in size.

He glanced in the door as Treyvan turned, a look of proprietary pride on his expressive face. Obviously he was waiting for a compliment. Inside, there were three chambers now, instead of the two Darkwind remembered; the fledglings', the adults', and a barren one, which would probably be the new nursery. The other two were basically large nests, piled deep with fragrant grasses that the pair had gathered down on the Plain, and changed periodically.

Treyvan's neck curved gracefully, and he faced his human friend eye to golden eye. "Well?" he demanded. "Whaaat do you think?"

"I think it's magnificent," Darkwind replied warmly—which was all he had time for, as the gryphlets heard and recognized his voice, and came tumbling out of their chamber in a ball of squealing fur-and-feathers. Darkwind was their favorite playmate—or play*thing,* sometimes he wasn't entirely certain which. But he'd used Treyvan and his mate the same way as a child, so turnabout only seemed fair.

Mostly . . . they tried to be careful, but they didn't always know their own strength—and they *were* very young. Sometimes they forgot just how long and sharp their claws and beaks were.

They hit him together, Lytha high, Jerven low, and brought him down, both shrieking in the high-pitched whistles that served the gryphons for howls of laughter.

Darkwind tried not to wince, but those whistles were enough to pierce his eardrums. *I'll be glad when their voices deepen. Human children are shrill enough as it is. . . .*

Lytha grabbed the front of his tunic in her beak and "worried" it; Jerven "gnawed" his ankle. He struggled; at least they were big enough now that *he* didn't have to watch what he did; he could fight against them in earnest and not hurt them, provided he didn't indulge in any real, killing blows. They seemed to have improved in their "playing" since the last time; he'd needed a new tunic when Jerven got through with him. Treyvan watched them maul him indulgently for a moment, then waded in, gently separating his offspring from his friend, batting at them so that they rolled into the far corners of the chamber, shrieking happily.

Darkwind *did* wince.

Treyvan whistled something at them; they bounced to their feet and bounded out the door. Darkwind still wasn't fluent in Gryphon, it was a very tonal language, and hard to master; but he thought it was probably the equivalent of "Go play, Darkwind needs to talk to Mother and Father about things that will bore you to sleep."

Treyvan shook his head, then turned, and settled himself into a graceful reclining curve, with his serrated, meat-rending bill even with Darkwind's chin, bare inches away, gazing into the human's face. "Your indulgenssss, old friend. They aaare veeeery young."

"I know," he replied, picking himself up off the floor, and dusting himself off. "I distinctly remember doing the same thing to you."

Treyvan's beak opened in a silent laugh. "Aaaah, but I wassss ssstill *thissss* ssssize, and you were much ssssmaller, yesss? The damagesss were much lessss."

"I think I'll survive them," Darkwind responded. "And I owe you both for more than just being gracious about playing 'monster' for me."

Treyvan shook his head. "Weee do not think of sssssuch," he said immediately. "Thissss issss what friendssss do."

Darkwind remained stubbornly silent for a moment. "Whether or not you think of it, I do," he said. "You two helped me cope with Mother's death; you've been mother and father to me since. It's not something I can forget."

The memory was still painful, but he thought it was healing. It certainly wouldn't have without their help.

"Sssstill," Treyvan objected. "You are uncle to the little onesss. At consssiderable perssonal damage."

He shrugged. "To quote your own words," he replied wryly, " 'that's what friends do.' I think they're well worth indulging. So, you've obviously enlarged the nest— and it's wonderful, the new chamber doesn't look tacked-on, it looks like it was built with the original. What else are you planning to do?"

"We thought, perhapsssss, a chamber for the young-lingssss to play in foul weather—"

They discussed further improvements for a moment until a shadow passed over Darkwind, and he looked up at the sound of his name whistled in Gryphon—

Then once again, he had to protect his eyes, as Hydona, Treyvan's mate, landed in the clearing before the nest, driving up a stronger wind with her wings than Treyvan had.

Darkwind rose to his feet to greet her. She was larger than Treyvan, and her dusty-brown coloration was a muted copy of his golden-brown feathers. There was more gray in her markings, and less black. Her eyes were the same warm, lovely gold as Treyvan's, though, and she was just as pleased to see him as her mate had been.

She nuzzled him and gripped a shoulder gently, purring loud enough to vibrate his very bones. He buried his hands in her neck-feathers and scratched the place at the back of her neck she could never reach herself; the most intimate caress possible to a gryphon, short of mating behavior. She and Treyvan had been extraordinarily open with him, especially after the death of his mother, allowing him glimpses of their personal life that most humans were never allowed to see. They were, all in all, quite private creatures; of all the Tayledras, only Darkwind was considered an intimate friend. They had not even allowed Dawnfire, who was possibly the best of all the k'Sheyna at dealing with nonhumans, to come that close to them.

"Ssssso," Hydona sighed, after a long and luxurious scratch. "Thisss is your patrol time—it musst be busssinesss that bringsss you. And bussinesss isss ssseriousss. How can we help?"

Darkwind looked into her brilliant, deep eyes. "I want to ask advice, and maybe some favors," he said. "I seem to have acquired a problem."

Hydona's ear-tufts perked up. *"Acquired* a problem? Interesssting word choicssse. Ssssay on."

He chose a comfortable rock, as she curled up beside her mate. "Well," he began. "It happened this way. . . ."

Skif

Chapter Nine

ELSPETH

Master Quenten reread the message from his old employer, Captain Kerowyn. *Herald* Captain Kerowyn, he was going to have to remember that. Not that the new title seemed to have changed her much.

"Quenten, I have a job for you, and a sizable retainer enclosed to make you go along with it. Important Personage coming your way; keep said Personage from notice if possible; official and sensitive business. Will have one escort along, but is capable of taking care of self in a fight. Personage needs either a mage-for-hire, a damn good one, or training. Or both. Use your own judgment, pass Personage on to Uncle if you have to. Thank you for your help. Write if you find a real job. Kerowyn."

He smiled at the joke; no, Kerowyn hadn't changed, even since becoming one of the white-clad targets for the Queen of Valdemar—although Quenten also had no doubts that she refused to wear the white uniform without a royal decree. Quenten thanked the courier for the message, and offered him the hospitality of the Post for his recovery-stay. It was graciously accepted, and the young man—one of King Faram's squires—offered to share gossip of the Rethwellan Court with him in return come dinner.

And people wonder how we get our information.

The squire was an affable youngster, fresh from the hill district, with the back-country burr still strong in his speech. He made Quenten quite nostalgic for the old days with the Skybolts; a good half of them came out of the hill district facing Karse, with their tough little ponies and all their worldly goods in a saddle-pack up behind them. What they lacked in possessions, they tended to make up for in marksmanship, tracking, and a tough-minded approach to life; something Kero had called "Attitude."

He had all of that, with a veneer of gentility that told Quenten he was from one of the noble families that hung on there, after fighting their way to the local high seat and holding it by craft, guile, and sheer, stubborn resilience. His eyes went round at Quenten's pair of mage-lights over the table, though he never said a word about them. He knew how to use the eating utensils though, which was more than Kero's hill lasses and lads generally did. He'd gotten that much out of civilization.

But because he was so new to Court, he couldn't tell Quenten what the mage really wanted to know—just who and what this Personage was.

"There's two of 'em, about a day behind me, I'd reckon," the young man said around a mouthful of Quenten's favorite egg-and-cheese pie. "One man, one girl, done up all in white, with white horses. Fast, they are, the horses I mean. I say about a day 'cause I started out a week ahead, but I reckon they've made it up by now, that's how fast them horses are."

Well, "done up all in white" in connection with the note from Kero meant they were Heralds out of Valdemar, but what Heralds could possibly want with a mage was beyond him. He recalled quite vividly his encounter with Valdemar's Border-protections. He didn't think they'd be able to pay *any* mage enough to put up with that.

Still, that wasn't for him to say; maybe there was a way around it. He'd have to wait and see.

But who were these Heralds? They'd have to be important for Kero to exert herself on their behalf—and equally important for King Faram to have sent one of his own squires on ahead with Kero's message to warn him that they were coming.

He put that question to the youngster over dessert, when the squire had sipped just enough of Quenten's potent, sweet wine to be a little indiscreet.

Ehrris-wine does it every time.

The young man rolled his wide blue eyes. "Well as to that," he replied, "No one's said for sure. But the young lady, I think she must be related. I overheard her call His Majesty 'Uncle,' when the King gave me the packet and instructions just before I left. I reckon she's Daren's get, though I'd never heard of her before."

Daren's child? Quenten snorted to himself with amusement. *And a Herald of Valdemar? Not unless the twins are aging a year for every month since they've been born. But Selenay's oldest child, now that's a possibility, though I wouldn't have thought they'd let her out of the city, much less the Kingdom. Interesting. Something must be going on in that war with Hardorn that I don't know about. I'd thought it was back to staring at each other across the Border.*

He sat back in his chair while the young man rattled on, and sipped his own wine. Suddenly the stakes were not just Kero asking a favor; not with a princess riding through Rethwellan incognito, looking for mages to hire. This had all the flavor of an intrigue with the backing of the Valdemaran Crown, and it promised both danger and the possibility of rapid and high advancement. Quenten had a good many pupils that would find those prospects attractive enough to chance the protections keeping mages out. *Maybe they even found a way to cancel them. That might be why they're finally coming down here now.*

In fact—now that Quenten was Master-Class, and could be a low-level Adept if he ever bothered to take the test—it was possible that it was attractive enough to interest *him.* It might be worth trying to find a way around those "watchers," whatever they were, if they hadn't been countered already.

Court Mage of Valdemar. . . . For a moment visions of fame and fortune danced in his head. Then he recalled *why* he wasn't a Court Mage now—the competition, the rivalry, and above all, the restrictions on what he could and could not do or say. He'd been offered the position and more than once. So had Jendar, as far as that went. Both of them had preferred to help friends to the post— friends who would tell them what was going on—and keep up casual ties with the rulers of the time. Sometimes a King preferred to go outside his Court for advice . . . to a mage, say, with no other (obvious) axes to grind.

He laughed at himself, then, and bent his attention to the amusing stories the young squire brought from Court. And remembered what he had once told Kero.

If I have to choose between freedom to do what's right, and a comfortable High Court position, I'll take the freedom.

She had shrugged, but her smile told him that she tacitly agreed with him. Which was probably why she was making a target of herself in Valdemar right now.

We're both fools, he thought, and chuckled. The squire, who thought the mage was chuckling at one of his jokes, glowed appreciatively.

Quenten used the same office and suite of rooms that the Captain had, back when Bolthaven was the Skybolts' winter quarters, and not a mage-school. Placed high up in a multistory tower that overlooked most of the town as well as the former fortress, he had a clear view of the main gate and the road leading to it, the exercise yard, and most of the buildings. Kero might not recognize the place at first sight anymore; the exercise yard had been planted and sodded, and turned into a garden, he'd had trees and bushes brought in and scattered about to provide shade, and most of the buildings had been refaced with brick. The barracks were a dormitory now, and looked it, with clothing drying on the sills, food or drink placed there to cool, kites flying from the rooftop, and youngsters sitting or hanging out of most of the windows. The main stable was a workshop, where anything that was likely to blow the place up could be practiced in relative safety. Only the smaller visitors' stable remained to house the few horses Bolthaven needed. While he kept the stockade, as a means of defining boundaries beyond which the students were not permitted without permission, the place didn't look like a fortress anymore, it looked like what it was; a school. And not just any school; the largest White Winds school in Rethwellan.

The only one that was larger was the school Kethry had attended, in Jkatha. Her son Jendar, Quenten's teacher, had founded a school near Petras, the capital of Rethwellan, in a little town called Great Harsey, but it had never been this large.

Then again, mage-schools can be dangerous for the innocent townsfolk. Sometimes things get a little out of hand. Townsfolk can get downright touchy over the occasional earth-elemental in the scullery. Can't imagine why. . . .

That hadn't been a problem for Quenten. The town of Bolthaven had been built around the garrison, the folk here depended on it for their custom. They'd been relieved to learn that there would still *be* custom here, and most of them had been able to turn their trades to suit young mages instead of young mercs. And, all told, an earth-elemental in the scullery did less damage—and was less of a hazard to the problematical virtue of the help—than any drunken merc bent on celebration.

The worst that ever came up from Bolthaven now was an urgent call for one of the teachers, followed by a polite bill for damages.

Quenten's desk was right beside the window; a necessity, since he spent very little time in doing paperwork—that's what he had clerks for—and a great deal of time in overseeing the pupils and classes. Some of that "overseeing" was conducted from his desk—an advantage mages had over mercenary captains. He could "look in" on virtually anything he chose, at any time, simply by exercising a little of the power that came with the rank of Master mage.

Just now he was keeping an eye on the road, in between considering the proposed theses of four would-be Journeymen. The messenger had departed early this morning; since then, he'd been waiting for the Personage. Not with impatience—a mage soon learned the futility of impatience—but with growing curiosity.

He wasn't certain what to expect, really. On rereading the note, he saw that Kero had said that he should give this girl training, something he hadn't taken a great deal of notice of the first time around. Now that was interesting—Kero herself was not a mage, but she had somehow managed to spot potential mages in the past and send them to either him or her uncle. Had she seen something in this girl?

Or was it simply something the girl herself wanted? Had she absorbed tales of what Kero's mages had done until she had convinced herself that she, too, could become a mage?

Well, that was possible, but not without the Talent for it. Unless you could See *and* manipulate the energies mages used, she could fret herself blue without getting anywhere.

Even those who followed the blood-paths had at least a little of the Talent. There were varying degrees in what mages could do, too. Not only did the strength of the Talent vary—thus dictating how much energy a mage could handle—but the kind of Talent varied—thus dictating the kind of energy he could handle. Some never became more than earth-mages and hedge-wizards, using their own life-energies to sense what was going on in the world around them, augmenting the natural attributes of plants and animals to serve them, and Healing. Not that there was anything wrong with that; Quenten himself had seen some very impressive merc work done by hedge-wizards with a firm grasp of their abilities and a determination to make the most of them. The tiniest change at the right moment can down a king . . . or an army.

But he rather doubted that being told she would never be anything other than a hedge-wizard would satisfy a headstrong princess. Nor would being told she could not be any kind of a mage at all.

He was prepared for just about anything, or so he told himself; from a spoiled brat who thought a white uniform and a coronet entitled her to anything she wanted, to a naive child with no Mage-Talent whatsoever, but many dreams, to someone very like some of his older pupils—

That would be the best scenario in many ways, to have her turn out to *be* teachable; with Mage-Talent present, but unused, so that he *could* give her what she wanted, but would not have to force her to unlearn bad habits. Theoretically, the discipline required by the Heralds' mind-magic would carry over, and give her a head start over Talented youngsters who had yet to learn the value of discipline.

A flash of white on the road just below the gate alerted

him, and he paused for a moment to key in his Mage-Sight. That, in particular, had improved out of all recognition since joining the Skybolts and his elevation to Master-class. If this child had any ability at all, he would be able to See it, even from the tower. *Then* he would know what to tell her if she asked for training. And he'd have some time to think about just how he was going to phrase it, be it good news, or bad.

Two dazzlingly white-clad riders on pure white horses entered the main gate and paused for a moment in the yard beyond before dismounting.

And that was when Quenten got one of the greatest shocks of his life.

Whatever he had been expecting—it wasn't what he Saw.

The ordinary young woman with the graceful white horse was—not ordinary at all. She *was* the bearer of an untrained, but major Mage-Gift; one so powerful it sheathed her in a closely-wrapped, sparkling aura in his Mage-Sight, that briefly touched everyone around her with exploratory fingers she was apparently unaware of. Quenten was astonished, and surprised she hadn't caused problems with it before this. *Surely* she must have Seen power-flows, energy-levels, even the nodes that he could See, but could not use. Surely she had wondered what they were, and how could she not have been tempted to try and manipulate them? Then he recalled something; these Heralds, one and all, had mind-magic and were trained in it. If they didn't know what Mage-Talent was—it could, possibly, be mistaken for something like Sight. And if she was told that this was just another way of viewing things, that she could not actually affect them, she might not have caused any trouble.

They have no idea how close they came. If she had ever been tempted to touch something. . . .

That was not the end of the surprises. She was carrying at her side something that radiated such power that it almost eclipsed her—and only long familiarity with Kero's sword enabled him to recognize it as Need. The sword had changed; had awakened somehow, and it was totally transformed from the relatively simple blade he had dealt with. Now there was no doubt whatsoever that it was a major magical artifact—and it radiated controlled power that rivaled the Adepts he knew.

It's a good thing I never tried mucking around with it when it was like this. It probably would have swatted me like a fly.

He wondered how he could have missed it when they were riding in; it must have been like a beacon. And how the mages at Faram's Court could have missed it—

He had his answer, as it simply—stopped what it was doing. It went back to being the simple sword he had known; magical, yes, if you looked at it closely enough, but you had to look very closely and know what you were looking for.

Did it put on that show for my benefit? he wondered. Somehow that idea was a little chilling. No one he knew could detect Mage-Sight in action; it was a passive spell, not an active one.

No one *he* knew. That didn't mean it couldn't be done. That notion was even more awe-inspiring than the display of power had been. Need was old; perhaps the ancient ways of magic it was made with harbored spells he couldn't even dream of.

The creature she was riding—not a horse at all, even if it chose to appear as one—rivaled both the young woman and the sword, but in a way few would have recognized. The aura enveloping it was congruent with the creature's skin, as if controlled power was actually shining *through* the skin. Which was very much the case. . . . Although few mages would have known it for what it was, Quenten recognized it as a Guardian Spirit of the highest order. And from the colors of its aura, it was superior even to the Ethereal Spirits he had once, very briefly, had conversation with when some of the Shin'a'in relatives came to Bolthaven for the annual horse-fair— the ones Kero's other uncle called "spirit-Kal'enedral," that served the Shin'a'in Goddess. The "veiled ones," shaman Kra'heera had called them; the unspoken implication being that only the spirit-Kal'enedral went veiled. They were to this "horse" what an eating knife is to a perfectly balanced rapier.

One blow after another, all within a heartbeat. He practically swallowed his tongue with shock and dropped his arms numbly to his sides.

For a moment, he felt like an apprentice again, faced with *his* Master, and the vision of what that Master had become after years and years of work in developing his Talent to its highest pinnacle placed before him. All that power—all that potential—and he hadn't the slightest idea what to do with it.

His mind completely froze for a moment as he stared at her. *I can't take her on!* his thoughts babbled in panic. *One slip—and she wouldn't just blow up the workshop, she could—she could—and that Guardian—and the sword—and—and—*

Only years of self-discipline, combined with more years of learning to think on his feet with the Skybolts, enabled him to get his mind working again so that he could stop reacting and start acting like a mage and a competent Master, instead of a dumbfounded apprentice.

And the first thing he did was to turn away from the window. With *her* out of his sight and Sight, he was able to take a deep breath, run his hand through his sweat-damp hair, and *think.* Quickly. He had to come up with an answer and a solution.

One thing was certain; it wasn't a question of whether she could be trained or not; she *had* to be trained. One day, she might be tempted to try to manipulate some of the energies she could sense all around her, and then—

No telling what would happen. Depends on what she touched, and how hard she pulled.

It could be even worse if she were in a desperate situation and she simply reacted instinctively, trying to save herself or others. With the thrust of fear driving her—

Gods. And the very first thing we are taught is never, ever, act in fear or anger.

She would be easy prey for anyone who saw her, and wanted to use her. There were blood-path Masters and even Adepts out there who wouldn't hesitate to lure her into their territory with promises of training, and then exploit her ruthlessly, willing or not. Anyone could be broken, and no mage had gotten to the Master level without learning the patience it took to break someone and subvert them, even if it took a year or more.

No, she had to be trained. Now the question was, by whom?

Kero said if I couldn't handle her to send her on to

old Jendar, her uncle. He's an Adept; hellfires, he taught me, he ought to be able to handle anyone. He can deal with her. I don't have to.

That burden off his hands, he sighed and relaxed. Gradually the sweat of panic dried, his heart went back to its sedate pace, his muscles unknotted. The problem was solved, but he wasn't going to have to be the one to solve it. He was glad now that he'd delegated one of the teachers—a very discreet young lady, who was, bless the gods, an Herbalist-Healer earth-witch with *no* Mage-Sight worth speaking of—to greet them when they arrived, just in case he suddenly found himself with his hands full.

God only knows what I'd have been like if I'd met them at the gate. Babbling, probably. Hardly one to inspire confidence. By the time word reached him that they had arrived, he was back to being the calm, unruffled image of a school-Master, completely in control of everything around him.

"Yes?" he said; the child poked his head inside, cautiously. All the apprentices were cautious when the Master was in his office. Quenten had been known to have odd things loose in the room on occasion, just to keep people from interrupting him. The legend of the constable's scorched backside was told in the dormitory even yet, and that had happened the first year the school had been founded.

"Sir, the people you expected are here. The lady's name's Elspeth, the gen'man is Skif, Elrodie says. If you're able, sir, you should come down, Elrodie says." The child looked the way he must have a few moments ago; it wasn't often an apprentice got to see the inside of the Master's office. Usually he met the youngsters on their own ground, and when he wasn't actually in the office, he kept it mage-locked, for his office also served as his secondary workroom. There were things in here no apprentice should ever get his hands on.

"I'll be right there," he said. The child vanished. He waited a few moments more to be certain his stomach had settled, then turned, and started down the stairs.

By the time he reached the ground, he felt close to normal, and was able to absorb the shock of his visitors' appearance without turning a hair. Outwardly, anyway.

The sword was "quiet"—but the girl and her so-called horse weren't.

So long as they don't do anything. . . .

He turned first to greet the young lady, as her companion held back a little, diffidently, confirming his guess that she was much higher-ranked than he was. And given her strong family resemblance to King Faram, she was undoubtedly the "Elspeth" that was Heir to the Valdemar throne. She took after the dark side of the family, rather than the blond, but the resemblance was there beyond a doubt.

To all outward appearances, she was no different than any other young, well-born woman of his acquaintance. Wavy brown hair was confined in a braid that trailed down her back, though bits of it escaped to form little tendrils at her ears. Her square face was not beautiful or even conventionally pretty and doll-like—it *was* a face that was so full of character and personality that beauty would have been superfluous and mere "prettiness" eclipsed. Like Kero, she was handsome and vividly alive. Her brown eyes sparkled when she talked; her generous mouth smiled often. If he hadn't had Mage-Sight, he would have guessed that she had Mage-Talent in abundance; she had that kind of energy about her.

She'd studied her Rethwellan; that was evident from her lack of accent. "I am very glad to meet you at last," she said, when she'd been introduced. "I'm Kero's problem child, Master Quenten. She's told me a lot about *you*, and since she's a pretty rotten correspondent, I guess you're rather in the dark about me." Her smile widened. "I know what her letters are like. The last time she was with the Skybolts, there was a flood that got half the town, and all she wrote was, 'It's a little wet here, be back when I can.' "

He chuckled. "Well, she neglected to supply me with your name and she kept calling you a Personage. I expect that was for reasons of security? You *are* the Elspeth I think you are—the one with a mother named Selenay?"

Elspeth nodded, and made a face. "I'm afraid so. That was part of what I meant by being a problem child. Sorry; can't help who my parents are. Born into it. Oh, this is Skif; he's also assigned to this job."

"By which she's tactfully saying that my chief duty is

to play bodyguard,'' Skif said, holding out his hand.
Quenten released his Mage-Sight just a little, and
breathed a silent sigh of relief. This young man was perfectly ordinary. No Magical Artifacts, no Adept-
Potential.

Except that he was also riding a Guardian Spirit. Not
as exalted a Spirit as the girl's, but—

The mare turned, looked him straight in the eye, and
gave him a broad and unmistakable wink.

He stifled a gasp, felt the blood drain from his face,
then plastered a pleasant smile on his lips, and managed
not to stammer. ''Since there is only one Elspeth with a
mother by *that* name that I know of—that Kero would
have been so secretive about—I can understand why you
are in that role,'' he said. ''It's necessary.''

''I know it is,'' they both said, and laughed. Quenten
noted that they both had hearty, unforced laughs, the
laughter of people who did not fear a joke.

Elspeth made a face, and Skif shrugged. ''We know
it's necessary,'' Skif replied for both of them. ''But that
doesn't mean Elspeth much likes it.''

Quenten had not missed the sword calluses on her
hands, and the easy way she wore her blade. She had the
muscles of a practiced fighter, too, though she didn't have
the toughened, hard-eyed look the female mercs had after
their first year in the ranks.

He coughed politely. ''Kero did, at least, tell me what
brings you here, and I have to be honest with you. I wish
I could help you, but I can't. None of my teachers are
interested in anything *but* teaching, and none of the
youngsters ready to go out as Journeymen are up to trying
to cross your borders and dealing with the magical guards
of that border. I assume you know about that; I couldn't
pass it when Kero first took the Skybolts north, and I
don't know that I could now that I'm a more practiced
Master with years in the rank.''

Elspeth's face fell; Skif simply looked resigned.

''What about you teaching us?'' she asked—almost
wistfully. ''I mean, I don't suppose either of us are teachable, are we?''

Do I tell her right now? He thought about that quickly;
well, it couldn't do any harm to tell her a little about her
abilities right off. It might make her a little more cau-

tious. "I'm afraid Skif isn't—but, young lady—you are potentially a *very* good mage. Your potential is so high, in fact, that I simply don't feel up to teaching you myself. And you have to be taught, there is absolutely no doubt about that."

Her face was a study in contradictory emotions; surprise warred with disappointment, elation with—was it fear? He hoped so; she would do well to fear that kind of power.

"I don't have the time," he said truthfully. "You're coming to the teaching late in your life, and as strong as you could be—well, it will require very personal teaching. One to one, in fact, with someone who will be able to deal with your mistakes. And I can't do it; it would take time away from the students I've already promised to teach. That wouldn't be fair to them. And I gather that you're under some time considerations?"

Both of them nodded, and Elspeth's "horse" snorted, as if in agreement.

Dearest gods, it's looking at me the way old Jendar used to when I wasn't up to doing a particular task and said so. Like it's telling me, "at least you know when not to be stupid."

"It wouldn't be fair to you to give you less attention than you need, especially given that."

Her shoulders sagged, and her expression turned bleak. "So I've come on a fool's errand, then?"

"Not at all," he hastened to assure her. "What I *can* and will do is send you on to my old master, Kero's uncle, Adept Jendar. He's no longer teaching in his school—he will, on occasion take on a very talented pupil like yourself. But without my directions, introduction, and safe-conduct, you'd never find him. He's very reclusive."

"I don't suppose we could get him to come back with us, could we?" Skif asked hopefully. "That would solve all our problems."

Quenten shrugged. "I don't know; he's very old, but on the other hand, magic tends to preserve mages. I haven't seen him in years and he may still be just as active as he always was. He's certainly my superior in ability and knowledge, he's just as canny and hard to predict as Kero, and I won't even attempt to second-guess him. The best I can offer is, ask him yourself.''

Skif looked a great deal more cheerful. "Thanks, Master Quenten, we will.''

Quenten felt as if a tremendous burden had just been lifted from his shoulders. *There's nothing quite like being able to* legitimately *pass the responsibility,* he thought wryly. And, feeling a good deal more cheerful himself, he told both of them, ''Even if I can't offer you the dubious benefits of my teaching, I can still offer the hospitality of the school. You *will* stay for at least the night, won't you? I'd love to hear what Kero's been up to lately. You're right, by the way," he concluded, turning with a smile for Elspeth, ''She's a terrible correspondent. Her letter about you was less than half a page; the letter I'm going to give you for Jendar is going to be at least five pages long, and I don't even know you that well!"

The young woman chuckled, and gave him a wink that was the mirror image of the one Skif's spirit-horse had given him. He racked his brain for the right name for them—Comrades? No, Companions, that was it.

''I can even offer something in the way of suitable housing for your—ah—friends," he said, bowing a little in their direction. ''Your 'Companions,' I believe you call them. I don't know what kind of treatment they're accustomed to at home, but I can at least arrange something civilized.''

Elspeth looked surprised at that; but the Companions themselves looked gratified. Like queens in exile, who had discovered that someone, at last, was going to give them their proper due.

''We have two loose-boxes, with their own little paddock, and you can fix the latch-string on the inside, so that they can open and shut it themselves," he said, hastily, trying to look as if he had visits from Guardian Spirits all the time. ''Kero always had Shin'a'in warsteeds, you know, and they needed that kind of treatment; they aren't Companions, of course, but they're a great deal more intelligent than horses.''

''That's lovely,'' Elspeth said as he fell silent, her gratitude quite genuine. ''That really is. I can't tell you how hard it is even in Valdemar to find someone who doesn't think they're just horses.''

"Oh, no, my lady," he replied fervently, convinced by the lurking humor in both sets of blue eyes that the Companions found him and his reactions to them very amusing. "Oh, no—I promise you—I know only too well that they aren't horses."

:And you don't know the half of it, friend,: whispered a voice in his mind.

For a moment he wasn't certain he'd actually heard that—then the light of amusement in the nearest one's eyes convinced him that he had.

I think I should ignore that. If they wanted me to treat them like heavenly visitors, they wouldn't look like horses, would they? Or would they? Do the Heralds know what they are? If they don't—no, I don't think I'd better tell them. If the Companions want them to know, they'll know. If not—no, it would not be a good idea to go against the wishes of a Guardian Spirit, in fact, it would be a very stupid idea—

He realized that he was babbling to *himself* now, and decided to delegate the tour of the stables and school to someone else. He was going to need a chance to relax before he dealt with these two again.

Dinner, held without being under those disturbing blue eyes, was far easier. They exclaimed over his mage-lights, and over the tame little fire-elemental that kept the ham and bread warm, and melted their cheese for them if they chose. They marveled at a few of his other little luxuries, like the stoves instead of fireplaces, which kept his quarters much warmer in winter, even without the aid of more fire-elementals. He exchanged stories with them of what he knew of Kero, and Faram and Daren, from the old days with the Skybolts, and what Kero was up to now, at least, as a Herald. He actually got quite a bit of useful Court gossip from her; she knew what to look and listen for.

But he got even more from Skif, who evidently didn't miss anything. *That* young man bore watching; he reminded Quenten of another one of the Shin'a'in, one he knew was trained as an assassin, who'd been one of the Skybolts' specialist instructors for a while—an instructor in techniques he *knew*, without being told, that he didn't want to know anything about.

There was a great deal more to Skif than met the eye. Quenten had the feeling that he was not only very resourceful, he could probably be quite dangerous. He also had the feeling that Skif's presence had a great deal to do with the reason why Elspeth hadn't been bothered by mages eager to use her before this.

Elspeth was, he discovered, an extremely well-spoken young lady, but in many ways she was still a girl.

She knew how she was treated inside Valdemar, and how her rank worked within that Kingdom, but had very little notion of how knowledge of her rank would affect people, for good or ill, outside it—or how they could and would exploit her given the chance.

"You see," Skif said, after he'd explained some of the ways in which she would have to be careful around local nobility. "I told you it was complicated down here."

She made a face, and the mage-light picked up golden glints in her eyes as she turned toward her partner. "You told me a lot of things, and some of them *I* was right about."

Quenten intervened. "It's not her fault, Skif; she's always dealt with very highly-ranked nobles. It's the local lordlings you have to be really careful with around here. I'd say that half of them were never born to their titles— or at least, weren't the first sons. They didn't get where they are now by being nice, and most of them want to climb a lot higher before they die. You can't even count on blood relations to be honest with you. Well, take Kero's brother, for instance. *He's* all right, but the Lady Dierna is pretty much an information-siphon for her relatives. And there are a couple of *them* that none of us trust, not even the King. Go to Lordan and within half a day every one of Dierna's relatives will know that something brought Heralds down out of Valdemar. Let Lordan know who and what you are, and I personally wouldn't vouch for your safety once you got off his lands. Ransom is too tempting a prospect."

"Huh," was Skif's only comment. He reached for another piece of smoked ham, thoughtfully. There were odd markings on his hands; old scars that looked like they might have been left by knife fights.

Interesting, Quenten thought. *A strange sort of partner for a princess.* For Skif *was* a partner and not "just a bodyguard;'' the body-language of both of them said that. *More than a partner, a lover, maybe?* That seemed likely at first—

Then again, maybe not. They were both Heralds, and the little he'd managed to pry out of Kero on the subject indicated that Heralds had an even closer brotherhood than the tightest merc company. Emotionally, sexually, whether the two were lovers didn't bear any thought after that; they were Heralds, and that was a good enough answer for Quenten.

"Even if you were left alone, they'd find a way to use your presence," he continued. "Believe me, the more you act like common folk, the better off you are." He waited for understanding to dawn, then said, patiently but forcefully, *"Get out of the white outfits."*

Skif snickered; Elspeth simply looked bewildered.

"Look, *common people* don't ride around in immaculate white outfits. The horses are bad enough, add the uniforms, and you might as well hire barkers to announce you in every little village. I'll get you some clothes before you leave; save the white stuff for when you need to impress someone. Your simple presence as someone's guest could lend weight to some quarrel they have that you know nothing about."

And I wish there was a way to dye the Companions, too, but I'm afraid the amount of magic energy they have simply by being on this plane is going to bleach them again before they get half a day down the road. That's assuming dye would take, which I wouldn't bet on.

Elspeth sighed, and finally nodded a reluctant agreement. "Damn. Being able to pull rank on someone who was being stupid would have been awfully useful. All right. You know more about the way things are around here than we do."

"That's why he's got Bolthaven as a freehold of the King," Skif put in unexpectedly. "As long as it's a freehold, none of the locals can try and bully each other by claiming he's with them." He turned to Quenten, gesturing with a piece of cheese. "Am I right?"

"Exactly," he replied, pleased with Skif's understanding. "Not that anyone who knew anything about magic would ever suspect a White Winds school of being on anyone's side. We don't do things that way."

Skif grinned crookedly. "I kind of got the impression from Kero that you folks were the closest thing there was to Heralds down here."

"Oh," he replied lightly, trying to keep away from that subject. The brotherhood of the White Winds mages wasn't something he wanted to confide to an outsider. There were things about White Winds people that weren't shared by any other mage-school, and they wanted to keep it that way. "We aren't that close."

:*I'll second that*,: whispered that voice in his mind. He started involuntarily.

"So what exactly are these 'mage-schools,' anyway?" Skif persisted, showing no notice of his momentary startlement. "I mean, some of you are real schools, and some of you seem to be philosophies, if you catch my meaning."

"We're—both," he replied, wondering who, or what, had spoken. Surely not the Companions? Surely he would have detected them "listening in" on the conversation. Wouldn't he?

"Each method of teaching *is* a philosophy," he continued, mind alert for other intrusions. "We differ in how we use our magic and how we are willing to obtain power."

How much should he tell them, and how much should he leave in Jendar's hands?

Better stick to the basics. "White Winds takes nothing without permission, and we try to do the least amount of harm we can. We also think that since Mage-Talent is an accident of birth, we have the obligation to use it for the sake of those who were never born with it." Then he grinned. "But there's no reason why a mage can't make a living at the same time, so long as he doesn't knowingly use his powers to abet repression or aid others who abuse their powers. But that's why you don't find many White Winds mages working with mercenary companies. When you're a merc, you can't guarantee that you're going to be working for the right side."

"At least we don't have to worry about that," Elspeth said. Skif simply raised an eyebrow—and Quenten had the distinct feeling that Skif was debating how much to tell *him*.

"I assume you've heard of blood-path mages?" he

asked, and was surprised when Skif shook his head. "Oh. Hellfire, I guess *I* had better tell you, then. They're mages who take their power from others." He waited expectantly, for them to make the connection, then added, a little impatiently, "By *killing* them. Usually painfully. And by breaking and using them, if they have the time to spare."

Elspeth's eyes widened. "That's what Ancar is doing—or at least, that's what some of the people who've escaped from Hardorn say he and his mages are doing. I didn't know there was a name for them."

Skif scowled. "So, which school teaches people to do *that?*" he asked, growling a little.

Quenten shrugged. "There are schools, but the moment anyone finds out about them, they're destroyed. If the mages haven't scattered first, which is what usually happens. No sane ruler wants that on his soil. But to tell you the truth, that kind of magic usually isn't taught in a school, it's usually one-to-one. A blood-path mage who decides to take an apprentice just goes looking for one. They try to find people who have potential but are untrained."

"And can't tell one mage from another?" Skif asked, with a hard look at him. Quenten nodded; Skif had already seen what he was driving at.

"Sometimes; sometimes they look for someone who is impatient, who is power-hungry and ruthless. That's the kind that usually rebels eventually; has a confrontation with his master, and either dies, wins, or has a draw that both walk away from. And that is how they reproduce themselves, basically." Quenten did *not* mention what happened in the first example; he decided, all things considered, it was better to wait until Elspeth was gone.

"Now, there's one thing I have to warn you about, and it's back to the same old story of 'you aren't in Valdemar anymore.' For every rule there's an exception—and this is the one to blood-magic. There are perfectly *good* people that practice a couple of forms of magic that require a blood-sacrifice. The Shin'a'in shamans, for one. Sometimes they spill their *own* blood, just a little, because any spillage of blood releases a lot of power. And in times of a very dire problem, a shaman or Swordsworn may actually volunteer as a sacrifice, as a kind of messenger to their Goddess that things are very bad, they need help, and they are willing to give up a lot to get it."

Elspeth's eyes got very wide at that. "You're joking—"

Quenten shook his head. "I am not joking. It's very serious for them. It hasn't happened in the last three or four generations—and the last time it did, the Plains were in the middle of a drought that had dried even the springs. People and herds were dying. One of the shamans threw himself off the top of the cliffs that ring the Plains. Right down onto an altar he'd set up down there."

"And?" Skif asked.

"And the drought ended. They say that he roams the skies of the Plains as a spirit-bird now. Some even say he transformed as he fell, that he never actually hit the ground." It was Quenten's turn to shrug. "I'm not their Goddess, it's not my place to make decisions. What's better; answer every little yelp for help, or make people prove they need it?"

"I don't know," Skif admitted. Elspeth just bit her lip and looked distressed. "But I can see what you mean; we really aren't home, are we?"

"There's a lot of gray out here, and precious little black and white," Quenten replied with a hint of a smile. "The Shin'a'in aren't the only odd ones, either. There're the Hawkbrothers, what the Shin'a'in call *Tale'edras*. Nobody except the Shin'a'in shamans knows anything about them, mostly because they tend to kill anybody that ventures into their territories."

Skif scrutinized him closely for a moment. "If you're waiting for a gasp of horror, Master Quenten, you aren't going to get one. There's a reason you told us this, and it has to do with the situation not being black and white. So? Why do they kill people who walk across their little boundary lines?"

Quenten chuckled. "Caught me, didn't you? All right, there's a reason that I think is a perfectly good one—and to be honest, they will *try* and turn you back; it's only if you persist that they'll kill you. The Shin'a'in say that they are the guardians of very destructive magics, that they 'purify' a place of these magics, then move on. And that they kill persistent intruders so that those intruders can't get their hands on that magic. Seems like a good reason to me.''

Skif nodded. ''Any evidence to support this?''

Quenten raised an eyebrow. ''Well, their territories *are* all in the Pelagirs, and there are more weird, twisted, and just plain evil things in there than you could ever imagine. And they *do* periodically vanish from a place and never come back, and once they're gone, anybody that moves in never has trouble from the oddling things again. So? Your guess is just as valid as mine. I'd believe the Shin'a'in, personally.''

Skif's eyes were thoughtful, but he didn't say anything. Elspeth stifled a yawn at that moment, and looked apologetic.

''It isn't the stories, or the company, Master Quenten,'' she said ruefully. ''It's the long ride and the wonderful meal. We started before dawn, and we got here just before sunset. That's a long day in the saddle; Skif's used to it, but I'm a lot softer, I'm afraid.''

''Well, I can't blame you for that,'' Quenten chuckled. ''The truth is, I'm not up to a day in the saddle myself, anymore. Why don't you find that bed I showed you? I was thinking of calling it a night, myself.''

''Thanks,'' she said, and finished the last of the wine in her glass, then pushed herself away from the table. She gave Skif an opaque look but didn't say anything.

''Good night, then,'' Quenten supplied. ''I'll see you off in the morning, unless you want to stay longer.''

''No, we're going to have to cover a lot of ground and we're short on time,'' she replied absently, then smiled. ''But thank you for the offer. Good night.''

Skif looked after her for a moment after the door had closed, then turned to Quenten. ''There's something else you didn't want her to hear,'' he said, ''About those blood-path mages. What is it?''

A little startled by Skif's directness, Quenten came straight to the point. ''It's about the ones who are looking for an 'apprentice'—or at least they call it that—who is untrained but powerful. The ones looking for someone who is totally naive about magic. Like your young friend there.''

Skif nodded, his eyes hardening. ''Go on.''

''What they're looking for is the exact opposite of

someone like themselves. They have two ways of operating, and both involve subversion." He paused to gather his thoughts. "The first is to corrupt the innocent."

"Not possible," Skif interjected. "Trust me on that one. If you've ever heard that Heralds are incorruptible, believe it."

Well, anyone who rides around on a Guardian Spirit probably is, no matter what people say about everyone having a price. I suppose Heralds do, too, but it's not the kind of price a blood-path mage could meet. "Well, the other is destruction. Luring the innocent into a place of power, then breaking him. Or her." Quenten gave Skif a sharp look. "And don't tell me that you can't be broken. *Anyone* can be broken. And a blood-path mage has all the knowledge, patience, and means to do so. Their places of power are usually so well guarded that it would take a small army to get in, usually at a terrible cost, and by the time they do, it's usually too late. That's if you can *find* the place because besides being protected, it will also be well-hidden."

Skif had the grace to blanch a little. "Nice little kingdom you have here."

"Oh, there aren't ever a lot of that kind, but they do exist," Quenten replied. "And that's why I'm warning you. *You* don't have the ability to see the kind of potential she carries—but I do, and so will anyone else of my rank who happens to see her. That's Master and above. And there are not only blood-path Masters, there are Adepts, trust me on that. One of *those* would be able to persuade you that he was your long-lost best friend if you weren't completely on the alert for someone like that. In fact, the truth is that unless you've got introductions like I'm going to give you, I would be *very* wary of anyone who seems friendly. The friendlier they are, the warier I'd be. There isn't a mage out here who has to go looking for pupils—they come to him. It's a matter of the way things work; power calls to power. So if someone is out looking, it usually isn't for anyone's purposes but his own. The only people as a group that you can trust without hesitation are the Shin'a'in and whoever they vouch for. Anyone else is suspect."

Skif's eyes narrowed. "And you say she looks—attractive?"

Quenten nodded soberly. "I hate to send you to bed with a thought guaranteed to create nightmares, but—yes. More than attractive. To put it bluntly, my friend, you are riding out into wolf territory with a young and tender lamb at your side. And the wolves can look convincingly like sheep."

Skif licked his lips, and the look in his eyes convinced Quenten that he hadn't been wrong. This man *was* very dangerous, if he chose to be. And he had just chosen to be.

Quenten could only hope the man was dangerous enough.

Chapter Ten

DARKWIND

Vree dove down out of the sky with no warning whatsoever, coming straight out of the sun so that Darkwind didn't spot him until the last possible second, seeing only the flash of shadow crossing the ground.

"Treyvan! Look out!" he shouted, interrupting whatever it was Hydona was about to say.

Treyvan ducked and flattened his crest, and Vree skimmed right over his head, his outstretched claws just missing the quill he'd been aiming for.

Then, without faltering in the slightest, he altered his course with a single wingbeat, and shot back up toward the clouds, vanishing to the apparent size of a sparrow in a heartbeat.

That was the single bad habit Darkwind had *never* been able to break him of. The gyre was endlessly fascinated by Treyvan's crest feathers, and kept trying to snatch them whenever the gryphon wasn't careful about watching for him.

"Sorry," Darkwind said, apologetically. "I don't know what gets into him, I really don't. . . ."

Hydona smothered a smirk. Treyvan looked up at the bird—who was now just a dot in the sky, innocently riding a thermal, as if he had never even *thought* about snatching Treyvan's feathers—and growled.

"Darrrrkwind, I do love you, but ssssome day I aaam going to *ssswat* that birrd of yourrrsss." Hydona made an odd whistling sound, half-choked; Treyvan transferred his glare to his mate.

"Sorry," Darkwind repeated, feebly. "Ah, Hydona, you were saying?"

"Oh, that therrre ssseems no rrreasssson for the Change-child to haave sssaved the *dyheli*." Hydona's eyes still held a spark of mirth as Treyvan flattened his crest as closely to his skull as he could. "Unlessss she trrruly meant to be altrrruissstic. And I sssuppose you could not judge how powerrrful a mage sssshee iss?"

He shook his head. "Not on the basis of a single spell. If I were an Adept trying to worm my way into a Clan, I'd probably try and make myself look as harmless as possible, actually."

"Shhheee isss Otherrr," Treyvan said, unexpectedly. Both Darkwind and his mate looked at him in surprise. "It iss the clawsss. Thossse cannot be changed from human bassse, only brrred in. Which meansss that she isss Otherrr, for the clawsss come frrrom the unhuman, and only the Othersss brrreed with them. Ssso ssshe is Otherrr, at least in parrrt."

Hydona nodded, slowly. "That iss trrue. I had forrgotten that."

Darkwind bit back a curse. That would make her even harder to slip past his father if he had to. A Changechild he might accept, with difficulty—but one who was even in part of the Others, the blood-path mages of the Outlands? Not a chance.

"But if she's Other, what was she doing, that close to k'Sheyna?" he asked.

Treyvan ruffled his feathers in the gryphon equivalent of a shrug. "It ssseemsss obviousss that sshe could haave many motivessss."

True. Darkwind could think of several. She could be a spy; she could still have been trying to escape a cruel master. She could even be an Adept herself, and have inflicted all those hurts on herself with the intent of lulling their suspicions.

"We could," Hydona offered unexpectedly, "quesstion her for you. We arrre asss effective asss the *vrondi* at sssensssing falsssehood. It isss insstinct.''

They are? That was news to him—though welcome news. Somehow the gryphons kept pulling these little surprises out of nowhere, keeping him in a perpetual state of astonishment.

''That would be—damned useful,'' he replied honestly. ''The Truth-Spell is still a *spell*, and I don't want to use it. Not this close to the border. I can't chance attracting things to the *hertasi* settlement, or to k'Sheyna, either.''

''It isss insstinct with usss,'' Treyvan repeated, to reassure him. ''Not a ssspell. Perhapsss, though, you ought to be therrre alsso. Ssshe will probably be verrry afrraid of usss.''

He smiled. ''Considering that you're large enough to *really* bite her head off if you wanted to, you're probably right,'' he said. ''And that might not be a bad thing, either. If we keep her frightened, we have a better chance of catching her in a lie, don't we?''

''Yesssss,'' Treyvan agreed. ''It doesss not affect the trrruth asss we sssenssse it, fearr.''

''Good; I'll be with you, so that she doesn't try to run, but you two *loom* a little bit. Be the big, bad monsters, and I'll be her protector.'' But another thought occurred to him, then. He'd been planning on what to do to find out more about her; he still had no idea what to do *with* her.

''What do I do with her if she seems all right?'' he asked. ''I can't possibly take her into the Vale.''

''Worrry about that when—and if—the time comesss,'' Treyvan said quietly. ''It isss eassy to make a decisssion about a frrriend. I would worrrry more about how to dissspossse of herrr. If ssshe issss falsssse, leave herrr to usss. If you like. We can dissspatch her.''

''No,'' he said, quickly. ''No, that's my job.'' It made him sick to think of killing in cold blood, but it *was* his job, and he would not put the burden on someone else. *Not them, especially. There's such an—innocence—about them. I won't see it stained with a cold-blooded murder, no matter how casually they think of doing it. It would matter to me, even if it doesn't seem to matter to them.*

Treyvan shrugged. "Very well, then," he said. "Ssshall we meet you therrre?"

"Fine," he replied. And couldn't help but grin. "Even if it *does* mean another trek through the marsh. The things I do for duty!"

Treyvan just laughed, and spread his wings. "Jussst keep that birrrd frrom my crrrest. He beginsss to look tasssty!"

And as Darkwind turned to head back, he was mortally certain that the gryphon was thinking of all those quill-snatching attempts by Vree, and chuckling at the notion of dining on the poor gyre. The gryphons were very catholic in what they considered edible; just as Vree would happily dine on a kestrel, a fellow raptor, the gryphons would probably be just as willing to make a morsel of Vree.

Except that Vree was Darkwind's. That alone was saving him from becoming Treyvan's lunch—in reality, if not in thought.

:Featherhead,: he Mindspoke up to the dot in the blue, *:You have no notion how close to the cliff you've been flying.:*

:Cliff?: responded Vree, puzzled. *:What cliff? Where cliff?:*

I can't tell if he's playing coy, or he really doesn't understand me.

Darkwind sighed, and waded into the murky water. *:Never mind. Just stop teasing the gryphons. Leave Treyvan's feathers alone, you hear me?:*

:Yes,: said Vree slyly. "Yes," that he'd heard Darkwind, not that he'd obey.

Darkwind groaned. *No wonder Father doesn't listen to me. I can't even get respect from a bird.*

Nera met him at the edge of the swamp, popping up out of nowhere right into his path and scaring a year out of him. He yelped, one foot slipped off the path and into who-knew-how-deep, smelly water, and he teetered precariously for a moment before regaining his balance.

He glared at the *hertasi*, snarling silently. Nera blithely ignored the glare. *:The winged ones are here,:* he Mindspoke. *:The creature you brought is also awake.:*

And with that, he vanished again, melting back into the reeds.

Darkwind closed his eyes for a moment and tried to think charitable thoughts. *He let me leave the girl here, and he's worried because of her, the threat she represents. He was startled to see the gryphons. He's preoccupied with other things. He forgets that I'm a lot clumsier in the swamp than he is.*

He grimaced. *Sure he does. And I'm the Shin'a'in Goddess.*

Not that it mattered; nothing was going to change Nera; the *hertasi* was far too fond of playing his little games of "eccentric old creature," and insisting that if Darkwind really *tried,* he could move as well as the *hertasi* could in the swamp. He *enjoyed* watching Darkwind come out of the reeds covered in muck.

Vree, Nera, Dawnfire, the gryphons. . . . With friends like these, why do I need to look on the border for trouble? All I need to do is sit and wait. They'll bring trouble to me.

But he did hurry his steps a little, as much as he dared without losing his footing. Nera would not have come looking for him if the *hertasi* weren't at least a little worried—truly worried—about the Changechild. And rightly; it *was* possible the girl was an Adept; she seemed a little young for the rank, but Darkwind had just attained Adept-class when the Heartstone fractured, and he had been younger.

And it didn't follow that she was as youthful as she looked. One of the commonest changes for a blood-path Adept to make in himself was to remove years. Most of them kept their bodies looking as if they were in their mid-twenties, but some even chose to look like children.

Those were the really nasty ones for Tayledras to cope with; given the Hawkbrothers' strong reaction to children, it was easy to play on their emotions until the enemy Adept had them in exactly the position he wanted them. K'Vala had been decimated by an Adept using that ploy several hundred years ago, back when their territory was on the eastern shore of the Great Crater Sea, the one the Outlanders called "Lake Evendim" now. Their lesson was one no Tayledras could afford to ignore.

He found himself thinking of his options if she *was* an

Adept, and how he might be able to trick her into revealing her abilities.

She'll have to pull power from the nearest node just to Heal herself, he thought, as he felt his way along the submerged path. *Treyvan should be able to sense that if she does; from what he told me, he's tied his magic into that node. If she's a Master, she'll draw from the leylines. That's going to be subtler, and harder to catch. Hmm.* If he had someone "trap" the lines, so that any interference would be noted, *she* might note it as well. What he needed was a Sensitive, someone who was so attuned to the local energy-flows that he would notice any deviation from the norm.

Wait a moment; didn't Treyvan tell me that the gryphlets are Sensitive to the power-flows in their birth area? That might work—assuming he can convince them to keep their minds on it.

He tried to think of something that would have convinced *him* to keep a constant watch for something when he was that young, and failed to come up with anything. Children were children, and generally as featherheaded as Vree.

Well, I'll mention it to the adults, and see what they say.

He emerged from the reeds to the walkways rimming the rice paddies and stopped long enough to dry his feet and put his boots back on. A quick look around showed him nothing amiss, which meant there had been no real need to hurry, only Nera's impatience.

Old coot. Just likes to see me lose my balance. And he's not happy unless he's the one in charge of everything.

He knew Nera was watching him, and he deliberately took his time.

On the hill above Nera's tunnel, two pairs of huge, waving wings told him that Treyvan and Hydona were waiting, too, but with more patience than the little *hertasi*.

He picked his way across the paddies, taking time to be courteous to the farmers who bent so earnestly over their plants. One of them even stopped him to ask a few questions about one of his kin who lived in the Vale—

and he could sense Nera's impatient glare even from the distant tunnel mouth.

He looked up, and sure enough, there was a shadow, just within the round entrance to the tunnel. He smiled sweetly at it and bent to answer the *hertasi's* questions, in detail and with extreme politeness. After all, he was the only Tayledras any of them saw regularly, and he *did* make a point to keep track of those Vale *hertasi* with relatives out here. They were so shy that they seldom asked him about their Vale kin, and it was only fair to give them a full answer when they did inquire.

And if Nera says anything, that's exactly what I'll tell him.

When he reached the hill and set foot on the carefully graveled trail leading up the side, he debated on going first to Nera's tunnel, but Treyvan's Mindspoken hail decided him in favor of the gryphons instead. It seemed that his charge was not only awake, but moving.

:Featherless son, your prize waits up here. She can walk, slowly, and there is more room for us up here. She did not ask what we were and does not seem particularly frightened.:

Well, that was a little disappointing. *:She must have known about you—or else she's seen gryphons before. So much for you playing monster. I'm on my way up.:*

When he reached the top of the sun-gilded bluff, he found his charge reclining on another of the stuffed grass mats, neatly bracketed between the two gryphons. They were also reclining in the cool, short grass, wings half-open to catch the breeze coming over the top of the hill.

His eyes went back to the Changechild as if pulled there. She seemed even more attractive awake, with sense in those slit-pupiled eyes and life in the supple muscles. He was only *too* aware of how fascinating she was; her very differences from humankind were somehow more alluring than if she'd been wholly human.

She nodded a greeting to him, then shifted her position a little, so that she could watch him and the gryphons at the same time. He noticed that she moved stiffly, as if more than her muscles were hurt.

"Sssso, your charrge iss awake," Treyvan said genially. "We have been having interessssting conversssation. Nyarrra, thisss iss Darrkwind."

She fixed him with an odd, unblinking gaze. "I remember you. You saved me," she said, finally, in a low, husky voice that had many of the qualities of a purr. "From the mist. You helped me get out when I fell."

"After you saved the *dyheli* herd," he pointed out. "It seemed appropriate—though I could not imagine why you aided them." He lifted an eyebrow. "I assume you had a reason."

"I was fleeing my own troubles when I saw them." She shrugged, gracefully. "I am what I am," she replied. "A Changechild, and not welcome among the Birdkin. When I saw the *dyheli* trapped, it came to me that it would be good to free them, and also that your folk value them. If I freed them, perhaps the door might be open for one such as I. And also," she added, looking thoughtful, "I have no love for he who trapped them."

"And who might that be?" Darkwind asked, without inflection. He could see what Treyvan had set up, even without a Mindspoken prompting; since the girl was not afraid of the gryphons, their planned positions would be reversed. *They* would be friendly, and *he* would be menacing.

A little harder to pull off, with her lounging on the ground like an adolescent male dream come to languid life, but certainly a good plan. It seemed that she was perfectly willing to believe that he would be hostile to her, even with her sexual allure turned up to full force.

"My master," she said, pouting a little at his coldness. "Mornelithe Falconsbane."

"Not a frrrriendly name," Hydona said, with a little growl.

"Not a friendly man," replied Nyara, with a toss of her head and a wince. "Not a *man* at all, anymore, for all that he is male—or at least, very little human. He has worked more changes upon his own flesh than he has upon mine."

"An Adept, then," Treyvan said with cheerful interest. "And one you did not carrre for, I take it? From yourrr hurtss, I would sssay he wasss even lesss kind than he wasss frriendly."

Nyara nodded, her supple lips tightened into a bitter line. "Oh, yes. I was the creature upon which he attempted his changes, and if they proved to his liking, he used them also. And he made his mistakes upon me, and often did not bother to correct them. Other things he did, too—beatings, and—''

Her eyes filled with tears and she averted her head. ''I—he hurt me, once too often. That is all I would say.''

''So, you ran away from him, is that it?'' Darkwind interrupted the attempt to play for sympathy rudely. ''How did you get away from someone as powerful as that? I don't imagine he let you simply walk away. And when you saw the *dyheli,* then what did you do?''

She blinked away the tears, and rubbed her cheeks with the back of her hand, without raising her head. ''I have stolen little bits of magic-learning from time to time. I have a small power, you see. When Mornelithe was careless, I watched, I learned. I learned enough to bend the spells of lock and ward and slip free of his hold. Then I went north, where I have heard from Mornelithe's servants that there were Birdkin, that he hated.'' She watched him out of the corner of her eyes. ''Do you think less of me, that I thought to use you? You are many, I am one. You have been the cause of some of my hurts, when *he* was angered with you and could not reach you. I thought—with Birdkin between me and him, he would ignore my flight and harry the Birdkin. He might even think I was with the Birdkin, and turn his anger on them. Then I saw the horned ones, and felt his magic upon them, and thought to buy myself sanctuary, or at least safe passage, with their freedom.'' Her head came up, and she looked defiantly into his eyes. ''You owe me safe passage, at least, Birdkin. Even though I thought to trick Mornelithe and set him on you. *You* have defeated him many times. I am but a small thing, and could not even defy him, and escaped him only with guile.''

He looked sideways at Treyvan, who nodded ever so slightly. Everything she'd said was the truth, then. It was probably safe enough to give her what she asked for.

''We do owe you that and a place to rest until you can journey again,'' he admitted, softening his icy expression a little. He caught the glint of scales out of the corner of his eye, and Mindspoke Nera, watching her closely to see if she detected the thoughts. *:Nera, this Change-child seems friendly, and she's going to need your help;*

shelter for a week or two at least, maybe more. Have you got any tunnels no one is using?:

The *hertasi* forgot whatever it was that had brought him, now that Darkwind had invoked his authority again. *:Hmm. Yes. The old one at the waterline that belonged to Rellan and Lorn, that flooded this spring. Again. They finally listened to me and moved out. Unless we have three or four weeks of rain, it should stay dry.:*

And it was right on the edge of the bluff, with the swamp on one side, a hillside too steep for someone in her condition to climb above, and all the *hertasi* between herself and freedom. That should do.

:Perfect,: he said.

And Nyara showed no signs of having heard the conversation.

:We will make it ready,: Nera told him, full of self-importance, and content now that he was a major part of whatever was going on. *:The creature can walk, but slowly—my Healer says that there are half-healed bones and torn muscles. Send her in a few moments and there will be a bed and food waiting.:*

"We can give you a place to stay for as long as you need it," he told her. "And I will see about getting you safe passage, once you're fit to journey again. I—don't think you can hope for sanctuary. The Elders of this Clan hate Changechildren too much."

"But you do not," she replied, her voice a caress.

"I—don't hate anyone," he said, flushing, and averting his eyes, much to Treyvan's open amusement. "But I don't determine what the Elders will say or do. At any rate, Nera and the others are moving some basic things in now, and as soon as you are ready, one of them will come show you where it is."

"I am grateful, Darkwind," she said, bowing her head a little and looking up at him from under long, thick lashes. "I am very grateful."

He felt his blood heating from that half-veiled glance, and wondered if she knew what she was promising him with it. Then he decided that she must know; sex was as much a part of her weaponry as her claws.

"Don't worry about being grateful," he said gruffly, while Treyvan hid his amusement. "Just get yourself healed up, so we can get you out of this Mornelithe's reach. The sooner you're gone, the safer we'll all be.''

They removed themselves to a place farther along the bluff, well out of earshot of the *hertasi* village, before any of them said anything.

It was a golden afternoon, near enough to nightfall for things to have cooled down, sunlight as thick and sweet as honey pouring over the gold-dusted grass of the bluff, with just enough breeze to keep it from being too warm. The gryphons fanned their wings out to either side of themselves, basking, their eyes half-lidded, and beaks parted slightly. Treyvan's crest was raised as high as it could go, and his chest feathers were puffed out.

They looked extraordinarily stupid. Darkwind had to fight off gales of laughter every time he looked at them.

Vree, on his good behavior now that both Darkwind and Treyvan were ready for his tricks, joined them on the grass. He had just taken a bath, and looked even sillier than the gryphons. Even though he was behaving, he kept eyeing the quills of Treyvan's crest with undisguised longing.

''Will the little ones be all right with you gone so long?'' Darkwind asked with concern.

Hydona nodded, slowly and lazily. ''The ruinsss are sssafe, tempo-rrrarrrily. We caught the *wyrrrsssa*. They were wild, masssterless.''

''What about that serpent you thought moved into the ruins this spring?'' he asked. ''The one I found the sign of. It's certainly large enough to make a meal of one of you, let alone Lytha or Jerven.''

''It made the missstake of basssssking on the sssame ssstone alwaysss,'' Treyvan replied, his voice full of satisfaction. ''It wasss delicioussss.''

''The little onesss will be fine,'' Hydona assured him. ''Their Mindsssspeech isss quite ssstrong now, and if they are threatened, they will call. We can be there verrrry quickly.''

Having seen the gryphons flying at full speed once, he could believe that. They were even faster than Vree, and that was saying something, for Vree was faster than any wild bird he had ever seen.

''So, was she lying about anything?'' Darkwind asked,

as he pulled the hair away from the back of his neck to let the sun bake into his neck and shoulder muscles. "Nyara, I mean."

"No," Hydona said. "Orrr—mossstly no."

"Mostly?" Darkwind said sharply. "Just how much was she lying about?"

"The one ssshe claimed wasss her massster," Treyvan said, slowly.

"Mornelithe Falconsbane," Darkwind supplied. "Sounds to me as if he really does hate Tayledras, if he's taken a use-name like that." Most Adepts assumed use-names; the Tayledras did it simply to have a name that was more descriptive of what they were, but the blood-path Adepts did so out of fear. Names were power, though not in the sense that the foolish thought, that knowing someone's "true name" would permit you to command him. No, by knowing the real name, the birth-name, of someone, you could discover everything there was to know about him, if you were thorough and patient enough—you could even see every moment of his past life, if you knew the spell to see into the past. And by knowing that about him, you knew his strengths and weaknesses. And most importantly, you could learn the fears that were the strongest because they were rooted in childhood. It was characteristic of blood-path Adepts that they had many, many weaknesses, for they generally had never faced what they were, and conquered those old fears. There had been cases of mere Journeymen besting Adepts, sometimes even by illusions, simply by knowing what those fears were, and playing to them.

But blood-path mage or any other kind, the use-name told the world something about what the mage was *now*. A name like "Mornelithe Falconsbane" did not call up easy feelings within a Tayledras.

"I do not like that name, Darrrkwind," Hydona said uneasily. "It does not sssit well in my mind."

"Nor mine, either," Darkwind admitted. "I don't imagine he cares much for anything with wings and feathers. *Mornelithe*, now, that's Old Tayledras; it's actually Kaled'a'in, the language we and the Shin'a'in had when we were the same people—"

"Yesss," Treyvan said, interrupting him. "We ssspeak Kaled'a'in. Fluently."

"You do?" he replied, surprised again. *That's something to go into with them later. In detail. Where on earth did they ever learn Kaled'a'in? I thought it was a dead language.* "Well, I knew what it was, but what's it mean?"

"*Hatrrred-that-returnsss,*" Treyvan said solemnly. "A name that sspeaksss of return over the agesss, not once, but many timesss. It isss not rebirrth, it isss actual returrn, and returrn looking for rrrevenge. It isss an evil word, Darrrkwind. Asss evil as you find 'Falconsssssbane' to be."

The words hung heavy and ill-omened between them, silencing all three of them for a moment, and bringing a chill to the air.

"Typical blood-path intimidation," Darkwind said in disgust, attempting to make light of it and dispel the gloom. "Trying to frighten people with a portentous name and a fancy costume. Frankly, *I'd* like to know where they're finding people willing to make clothing like that, those ridiculous cloaks and headdresses. They look as if they were designed by an apprentice to traveling players with delusions of grandeur. Half the time they can't even walk or see properly in those outfits."

Treyvan laughed. "Oh? And who isss it hasss an entire collection of Ravenwing'sss feather masssksss on hisss wallsss?"

"That's different," he replied, defending himself. "That's art. Back to the subject; what was it Nyara lied about in connection with her master? Wasn't he her master after all?"

"Oh he wasss her massster, yesss. But he wasss more. Sssomething more—intimate." Treyvan shook his head and looked over at his mate, who nodded.

"Yesss," said Hydona. "But not intimate, asss in loversss. There isss no love there. It wasss something elsssse."

Darkwind tried to puzzle that one out, then gave it up. "I'll think about that for a while; maybe the connection will come to me. She *did* escape, though, right?"

"Oh, yesss," Hydona replied emphatically. "Yesss, sshe did essscape, and wass purssued. I would ssay that her sstory isss trrrue—all of it that ssshe told usss, that isss."

"I wish I'd been able to ask her more questions," he said, chewing at his lower lip as he thought. "I wish I'd been able to *think* of more questions."

"It ssseemss clear enough," Treyvan said lazily, stretching his forelegs out into the sun a little more. "Ssshe isss exactly what sshe ssseemsss."

"A Changechild, used to try out the changes her master wanted to perform on his own body—used as a sex toy when he wished."

"Yesss," Hydona nodded. "And usssed alssso to rrraissse and hold powerrr for him. You did not ssssee that upon herrr?"

He looked up at the sky in exasperation. "Of course! I missed that aspect completely! I could not imagine why Falconsbane would allow her to keep her Mage-Gift intact, when an Adept should be able to block it or render it useless by burning the channels. But if she didn't have enough to challenge him—but *did* have enough to carry power—"

"Ssshe would make the perrrfect vesssel," Treyvan concluded.

"Exactly," Hydona replied. "He could ussse herrr to carrrry powerrr from hisss sacrificesss; he could generrrate powerrr *frrrom* herrr by hurrrting herrr."

"And best of all," Darkwind concluded grimly, "he could exhaust *her* power without touching his own. That made it possible for him to work spells that don't disturb the energy-flows around here at all, because it's all internal power. *That* is how he's been doing things without my sensing them!"

"Sssensing them?" Treyvan opened one eye. "I thought you had given up yourrr mage-sssskillsss."

"I have," he replied firmly. "But I can still sense the power flows and the disturbances when someone tampers with them. As long as I'm not inside the Vale, that is."

"That Heartsssstone isss a problem, Darrrkwind," Treyvan said, unexpectedly. "It isss distorting everrrything in the area of the Vale, asss if it were a thick, warped pane of glasss. And when thingsss come into thiss area, like the ssserpent, it isss attracting them. I am ssssurprisssed that no one in therre hasss noticed the problemsss."

Darkwind shook his head, compressing his lips tightly.

"If I say what I'd like to—well, that's Vale business, and the Elders' business, and you—"

"Are Outssssidersss," Treyvan replied, rolling his eye in exasperation. "And if your father dissscovered you had been ssspeaking of Vale busssinesss to Outssssiderssss, what then? Would he cast you out? It might be worth it, Darrkwind. Thisss isss involving more than jussst k'Sssheyna. The broken Heartssstone beginsss to affect the area out-ssside the Vale."

"No." He shook his head emphatically. "I have a duty to my Clan, and to what the Tayledras are supposed to be. I guess—" he thought for a moment, "I suppose I'm just waiting for the moment that they all bury themselves, and I can find out where k'Vala or k'Treyva are now, and I can go get some help."

"May that be sssoon," Hydona sighed.

"Too true." He eyed the sun and stood up, then hesitated a moment. "You know my personal reasons for giving up magic—and—well, I wouldn't admit it to anyone but you, but—I'm beginning to think that may have been, well, a little short-sighted."

Treyvan tilted his head. "I will not ssay that I told you the ssame."

"I know you did. But now," he frowned, "if the Heartstone is attracting uncanny things, it is probably a good idea not to rescind that vow. Look what happened to the one mage who *tried* casting spells outside the Vale."

"A good point," Treyvan acknowledged. "But you ssstill show Adept-potential, do you not? Would that not attract creaturesss asss well ass ssspellcassssting?" He tilted his head the other way. "A dissstinct liability to a ssscout, I would sssay."

He flushed. "Treyvan, I'm not stupid. I thought of that. I swore I wouldn't spellcast. I *never* swore I wouldn't keep my shields."

Treyvan laughed aloud. "Good. You are asss canny as I could wish, flightlesss ssson."

He had to laugh, himself. "Well, Nera has things well in hand for now, you have youngsters to get back to, and I—I guess I'd better finish out my patrol, tell Dawnfire the good news if she doesn't know already, and figure out how best to phrase Nyara's request to the Elders."

Treyvan chuckled. "Ssshe won't be moving far or fasst for a few dayss, if I'm any judge of human ssshapesss. You'll have ssome time to think."

Darkwind sighed. "I hope so," he replied. "It isn't going to be easy. Starblade is *not* going to like this."

Chapter
Eleven

ELSPETH

Skif peered through the foggy gloom of near-dawn, wishing he had eyes like a cat. He watched for possible trouble, as Elspeth stood—literally—on her saddle, trying to read the signpost in the middle of the crossroads. Gwena stood like a stone statue; a distinct improvement over a horse in a similar situation.

Before they had left Bolthaven, Elspeth had taken Quenten's advice quite literally—and very much to heart. For one thing, she'd consulted with him about disguises, in lieu of being able to ask Kerowyn. Now they wore something more in the line of what a pair of prosperous mercenaries would wear. "Mercs would be best," Quenten had decided, after a long discussion, and taking into consideration the fact that no amount of dye would stain the Companion's coats. "Tell people who ask you've been bodyguards for a rich merchant's daughter, and that's where you got the matched horses. If you say you're mercs, no one will bother you, and you can wear your armor and weapons openly. Just put a coat of paint on those shields, or get a cover for them."

They'd given him carte blanche, and a heavy pouch of coin. He'd grinned when Skif lifted an eyebrow over the selection of silks and fine leathers Quenten's agent brought back from the Bolthaven market, clothing that was loose and comfortable, and so did not need to be tailored to them to look elegant.

"We want you two to look prosperous," he'd said. "First of all, only a prosperous merc would be able to afford horses like yours, even if you did get them in the line of duty. And secondly, a prosperous merc is a *good* fighter. No bandit is ever going to want to bother a mercenary who looks as well-off as you will. The *last* place a merc puts his money is in his wardrobe. If you can afford this, *you're* not worrying about needing cash for other things."

"But the jewelry," Skif had protested. "You've turned most of our ready cash into jewelry!"

"A free-lance merc wears his fortune," Quenten told him. "If you need to buy something, and you don't want to spend any of those outland gold coins because it might draw attention to you, break off a couple of links of those necklaces, take a plate from the belt, hand over a ring or a bracelet. That's the way a merc operates, and no one is going to turn a hair. Very few mercs bother with keeping money with a money-changing house, because it won't be readily accessible. In fact, only about half of even bonded mercs have a running account with the Mercenary's Guild, for the same reason. Where you're going, every merchant and most good inns have scales to weigh the gold and silver, and they'll give you a fair exchange for it."

Skif thought about what he said, then sent Quenten's agent back to the bazaar to exchange the rest of their Valdemaren and Rethwellan gold and silver for jewelry. He had to admit that the ornaments he got in exchange, a mixture of brand new and worn with use, were a great deal less traceable than the Valdemaren coin. He felt like a walking target—his old thief instincts acting up again— but he knew very well that when *he* was a thief, he'd never, ever have tackled *two* wealthy fighters, especially when they walked with their hands on their hilts and never drank more than one flagon of wine at a sitting. Quenten had been right; a wealthy, cautious fighter was someone that tended not to attract trouble. Still, he'd complained to Elspeth their first night on the road that he felt like a cheap tavern dancer, with his necklaces making more noise than his chain-mail.

Elspeth had giggled, saying *she* felt like a North-Province bride, with all her dowry around her neck, but she had no objections to following Quenten's advice.

He still resented that, a little. He'd made a similar suggestion—though he had suggested they dress as a pair of landed hill-folk rather than mercs—and she had dismissed the notion out of hand. But when *Quenten* told them to disguise themselves, she had agreed immediately.

Maybe it was simply that he'd suggested plain, unglamorous hill-folk, and Quenten had suggested the opposite. Skif had the feeling she was beginning to enjoy this; she was picking up the kind of swaggering walk the other well-off mercs they met had adopted, and she had taken to binding up her hair with bright bands of silk, and some of the strands of garnet and amethyst beads Quenten had bought. There were eye-catching silk scarves trailing from the hilt of Need, and binding the helm at her saddlebow. She looked like a barbarian. And he got the distinct impression she *liked* looking that way. Her eyes sparkled the moment they crossed into a town and found a tavern, and she began grinning when other mercs sought them out to exchange stories and news. One night she'd even taken up with another prosperous female free-lance, Selina Ironthroat, and had made the rounds of every tavern in town.

The gods only know what they did. I don't even want to think about it. At least she came back sober, even if she was giggling like a maniac. If half the stories those other mercs told me about Selina are true, her mother would never forgive me.

Not only that, she took the inevitable attempts at assignations with a cheerful good humor that amazed him.

He'd expected her to explode with anger the first time it happened. She had been the center of a gossiping clutch of Guild mercs, but as the evening wore on, one by one, they'd drifted off, leaving her alone for a moment. That was when a merc with almost as much gold around his neck as she wore had tried to get her to go off with him— and presumably into his bed.

He readied himself for a brawl. Then she'd shocked

the blazes out of him. She'd *laughed,* but not in a way
that would make the man feel she was laughing *at* him,
and said, in a good approximation of Rethwellan hill-
country dialect, "Oh, now that is a truly tempting offer,
'tis in very deed, but I misdoubt ye want to make me
partner there feel I've left 'im alone."

She'd nodded at Skif, who simply gave the merc The
Look. *Don't mess with my partner.* And turned back to
his beer, with one cautious eye on the proceedings.

"He gets right testy when he thinks he's gonna be
alone, truly he does," she continued, a friendly grin on
her face, her eyes shining as she got into her part. "Ye
see, his last partner left 'im all by 'imself one night, and
some sorry son of a sow snuck up on 'im when he wasn't
payin' attention, an' hit 'im with a bottle." Her face
went thoughtful for a moment. " 'Twas sad, that. 'E not
only took it out on 'is partner, gods grant th' puir man
heals up quick, 'e took it out on th' lads as took the puir
fellow off. He hates havin' no one to watch 'is back, he
truly do."

The other merc looked at Skif, who glowered back;
gulped, and allowed as how he, too, hated having no one
to guard his back.

"Then let's buy you a drink, lad!" she'd exclaimed,
slapping him so hard on the back that he'd staggered.
"When times be prosperous, 'tis only right t' share
'em. No hard feelin's among mercs, eh? Now, where are
ye bound for?"

Oh, yes, indeed, she *looked,* and acted, the part; a far
cry from the competent but quiet princess of Valdemar,
who never had seen the inside of a common tavern in her
life.

As he waited for her to decipher the sign, he wondered, as he had wondered several times before this, if
she wasn't enjoying it a bit too much.

She dropped down into her saddle by the simple ex-
pedient of *doing* just that, her feet slipping down along
the sides as she fell straight down—and he winced. That
was one of Kero's favorite tricks, and it *always* made
men wince.

"We're on the right road if we go straight ahead," she
said. "That's 'Dark Wing Road,' and we don't want it;
it's going into the Pelagiris Forest in a couple of leagues,

and it doesn't come out until it hits the edge of the Dhorisha Plains. No towns, no inns, no nothing. We want this one; it's still the Pelagiris Road, and in a while it'll meet the High Spur Road, and *that* takes us to Lythecare.''

On the map, this "Dark Wing Road" had looked to be a very minor track, but it was just as well-maintained in reality as the High Spur Road they expected to take. Of course, now that she'd pointed out what it was, it was obvious that it went in the wrong direction, but with all this dark mist confusing his senses—"I'm all turned around in this fog,'' he complained.

"That's what you get for being a city boy,'' she replied, ridiculously cheerful for such an unholy hour. "Get you off of the streets, and you can't find your way around.'' She sent Gwena to join him, then took the lead. His Companion followed after with no prompting on his part, the fog muffling the sounds of hooves and the jingle of harness.

His nose was cold, and the fog had an odd, metallic taste and smell to it. He hated getting up this early at the best of times; the fog made it that much worse.

"You're just as much city-bred as me,'' he countered, resentfully, a harder edge to his voice than he had intended. "Since when did you get to be such an expert on wilderness travel?''

She swiveled quickly and peered back at him, hardly more than a dark shape in the enshrouding fog. "What's wrong with you?'' she asked, astonishment and a certain amount of edge in her voice as well.

"Nothing,'' he said quickly—then, with more truth—"Well, not much. I hate mornings; I hate fog. And there's something that's been bothering me—you're different. It's as if you're turning into Kero.''

Or even Selina Ironthroat.

"So what if I am?'' she countered. "Who would you rather have next to you in trouble—Kero, or mousy little princess Elspeth, who would have let *you* try and figure out where we were going and what we were doing? What's wrong with turning into Kero? That's assuming that I *am;* I happen to think you're wrong about that.''

Now it was his turn to be surprised. He'd never heard her refer to herself as a "mousy little princess'' before. And while she had sometimes railed *about* things to him, she'd never turned on him before. ''Uh—'' he replied, cleverly.

''Or is it just that I won't let you take care of me? Is that the problem?'' He heard the annoyance in her voice that meant she was scowling. ''You've been sulking since we left Bolthaven, and I'm getting damned tired of it. As long as I let *you* make all the decisions, everything was fine—but this is *my* trip, and I'm the one with the authority, and you know it. I pull my own weight, Skif. I was perfectly capable of doing this trip by myself, in fact, I was ready to. I admit I didn't think about disguises—and you *were* right about that idea. But the fact is, if I'd been able to go on my own, I was intending to travel by night and hide by day. And if anyone saw me, I was going to pretend I was a ghost-rider and scare the blazes out of him.''

''It's not that you're making the decisions. It's just the changes in you. You're so—hearty,'' he said feebly. ''You're kind of loud, actually. Everybody notices us, wherever we go. I thought the point was to keep from drawing attention to ourselves.''

She snorted, and it wasn't ladylike. ''You think these costumes *aren't* going to draw attention to us? Come on, Skif, we're walking advertisements for the life of the merc! Sure, I'm loud. That's what a woman like Berta *would* be. Like Selina Ironthroat. I spent that night studying her, I'll have you know. I'm competing for men's money in a man's world, and I'm doing damn well at it, and the more I advertise that fact, the more jobs I'll be offered. In fact, I've *been* offered jobs, quite a few of them; I turned them down, saying we were going off to take another job with a caravan we were picking up at Kata'shin'a'in.''

''Oh,'' he replied, feeling overwhelmed. Admittedly, he hadn't thought much about the part he was supposedly playing. Certainly not the way she had. She had everything; motives, background, character—even an imaginary job that would give them an excuse to turn down any other offers.

''Don't *cosset* me, Skif,'' she said, her voice roughened with anger. ''I'm sick to death of being cosseted. Kero wouldn't, and you know it. This is exactly the kind of job she'd love. She'd be right beside me, slapping those drunks on the back—and if she had to, I bet she'd be hauling them off to bed with her, too."

"*Elspeth!*" he yelped, before he thought.

"There!" she said triumphantly. "You see? What's the matter, don't you think I know about the simple facts of a man and a woman? An *ordinary* man and woman, not Heralds, the kind of people who are driven by the needs of the moment? Just what, exactly, are you trying to protect me from? The idea that drunk strangers grab each other and hop into strange beds and proceed to forn—"

He tried, but he couldn't help himself. He emitted an inarticulate moan.

"—each other's tails off?" she finished, right over the top of him. "And I deliberately didn't use any of the ten or so rude words I know for the act, just to avoid bruising your delicate sensibilities. I can swear with the worst of the mercs if I have to, and I know hundreds of filthy jokes, and furthermore, I know exactly what they mean! I've spent lots of time with Kero's Skybolts, and they treated me just like one of them. Skif, I *grew up*. I'm not the little sister that you used to leave candy for. *And I don't need you to shelter me from what I already know!*" A pause, during which he tried to think of something to say. "Stop treating me like a child, Skif. I'm not a little girl anymore. I haven't been for a long time."

And that's the problem, he thought, unhappily. She *wasn't* a little girl anymore, and he wasn't sure how to act around her. It wasn't that competence in women bothered him—he loved Talia dearly, and he looked up to Kero as to his very own Captain, for she was one of the few at Court to whom his background meant nothing in particular. It was seeing that confidence in *Elspeth* that bothered him. He couldn't help but think that it wasn't confidence, it was a foolish overconfidence, the headiness of freedom.

The warnings Quenten had given him had made him wary to the point of paranoia. Every time someone approached her, he kept examining them for some sign that they weren't what they seemed, that they were really blood-path mages stalking her, like a cat stalking a baby rabbit.

:*She just doesn't understand,*: he confided to his Companion, thinking that she, at least, would sympathize.

:There're all those mages out there Quenten warned us about. She doesn't even think about them, she doesn't watch for them, and she's not trying to hide from them.:

:But you warned her about everything Quenten said,: Cymry said, answering his thought. *:You told her everything you knew. She may be right about hiding in plain sight, you know. Why would a mage look for someone like her to have Mage-Gift? Everyone knows mages can't be fighters. Besides, don't you think she's as capable as you are of telling if someone is stalking her?:*

:Yes, but—:

:In fact,: she continued, thoughtfully, *:it's entirely possible that she would know sooner than you. She does have mage abilities, even if they aren't trained. Quenten said that power calls to power, and she's keeping a watch on the thoughts of everyone around her. Don't you think she'd know another mage if one came that close to her?:*

:Yes, but—: He lapsed into silence. Because that wasn't all, or even most, of what was bothering him.

She'd grown up, all right. She was no longer anything he could think of as a "girl." And whether it was the new attitude, or the new clothing, or both—he couldn't help noticing just how much she had grown up. Certainly the new clothing, far more flamboyant than anything she wore at home, enhanced that perception. It seemed almost as if she had taken on a new life with the new persona.

Maybe it was also, at least in part, the fact that no one was *watching* them together. There was no one to start rumors, no one to warn him that she was not exactly an appropriate partner for an ex-thief; no one to wink and nod whenever he walked by with her, no one to ask, with arch significance, how she was doing lately. The friends had been as annoying as the opponents.

But now both were gone, far out of distance of any gossip. And he was free to look at her as "Elspeth" instead of The Heir To The Throne.

And he was discovering how much he liked what he saw. She was handsome in the same vibrant way Kero was—*and, admit it*, he thought to himself, *you're more than half in love with Kero.* Clever, witty, with a ready laugh that more than made up for her whiplash temper.

Oh, she was a handful, but a handful he wouldn't mind having by his side. . . .

Dear gods. A sudden realization made him blush so hotly he was very glad that the fog was still thick enough to hide it. It wasn't outraged sensibilities that made him yelp at the idea of her entertaining one of those mercs in bed—it was jealousy. The very last emotion he'd ever have anticipated entertaining, especially over Elspeth.

He didn't *want* her running off with someone else, he wanted her to run off with *him*.

He must have been giving an ample demonstration of his jealousy over the past few days; surely she had guessed long before he had.

But now that he thought about it, she didn't seem to notice anything except his increasing protectiveness—"mother-henning," she called it. This wasn't the first time she'd complained about it.

But it was the first time she had done so at the top of her lungs. She might not have noticed his attraction, but she had certainly noticed the side effects.

I guess she's really mad, he thought guiltily. And cleared his throat, hoping to restart the conversation, and get it turned back onto friendlier ground.

She didn't say anything, but she didn't turn around and snap at him, either. The growing light of dawn filtered through the fog, enveloping them both in a glowing, pearly haze—and it was a good thing they *were* both wearing their barbaric merc outfits; the Companions just faded into the general glow, and if they'd been wearing Whites, they'd have lost each other in a heartbeat. This kind of mist fuddled directions and the apparent location of sound, too. He peered at her fog-enshrouded shape up ahead of him; it looked uncannily as if she was bestriding a wisp of fog itself.

Try something noncommittal. Ask something harmless. "Did Quenten say why Adept Jendar is living in Lythecare, when the school he founded is all the way back up near Petras in Rethwellan?" he asked, trying to sound humble.

"Don't try to sound humble, Skif," she replied waspishly. "It doesn't suit you." Then she relented and unbent a little; he thought perhaps she turned again to make certain he was still following, and hadn't halted his Companion in a fit of pique. "Sorry. That wasn't called for. Ah—he did tell me some. Jendar wants to be down here in Jkatha so he's somewhere nearer his Shin'a'in relatives, but he doesn't want to be in Kata'shin'a'in, because it's really just a trade-city, and it practically dries up and blows away in the fall and winter."

"What did he mean by that?" Skif asked, puzzled. "I should think a trade-city would have anything he'd want."

She paused. "Let me see if I can do a good imitation of Quenten imitating Jendar."

Her voice shifted to that of a powerful old man's, with none of the querulousness Skif expected.

" 'I want fabulous food! Carpets! Hot bathhouses and decent shops! Beautiful women to make a fool of me in my old age! Servants to pamper me outrageously, and merchants to suck up to me when I'm in the mood to buy something!' "

Skif chuckled; Elspeth did an excellent imitation when she was in a good mood—and from the sound of it, she had shaken her foul humor. *I have the feeling I'm going to like Kero's uncle as much as I do her.*

"I think I'm going to like the old man," she said, echoing his thought. "Quenten also said that there were two reasons Jendar didn't retire in Great Harsey, even though the school and the village begged him to. The first was that Great Harsey is a real backwater, too far for a man his age to travel to get to Petras, even if it is less than a day's ride away. The other is that he said that if he stayed, the new head would never *be* a head, he'd always be 'consulting' with Jendar and never making any decisions for himself. He thought that would be a pretty stupid arrangement." Her voice shifted again. " 'Let the youngster make his own mistakes, the way I did. *You* certainly haven't been hanging on my coattails, Quenten, and you're doing just fine.' "

She paused again, and said, significantly, "Jendar obviously believes in letting people *grow up.*"

"I get the point," Skif muttered. "I get the point."

It wasn't far now to the turnoff, but Elspeth was beginning to wonder if she'd make it that far. And she wondered also what happened to a Herald who murdered his Companion. . . . Once in a while, she wished there was such a thing as repudiation by the *Herald,* and this was one of those times. The summer heat was bad down here; it was worse, without trees to give some shade. The Pelagiris Forest lay somewhere to their right, but there wasn't a sign of it along this road way, except for the occasional faint, fugitive hint of pine.

:Well, you're certainly smug today,: Elspeth finally said to Gwena, when, for the fourth time, a sensation as of someone *humming* invaded the back of her mind. She pushed her hat up on her forehead and wiped away the sweat that kept trickling into her eyes.

:What?: Gwena replied, her ears flicking backwards. *:What on earth do you mean?:*

:You were humming to yourself,: Elspeth told her crossly. *:If you were human, you'd have been whistling. Tunelessly, might I add. It's damned annoying when someone is humming in* your *head; it's not something a person can just ignore, you know.:*

:I'm just feeling very good,: Gwena replied defensively, picking up her pace a little, to the surprise of Cymry, who hurried to match her, hooves kicking up little clouds of dust. *:Is there anything wrong with that? It's a lovely summer day.:*

Oh, really? *:A candlemark ago you were complaining about the heat.:*

:Well, maybe I'm getting used to it.: Gwena tossed her head, her mane lashing Elspeth's wrist, and added, *:Maybe it's you. Maybe you're just being testy.:* Her mind-voice took on a conciliating tone. *:Is it the wrong moon-time, dear?:*

:No it's not, as you very well know. Besides, that has nothing to do with it!: Elspeth snapped, without thinking. *:Skif is being a pain in the tail.:*

:Skif is falling in love with you,: Gwena replied, dropping the conciliating tone. *:You could do worse.:*

:I know he is, and I couldn't *do worse,:* she said, conscious only of her annoyance. *:I'm not talking about differences in rank or background, either. And don't you start playing matchmaker. He's a very nice young man, and I'm not the least interested in him, all right?:*

:All right, all right,: Gwena said, sounding surprised at her vehemence. *:Forget I said anything.:*

Gwena closed her mind to her Chosen, and Elspeth

sighed. It wasn't just Skif and his problem that was bothering her—or even primarily Skif. It was something else entirely.

It was a feeling. One that had been increasing, every step she rode toward Lythecare. The feeling that she was being *herded* toward something, some destiny, like a complacent cow to the altar of sacrifice.

As if she were doing what she "should" be doing.

And she didn't like it, not one tiny bit.

Everything had fallen into place so very neatly; she could almost tally up the events on her fingers. First, Kero showed up, with a magic sword. Then, Elspeth, having seen real magic at work, firsthand, just *happened* to get the idea that Valdemar needed mages. Then, Kero just *happened* to back that up, having had to deal with mages herself in her career.

All that could have been mere coincidence. But not the rest. Why was it that within a month, *she* was attacked by an assassin who may have been infiltrated into Haven magically, there was a magic attack on a major Border post—manned by Kero's people, so an accurate report got back, *and* the Council, for some totally unknown reason, seemed to be forced into letting her go look for mages?

And lo, as if in a book, Kero just *happened* to have kept up contact with her old mage, who *happened* to have kept up contact with his old teacher, who *happened* to be Kero's uncle and doubly likely to cooperate. No one had stopped them on this trek, no one had even recognized them as far as Elspeth knew. Everyone was so helpful and friendly it was sickening. Even the mercs seemed to take her stories at face value. There was no sign of Ancar or his meddling. Everything was ticking along quietly, just like it was *supposed* to occur.

They were barely a candlemark away from the turnoff for Lythecare. And the Companions were so smug about something she could taste it.

Gwena was humming again.

And suddenly she decided that she had had enough.

That is it.

She yanked so hard on her reins that Gwena tripped, went to her knees, and scrambled back up again with a mental yelp—and Cymry very nearly ran into her from behind.

She turned to look at Skif; he stared stupidly back at her, as if wondering if she had gone mad.

"That's it," she said. "That is *it*. I am *not* playing this game anymore."

"What?" Now Skif looked at her as if *certain* she had gone mad.

"I am being herded to something, and I don't like it," she snapped, as much for Gwena's ears as his. "I did want to do this, and Valdemar certainly needs mages, but I am *not* going to be guided by an invisible hand, as if I were a character in a badly-written book! This is *not* a foreordained Quest, I am *not* in a Prophecy, and I am *not* playing this game anymore."

With that, she dismounted and stalked off the side of the road to a rough clearing. Like seemingly all wayside clearings in this part of Jkatha, it was a bit of grass, surrounded by fenced fields of grain, with a couple of dusty, tall bushes, and a very small well. She sat down beside the well defiantly and crossed her arms.

Skif dismounted, his expression not the puzzled one she had expected but something she couldn't read. He walked slowly over to her, the Companions following with their reins trailing on the ground.

"Well?" she said, staring up at him.

He shrugged, but the conflicting emotions on his face convinced her that he knew something she didn't.

"I am not moving," she said, firmly, suppressing the urge to cough as road dust went down her throat. "I am not moving, until you tell me what you know about what's going on."

He looked helplessly from side to side; then his Companion whickered, and looked him in the eyes, nodding, as if to say, "You might as well tell her."

I thought so. She glared at Gwena, who flattened her ears. *:You should have told me in the first place.:*

"It—was the Companions," Skif said, faintly. "They, well, they sort of—ganged up on their Heralds, when you first wanted to go looking for mages. The Heralds that didn't want to let you go, like your mother—well, they kind of got bullied."

"They *what?*" she exclaimed, and turned to Gwena,

surprise warring with other emotions she couldn't even name.

:It had to be done,: Gwena replied firmly. *:You had to go. It was important.:*

"That's not all," Skif said, looking particularly hangdog. "For one thing, they absolutely forbid you to be told what they were doing. For another, they're the ones that suggested Quenten in the first place. They said he was the only way to an important mage that they could trust."

"I *knew* it!" she said, fiercely. "I knew it, I *knew* it! I knew they were hock-deep in whatever was going on! I *knew* I was being herded like some stupid sheep!"

She turned to Skif, ignoring the Companions. "Did they say anything about the Shin'a'in?" she demanded. "If I'm going to do this, I am by *damn* going to do it my way."

"Well," he said, slowly, "No. Not that I know of."

:We don't know anything about the Shin'a'in Goddess,: Gwena said, alarm evident in her mind-voice. *:She's not something Valdemar has ever dealt with. We're not sure we trust Her.:*

"You can't manipulate Her, you mean," she replied flatly.

:No. She could be like Iftel's God; She could care only for the welfare of Her own people. That's all. We know some of what She is and does—but it's not something we want to stake the future of Valdemar on.: Gwena's mind-voice rose with anxiety. Elspeth cut her off.

"What do *you* have to say about this?" she asked Skif. "You, I mean. Not the Companions."

"I—uh—" he flushed, and looked horribly uncomfortable. "I—don't know really what the Companions think of it."

He's lying. His Companion is giving him an earful.

"But I—uh, from everything Kero's said, the Shin'a'in probably could give you the teaching, and if *they* couldn't, they would know someone who could." He gulped, and wiped sweat from his forehead with his sleeve. "Kero trusts them—not just her relatives, I mean—and so does *her* Companion, I know that much."

Gwena snorted. *:Of course Sayvil says she trusts them. Contrary old beast, she'd say that just to be contrary.:*

Elspeth ignored the waspish comment. "Fine." She turned to stare into Gwena's blue eyes. "I am going to Kata'shin'a'in, and I am going to see if the Shin'a'in know someone to train me." She turned the stare into a glare. "That *is* where I am going, and you are not going to stop me. I'll *walk* if I have to. I'll buy a plowhorse in the next village. But I am *not* going to Lythecare. And that is my final word on the subject." She raised her chin and stared defiantly at all of them. "Now, are you with me, or do I go on alone?"

Less than a candlemark later, they passed the turnoff to Lythecare, heading straight south, to Kata'shin'a'in.

And Gwena was giving her the most uncomfortable ride of her life, in revenge.

But every bruise was a badge of victory—

And I hope I'll still believe that in the morning when I can't move. . . .

© 91 Larry Dixon

Dawnfire

Chapter Twelve

DARKWIND

This patrol—like all the others lately—had been completely uneventful. *This is almost too easy,* Darkwind thought, making frequent checks of the underbrush beside the path for signs of disturbance. *A week now, that Nyara's been hiding with us, and there's nothing from the other side. Nothing hunting her, except that couple of wyrsa I caught on her trail, no magic probes, nothing.*

The very quietude set all his nerves on edge. *Of course, her shielding is really outstanding. Falconsbane might not know she's here, or even that she headed this way when she ran. He could be hunting for her in another direction altogether.*

That was what Treyvan said; Hydona was of the opinion that Falconsbane knew very well she'd come this way but assumed she was in the Vale. She pointed out that in all the time Falconsbane had been on their border—and everything Nyara said indicated that he had been there for a very long time—he'd never directly challenged k'Sheyna. He was only one Adept, after all, and there were at least five Adepts and ten times that many Masters in k'Sheyna. And even though none of them were operating at full strength, the mages of k'Sheyna could still be more than he cared to meet in conflict. Especially when the conflict was over the relatively minor matter of the loss of a single Changechild.

"He can alwaysss make anotherrr," Hydona had said, callously. "It isss unussual for one like himssself to keep a pet forrr longerrr than a few yearsss."

And oddly enough, Nyara agreed with Hydona's analysis.

"If he was angered at all, his anger would have been for a loss; not for the loss of *me*," she'd said, more than a little piqued at having to admit that she was worth so little to her former master. "As an individual, I mean very little to him. He has threatened many times to create another, to then see how I fared among his lesser servants as their plaything. All that would goad him into action was that he had lost a possession. If something distracted him from that anger, he would have made only a token attempt to find me, more to appease his pride than to get me back."

So it seemed, for other than the pair of *wyrsa*, there had been nothing in the way of activity—not along Darkwind's section, nor Dawnfire's—not, for that matter, anyone else's. Except for Moonmist; *she* ran into a basilisk who'd decided her little patrol area was a good one to nest in. Prying *that* thing out had taken five scouts and three days. They didn't want to kill it if they didn't have to; basilisks were stupid, incredibly dangerous, and ravenous carnivores who would eat anything that couldn't run away from them—but they weren't evil. They had their place in the scheme of things; they dined with equal indifference on their own kills or carrion, and there were few things other than a basilisk that would scavenge the carcasses of cold-drakes or *wyrsa*.

But no one wanted a basilisk for a near neighbor, not even the most ardent animal lover. Not even Earthsong, who had once unsuccessfully tried to breed a vulture for a bondbird.

But that was the only excitement there had been for days, and there was no way that incident could have been related. No one could herd a basilisk. The best you could do was to make things so unpleasant for it that it chose to move elsewhere. No one, in all the history of the Tayledras, had ever been able to even *touch* what passed for one's mind, much less control it. The histories said they were a failed and abandoned experiment, like so many other creatures of the twisted lands; a construction of one of the blood-path mages at the time of the Mage Wars. But perversely, once abandoned, the basilisk continued to persist on its own.

It's just a good thing they only lay two or three fertile eggs in a lifetime, he thought wryly, *or we'd be up to our necks in them.*

A broken swath of vegetation caught his attention, and he looked closer, only to discover the spoor of a running deer and the tracks of its pursuer, an ordinary enough wolf pair. From the small hooves, it was probably a weanling, separated from its mother; it wouldn't have broken down the bushes if it had been an adult.

This is ridiculous, he thought. *I might as well be a forester in the cleansed lands. There hasn't been anything worth talking about out here for the past week.*

That was the way the area around a Vale was *supposed* to look, just before a Clan move to a new spot. No magic-warped creatures like the giant serpent, no mage-made things like the basilisk; just normal animals, relatively normal plant life.

Maybe Father's been right about sitting and waiting for the Hearthstone to settle. . . .

Up ahead, the forest thinned a little, the sunlight actually reaching the ground in thick shafts. These golden lances penetrated the emerald leaf canopy, bringing life to the forest floor, for the undergrowth was thicker here, and there was even thin grass among the wild plum bushes. He looked up at the hot blue eye of the sky as he reached a patch of clearing; framed by tree-branches, Vree soared overhead, calmly. *He* hadn't seen anything either; in fact, he'd been so bored he'd taken a rock-dove and eaten it while waiting for Darkwind to catch up. It had been a long time since he'd been able to hunt and eat while out on scout.

Starblade's answer to the fracture of the Heartstone had been to wait and see what would happen. He'd insisted that the great well of power would drain itself, slowly— Heal itself, in fact—until it was safe to tap into it, drain the last of its energies, construct a Gate, and leave.

Darkwind had disagreed with his father on that, as he had seemingly on everything else. And up until the past week, it certainly hadn't looked as if the Heartstone was following his father's predictions. In fact, if anything, the opposite was true. There had been *more* uncanny creatures; more Misborn attracted, more actually trying to penetrate the borders. And recently, there had been the other developments; the fact that the mages within the Vale had been unable to sense the changes in energy flows outside it, the fact that now most of the scouts' bondbirds refused to enter the Vale itself, the perturbations that Treyvan sensed.

But maybe that was all kind of the last gasp—maybe things have settled down. Maybe Father's right.

But when he considered that possibility, all his instincts revolted.

Yes, but what if I just feel that way because if Father is right, it means that I am wrong? What if I am wrong, what does it matter? Other than if I'm wrong, Father will never let me forget it. . . .

He stopped for a moment, hearing a thudding sound— then realized it was only a hare drumming alarm, hind foot beating against the ground to alert the rest of his warren—probably at the sight of Vree.

Is it just that I can't admit that sometimes he might be right?

On the other hand, there was a feeling deep inside, connected, he now realized, with the mage-senses he seldom used, that Starblade was wrong, dead wrong. A Heartstone that badly damaged could not Heal itself, it could only get worse. And this calm they were experiencing was just a pause before things degenerated to another level.

I guess I'll enjoy it while it lasts, and stay out of the Vale as much as possible.

He sent another inquiring thought at Vree, but the gyre had no more to report than the last time.

It was very tempting to cut everything short and go to see how Nyara was doing. So tempting, that he fought against the impulse stubbornly, determined to see his patrol properly done. It might make up for the other days he had neglected it.

Not really neglected it—there were the dyheli, *and then* Nyara.

His efforts at appeasing his conscience came to nothing. *It still wasn't done. And if I hadn't been very lucky, things could easily have slipped in.*

He no longer worried that these temptations were caused by anything other than his own selfish desire to spend more time with the Changechild. Nyara was good company, in a peculiar way. She was interested in what he had to say and just as interesting to listen to.

At least I can appease my conscience with the fact that I'm learning something about our enemy.

She was also as incredibly attractive as she had been the first time he'd seen her. If he had been a less honorable man, her problematic virtue wouldn't have stood a chance. Which led him to revise his earlier assumptions; to think that she *wasn't* in control of that part of herself. She might even be completely unaware of it.

That would fit the profile of her master.

Mornelithe Falconsbane would not have wanted her in control of anything having to do with sexual attraction; *he* would have wanted to pull the strings there. Which was one reason why Darkwind had continued to resist letting her lure him to her bed. He had no prejudice against her, but he was not sure what would happen, what little traps had been set up in her makeup, that a sexual encounter would trigger.

That would fit Falconsbane's profile, too. Make her a kind of walking, breathing trap that only he could disarm. So anyone meddling with the master's toy would find himself punished by the thing he thought to enjoy.

With a set of claws—and sharp, pointed teeth—like she had, he didn't think he was in any hurry to find out if his speculations were true, either. Darkwind was not *about* to risk laceration or worse in a passionate embrace with her.

He was so lost in his own thoughts that he almost missed the boundary marker, the blaze that marked the end of his patrol range and the beginning of Dawnfire's. He glanced at the sun, piercing through the trees, but near the horizon; it was time for Thundersnow to take over for him. And if he hurried, he *would* have a chance to chat with Nyara before he went to the council meeting.

He was already on the path to the *hertasi* village before the thought was half finished.

* * *

"I think this is the best chance I'm going to have; things have been so quiet, they can't blame disturbances on your presence. So I'm going to tell the Council about you, and put your request to them," he told her as they both soaked up the last of the afternoon's heat on the top of the bluff.

She didn't answer at first; just turned on her back and stretched, lithe and sensuous—and seemed just as innocent of the effect it had on him as a kitten. She wasn't even watching him, she was watching a butterfly a few feet away from them.

That didn't stop his loins from tightening, or keep a surge of pure, unmixed lust from washing over him, making it difficult to think clearly for a moment.

He sought relief in analyzing the effect. *That sexual impact she has can't be under conscious control. She couldn't fake the kind of nonchalance she's got right now.*

"When?" she asked, yawning delicately. "Is it tonight, this meeting?"

He nodded; he'd explained to her the need to wait until a regular meeting so that her appearance would seem a little more routine. She'd agreed—both to his reasons and to the need to wait.

But in fact, his real reasons were just a little different. He'd put off explaining what had happened in its entirety until he wouldn't have to face his father alone. Starblade in the presence of the rest of the Elders was a little easier to deal with than Starblade in the privacy of his own *ekele,* where he could rant and shout and ignore anything Darkwind said—and he tended not to take quite so much of his son's hide in public, where there were witnesses both to his behavior and to what Darkwind told him.

"It is well," Nyara purred, satisfaction brimming in her tone. She blinked sleepily at Darkwind, her eyes heavy-lidded, the pupils the merest slits. "Though I still cannot travel, should they grant me leave. You *will* say that, yes?"

"Don't worry," he replied, "I'm going to make that very clear."

In fact, that was one of the points he figured he had in his favor; Nyara obviously could not move far or fast, and he wanted to have a reason for why he had left her with the *hertasi,* instead of putting her under a different guardian. "More competent," Starblade would undoubt-edly say. "Less sympathetic," was what he would mean.

And if worse came to worst, he wanted to have a rea-son for continuing to leave her here, instead of putting her with a watcher of Starblade's choice.

"You still seem fairly weak to me," he continued, "and Nera's Healer seems to think it's a very good idea for you to stay with us until those cracked bones of yours have a chance to heal a bit more. And that reminds me; have you had any problems with the *hertasi?*"

"Have they complained of me?" she snapped sharply, twisting her head around to cast him a look full of sus-picion.

He was taken a little aback. "Why, no—it's just that I wanted to make certain you were getting along all right. If there was any friction, I could move you—maybe to the ruins where the gryphons are. It's pretty quiet there—"

"No, no!" she interrupted, her voice rising, as if she were alarmed. Then, before he could react, she smiled. "Your pardon, I did not mean that the way it may have sounded. Treyvan and Hydona are wonderful, and I like them a great deal—as I expected to like anything Mor-nelithe hated. I learned early that whatever thwarted him he hated—and that what he hated, I should be prepared to find good."

"He knows about Treyvan and Hydona—"

"No, no, *no,*" she interrupted again, hastily. "I am saying things badly today. No, it is only gryphons in general that he hates. As he hates Birdkin, so I was pre-pared to like you. He never told me why." She shrugged indifferently, and by now Darkwind knew he'd get noth-ing more out of her on the subject. She had all the ability of a ferret to squirm her way out of anything she didn't want to talk about.

But if she likes them, why wouldn't she want to stay near them?

"It is the little ones," she sighed, pensively, as if an-swering his unspoken suspicion. "I am very sorry, for I am going to say something that will revolt you, Birdkin, but I cannot *bear* little ones. No matter the species." She shuddered. "Giggling in voices to pierce the ears, running about like mad things, shrieking enough to startle the dead—I cannot *bear* little ones.'' She looked him squarely in the eyes. ''I have,'' she announced, ''*no* motherly instinct. I do not *want* motherly instinct. I do not want to see little ones for more than a short time, at *long* intervals.''

He laughed at her long face. ''I can see your point,'' he replied. ''They are a handful—''

''And soon there will be two *more*, this time the *very* little ones, who cry and cry all night, and will not be comforted; who become ill for mysterious reasons and make messes at both ends. No,'' she finished, firmly. ''I care much for Treyvan and Hydona, but I will not abide living with the little ones.''

''You've been getting along all right with the *hertasi*, though?'' he asked anxiously. If he had to leave her here for any length of time, it would be a good idea to make sure both parties were willing. Nera had indicated that *he* had seen no trouble with her, but Darkwind wanted to be sure of that. Sometimes the *hertasi* were a little too polite.

''As well as one gets along with one's shadow.'' She shrugged. ''They are quiet, they bring me food and drink, they are polite when I speak to them, but mostly they are not there—to speak to, that is.'' A wry smile touched the corners of her mouth, and the tips of her sharp little canine teeth showed briefly. ''I am well aware that they watch me, but in their place, *I* would watch me, so all is well. I pretend to ignore the watchers, the watchers pretend they are most busy counting grass stems, we both know it is pretense, and politeness is preserved.''

Darkwind laughed; she smiled broadly. *Now I know why Nera called her ''a very polite young creature.''*

''As long as you're doing all right here—'' he glanced at the setting sun. ''I have to get back for that meeting. I expect to have some trouble with it.''

Nyara's smile faded to a wistful ghost. ''I wish I could tell you it would be otherwise, but I doubt it will be so. I only hope you do not come to regret being my champion.''

He sighed, and got to his feet. ''I hope so, too.''

The windows of the *ekele* shook as his father pounded the table with his fist. ''By all the gods of our fathers,''

Starblade stormed, "I *never* thought my own son would be so much of a fool!"

Darkwind stared at a patch of the exposed bark of the parent-tree, just past his father's shoulder, and kept his face completely expressionless. At least it sounded like most of the tirade was over. This was mild compared to the insults Starblade had hurled at him at the beginning of the session.

Then again, it might simply be that Starblade had run out of insults.

Starblade shook his fist in the air, not actually threatening Darkwind but the implication was there. "If I didn't know better, I'd swear I couldn't be your father! I've never—"

"That's enough, Starblade," interrupted old Rainlance tiredly. "That is quite enough."

The quiet words were so unexpected, especially coming from Rainlance, that both Starblade and his son turned to stare in surprise at the oldest of the four Elders. Rainlance never interrupted anyone or raised his voice. Except that he had just done both.

"By now we all know that you think your s—hmm, Darkwind—is the greatest fool ever born. We also know precisely why you think that." Rainlance leveled a penetrating stare at Starblade that froze him where he sat. "The fact is, I've known you a great deal longer than Darkwind, and I think there are times when you allow some of your opinions to unbalance your judgment. This is one of them. It just so happens I've never shared your peculiar prejudice against the Changechildren. I won't go into why, right now, but I have several good reasons, strong ones, to disagree with you on that. And I *also* do not share your view of Darkwind's incompetence." He coughed, and shook his head. "In point of fact, I think Elder Darkwind has done a fine job up until now, a *very* fine job. His peers trust him, he has never let *his* private opinions interfere with his judgment, and I don't see any reason to make a snap decision about this Other of his. I don't see any reason, in fact, why we *shouldn't* continue to help her."

Rainlance looked pointedly at the other Elder, Iceshadow, who shrugged, the crystals braided into his hair tinkling like tiny wind chimes. "She's not a danger where she is,'' Iceshadow said. ''She hasn't caused any trouble—''

''That we know of,'' snapped Starblade.

Iceshadow gave Starblade a look of disapproval, and Darkwind knew he'd scored at least one point. Iceshadow hated to be interrupted. ''Very well. If you insist on that phrasing. That we know of. Frankly, I see no harm in letting her stay where she is until she's healthy, and considering her request for safe passage then.''

Rainlance nodded. Starblade frowned angrily, then pounced. ''Under *strict watch*. Darkwind may be a gullible boy being led by a pair of come-hither eyes and a sweet voice, but I'm not so sure this Other may not be playing a deeper game. I say she stays under *strict* watch, with careful observers.''

''You can't get more careful than *hertasi*,'' Iceshadow remarked to the ceiling of his *ekele*. ''And if she's leading Darkwind around by his urges, that ploy won't work on *hertasi*. Even stubborn, pigheaded old—ah—mages will admit to that.''

It was Iceshadow's turn to receive a glare, but the Elder ignored it, winking broadly at Darkwind when Starblade turned away in disgust.

''I think the *hertasi* will do as watchers,'' Rainlance said smoothly, soothingly, as he sought to heal the split in the Council. ''They are certainly quite competent. But I do agree she should be kept as far from the Vale itself as possible. And if she causes any trouble—''

''If she even *looks* like she's causing any trouble,'' Starblade growled.

Rainlance raised his voice a little, and annoyance crept into it. ''—she'll have to be dealt with.''

''She'll find herself bound and staked, and you can tell her so!'' Starblade shouted.

''*Are* you quite finished?'' Rainlance shouted back, his temper frayed to the snapping point. ''I'd like to get on with this if I may!''

Starblade sank back into his seat with an inarticulate mumble, confining himself to angry glares at anyone who happened to glance at him.

Rainlance closed his eyes for a moment and visibly forced himself to calm down. Darkwind had no sympathy to spare for him; he'd been on the receiving end of his father's tempers too often to feel sorry for anyone else.

"Really, Darkwind," Rainlance continued, opening his eyes, his voice oozing reason and conciliation. "You must see this in the perspective of the Vale and Clan as a whole. We really can't take her into the Vale. We can't take the chance, however slim, that she might be some kind of infiltrator."

"I'm not asking for her to be brought into the Vale," Darkwind replied, echoing Rainlance's tone as much as he was able. "I'm just asking that she be allowed nearer. Right now she's in jeopardy; she's hurt, and she can't run the way the *hertasi* can. I doubt she'd be able to get away if something comes over the border, especially if it's something that's come hunting especially for her. She can't run, she can't hide, and Mage-Gifted or not, she probably can't protect herself from any kind of trained mage."

Iceshadow shook his head regretfully; Darkwind got the feeling that if this hadn't been so serious an issue, he was so annoyed with Starblade right now that he would have been glad to agree with Darkwind just for a chance to spite his father. "No. It's just not possible. And I'm sure she realizes that, even if you don't. After all, look at what she is and what we are—we're enemies. Or at least, she's been on the enemy side. And yet she came to us, supposedly for help. She *admitted* she was going to use us as a kind of stalking horse. No, she stays where she is, and that's the end of it."

"Well," said Starblade, his voice penetrating the silence that followed Iceshadow's speech like a set of sharp talons, his eyes narrowed, and a tight little smile on his lips. "Since you seem so worried about her, since you brought her into our boundaries in the first place—and since she *is* in your territory—I think it's only fair that you be the one to undertake her protection. Even if it means you have to fall back on magery." He looked around at the other Elders. "Isn't that fair?"

"I don't know—" Rainlance began.

"*I'd* say it is," Iceshadow said firmly. "I've never been happy that when Songwind left us, his magic did as well, Darkwind. I understand your feelings, but I've never been happy about it. You could be quite a mage if you'd give it another try.''

Rainlance shrugged. Starblade cast his son a look of triumph. "It seems there's a consensus," he said smugly.

Darkwind managed not to jump up and hit him, scream at the top of his lungs, or do anything else equally stupid and adolescent. In fact, his reaction, so completely under control, seemed to disappoint his father. He thought quickly, and realized that, unwittingly, his father had not only left him an out, he'd given the scout a chance to do something he'd been campaigning for all along. He'd have to phrase this very carefully.

"Very well, Elders," he replied, nodding to each of them in turn. "I am overruled. Nyara may stay, under the eyes of the *hertasi*. I will undertake to keep the Changechild protected—using all the resources at my disposal. Is that your will?"

Rainlance nodded. "That's fine," Iceshadow said. Starblade looked suspicious, but finally gave his consent.

"Done," said Rainlance. "You have the Council's permission, as stated."

"Good," Darkwind said. "Then if that is the consensus, I will have the other scouts keep an eye out for her and stand by for trouble, I will recruit whatever *dyheli* I can find to stand guard, and I have no doubt there will be plenty of volunteers, since she helped save one of their herds—I will ask Dawnfire to look for help among the *tervardi,* and I will see if the gryphons are willing to work some of their protective magics."

He managed *not* to grin at Starblade's expression. For once, he'd managed to outmaneuver his father.

But there was no feeling of triumph as he left the meeting; the fight had been too hard for that. Instead, he was weary and emotionally bruised.

Like someone's been beating me with wild plum branches.

He climbed down out of the *ekele* before anyone else. It would have been a courtesy to wait for the eldest to descend first, but he wasn't feeling particularly courteous right now—and he really didn't want to chance his father ambushing him for a little more emotional abuse. It was dark enough around here that he should be able to escape, provided he did the unexpected. And he was getting rather good at doing that. . . .

So he hurried off into the cover of the thick undergrowth, taking exactly the *wrong* path—one leading to the waterfall at the head of the Vale, instead of the exit. It passed the Heartstone, though not near enough to see the damaged pillar of stone, its cracked and crazed exterior only hinting at the damage echoed across the five planes, and visible to anyone with even a hint of Mage-Sight.

He felt it, though, as he passed; an ache like a bruised bone, a sense of impending illness, a disharmony. If he'd had any doubts about it Healing itself earlier, they were dispelled now. It hadn't Healed itself, it had only gotten worse. Now it left a kind of bitter, lingering aftertaste in the back of his mind; if it had been a berry he'd tasted, he would have labeled it "poisonous" without hesitation.

So he did something he had never thought he would do in his lifetime. He shielded himself against it.

The air immediately seemed cleaner, and the sour sense of sickness left him. There was only the hint of incenselike smoke from the memorial brazier at its foot, the flame that commemorated the lives lost when the Heartstone fractured. Now all he had to contend with was the bad taste the meeting had left in his mouth.

He started to look for a way to double back to the path he wanted to take, when he remembered that there was another hot spring at the foot of the waterfall. It wasn't a big waterfall, but it was a very attractive one; it had been sculpted by Iceshadow himself, back when the Vale had first been constructed, and the cool water of a tiny stream fell into a series of shallow rock basins to end in the hot pool of the spring below. Each of the basins had been tuned, although Darkwind had no idea how something like that was done. The music of the falls was incredibly soothing.

Just what I need right now.

That decided him; instead of retracing his steps, he took the path all the way to the end. And as if to confirm that he had made the right decision, as he entered the clearing containing the pool, the moon rose above the tree level, touching the waterfall, and turning it into a shower of flowing silver and diamond droplets. *If you didn't know better, you'd swear there was nothing wrong here in the Vale, it's that peaceful.*

And no one, absolutely no one, was there.

Of course, that might have been because this particular pool had once been a popular trysting spot, and there was not a great deal of romance going on in the Vale anymore. Most of the young Tayledras were scouts, and they seldom came this far in now. As for the rest—Darkwind suspected the mages were suffering, perhaps without realizing it, from the same, sickened feeling the Heartstone induced in him. That was not the sort of sensation likely to make anyone think of lovemaking. . . .

He wondered how many of them had thought to cut themselves off from the Stone. *Not many,* he decided, shedding his clothes and leaving them in a heap beside the pool. *It's their power, their lifeblood. They'd rather feel ill than lose their connection to it. They wouldn't be able to draw on it if they shielded themselves against it.*

Idiots.

Then he left all thought of them behind, as he plunged in a long, flat dive into the hot water of the pool.

He came to the surface, and floated on his back, letting it soothe the aches in his muscles as it forced him into a state of relaxation. Only then did he realize how tightly he had been holding himself, and how many of those aches were due to tension.

He drifted for a while, losing himself deliberately in the sound of the falling water, the changing patterns of the sparkling droplets, the silence.

"Turning merman?" said a shadow at the entrance.

He swam lazily to the edge, rested his arms on the sculpted rim, and looked up into Dawnfire's amused eyes. She looked down on him, a faint smile playing on her lips, her hair loose, her boots in her hand. "Not that I'm aware of," he said lightly. "Unless you saw something I didn't know about."

"Probably not." She knelt down beside him, put her boots down beside her, then unexpectedly seized his head in both her hands, leaned down to water-level, and presented him with the most enthusiastic—and expert—kiss he'd ever had from her. His mouth opened under her questing tongue, and he clutched the rim with both hands, convulsively.

What—she never *gets aggressive*— He became aware that not all the heat coursing through his veins was due to the temperature of the water. He closed his eyes, went passive, and let her lips and tongue play with his, until he was breathless. Her hair fell around him, enveloping him in her own silken waterfall.

She released him, and he nearly slid under.

"*That* was for going back and saving my *dyheli*," she said, sitting back on her heels, balancing there as if she had no weight at all.

"I didn't—exactly—" He regretted having to confess that he had very little to do with it, if *that* was what she had in mind for a reward.

She dismissed everything he was going to say with a wave of her hand. "I know, there's that Changechild involved in it, and it did the magic—but *you* stayed with them, and *you* Mindcalled them. They'd never have found their way out without that."

"*It*" did the magic. She doesn't know Nyara is female. . . .* His attention was captured and held, as she began removing her clothing in the most provocative way, slowly, teasingly. He found himself watching her with parted lips. First the tunic—lacings loosened, then pulling the garment slowly over her head. Then the breeches, inching them down over her hips, sliding them a little at a time down her long, lithe legs—all the while maneuvering so that the shirt covered all the strategically important parts of her. Then the shirt followed the tunic at the same tantalizingly slow speed.

At that moment she seemed just as exotic as Nyara, and just as desirable.

Nyara— If she doesn't know Nyara's a female, there's no harm in not telling her—

She was down to a short chemise now, and she winked, once, then vanished into the shadows, reappearing before he had time to think why she had left.

"I put the 'in use' marker at the entrance," she said. "Not that there's anyone likely to be here tonight. I knew you were at the meeting, and I waited to catch you to thank you properly. But you didn't go the way I thought you would. I had to chase you, loverhawk."

She stood in an unconscious pose at the rim, moonlight softening the hard muscles, and turning her into something as soft and quicksilver as a Changechild.

"I wanted to avoid Father," he said, filling his eyes with her.

"I thought so," she said, and laughed. "I figured, knowing you, that as long as you were here you'd probably decide to soak him out of your thoughts. I've been checking every pool between here and Rainlance's *ekele*."

"I'm glad you found me," he said softly.

She sat on the rim, slid out of the chemise, and into his arms. "So am I," she whispered, and buried her hands in his damp hair, her lips and tongue devouring him, teasing him, doing things no woman had ever done to him before.

His hands slid down her back, to cup her buttocks and hold her against him. She strained into the embrace, as if she wanted to reach past his skin, to merge with him. Her kiss took on a fiercer quality, and she worked her mouth around to his neck, biting him softly just beneath his ear, while he ran his hands over every inch of her, re-exploring what had become new again, and making her shiver despite the heat of the pool. He gasped as she nuzzled the soft skin behind his ear, then worked her way back to the hollow of his throat, and gasped again when she untangled her fingers from his hair, and slid them down *his* chest, slowly—teasingly.

"Not in here—" he managed to whisper, as he grew a little light-headed from the combined heat of the water and his blood.

She laughed, low and throatily. "All right." She began to back up, one tiny step at a time, rewarding him for following her with her clever fingers, which were now hard at work well below the waterline and threatening to make his knees go to jelly at any moment.

They reached the edge of the pool, right beside the waterfall, where some kind soul had left a pile of waterproof cushions and mats. She turned away from him to hoist herself up on the rim.

He caught her by the waist, lifted her up, and held her there, nibbling his way up the inside of her thighs until it was her turn to gasp. She buried her hands in his wet hair and her fingers flexed in time with her breathing.

Then she clutched two fistfuls of hair, pulled him away, and swore at him, half laughing. "Get up here, you oaf!" she hissed, "Or I'll get back in the water and do the same to you! You *just* might drown!"

"We can't have that," he chuckled, and joined her; tumbling her into the cushions, nibbling and touching, making her squeal with laughter and surprise.

He only had the upper hand for a moment. Then she somehow squirmed out from beneath him, and pulled a wrestler's trick on him. Then she had him on *his* back, bestriding him, a wicked smile on her face as she lowered herself down, a teasing hair's breadth at a time.

He arched to meet her, his hands full of her breasts, catching her unawares. She cried out and arched her back, driving herself down onto him.

Their minds met as their bodies met, and the shared pleasures enhanced their own, as she felt his passion and he experienced every touch of his fingers on her flesh.

She roused him almost to the climax, again and again, building the passion higher and higher, until he thought he would not be able to bear another heartbeat—

Then she loosed the jesses, and they soared together.

"Dear—gods," he whispered, as they lay together in a trembling symmetry of arms and legs.

She giggled. "The reward of virtue."

"I think I shall strive to be virtuous," he mumbled, then exhaustion took him down into sleep before he could hear her reply. If she even made one. Verbally.

When he woke, she had moved away from him to lie in a careless sprawl an arm's length away. He'd expected as much; he'd learned over the past few months that she was a restless sleeper—after more than once finding himself crowded onto a tiny sliver of sleeping pad. The moon was just retreating behind the rock of the waterfall. He slipped into the pool for a moment, to rinse himself off after his exertions, warm up his muscles, and to cross to the other side without rustling the undergrowth. *That* would surely wake her, as the sound of someone swimming would not.

On the other side of the pool, he used his shirt to dry

himself and pulled on the rest of his clothing. He hated
to leave her like that.

*But she is as curious as two cats, and I am not certain
I want to answer all the questions she is likely to have
when she wakes.*

She *would* ask about the rescue, and she would also
want to know about the Changechild. And when she
found out that Nyara was female—

I am not ready to fend off fits of jealousy, he thought,
wearily. *Father's accusations are bad enough. Hers would
be worse. And there is no reason for them.*

Yet. Not that he hadn't entertained a fantasy or two.

But they are only fantasies and will remain so, he told
his conscience firmly. *Still, they are things I would rather
she did not know about. She is not old enough to accept
them calmly, for the simple daydreams that they are.
However satisfying. Or accept that sometimes the fantasy
can be as fulfilling as the reality.*

He moved quickly and quietly along the paths of the
Vale, pausing now and then to take his bearings. Once
outside, he went on alert. Although this *was* where the
scouts had their *ekeles,* they did not equip them with
retractable ladders for nothing.

But the night lay over the forest as quietly as a blanket
on a sleeping babe. Only twice did he pause at an unusual sight or sound. The first time, it was a pair of
bondbirds, huge, snow-winged owls, chasing each other
playfully. He recognized them as K'Tathi and Corwith,
and relaxed a little. If they were up, it meant the trail
was under watch. The second time he stopped was to
hail his older half brother, Wintermoon, the bondmate
of those owls, who knelt beside the trail, dressing out a
young buck deer.

Wintermoon, one of two children of Starblade's con-
tracted liaison with a mage of k'Treva, had none of either
parent's Mage-Talents, and only enough of Mind-magic
to enable him to speak with his bondbird. The other child,
a girl, had apparently inherited it all, but *she* was with
k'Treva and out of Starblade's reach. The Adept had never
forgiven his eldest son for his lack of magery, and Wintermoon had responded by putting as much distance between himself and his father as Clan and Vale would
permit. He had no wish to leave k'Sheyna; he had an

amazing number of friends and lovers for so taciturn and elusive an individual—it was simply that he also had no wish to deal with a father who had nothing but scorn for him.

"Good hunting," Darkwind said with admiration, eyeing the size of the buck's rack. "Wish I could do that well in the daylight!" He had no fear that Wintermoon had taken anything other than a bachelor; his brother was too wise in the stewardship of the forest to make a stupid mistake in his choice of prey.

Wintermoon laughed; part of his attempt to put distance between himself and Starblade had been to bond exclusively to owls. He had become completely nocturnal, and was one of the night-hunters and night-scouts, and encountered his father perhaps twice in a moon, if that often. "It becomes easier as time goes on. And K'Tathi there lends me his eyes; that's most of it."

"How does—" Darkwind began, puzzled.

Wintermoon followed the thought with quicksilver logic. "He perches above my head. I simply have to adjust my aim to match. Practice enough against trees, and it's not so bad. So, little brother, do you want any of this?"

Darkwind shook his head. "No, I'm fine for the next few days. Dawnfire could use some, though. She was telling me her larder was a little bare."

That should make up for my leaving her like that.

"I'll see she gets it. All's clear the way back to your place. Fair skies—"

That was a clear dismissal—and really, about as social as Wintermoon ever got outside of the walls of his *ekele*. "Wind to thy wings," Darkwind responded, and continued up the trail. He didn't entirely release his hold on caution, but he did relax it a little. Wintermoon was completely reliable; if he said it was clear, he didn't mean just the trail, he meant for furlongs on either side.

Once at his *ekele*, he woke Vree up to let down the ladder-strap for him. There was still enough moon for the gyre to see, though he complained every heartbeat, and went back to sleep immediately, without waiting for Darkwind to climb up.

Even though he was relaxed and utterly weary, he couldn't help thinking about Nyara, as he drifted off to sleep. He found himself thinking of her suspiciously, the way his father would.

Or Wintermoon, for that matter. He's more like Father than he knows. Or will admit.

He wished he'd been able to persuade the Elders to allow her closer. And not just for her protection. No, it would have been much easier to keep a watchful eye on her, if she'd been, say, in one of the dead scouts' abandoned *ekeles*.

Of course, Starblade would have opposed that out of its sheer symbolism.

Still, she was within reach. The *hertasi* were clever and conscientious. There were the gryphons, three or four *tervardi*, several *dyheli* herds, and Dawnfire between here and the Vale, and her only other escape routes lay across the border, into the Outlands.

I can't see her going back that way, he yawned, finally giving in to sleep. *She was running away. Why in the name of the gods would she ever run back?*

©91 Larry Dixon

Nyara

Chapter Thirteen

INTERLUDE

Nyara huddled before her father, abject terror warring with another emotion entirely.

Pure, wanton desire.

She hated it, that need, that fire that drove her to want him—and even as she hated him, she hated herself for feeling it.

Even though she could not control that need, even though she knew it was built into her; as he had sculpted her flesh to suit him, he had also sculpted her mind and her deepest instincts.

It didn't matter; none of it mattered. Half the time she suspected he had inserted that same self-hatred into her, purely for amusement.

And when he had called her this night, she had obeyed the call. *That* was built into her, too, for all that she had run away from him, for all that she had deluded herself, telling herself that she could, would resist him. She could not, and had not, and now she groveled here at his feet, longing for his touch, hating and fearing it. Despising herself for thinking that she could escape him so easily.

It had been no trouble to deceive the little *hertasi* who guarded her; they were not creatures of the night, and a simple illusion of her slumbering form in the darkness of the little cave they had given her was enough to satisfy them.

She had not lied. Until tonight, she *had* thought she could escape his reach. She had not purposefully misled the *hertasi* Healer, either—her weakness and pain were not feigned, nor were her injuries. But what the Healer did not know, was the extent to which she could ignore pain and fight past weakness when she had to.

That was how she had found the strength to counter her father's magic and free the *dyheli* herd. That was how he had forced her to come to him when he called, overriding the pain with his own commands.

And, as usual, he said nothing at first; merely smiled and waited until she had abased herself sufficiently to drive home how helpless she was, how much of her life lay within his power.

If she resembled a cat, Mornelithe Falconsbane *was* a feline; one that stood upon two legs, and walked, and talked, but there his connection with humanity ended. Long silky hair poured uncut down his back, the color a tawny gold that he maintained magically, else he would have been as bleached-silver as any Tayledras Adept. Long, silky hair grew on most of his face, carefully groomed and tended by a made-servant whose only role was to brush her master whenever he called. His slit-pupiled eyes were a golden-green, like watery beryls; his canines sharper and more pronounced than hers. His pointed ears were tufted at the tips, and the silky hair continued down his spine in a luxurious crest, ending at the clefts of the buttocks. For the rest, he was as perfectly formed and conditioned as a human could be, with a body any sculptor would have wept to see.

As Nyara knew, intimately.

Since he had emerged from his stronghold to call her to the border of k'Sheyna and the beginnings of his domain, he had chosen to dress for the occasion in soft, buckskin leather that perfectly matched his hair. Darkwind's disparaging comments to the contrary, Mornelithe seldom wore elaborate costumes; in fact, within his own quarters, he went nude as often as not.

Which Nyara *also* knew, intimately.

She knelt before him until her legs ached from the stones and bits of branch beneath them—which he would not permit her to clear away. He lounged on a blanket of fur spread over a fallen tree trunk by a servant, making him an impromptu throne. The golden mage-light above his head glistened on his hair, the tips of the fur, and on the bat-wings of his two giant guardian-beasts, half wolf, half something she could not even name, creatures whose heads loomed even with his when he stood.

Some of her scars had come from the teeth of those beasts, lessonings in her proper place in the scheme of things, and the proper demeanor to display. Thus she had learned not to move until told, or speak until spoken to.

"Well," he said at last, his voice deep, calm, smooth and soothing. There was a wealth of warm amusement in his voice, which meant he was pleased. She soon discovered why.

"You took my invitation to flee to the Birdfools as if you had thought of it yourself, dear daughter," he chuckled. "I am proud of you."

She burned with humiliation. So it had all been *his* idea, from the inattentive guards, to the captive *dyheli* herd. Without a doubt, he had planned everything, knowing how she would react to anything he presented in her path. She should have known. . . .

"You followed my plan to the letter, my child," he said with approval. "I am very pleased with you. I assume that they invoked a Truth-Spell upon you?"

"Of a kind," she whispered, shivering with shamed pleasure as his approval warmed and excited her. "The Birdkin do not trust me, yet. They keep me in a dwelling of sorts at the border, with *hertasi* and one Birdkin scout to watch."

"One scout only?" Mornelithe threw back his head and laughed, and the guardian-beasts hung out their tongues in frightening parodies of a canine grin. "They trust you more than you think, little daughter, if they set only one to watch you. Are there no other watchers on you?"

She could not help herself; she was compelled to answer truthfully. But she *could* make him force it out of her a word at a time, and perhaps he would grow tired before he learned all the truth. Let him think it was fear that tied her tongue. "Two," she whispered.

"*Hertasi?*"

She shook her head. He frowned, and she trembled. *"Tervardi,* then?"

She shook her head again, hope growing thin that he would lose interest.

"Surely not *dyheli?* No?" His frown deepened, and she lost any hope of hiding her friends' identities. "What are they? Speak!"

He reached out a tendril of power to curl about her. A hand of pain tightened around her mind, though not so much that she could not speak. Her body convulsed. "Gryphons," she whimpered, through tears of agony and anger. "Gryphons."

The pain ceased, and she slumped over her knees, head hanging, hands clasped together tightly. She fought to control her tears, so that he would not know how she had come to like the pair, and so have yet another weapon to hold over her.

"Gryphons." His voice deepened, and the guardian-beasts growled. "Gryphons, *here.* This requires—thought. I will have more of these gryphons out of you, my child. But later."

She looked up, cheeks still wet with tears. He was looking past her, into the dark forest, his mind elsewhere than on her. Then he took visible hold of himself, and gazed down on her, smiling when he saw her tears. He leaned down, and lifted a single drop on a long, talon-tipped finger, and licked it off, slowly, with sensuous enjoyment, his eyes narrowed as he watched her closely.

She shook with a desire she could not control, and that only he could command. He smiled with satisfaction.

"This Birdfool," he said, leaning back into his fur. "His name."

"Darkwind," she told him.

His eyes lit up from within, and again he laughed, long and heartily, and this time the beasts laughed with him in gravelly growls. "Darkwind! The son of my *dear* friend Starblade! What a delicious irony. Has Starblade seen you, my dearest?"

She shook her head, baffled by his words.

"What a pity; he'd have been certain to recognize you, as you would recognize him if you saw him." He laughed again, and she dared a question.

"I have seen him, this Starblade?"

"Of course you have, my precious pet. He was my guest here for many days." Mornelithe's smile deepened, and he licked his lips. "Many, many days. You dined upon his pet bird, do you not recall? And I gave him the crow to replace it, once he learned his place beneath me."

Nyara's eyes widened, as she remembered the Tayledras Mornelithe had captured and broken; how she had been so jealous of the new captive, who had taken *her* place, however briefly, in Mornelithe's attentions. How she had so amused Mornelithe with her jealousy that he had chained her in the corner of his bedroom, like a pet dog, so that she was forced to watch him break the new captive to his will.

And he, the former captive, without a doubt would remember her.

"My little love, if you can contrive a way for Starblade to see you, I should very much be pleased," Mornelithe said caressingly. "It would enlarge my vengeance so well, to know that *he* knew that I had an agent in place on his ground, subverting his beloved son. It would be delicious to know how his mind must burn, and yet he could do and say nothing about it."

"I do not think I can manage that," she told him timidly. "He never leaves the Vale, and I may not go within it."

"Ah, well," Mornelithe said, waving the idea aside. "If you can, it would be well. But if not, I am not going to contrive it at the moment."

His expression grew abstracted for a moment.

She ventured another question. "Is there something that I should know, my lord?"

He looked down at her, and smiled, shaking his head. "It is no matter. There are other matters requiring my attention just now, a bit weightier than this. My vengeance has waited long, and it can wait a little longer."

She sighed with relief, thinking that he was finished with her, that he had forgotten about Treyvan and Hydona—

Only to have her hopes crushed.

"The gryphons," he said, suddenly looking down at her again, and piercing her with his eyes. "Tell me about the gryphons. *Everything.*"

Compelled by his will, she found herself reciting all that she knew about them, in a lifeless, expressionless voice. Their names, the names of their two fledglings; what they looked like, where they nested. *Why* they had chosen to nest there.

And that there was going to be another mating flight shortly.

He sat straight up at that—and she huddled in on herself, shivering, her teeth chattering, free from his compulsion and sick inside with her own treachery.

She looked up at him, from under her lashes. His eyes were blank, his thoughts turned entirely within. Even his guardian-beasts were quiet, holding their breath, not wanting to chance disturbing him.

Then—he stared down at her, and pointed his finger at her, demandingly, the talon fully extended. "More!" he barked, his words and will lashing her like barbed whips. "Tell me more!"

But she had nothing more to tell him, and so he punished her, lashing her with his mind, inflicting pain that would leave no outward signs, nor anything that a Healer could read, but whose effects would linger for days.

And the more he hurt her, the more she yearned for him, burned for him, until the pain and desire mingled and became one obscene whole. She groveled and wept, and did not know whether she wept because of her shame or because of her need.

Finally he released her, and she lay where he left her, panting and spent, but still afire with longing for him.

"Enough," he said, mildly, softly. "You will learn more. I will call you again, when my other business has been attended to, and you will tell me what you have learned. You will try to ensnare Darkwind, if you can, but you *will* learn more of the gryphons."

"Yes," she whispered.

"You will return here to me when I call you."

"Yes," she sobbed.

"You will remember that my reach is long. I can punish you even in the heart of the k'Sheyna Vale if I choose. Starblade has put *my* stamp on their Heartstone, and I can reach within at my will." His eyes glittered, and he licked his lips, slowly, deliberately.

"Yes."

"Do not think to truly escape me. I created you, flesh of my flesh, my dearest daughter, and I can destroy you as easily as I created you." He reached down and ran a talon along her chin, lifting her eyes to meet his, and in spite of herself, she thrilled to his touch.

She said nothing; she only looked helplessly into his eyes, his glittering, cold, cruel eyes.

"Should you try to hide, should you reach k'Sheyna Vale I will call you even from there. And when you come to me, you will find that what you have enjoyed at my hands will be paradise, compared to what I deal you then." He held her in the ice of his gaze. "You do understand, don't you, my dear daughter?"

She wept, silent tears running down her cheeks, and making the mage-light above his head waver and dance—but she answered him. Oh, yes, she answered him.

"Yes, Father."

"And what else?" he asked, as he always asked. "What does my daughter have to tell her doting father?"

And she answered, as she always answered.

"I l-l-l-love you, Father. I love you, Father. I love and serve only you." And her tears poured down her cheeks as she repeated it until he was satisfied.

Chapter Fourteen

ELSPETH

Kata'shin'a'in was a city of tents.

At least that was the way it looked to Elspeth as she and Skif approached it. They had watched it grow in the distance, and she had wondered at first what it was that was so very odd about it; it looked *wrong* somehow, as if something about it was so wildly different from any other city she had ever seen, that her mind would not accept it.

Then she realized what it was that bothered her; the colors. The city was nothing but a mass of tiny, brightly-colored dots. She could not imagine what could be causing that effect—was every roof in the city painted a different color? And why would anyone do something as odd as that? Why *paint* roofs at all? What was the point?

As they neared, the dots resolved themselves into flat conical shapes—which again seemed very strange. Brightly colored, conical roofs? What kind of odd building would have a conical roof?

Then she realized: they weren't buildings at all, those were *tents* she was looking at. Hundreds, perhaps thousands, of tents.

Now she understood why Quenten had said that Kata'shin'a'in "dried up and blew away" in the winter.

Somewhere amidst all that colored canvas there must be a core city, with solid buildings, and presumably inns and caravansaries. But most of the city was made up of the tents of merchants, and when trading season was over, the merchants departed, leaving behind nothing at all.

She glanced over at Skif, who was eyeing the city with a frown.

"What's the matter?" she asked.

"Just how are we ever going to find the Tale'sedrin in there?" he grumbled. "Look at that! There's no kind of organization at all—"

"That *we* can see," she interrupted. "Believe me, there's organization in there, and once we find an inn, we'll find someone to explain it to us. If there *wasn't* any way of organizing things, no one would ever get any business done, they'd be spending all their time running around trying to find each other. And when in your entire life have you ever known a successful disorganized trader?"

His frown faded. "You have a point," he admitted.

:*I don't like this,*: complained Gwena.

:*I am perfectly well aware that you don't like this,*: Elspeth replied crisply.

:*I think this is a mistake. A major mistake. It's still not too late to turn back.*:

Elspeth did not reply, prompting Gwena to continue. :*If you turned around now, we could be in Lythecare in—*:

Elspeth's patience finally snapped, and so did the temper she had been holding carefully in check. :*Dammit, I told you I* won't *be herded into doing something, like I was the gods' own sheep! I don't believe in Fate or Destiny, and I'm not going to let you lot move me around your own private chessboard! I* will *do this my way, or I won't do it at all, and you and everyone else can just find yourself another Questing Hero! Do you understand me?*:

Her only answer was a deep, throaty chuckle, and that was absolutely the final insult. She was perfectly ready to jump out of the saddle and *walk* to Kata'shin'a'in at that point.

:*And. Don't. Laugh. At. Me!*: she snarled, biting off each mental word and framing them as single words, instead of an entire thought, so that her anger and her meaning couldn't possibly be misunderstood.

Absolute mental silence; then Gwena replied—timidly, as Elspeth had *never* heard her speak in her life with her Companion, *:But I wasn't laughing.:*

Her temper cooled immediately. She blinked.

It hadn't really *sounded* like Gwena. And she'd never known a Companion to lie. So if it wasn't Gwena—

:Who was it?: she asked. *:If it wasn't you, who was it?:*

:I—: Gwena replied hesitatingly, lagging back a little as Skif rode on ahead, blithely oblivious to what was going on behind him. *:I—don't know.:*

A chill crept down Elspeth's spine; she and Gwena immediately snapped up their defensive shields, and from behind their protection, she Searched all around her for someone who could have been eavesdropping on them. It *wasn't* Skif; that much she knew for certain. The mind-voice had a feminine quality to it that could not have been counterfeited. And it wasn't Cymry, Skif's Companion; other Companions had only spoken to her *once*, the night of Talia's rescue. She could not believe that if any of them did so again that it would be for something so petty as to laugh at her. *That* was as unlikely as a Companion lying.

And besides, if it *had* been Cymry, Gwena would have recognized her Mind-voice and said something.

Kata'shin'a'in stood on relatively treeless ground, in the midst of rolling plains. While there were others within Mindhearing distance—there were caravans both in front of and behind them—there was no one near. Certainly not near enough to have provoked the feeling of intimacy that chuckle had.

In fact, it was incredibly quiet, except for the little buzz of ordinary folk's thoughts, like the drone of insects in a field.

The chill spread from her spine to the pit of her stomach, and she involuntarily clutched her hand on the hilt of her sword.

:You—: said a slow, sleepy mind-voice gravelly and dusty with disuse as she and Gwena froze in their places. *:Child. You are . . . very like . . . my little student Yllyana. Long ago . . . so very, very long ago.:*

And as the last word died in her mind, Elspeth gulped; her mind churned with a chaotic mix of disbelief, astonishment, awe, and a little fear.

It had been the *sword* that had spoken.

Skif looked back over his shoulder. "Hey!" he shouted, "Aren't you coming? You're the one who wanted to go here in the first place."

But something about their pose or their expressions caught his attention, and Cymry trotted back toward them. As he neared them, his eyebrows rose in alarm.

"What's wrong?" he asked urgently. Then, when Elspeth didn't immediately reply, he brought Cymry in knee-to-knee with her and reaching out, took her shoulders to shake her. "Come on, snap out of it! What's wrong? Elspeth!"

She shook her head, and pushed him away. "Gods," she gulped, her thoughts coming slowly, as if she was thinking through mud. "Dear gods. Skif—the sword—"

"Kero's sword?" he said, looking into her eyes as if he expected to find signs that she had been Mindblasted. "What about it?"

"It talked to me. Us, I mean. Gwena heard it, too."

He stopped peering at her and simply *looked* at her, mouth agape. "No," he managed.

"Yes. Gwena heard it, too."

Her Companion snorted and nodded so hard her hackamore jangled.

"A sword?" He laughed, but it was nervous, very nervous. "Swords don't talk—except in tales—"

:But . . . I am a sword . . . from a tale. Boy.: The mind-voice still had the quality of humor, a rich, but dry and mordant sense of humor. *:And horses don't talk . . . except in tales, either.:*

Skif sat in his saddle like a bag of potatoes, his mouth still gaping, his eyes big and round. If Elspeth hadn't felt the same way, she'd have laughed at his expression. He looked as if someone had hit him in the back of the head with a board.

His mouth worked furiously without anything coming out of it. Finally, "It talks!" he yelped.

:Of course I talk.: It was getting better at Mindspeech by the moment, presumably improving with practice. *:I'm as human as you are. Or I was. Once:*

"You were?" Elspeth whispered. "When? How did you end up like *that?* And why—"

:*A long story,*: the sword replied. :*And one that can wait a little longer. Get your priorities, child. Get in there, get shelter. Get a place to sit for a while. Then we'll talk, and not before.*:

And not one more word could any of them get from it, although the Companions coaxed and cajoled along with the two Heralds. And so, with all of them wondering if they'd gone quite, quite mad, they entered the trade-city of Kata'shin'a'in.

The inn was an old one; deep paths had been worn into the stone floors and the courtyard paving, and the walls had been coated so many times with whitewash that it was no longer possible to tell whether they had been plaster, brick or stone. The innkeeper was a weary, incurious little old man, who looked old enough to have been the same age as his inn. The stone floors and the bathhouse indicated that the place had once catered to prosperous merchants, but that was no longer the case. Now it played host to a variety of mercenaries, and the more modest traders, who would form caravans together, or take their chances with themselves, their own steel, and a couple of pack animals.

Their room was of a piece with the inn; worn floor, faded hangings at the window, simple pallet on a wooden frame for a bed, a table—and no other amenities. The room itself gave ample evidence by its narrowness of having been partitioned off of a much larger chamber.

At least it was clean.

Elspeth took Need from her sheath, laid the sword reverently on the bed, and sat down beside it—carefully—at the foot. Skif took a similar seat at the head. The Companions, though currently ensconced in the inn's stable, were present in the back of their minds.

So now is the time to find out if I'm having a crazy-weed nightmare.

"All right," she said, feeling a little foolish to be addressing an apparently inanimate object, "We've gotten a room at the inn. The door's locked. Are you still in there?"

:Of course I'm in here,: replied the sword acerbically. Both she and Skif jumped. *:Where else would I be?:*

Elspeth recovered first, and produced a wary smile. "A good question, I guess. Well, are you going to talk to us?"

:I'm talking, aren't I? What do you want to know?:

Her mind was a blank, and she cast an imploring look at Skif. "What your name is, for one," Skif said. "I mean, we can't keep calling you 'sword.' And 'Hey, you' seems kind of disrespectful."

:My holiest stars, a respectful young man!: the sword chuckled, though there was a sense of slight annoyance that it had been the male of the two who addressed her. *:What a wonder! Perhaps I have lived to see the End of All Things!:*

"I don't think so," Skif replied hesitantly. "But you still haven't told us your name."

:Trust a man to want that. It's—: There was a long pause, during which they looked at each other and wondered if something was wrong. *:Do you know, I've forgotten it? How odd. How very odd. I didn't think that would happen.:* Another pause, this time a patently embarrassed one. *:Well, if that doesn't sound like senility, forgetting your own name! I suppose you'd just better keep calling me 'Need.' It's been my name longer than the one I was born with anyway.:*

Skif looked at Elspeth, who shrugged. "All right—uh—Need. If that doesn't bother you."

:When you get to be my age, very little bothers you.: Another dry mental chuckle. *:When you're practically indestructible, even less bothers you. There are advantages to being incarnated in a sword.:*

Elspeth saw the opportunity, and pounced on it. "How *did* you get in there, anyway? You said you used to be human."

:It's easier to show you than tell you,: the blade replied. *:That's why I wanted you locked away from trouble, and sitting down.:*

Abruptly, they were no longer in a shabby old room in an inn that was long past being first quality. They were somewhere else entirely.

* * *

A forge; Elspeth knew enough to recognize one for what it was. Brick-walled, dirt-floored. She seemed to be inside someone else's head, a passive passenger, unable to do more than observe.

She rubbed the sword with an oiled piece of goatskin, and slid it into the wood-and-leather sheath with a feeling of pleasure. Then she laid it with the other eleven blades in the leather pack. Three swords for each season, each with the appropriate spells beaten and forged into them.

A good year's work, and one that would bring profit to the Sisterhood. Tomorrow she would take them to the Autumn Harvest Fair and return with beasts and provisions.

Her swords always brought high prices at the Fair, though not as high as they would be sold for elsewhere. Merchants would buy them and carry them to select purchasers, in duchys and baronies and provinces that had nothing like the Sisterhood of Spell and Sword. But before they were sold again, they would be ornamented by jewelers, with fine scabbards fitted to them and belts and baldrics tooled of the rarest leathers.

She found this amusing. What brought the high price was what she had created; swords that would not rust, would not break, would not lose their edges. Swords with the set-spell for each season; for Spring, the spell of Calm, for Summer, the spell of Warding, for Fall, the spell of Healing, and for Winter, the spell that attracted Luck. Valuable spells, all of them. Daughter to a fighter, and once a fighter herself, though she was now a mage-smith, she knew the value of being able to keep a cool head under the worst of circumstances. Spring swords generally went to young fighters, given to them by their parents. The value of the spell of Warding went without saying; to be able to withstand even some magic was invaluable to—say—a bodyguard. With one of her Summer swords, no guard would ever be caught by a spell of deception or of sleep. Wealthy mercenaries generally bought her Fall swords—or the noble-born, who did not always trust their Healers. And the younger sons of the noble-born invariably chose Winter blades, trusting to Luck to extract them from anything. The ornamentation meant nothing; anyone could buy a worthless Court-

sword with a mild-steel blade that bore more ornament than one of hers. But her contact had assured her, over and over again, that no one would believe her blades held power unless they held a trollop's dower in jewels on their hilts. It seemed fairly silly to her; but then, so did the fact that most mages wore outfits that would make a cat laugh. Her forge-leathers were good enough for her, and a nice, divided wool skirt and linen shirt when she wasn't in the forge.

Once every four years, she made eleven swords instead of twelve, and forged all four of the spells into a single blade. Those she never sold; keeping them until one of the Sisterhood attracted her eye, proved herself as not only a superb fighter, but an intelligent and moral fighter. Those received the year-swords, given in secret, before they departed into the world to earn a living. Never did she tell them what they had received. She simply permitted them to think that it was one of her remarkable, nearly unbreakable, nonrusting blades, with a simple Healing charm built in.

After all, why allow them to depend on the sword?

If any of them ever guessed, she had yet to hear about it.

There was one of those blades waiting beneath the floor of the forge now. She had yet to find someone worthy of it. She would not make another until this one found a home.

:That's what I was,: whispered the sword in the back of Elspeth's mind.

The scene changed abruptly. A huge building complex, built entirely of wood, looking much like Quenten's mage-school. There were only two differences that Elspeth noticed; no town, and no stockade around the complex. Only a forest, on all four sides, with trees towering all about the cleared area containing the buildings. Those buildings looked very old—and there was another difference that she suddenly noticed. Flat roofs: they all had flat roofs and square doorways, with a square-knot pattern of some kind carved above them.

She was tired; she tired often now, in her old age. A lifetime at the forge had not prevented joints from swelling or bones from beginning to ache—nor could the Healers do much to reverse her condition, not while she continued to work. So she tottered out for a rest, now and then, compromising a little. She didn't work as much anymore, and the Healers did their best. While she rested, she watched the youngsters at their practice with a critical eye.

There wasn't a single one she would have been willing to give a sword to. Not one.

In fact, the only girl she felt worthy of the blade wasn't a fighter at all, but was an apprentice mage—now working out with the rest of the young mages in the same warm-up exercises the would-be fighters used. All mages in the Sisterhood worked out on a regular basis; it kept them from getting flabby and soft—as mages were all too prone to do—or becoming thin as a reed from using their own internal energies too often. She watched that particular girl with a measuring eye, wondering if she was simply seeing what she wanted to see.

After all, she had started out a fighter, not a mage. Why shouldn't there be someone else able to master both disciplines? Someone like her own apprentice, Vena, to be precise.

Vena certainly was the only one who seemed worthy to carry the year-blade. This was something that had never occurred in all the years she'd been forging the swords. She wasn't quite certain what to do about it. She watched the girls stretching and bending in their brown linen trews and tunics, hair all neatly bound in knots and braids, and pondered the problem.

The Sisterhood was a peculiar group; part temple, part militia, part mage-school. Any female was welcome here, provided she was prepared to work and learn some useful life-task at the same time. Worship was given to the Twins; two sets of gods and goddesses, Kerenal and Dina, Karanel and Dara; Healer, Crafter, Fighter, and Hunter. Shirkers were summarily shown the door—and women who had achieved self-sufficiency were encouraged to make their way in the outside world, although they could, of course, remain with the Sisterhood and contribute some or all of their income or skills to the upkeep of the enclave.

All this information flashed into Elspeth's mind in an eyeblink, as if she had always known it.

Those girls with Mage-Talent were taught the use of it;

*those who wished to follow the way of the blade learned
all the skills to make them crack mercenaries. Those who
learned neither supported the group by learning and
practicing a craft or in Healing—either herb and knife
Healing, or Healing with their Gifts—or, very rarely, taking their place among the few true Priests of the Twins
at the temple within the Sisterhood complex.*

*The creations of the crafters in that third group—and
those mages who chose to remain with the enclave—
supported it, through sales and hire-outs. The Sisters
were a diverse group, and that diversity had been allowed for. Only one requirement was absolute. While she
was with the Sisterhood, a woman must remain celibate.*

That had never been a problem for the woman whose
soul now resided in the blade called "Need."

Interesting, though—in all her studies, Elspeth had
never come across anything about the "Twins" or the
"Sisterhood of Sword and Spell." Not that she had covered the lore of every land in the world, but the library
in Haven was a good one—there had been information
there on many obscure cults.

On the other hand, there had been nothing in any of
those books about the Cold Ones, and Elspeth had pretty
direct experience of *their* existence.

*She'd never found any man whose attractions out-
weighed the fascination of combining mage-craft with
smithery. Of course, she thought humorously, the kind of
man attracted to a woman with a face like a horse and
biceps rivaling his own was generally not the sort she
wanted to waste any time on.*

She sighed and returned to her forge.

The scene changed again, this time to a roadway running through thick forest, from a horse-back vantage
point. The trees were enormous, much larger than any
Elspeth had ever seen before; so large that five or six
men could scarcely have circled the trunks with their
arms. Of course, she had never seen the Pelagiris Forest;
stories picked up from mercs along the way, assuming
those weren't exaggerated, had hinted of something like
this.

*The Fair was no longer exciting, merely tiring. She was
glad to be going home.*

But suddenly, amid the ever-present pine scent, a whiff of acrid smoke drifted to her nose—causing instant alarm.

There shouldn't have been any fires burning with enough smoke to be scented out here. Campfires were not permitted, and none of the fires of the Sisterhood produced much smoke.

A cold fear filled her. She spurred her old horse which shuffled into a startled canter, rolling its eyes when it scented the smoke. The closer she went, the thicker the smoke became.

She rode into the clearing holding the Sisterhood to face a scene of carnage.

Elspeth was all too familiar with scenes of carnage, but this was the equal of anything she'd seen during the conflicts with Hardorn. Bodies, systematically looted bodies, lay everywhere, not all of them female, none of them alive. The buildings were smoking ruins, burned to blackened skeletons.

Shock made her numb; disbelief froze her in her saddle. Under it all, the single question—why? The Sisterhood wasn't wealthy, everyone knew that—and while no one lives without making a few rivals or enemies, there were none that she knew of that would have wanted to destroy them so completely. They held no secrets, not even the making of the mage-blades was a secret. Anyone could do it who was both smith and mage, and willing to spend one month per spell on a single sword.

Why had this happened? And as importantly, who had done it?

That was when Vena came running, weeping, out of the forest; face smudged with ash and smoke, tear-streaked, clothing and hair full of pine needles and bark.

Again the scene changed, to the forge she had seen before, but this time there was little in the way of walls or ceiling left. And again, knowledge flooded her.

Vena had been out in the forest when the attack occurred. She had managed to scale one of the smaller trees and hide among the branches to observe. Now they both knew the answer to her questions.

"Who" was the Wizard Heshain, a mage-lord who had never before shown any notice of the Sisterhood. Vena had described the badges on shields and livery of the large, well-armed force that had invaded the peaceful enclave, and she had recognized Heshain's device.

"Why—"

His men had systematically sought out and killed every fighter, every craftswoman, every fighter apprentice. There had been mages with them who had eliminated every adult mage.

Then they had surrounded and captured every apprentice mage except Vena. They fired the buildings to drive anyone hiding into the open and had eliminated any that were not young and Mage-Talented.

The entire proceedings had taken place in an atmosphere of cold efficiency. There were no excesses, other than slaughter, not even rape—and that had struck Vena as eerily like the dispassionate extermination of vermin.

Afterward, though, the bodies of both sides had been stripped of everything useful and anything that might identify them. There had still been no rapine, no physical abuse of the apprentices; they had been tied at the wrists and hobbled at the ankles, herded into carts, and taken away. Vena had stayed in the tree for a full night, waiting for the attackers to return, then she had climbed down to wander dazedly through the ruins.

Vena had no idea why the wizard had done this—but the kidnapping of the apprentices told her all she needed to know.

He had taken them to use, to augment his own powers. To seduce, subvert, or otherwise bend the girls to his will.

They had to be rescued. Not only for their own sakes and that of the Sisterhood, but because if he succeeded, his power would be magnified. Considerably. Quite enough to make him a major factor in the world.

A man who sought to increase his power in such a fashion must not be permitted to succeed in his attempt.

He had to be stopped.

Right. He had to be stopped.

By an old, crippled woman, and a half-trained girl.

This was a task that would require a fighter of the highest skills, and a mage the equal of Heshain. A healthy mage, one who could ride and climb and run away, if she had to.

But there was a way. If Vena, a young and healthy

girl, could be endowed with all her skills, she might well be able to pull off that rescue. One person could frequently achieve things that an army could not. One person, with all the abilities of both a mage of some strength—perhaps even the superior of Heshain—and a fighter trained by the very best, would have advantages no group could boast.

That was their only hope. So she had sent Vena out, ostensibly to hunt for herbs she needed. In actuality, it was to get her out of the way. She was about to attempt something she had only seen done once. And that had not been with one of her bespelled swords.

She took the hidden sword, the one with the spells of all four seasons sealed to it, out of its hiding place under the floor of the forge. She heated the forge, placed it in the fire while she wrought one last spell—half magic, and half a desperate prayer to the Twins.

Then, when the blade was white-hot, with fire and magic, she wedged it into a clamp on the side of the forge, point outward—

And ran her body onto it.

Pain seared her with a white-hot agony so great it quickly stopped being ''pain'' and became something else.

Then it stopped being even that, and what Elspeth felt in memory was worse than pain, though totally unfamiliar. It was not a sensation like anything Elspeth had ever experienced. It was a sense of wrenching dislocation, disorientation—

Then, nothing at all. Literally. No sight, sound, sense of any kind. If she hadn't had some feeling that this was all just a memory she was reexperiencing, she'd have panicked. And still, if she had any choice at all, she never, ever wanted to encounter anything like this again. It was the most truly, profoundly horrifying experience she had ever had.

A touch. Connection. Feelings, sensations flooded back, all of them so sharp-edged and clear they seemed half-raw. Grief. Someone was weeping. Vena. It was Vena's senses she was sharing. The spell had worked! She was now one with the sword, with all of her abilities as mage and as fighter, and everything she had ever learned, intact.

Experimentally, she exerted a bit of control, moving Vena's hand as if it had been her own. The girl plucked at her tunic, and it felt to her as if it was her own hand she was controlling. Good; not only was her knowledge intact, but her ability to use it. She need only have the girl release control of her body, and an untrained girl would be a master swordswoman.

Vena sobbed helplessly, uncontrollably. After the first rush of elation, it occurred to her that she had probably better tell the child she wasn't dead. Or not exactly, anyway.

The sword released its hold on them, and Elspeth sat and shook for a long time.

It was a small comfort that she recovered from the experience before Skif did. She had never been so intimately *one* with someone's thoughts before. Especially not someone who had shared an experience like Need's death and rebirth.

She had never encountered anyone whose thoughts and memories were quite so—unhuman. As intense as those memories were, they had *felt* old, sounded odd, as if she was listening to someone with a voice roughened by years of breathing forge smoke, and they contained a feeling of difference and distance, as if the emotions Need had felt were so distant—or so foreign—that Elspeth couldn't quite grasp them. Perhaps that made a certain amount of sense. There was no way of knowing quite how old Need was. She had gotten the distinct impression that Need herself did not know. She had spent many, many lifetimes in the heart of the sword, imprisoned, though it was by her own will. That was bound to leave its mark on someone.

To make her, in time, something other than human? It was possible.

Nevertheless, it was a long time before she was willing to open her mind to the blade again, and to do so required more courage than she had ever mustered up before.

:I wish you wouldn't do that,: the sword said, peevishly, the moment she reestablished contact.

"What?" she replied, startled.

:Close me out like that. I thought I made it clear; I

can only see through your eyes, hear through your ears. When you close me out, I'm deaf and blind.:

"Oh." She shivered with the recollection of that shared moment of pain, disorientation—and then, nothing. What would it be like for Need, in those times when she was not in contact with her wielder?

Best not to think about it. "Can you always do that?" she asked instead. "As long as you aren't closed out, I mean."

Skif showed some signs of coming out of his stunned state. He shook his head, and looked at her, with a bit more sense in his expression, as if he had begun to follow the conversation.

:Once I soul-bond, the way I did with Vena, and most of my other wielders, yes. Unless you deliberately close me out, the way you just did. I had forgotten that there were disadvantages to bonding to someone with Mindspeech.: Need seemed a little disgruntled. *:You know how to shield yourselves, and unless you choose to keep me within those shields with you, that closes me out.:*

Given some of what Kero had told her about her own struggles with the sword, Elspeth was a little less inclined to be sympathetic than she might ordinarily have been. Need had tried, not once, but repeatedly, to get the upper hand and command the Captain's movements when she was young. And she *had* taken over Kero's grandmother's life from time to time, forcing her into situations that had often threatened not only her life, but the lives of those around her. Granted, it had always been in a good cause, but—

But Kero—and Kethry—had occasionally found themselves fighting *against* women, women or things in a woman's shape. Creatures who were frequently the equal in evil of any man. And when that happened, Need had not only not aided her wielder—she had often fought her wielder.

More than once, both women had found themselves in acute danger, with Need actually helping the enemy.

Given that, well . . . it was harder to be in complete sympathy with the sword.

Poor Kero, Elspeth thought. *I'm beginning to understand what it was she found herself up against, here. . . .*

And that made something occur to her. "Wait a minute—Kero had Mindspeech! Why didn't you talk to her before this?''

:*I was asleep.*: the sword admitted sheepishly. :*There was a time when all I could bond to were fighters, with no special abilities whatsoever. During that rather dry spell, there was a long period between partners. I am not certain what happened; I didn't get a chance to bond properly, because she didn't use me for long. Perhaps my wielder put me away, perhaps she sold me—or she might even have lost me. I don't know. But my bond faded and weakened, and I slept, and my wielders came to me only as dreams.*:

"What woke you?" Skif asked. He sounded back to his old curious self.

:*I think, perhaps, it was the one before you. Kerowyn, you said? She began to speak to me, if crudely. But because I had been asleep for so very long, I was long in waking. Then, as I gradually began to realize what was going on and came to full wakefulness, she brought me to your home.*:

Need fell silent, and all of them—Elspeth Felt Gwena back with her again—waited for her to speak. Gwena finally got tired of waiting.

:*Well?*: she snapped. :*What then?*:

Elspeth clearly felt the sword react with surprise.

:*What then? I stayed quiet, of course! The protections about your land are formidable, horse. Someone has changed the nature of the* vrondi *there. They—*:

"The what?" Elspeth asked, puzzled by the strange reference.

:*The* vrondi, *child,*: Need responded, impatiently. :*You know what they are! Even though you have no mages within your border, you use the* vrondi *constantly, to detect the truth!*:

Unbidden, the memories of first learning the Truth-Spell sprang into her mind.

''*Think of a cloud with eyes,*'' said Herald Teren. ''*Think of the spell and concentrate on a cloud with eyes.*''

She must have spoken it aloud, for the sword responded. :*Exactly,*: Need replied with impatience. :*Clouds with eyes. Those are* vrondi. *Did you think they were only creatures of imagination?*:

Since that was precisely what she had thought, she prudently kept that answer to herself.

:Someone, somehow, has changed the nature of the vrondi, *and they are not the same in your land,:* the blade said peevishly. *:They look now, they look for mage-energies. When they see them, they gather about the mage, and watch, and* watch, *and they do not stop watching unless they see that the mage is also a Herald, and has one of your talking horses with him.:* If a sword could have produced a snort, this one would have. *:So I kept silent. What else was I to do? I did not wish to call attention to myself. That was when I drifted back to sleep again.:*

:Not as deeply, I trust,: Gwena responded, dryly.

:Well, no. And I waited, not only to be able to leave your land, but to be passed to the one I had sensed— you. Not only a fighter, but one with Mage-Talent as well, and Mindspeech.:

"Then I took you out—"

:And I woke. Just as well, I think. If you will forgive me, child—you need me.:

Elspeth groaned inwardly, though not at the pun. The last thing she had any use for was yet another creature with an idea of what she "should" be doing.

Oh, gods, she thought. *Just what I wanted. Another guardian. Someone else with a Quest.*

That was not the end of her troubles, as she soon learned.

Both she and Skif were exhausted, but Skif seemed a little more dazed than she. Possibly it was simply a matter of sex; Need had shown herself to be a little less than friendly to males, and Elspeth had no doubt that the sword had not made mental contact easy on him.

Skif lay down on the bed, his face a little dazed. Elspeth, though she was tired, also felt as if she needed to get on with her plans quickly, before Need could complicate matters.

It was possible, of course, that *Need* could prove to be the magic-teacher she so eagerly sought. Possible—but a last resort, to be considered only when she had exhausted all others. Including seeking the Adept in Lythecare. She wasn't certain of Need's powers, and she wasn't certain if the blade was entirely to be trusted. If she would run roughshod over Skif, what would she do to handicap other Valdemaran males? Would she actually sabotage *their* training? Elspeth couldn't be sure, so she wasn't going to take the chance.

When the sword had been put in her sheath, with a promise that Elspeth would not again block Need out of her mind without ample warning and cause, she went out for a breath of air, and to begin to explore the tent city. As she had been expecting, there *was* a logical pattern to the "streets" of Kata'shin'a'in. The farthest tents, those all the way downwind, belonged to the beast sellers. Near to them were those who sold the things one would need for a beast, everything from simple leads and halters for sheep and collars for dogs, to the elaborate tack for parade horses.

Then came leather workers in general, then the makers of glass, metal and stonework.

Then textile merchants, and finally, nearest the core city, sellers of food and other consumables.

The core city itself contained a very few shops. It consisted mostly of the dwellings of those few who remained here all year and the inns.

There were dozens of those inns, ranging in quality from a mud-walled, dirt-floored, one-room ale house, to a marble palace of three stories, whose supposed amenities ranged from silk sheets through mage-crafted delicacies to the very personal and intimate attendance of the servant of one's choice.

The innkeeper had not gotten any more explicit than that, but Elspeth reckoned wryly that a whore by any other name still plied his or her trade—presumably, with expertise.

It might be nice to experience service like that, one day—*though without,* she thought with a little embarrassment, *anything more personal than a good massage.*

But for now, she had a great deal more on her mind than that. For one thing, she had to find Shin'a'in. This was Kata'shin'a'in, "City of the Shin'a'in," after all. Once she found Shin'a'in, she had to get them to talk to her. Then she had to find someone willing and able to put her in touch with Tale'sedrin, Kero's Clan.

And she reckoned that the best place to find the

Shin'a'in would be in the beast market. They not only bred horses, after all, they also had herds of sheep and goats; presumably they bought and sold both.

Failing that, she would try the textile merchants. The Shin'a'in were great weavers and among those who treasured such pieces of art, their carpets, blankets, and other textiles and embroideries were famed all the way up into Valdemar.

So she went out to scout the beast market first.

She had hoped to slip away without disturbing Skif, who had fallen asleep on the bed, exhausted by the strain of the strange day.

But no matter what Need claimed about her own powers, evidently "attracting Luck" was no longer one of them. She had no sooner gotten outside the door of the inn when Skiff came panting up behind her.

She sighed and kept from snapping at him. It was fairly obvious that he was not going to let her go out alone. And it wasn't simply more of his mother-henning. The peculiar look in his eyes told her all she needed to know.

He was infatuated with her.

And I ought to recognize infatuation when I see it, since I've suffered under it myself.

He undoubtedly had convinced himself that he was in love with her.

Wonderful, she thought to herself, as she headed determinedly toward her goal, despite having him trailing along behind her. *Just wonderful. My partner thinks he's in love with me, my Companion wants me to become some kind of Foretold Hero, my sword has a mind of its own, and I'm going to have to find someone from an elusive tribe of an elusive people all on my own, in a city where I don't even speak the language.*

No, somehow I don't think that attracting Luck is on the list of active spells. . . .

Chapter Fifteen

DARKWIND

Treyvan roused his feathers, fluffing his crest and shaking his head, his claws digging long furrows into the thick weedy turf. He held his head high, his muscles stiff with impatience. Darkwind glanced sideways at him and smiled a little.

A shadow passed over the scout, and he looked up automatically, but it was only a cloud passing across the sun. Vree was waiting for him back in the forest, away from the temptation of Treyvan's crest feathers. "How long have you and Hydona been mated?" he asked, with pretended innocence.

"Twelve yearsss," the gryphon replied, rousing his feathers again, and casting his own glance upward. "What'sss that got to do with anything?"

"And you've made quite a few mating flights, haven't you?" the scout continued, his smile broadening. Treyvan was so preoccupied he didn't even realize that Darkwind was teasing him.

"Well," Treyvan said, with a sidelong glance at Hydona. Hydona only roused her own feathers, watching him coyly. "Yesss."

"If you've got so much experience at it," he laughed, reaching up to scratch behind Treyvan's ear-tufts, "don't you think you ought to be able to take your time about this one?''

Treyvan closed his eyes, wearing an expression of long-suffering patience. ''You, a human, *alwayss* in ssseason, with matesss ambusshing you even when you are bathing—you tell *me* that? You crrreaturess neverrr *ssstop.*''

Hydona made a choking sound; her mate pointedly looked away from her. Darkwind knew that faint gargling from past exchanges with the pair; she was trying not to chuckle. He raised his eyebrows at her, then gave her a broad wink. She hid her head by turning it to the side, but her shaking shoulders told him she was stifling out-right laughter.

''Anyway,'' Treyvan continued, in an aggrieved tone, ''you know very well that I casst the initial ssspell thiss morrrning. *And* you know verrry well that until we complete it with the sssecond ssspell, it'sss going to make me itchierrr than a plague of sssand-fleasss. I explained it to you often enough.'' He shook his head and made a grinding sound with his beak. ''I feel asss if my ssskin isss too tight,'' he complained.

Darkwind bit his tongue to keep from making a retort to that particular complaint. ''In that case,'' he said, soothingly, ''I had probably better leave you two alone.''

''Oh, he'll live,'' Hydona countered, controlling herself and her humor admirably. ''Trrruly he will. You're rrready for what we'll do thisss time, I hope? Not like the lassst time?''

He flushed at the memory of the ''last time,'' when he had been much younger. He had been close enough to them, and unshielded, so that he had gotten caught up in the extremely potent magic of their mating spell. The first spell that Treyvan had mentioned was what actually made the mating fertile; otherwise their sexual activity was purely for enjoyment. The second would ensure conception. And despite Treyvan's acerbic comment about ''humans always being in season,'' the fact was that the gryphons were at least as active in that area as any humans Darkwind knew.

''I'll be fine,'' he told her. ''I'm not fourteen anymore.''

Hydona laughed. ''I'd notisssed,'' she teased.

"Essspecially around Dawnfirrre. When will *you* be picking a mate?"

"Uh—" the question took him by surprise, so he settled for a gallant answer. "When I find a mate as magical as you are."

"Flattererrr," she replied, dryly. "Well, when you do, perhapsss we'll all be rrready to ssssettle a new place together, ssso that we can keep eyesss on each other'sss sssmall onesss." She looked over his head a moment, off into the distance. "That isss the ultimate goal of ourrr being herrre, you know," she said thoughtfully. "We'rrre pioneersss, of a sssort. Our kind came from sssomewhere about herrre, you know, very, very long ago, and Trrreyvan and I are here now to sssee if it isss the time to rrreturn."

"So you told me," he said, "A long time ago."

She nodded as Treyvan sighed and lay down in the long grass with a long-suffering look.

"Oh, yesss," she said, ignoring her mate, with a mischievous twinkle in her eyes. "We arrre herrre to sssee if we can raissse little ones, brrring them into the magic of the land, and prosssper. If we do well, more will come. You know, ourrr people and yoursss arrre ancient parrrtnersss, from the daysss of the Kaled'a'in. The *hertasi*, too, and othersss you may not have everrr sssseen beforrre. It would be good if we could be partnersss again."

Another surprise; this time, a much greater surprise. He'd been astonished to learn that the gryphons were fluent in the ancient tongue of Kaled'a'in, a language so old that very few of either the Tayledras or the Shin'a'in could be considered "fluent," despite the fact that both their current languages were derived from that parent. But this revelation was a total surprise, for there was nothing in the Tayledras histories to indicate that the two species had been so close.

While he pondered the implications of that, Hydona reached over and gently bit Treyvan's neck. The male gryphon's eyes glazed and closed, and the cere above his beak flushed a brilliant orange-gold. Obviously, her mind was no longer on the far past, but on the immediate future. And from the look on Treyvan's face, his mind had been there for some time.

Darkwind coughed. "Uh—Hydona?"

"Hmm?" the gryphon replied dreamily, her own eyes bright, but unfocused, her thoughts obviously joined to Treyvan's.

"Who's watching the little ones?" he asked. "I can't; I've got to be out on patrol. I don't trust this quiet."

"They'll be fine," Hydona replied, releasing her mate long enough to reply. "They've been told not to leave the nessst, and if they called, nothing could get to them beforrre we'd be on top of it."

"Are you sure?" he persisted, but Hydona was nuzzling Treyvan's neck again and he knew there was no way he was going to get any sense out of her at the moment.

"They'll be fine," she mumbled, all her attention centered once more on her mate.

Despite being under shielding, the sexual euphoria began penetrating even his careful defenses. This was obviously the time to leave.

As he picked his way through the ruins, a feeling of light-headedness overcame him for a moment. He looked back over his shoulder to see the two of them surging up into the cloudy sky, Hydona a little ahead of Treyvan. Even as he watched, they began an elaborate aerial display, tumbling and spiraling around each other, in a dance that was half-planned and half-improvisation. This "dance" itself was part of the spell; the rest—Treyvan's extravagant maneuvers—were designed to inflame himself and his mate.

And judging by the faint excitement *he* was feeling, even through his shields, it was having the desired effect.

As he turned his eyes back toward the ground, another moving speck caught his eye. Though it was very high, long experience enabled him to identify it as a red-shouldered hawk, one of the many breeds often used as bondbirds by the Tayledras.

That made him think reflexively of Dawnfire, whose bird *was* a red-shouldered. And that—given all that he'd been exposed to in the past few moments—made his thoughts turn in an entirely different direction than they *had* been tending.

Dawnfire rode the thoughts of her bondbird with the same ease that the bird commanded the currents of the sky. Theirs was a long partnership, of seven years' standing, for she had bonded to Kyrr at the tender age of ten. Darkwind's Vree had been with him only four or five years; the bird he had bonded to before that had been a shorter-lived shriek-owl, gift of his older brother.

A shriek-owl was not a practical bird for a scout, but the tiny creatures were perfect for a mage, which was what Darkwind had been in that long-ago, peaceful time. Shriek-owls in the wild seldom lived beyond three years—the bondbird breed in general tripled that lifespan. That was nothing near like the expected lifespan of the scouts' birds—twenty-five to fifty years for the falcons, larger owls, and hawks, and up to seventy-five years for the rarer eagles. And shriek-owls were tiny; scarcely bigger than a clenched fist. They ate mostly insects, flew slowly, and generally flitted from tree to tree inside a very small territory. They could hardly be counted on to be an effective aid either on a scouting foray or to aid in an attack. But the owls were charming little birds, by nature friendly and social—in the wild they nested several to a tree—and the perfect bird for a mage who only needed a bird to be occasional eyes and ears and to pass messages. A mage did not necessarily need to bond to his bird with the kind of emotional closeness that a scout did, nor did he need a bird with that kind of long expected lifespan. All of the mages that Dawnfire knew that she liked, personally, *did* bond closely with intelligent birds, but it was not as necessary for them as it was for scouts.

Scouts had to develop a good working, partner-like relationship with their birds, and that required something with a long anticipated lifespan. Scouts spent as much as a year simply training their birds, then it took as much as four or five more years to get the partnership to a smooth working relationship. Like the scouts, the lives of the bondbirds were fraught with danger. There had already been casualties among the birds, and Darkwind had warned his corps to expect more. Their enemies knew the importance of the birds, as well as the impact a bird's violent death had on his bondmate, and often made the birds their primary targets. Dawnfire tried not to think about losing Kyrr, but the fact was that it could happen.

Darkwind's father Starblade had lost *his* bird in circumstances so traumatic that the mage had returned to the Vale in a state of shock, and actually could not recall what had occurred. Since he had been investigating a forest fire ignited by firebirds, and since the birds themselves seldom reacted so violently that they set their homes aflame, the other Tayledras assumed that whatever had frightened the firebirds had probably caught and killed Starblade's perlin falcon. That had been a set of very strange circumstances, actually; Dawnfire remembered it quite vividly because her mother had been one of the scouts who had found the mage and had talked it over one long night with friends in her daughter's presence.

There had been a sortie that had drawn most of the fighters off when word of the fire had reached the Vale. Starblade had gone out to take care of it.

He had then vanished for many days. He was found wandering, dazed, within the burned area, near nightfall on the third day. His bondbird was gone, and he himself could not remember anything after leaving the Vale. Injured, burned, dehydrated, no one was surprised at that—but when days and weeks went by and he still could not remember, and when he chose to bond again with a crow, from a nest outside of the Vale—some people, like Dawnfire's mother, wondered. . . .

Darkwind had once said something after another of his angry confrontations with his father—something about his feeling that Starblade had changed, and was no longer the father he had known. *He* blamed the change on the disaster, Dawnfire wasn't so sure.

Starblade had not been that close, emotionally, to Darkwind's mother, though Darkwind had never accepted that. Dawnfire was not at all certain that Starblade would have been so badly affected by her death that his personality had changed. She blamed the change on the death of Starblade's bird. It seemed to *her* and her own mother that Starblade had become silent and very odd afterward. And that crow he'd bonded to was just as odd. . . .

She pulled her thoughts away from the past and returned them to the present. She was off-duty today and had decided to indulge her curiosity in something.

Darkwind's gryphons.

She had been terribly curious about them for a very long time, and had even gone to visit them a time or two. But the gryphons, while still being cordial and polite, had made one thing very clear to her: the only visitor they truly welcomed was Darkwind.

That—had hurt. It had hurt a very great deal, and not even Darkwind knew how much it hurt. She brooded on that, as Kyrr neared the the ruins, coming in high over the forest.

I've never had anyone rebuff me like that, she thought resentfully. *Every other nonhuman I've ever met seems to think I'm a good person to deal with and to have as a friend.* Tervardi, kyree, dyheli, hertasi—*even firebirds, teyll-deer, wolves, the nonsentients. . . . Why don't the gryphons want me around?*

She'd asked that question any number of times. Darkwind wouldn't tell her a great deal, citing the gryphons' desire for privacy. That had only inflamed her curiosity— at the same time, she felt she had to respect that need. But why wouldn't they be willing to meet with her, once in a while, away from their nest? Why was it that only Darkwind was worthy of their attention?

Over the months and years, the unfulfilled questions ate at her, and she had slipped over to the ruins more than once to watch the gryphons and their offspring from a distance. Darkwind had never forbid her that; in fact, he said once that she had eased one of his worries, helping to keep an eye on the young ones while the adults were off hunting.

They had to spend a great deal of time in hunting; they were very large, flighted carnivores, like the birds-of-prey they resembled, and they needed a lot of meat. They ranged very far in order to keep from overhunting any area, and they often spent an entire morning or afternoon away from the nest. Dawnfire had taken this tacit approval as permission to watch them whenever she wasn't otherwise occupied, so long as she did it from afar, feeling that she might be able to earn the acceptance of the adults with her unofficial guardianship of their offspring.

But then, a week or so ago, Darkwind had specifically forbidden her to go anywhere near the ruins today, without giving any explanation. And that had driven her curious nature wild, as well as rousing resentment in her that he had simply ordered her as if it was his right.

He probably shouldn't have told me, she admitted to herself, as her bird soared just at the border of the gryphons' territory. *If he hadn't told me, I probably wouldn't be doing this—*

But then anger at him and his authoritative attitude burned away that thought—an anger nearly a week old, born of resentment, and nurtured on his continued silence. How *dare* he forbid her to go where she wanted to go on her own time? He had no authority over her, over her freedom! He hadn't *asked* her, simply and politely, he'd *demanded* that she promise, then and there, refusing to answer any questions, either before she reluctantly promised, or after. He refused to explain himself, or even talk about it. Her anger smoldered, hot, and grew hotter with every day that passed.

Following anger had come suspicion, slowly growing over the course of several days; a feeling that he was hiding something, and nothing had alleviated it since.

Her suspicions centered around the Changechild. He was always with the gryphons—he was with them, and with that Changechild. He wouldn't talk about either. It was not unreasonable to suppose that the two were connected—and that there was something about the Changechild that Darkwind didn't want her to know.

He'd never hidden anything from her before. There was no reason why he should want to start now.

Or so she had thought. Until this morning, when an overheard comment told her something very important that Darkwind had somehow left out of his few stories about the Changechild.

"Has Darkwind said anything more about the Changechild?" Ice-shadow asked someone. "Is she ready to leave, yet?"

She? This Changechild, neuter in her mind, suddenly took on a different face. "It" was a *she.*

Suddenly the senseless questions had sensible answers. And there were plenty of reasons why Darkwind would want her kept in the dark about this female. Especially if she was attractive.

And Dawnfire's imagination painted her as very attractive. Most Changechildren were. And there were the attractions of the exotic, of course. . . .

Not that I care if he's enamored with the girl, she told herself, as Kyrr soared a little closer to the gryphons' nest. *It's not as if we're lifebonded or something. We haven't even traded bondbird primary feathers. I would if he offered, but we haven't, just coverts. I don't exactly have a hold on him. . . .*

Excuses, excuses, and none of them meant anything, not really.

Damn him, anyway.

She had given a promise, and she never broke one—no matter what.

Even if the person she had given the promise to turned out to be a worthless sneak.

So she had spent most of the morning trying to think of a way around that promise, so that she could see what Darkwind was really up to when he slipped off to his gryphon friends. She wasn't entirely certain why she was tormenting herself, it was as if she kept biting at a sore tooth. It hurt, but she just couldn't seem to stop doing it.

Then the answer to her dilemma had occurred to her; she had promised that *she* wouldn't go near the gryphons, but she hadn't promised that Kyrr would stay away. And what Kyrr saw, she could see. Kyrr could be her way to see just what Darkwind was really up to.

The only problem was that to do that, she would have to hole up in her *ekele* and go into a full trance. That was something she was secretly ashamed of; that she could not make full contact with Kyrr's mind unless she performed a full bonding. She didn't know why; scouts generally had no trouble using their bird's senses. There *were* one or two others who had the same trouble, but no more than that. Darkwind had speculated that she found the experience of having her consciousness split to be too traumatic to deal with unless she was in a full trance—since in a full trance, her consciousness wasn't really split.

Normally this wasn't a handicap; her communication with Kyrr was otherwise excellent. The big hawk was one of the most intelligent of all the scouts' bondbirds, and had no trouble with simply *telling* her what she needed to know. Kyrr could "speak" in full sentences, she had a sense of humor, and had no trouble in cooperating with her bondmate. There had never been any rebellion or any real disagreements with Kyrr.

But Kyrr could not read facial expressions; she could not pick up the nuances of behavior that Dawnfire needed to know. She wanted to *know* how he really felt about this Changechild. Kyrr only understood things as they related to raptor feelings and instincts. And she didn't want Kyrr to misinterpret things that she saw in light of those instincts. After all, it was entirely possible that Darkwind had other reasons for keeping her away, legitimate reasons.

It's entirely possible that pigs will fly, too, she thought sourly.

Darkwind wasn't at the gryphons' nest, and neither were the gryphons. Surprised, she sent Kyrr ranging out to find them. After a bit of searching, she spotted them, near the edge of the ruins, where the forest began; she must have passed them at a distance when Kyrr flew in. Darkwind's figure blended into the landscape of tumbled stones and overgrown hillocks, rendering him very difficult to see, but the gryphons stood out against the ruins very clearly. More clearly than she remembered, in fact; their feathers shone with color, gold and red-brown, and they seemed to capture and hold the sunlight, shining in all the colors that Kyrr could see and she couldn't. For a moment, their striking beauty drove all other thoughts from her mind.

Then she wrenched her attention away, to look for anything that might be the Changechild. But there were only the gryphons and Darkwind, with no sign of anyone else, nor any of the signs that several days of occupancy would put around a hiding place in the ruins. Unless they were trying to conceal it—and they had no reason to—there would be distinctive signs of habitation.

Her anger faded and died, giving way to embarrassment.

Was I wrong? she wondered, as the gryphons fanned their wings in the sun, and she and Kyrr circled nearer. She had never felt so stupid in her life. She was just glad that she hadn't made this blunder in public. *Was I just a suspicious, jealous bitch? Was I overreacting to something that hadn't even happened?*

It certainly looked like it. As Darkwind bade farewell to his two friends and slipped into the shadows of the forest, she very nearly sent Kyrr home. But sheer curiosity kept her aloft, circling above the two gryphons, and something about their colors nagged at the back of her mind, reminding her of a memory she couldn't quite put her finger on.

Then it came to her, as the larger of the two gryphons bit the neck of the smaller one in an unmistakable act of sexual aggression.

Gods and ancestors—they're going to mate. That's why he didn't want me around them.

For a moment, that was even more embarrassing. She felt as if she'd been caught watching the *dyheli* stallions and their mares for the sheer, erotic amusement of it. . . .

But they'd had mating-flights before, lots of them, and Darkwind had never forbidden her to go near. What was it that was so different this time?

Curiosity overcame embarrassment. Whatever it was, she was going to find out.

As first one, then the other of the gryphons launched themselves into the air, she circled the sky around them, keeping them in sight at all times.

The male—Treyvan—wheeled and stooped and circled his mate, who hovered as he circled, followed him in his dives, and climbed beside him as he dove upward again. This was not simply "flight"—this was an aerobatic dance, breathtaking and beautiful, and as impressive as anything she had ever witnessed.

The gryphons moved higher with every turn of the dance, gaining altitude as the dives grew shallower, the climbs steeper, and the circles more fluid and sensuous. They came even with Kyrr, then climbed above her, continuing to climb higher as she tried to follow. Finally they climbed into regions where she couldn't follow, leaving her gazing in wonder from below. . . .

Then there was just one single dot in the blue. And it was growing larger.

Dear gods—they mate on the wing, like eagles—

For two minutes they fell together, claws locked in

ecstasy—plummeting toward the earth so fast that the wind whistled in their feathers, eyes closed—

—*they aren't going to*—

At the last possible moment they broke apart, spreading their wings with a *crack* as they caught the air and shot upward again, side by side, beauty so incredible that she couldn't breathe—

When the beauty of the moment was shattered by the *thunk* of a heavy crossbow firing, and a bolt streaking toward Hydona.

Dawnfire was watching the female at the moment that the broad-bladed bolt ripped through the air, changing its arc to meet the wing and shred it.

The female screamed as the wing collapsed; the uninjured wing flailed wildly as she fell in a barely-controlled spiral towards the ground.

The male's scream of rage echoed his mate's scream of pain; he did a wing-over and turned his climb into a killing dive, claws extended, as he followed his mate down.

The female crashed into the trees at the edge of the forest and was lost to sight; the male followed an eye-blink behind her.

Then a sudden flare of light from beneath the trees enveloped him in a tongue of white flame; he screamed again, but this time in pain, not in rage. The light held him suspended for a moment, as he went limp. Then he simply dropped, unconscious, through the leafy roof of the forest.

All that saved him from a broken neck was the fact that it was a relatively short drop.

Anger filled her, white-hot anger, and the urge to kill.

Without stopping to think, Dawnfire sent Kyrr in a near-vertical stoop down after them; Kyrr's instinct was to shriek with rage, but Dawnfire clenched the hawk's beak shut. No point in warning whoever it was that had perpetrated this—outrage.

As she dove through the branches, snaking through the obstacle course with desperate adjustments of her wings, Kyrr's blood boiled with rage. It was all that Dawnfire could do to keep her under control and quiet. The bond-bird wanted blood, she wanted it *now,* and she wasn't going to accept less.

:Kill!: she shrilled in Dawnfire's mind. *:Kill them all!:*

Dawnfire gritted mental teeth, and held to her tenuous control as they penetrated the last of the branches and broke out into the clear air beneath the forest canopy. *If I lose her now, I lose her for all time. I'll never be able to control her in a rage again—*

There were two men with the unconscious gryphons; she saw that in a moment. One, the one with the crossbow, was standing guard over the unconscious male who lay in a pathetic and boneless heap at his feet.

The other was beside the female, who was, at least, semiconscious. He was unarmed, dressed in close-fitting leather—and he was without a doubt a mage, one of the Others, who had manipulated himself into a form that was scarcely more than half human.

And he was doing something to the female gryphon.

Dawnfire barely had time to take that all in; at that moment, the female gryphon sent up a shriek of heart-rending agony. The scream goaded Kyrr into a rage that tore her loose from Dawnfire's control.

Not that it mattered, because Dawnfire herself was so angered that she released control to Kyrr, to give her all the edge she needed.

Screaming outrage, they dove together in a full-scale attack, claws extended and aimed for the mage's eyes.

He looked up—

And his eyes were all Dawnfire could see—just before something slammed into her, and darkness swallowed her. His eyes—his slitted eyes. . . .

And his hate-filled, sharp-toothed smile. . . .

Chapter
Sixteen

ELSPETH

Elspeth swore silently as she caught a familiar profile out of the corner of her eye. Skif was following her again.

The turbaned merchant implored her to examine the clever workmanship of the leather pouch she was holding, conveying grief that his profit margin had already been slashed to nothing. Elspeth lingered over her purchase, haggling a few more coppers off the price of the belt-pouch, as she watched Skif ghosting around the edge of the crowd, keeping an eye on her. He was very good; it was unlikely that anyone around her realized that he was shadowing her. In a bazaar full of foreigners of all shapes, sizes and costumes, neither of them stood out from the crowd. Trade season was at its height, and the crowds of small traders, mercs, and the occasional pleasure traveler filled the aisles between the tent-booths. It was not the easiest thing to spot Skif as he skillfully used the crowds to cover his movements, but *he* had trained *her*, and she knew his moves better than anyone else could.

It was just a good thing that she was conscientious enough to keep her own watch out for other followers. He could easily be distracting her enough to put her at hazard.

The scent of fine leather rose from the pouch in her hands as she pretended to examine it further. The merchant swore she was impoverishing him.

This was getting annoying. No, it had gotten annoying already. She had begun to lose her patience with him.

Twice now, she had gotten close to someone who had hinted he might know a Shin'a'in or two—and twice, it had come to nothing. The Clansmen were proving incredibly elusive.

"Alas, you should have been here in the spring," said the folk in the fabric bazaar. "They are only here in the spring. But I have some fine Shin'a'in rugs, and you couldn't get a better bargain on them from a Clansman herself. . . ."

"Oh, you should wait until the fall," said the horse traders. "They never come here except in the fall. Now, I have some outstanding Shin'a'in saddle mares. . . ."

"Well, they were just here," said the shepherds, in a dialect so thick she could scarcely make out what they were saying. "Tale'sedrin, you say? That's the blonds, no? Ah, you just missed them; here last week, they were, buying up them new long-haired goats."

Here last week, here last season, not here yet—the herders were the closest she had gotten; at least they knew that Kero's Clan had a number of blond members, legacy of Kero's grandmother Kethry.

But the Shin'a'in were proving horribly hard to find. It seemed that no matter where she went, they had either been and gone, or they had not yet appeared.

"Cakes yesterday, cakes tomorrow, but never cakes today," she muttered to herself, keeping one eye on Skif as she paid for the leather pouch and attached it to her belt. Clever pouch; well worth having, with a catch designed to foil pickpockets, and a belt loop with woven wire glued between two layers of leather, to outwit cutpurses.

Well, she wasn't going to get anywhere today. The leather market was as empty of contacts as any other. It was time to try something else.

But before she did that, she was going to have to deal with Skif. Before he drove her to give him a bloody nose.

The crowds hadn't thinned any; sometimes she wondered what they were all doing here, they couldn't all be selling to each other, or there wouldn't be anyone in the booths. But there were smaller merchants who had no booths, picking up bargains for the luxury trade; there were plenty of people who seemed to be here just to shop and enjoy themselves. Kata'shin'a'in seemed to provide a kind of ongoing Fair that lasted for months. The security provided by the discreet bazaar guards encouraged folk to wear their finery and indulge themselves. She headed back to the inn with her other purchases, fruit and cheese and fresh bread, in a string bag at her side. She moved through the crowd briskly, at a fast walk, taking Skif by surprise so that she managed to lose him around a corner.

Well, while *he* had been busy following her, she had been paying attention to the layout of the bazaar. She took a shortcut through the saddlers, coming out in the midst of the rug sellers; from there it was a another skip across to the food vendors. She stopped just long enough to buy a parchment bag full of sugared fried cakes; her nose caught the scent and she discovered she couldn't resist the rich, sweet odor. Then she cut down the aisle of the scent sellers and from there, she strolled directly into the inn.

She unlocked the door of their room; and as she had expected, she had beaten him back. Since he was *supposed* to have been taking a nap—

:*I wish you'd take me with you,*: Need said querulously, from beneath the bed. :*It may be just a bazaar, but you know very well there are people who are out there looking for you.*:

Wonderful. Another mother hen. "I can't take you with me," she said, trying to keep her patience intact. "It's bazaar rules; no long weapons in the bazaar, nothing longer than a knife, unless it's a purchase, and then it has to be wrapped up."

:*You could carry me wrapped,*: the blade suggested hopefully. :*There wouldn't be any problem then.*:

"Then you'd do me about as much good as a stick," she snorted. "Less; you're not much good as a stick, you're too awkward and not long enough."

Before the sword could retort, there was a sound of a key in the door, and it opened as soon as the lock disengaged.

''Welcome back,'' she said dryly.

''Uh. Hello,'' Skif said, first startled, then sheepish.

''I suppose you couldn't sleep, hmm?'' She put her purchases on the rickety little table that was supplied with the room. ''You know, there's a little story I've been meaning to tell you—I wonder if you've ever heard it? It's about Herald Rana and her old suitor from home.''

He shook his head, baffled.

:You're a cruel child,: said Gwena.

:I'm getting tired of this,: she replied.

''Herald Rana went back home for a visit last year, and a young man who wouldn't give her a second glance back when she was the cheesemaker's daughter decided that she was the most wonderful woman he'd ever seen.'' She shrugged. ''It might have been the Whites, it might have been that she'd matured quite a bit since the last time he saw her. It really doesn't matter. He followed her back to Haven and then out on her circuit. He got to be such a nuisance that she decided to do something about him. So the next time he came up behind her in a market and put his arms around her, she put him to the ground.'' She raised one eyebrow at him. ''That wasn't enough for him, apparently, because he kept following her, but at a distance. So she waited until he followed her out into the forest when she went to hunt a little fresh meat.''

She paused, significantly.

''Well?'' Skif finally responded.

''She ambushed him and planted an arrow right between his legs. I'm given to understand that she came close enough to his assets to shave them.''

Skif gulped.

''I trust you take my point.'' She turned away from him, drew her knife, and lopped off the tip of the cheese roll with an obvious enthusiasm that made him wince. She stabbed the piece and offered it to him. He declined.

:You are a very cruel child.: Gwena sounded more amused than accusatory.

:Very practical,: Need retorted, with a chuckle.

:Very weary,: she replied to both of them. And took the cheese herself. *:Let's hope he gets the point—before I have to give it to him.:*

The sword and Gwena joined in laughter. *:Oh, I think*

he did,: Gwena chuckled. *:I'll have a talk with Cymry and see if she can't have a word with him.:*

:She'd better do something,: Elspeth replied grimly. *:Or I will. And this time, Herald or not, I'll be more direct.:*

Priests and other religious travelers had their own special camping ground reserved for them away from the bazaar, on top of a rise. Shaman Kra'heera shena Tale'sedrin looked out over the crowded tents of the bazaar from his vantage point above it and smiled a little. Somewhere down there was a young woman, accompanied by a tall young man, who was looking for them.

Not them, specifically. Just the Tale'sedrin. Since he and Tre'valen had arrived late this afternoon, no less than four traders had come strolling up to their tent with the casually proffered information that someone was looking for Tale'sedrin.

To each of those four, Kra'heera had said nothing. He had simply gone about his business of raising their tent. His apprentice, Tre'valen, had thanked them politely, but when he had shown no further interest in the subject, the four had strolled onward, ostensibly to visit some other tent dweller farther on. But Kra'heera read the set of their shoulders, and knew that they went away disappointed because he had not been interested in buying the rest of their information. There was as much traffic in information in the bazaars of Kata'shin'a'in as there was in material goods.

He had not bought their intelligence because he did not need to. And he let them know by his manner, since they were no fools, that he had his own ways of information. Reinforcing the shamans' reputation for uncanny, timely knowledge never hurt.

As sunset touched the tops of the tents with a sanguine glow, another visitor reached the encampment of the Shin'a'in, but this visitor had no interest in selling her information. Not to folk of the People of the Plains; not when her own son rode with them, adopted into the Clan of Tale'sedrin by marriage.

This scarlet-clad visitor was welcomed within the newly-pitched tent with jokes and news; the brazier was fired for her, and cakes and sweet tea were offered and accepted. And when all the civilized amenities were completed, and *only* then, did rug seller Dira Crimson say what she came to say.

She, Kra'heera, and Tre'valen sat comfortably on over-stuffed cushions, placed on a carpet any of the rug traders would have offered their firstborn offspring for. "There is a girl," the woman said, her plump, weathered face crinkling with a smile as she arranged the folds of her scarlet skirt about her feet. "She is a stranger, and speaks with an accent that I would not know, had I not journeyed once into Valdemar with the Clan—where we had much profit, the gods be praised."

Kra'heera's lips curled up in his own smile, and he filled her cup with more tea. "I think that the gods had less to do with that than your own wit and fine goods, trade-sister."

She waved the suggestion aside. "Na, na, one does one's best, and the gods decree the rest. So. There is a girl. There is a young man with her. *She* looks for Tale'sedrin. *He* watches her with the eyes of a young dog with his first bitch."

Kra'heera laughed at the old woman's simile. There was no repressing Dira; she told things as she saw them, and if anyone objected, why, she felt they need not listen.

"Young men are ever thus. What of this girl of Valdemar, who seeks the Children of the Hawk?" he asked.

"Well, it is said that she comes from Kerowyn, on whom be peace and profit, if such a thing is possible for one whose livelihood is by the sword. It is said that she bears the mage-sword given her from the hand of Kerowyn as a token of this." The old woman's black eyes peered at him sharply, from within a nest of wrinkles. "This is the sword of Clan-Mother Kethryveris, the blade called 'Need.' "

"It is said?" Kra'heera pondered the information. "You have seen this?"

Dira shook her head. "No, not with my own eyes. Nor have I heard her claim this with my own ears. I have spoken with her but briefly, a few words at most. She seems honest. That is all I can say."

Kra'heera nodded, and Dira smiled her satisfaction. No Shin'a'in ever moved on purely hearsay evidence. No

Shin'a'in dared move on hearsay. But Dira had reported what she knew, and Kra'heera would not be caught by surprise.

The last of the light faded, and Tre'valen lit the scarlet lamps that marked the tent as priestly and not to be disturbed. They exchanged a few more pleasantries, and Dira took herself back to her own tent, somewhere in the labyrinthine recesses of the rug seller's bazaar.

Kra'heera nodded to his apprentice to take her place beside the brazier. The elder shaman sat in thought while his apprentice seated himself. "Will you do nothing about this Outlander?" Tre'valen wondered aloud. "Will you seek her out?"

"Perhaps." Kra'heera studied the bottom of his paper-thin porcelain teacup. "Perhaps. She may be of some use to us, whether she speaks the truth or no. But we have a more urgent appointment, you and I."

"We do?" Tre'valen asked, surprised, his black brows arching upwards in surprise. Tre'valen was one of the pure-blood Shin'a'in—by no means the majority among the mixed-blood Clan of Tale'sedrin. His ice-blue eyes were startling to an outsider, set beneath his raven-black hair, in an angular, golden-skinned face.

"Surely you did not think that we came riding over the Plains in the heat of summer for the pleasure of it?" Kra'heera responded wryly. "If that is so, you have an odd notion of pleasure."

Tre'valen flushed a little but held his tongue. Kra'heera's wit sometimes tended to the acidic, but his apprentices had to grow used to it. That was part of becoming a shaman; to be able to face any temperament with calm.

"We go out now," Kra'heera announced, standing up from his cross-legged position with an ease many younger men would envy. *That* took Tre'valen by surprise; the apprentice scrambled to his feet awkwardly, just in time to follow his superior out into the night. To Kra'heera's veiled amusement, Tre'valen first turned toward the bazaar, and only altered his steps when he realized that the shaman was heading into the Old City.

And not just the Old City, but the oldest part of the city. The city swallowed them, wrapping them in a blanket of sound and lights. Kata'shin'a'in did not sleep in trade season; business went on as usual after nightfall, although the emphasis shifted from the general to the personal, from the mundane to the exotic. In the bazaar the perfume sellers, the jewelers, the traders in mage-goods would be doing brisk business. In the Old City, within the inn walls, food, drink, and personal services were being sold. Kra'heera wondered if his apprentice felt as odd as he did, moving silently between walls, with the sight of the land and much of the sky blocked out by masonry. The wind could not move freely here, and the earth beneath their feet had been pounded dead and lifeless by the countless hooves of passing beasts.

Yet the Shin'a'in had once known cities—or rather *a* city, one that had once stood in the precise middle of the Dhorisha Plains. Once, and very long ago, that had been the home of the Kaled'a'in.

Kra'heera led the way confidently between the walls of alien stone, through the scents and sounds that were just as alien, the evidences of Outlanders conducting further business—or pleasure. He moved without worry, for all the fact that he wore a sword at his back, for the rule of the bazaar did not apply to Shin'a'in; not here, in their own city, where they only visited, but never lived.

The deeper they went into the core city, the darker and quieter it became—and the stranger grew the scents and the sounds. Voices babbling in chaos became voices chanting quietly in unison; raucous song became the sweet harmony of a pair of boy sopranos. The mingled scents of perfume, wine, and cookery gave way to the smoke of incense and the fragrance of flowers. This was the quarter of the temples, and the doors spilling forth yellow light yielded to those with lanterns on either side, held invitingly open for the would-be worshiper.

Yet these were all Outlander places of worship, not places that belonged to the Shin'a'in. Kra'heera continued past them as Tre'valen gazed about in interest. The lanterns at the temple doors became fewer; the doors, closed and darkened, until there was no light at all except what came from the torches kept burning at intervals along the street. Sound faded; now they heard the dull scuff of their own boot soles along the hard-packed dirt of the street.

Finally they reached their goal, near where the street

ended in a blank wall; a single, closed door, with a lantern burning low beside it. Kra'heera knocked in a pattern long familiar to his apprentice as the beginning of one of the drum chants.

The door opened, and Kra'heera again hid his amusement to see Tre'valen's shock. She who opened the door for them was Kal'enedral, Swordsworn—and at first glance, she looked to be garbed in black, the color of blood-feud.

A closer look as she closed the door behind them, however, showed Tre'valen what Kra'heera already knew; the color of her costume was not black, nor brown, but deep midnight blue.

Which was *not* a color that Swordsworn ever wore.

"What—" said Tre'valen.

"She is special," Kra'heera said, anticipating his question. "She is Sworn, not only to the Warrior, but the Crone as well. She bears her blade—but she uses it to guard wisdom. There are a dozen more like her here, and this is the only place where you will find them."

The Kal'enedral led them down the corridor, into a single, square room, with a roof made of tiny, square panes of glass set in a latticework of lead. The full moon had just begun to peer through the farther edge of the window-roof. Tre'valen stared at it in fascination; glass windows were a wonder to a Shin'a'in, and a glass roof a marvel past expectation. He almost stumbled onto the weaving carpeting the floor of the room; Kra'heera caught him before his foot touched the fragile threads, and steadied him as he looked down in confusion.

"It is too old to hang," he explained. "And besides, as you know, there are things that need the moon to unlock."

The Kal'enedral slipped out of the room unnoticed; Kra'heera took a seat on one of the many cushions placed around the woven tapestry at the periphery of the room. After a moment's hesitation, Tre'valen joined him.

"You know the story of our people," Kra'heera said softly, as he waited for the moon to sail above the walls, shine down through the window, and touch the threads of the weaving. "Let me remind you again, to set your mind upon the proper paths."

Out of the corner of his eye he saw Tre'valen nod, and

waited for a moment, absorbing the silence—and the dust
of centuries rising from the weaving.

"In the long-ago time, we and the Hawkbrothers were
one people, the Kaled'a'in. We served and loved an overlord, one of the Great Mages, and when he became drawn
into a war, so, too, did we. The end of that war brought
great destruction, so great that it destroyed our homeland. The mage himself had great care for his people,
and he gave the warning and the means for us to escape
before the destruction itself was wrought. It took us many
years to return from whence we had escaped; when we
came here, to this very spot—"

The moon crept through the roof-window; it had been
edging down toward the weaving. He had paced his words
to coincide with it reaching the first threads of the border, as he reached with the power She gave her shamans,
and invoked the magic of the weaving.

"—this is what we saw."

*Shaman Ravenwing passed her hand over her eyes,
wishing she could change the reality as she blotted out
the sight.*

*The debris that they had encountered on their way
here, the flattened trees, complete absence of animal and
bird life, the closer they came to the site, had given them
some warning. The ridge of earth they had approached
had told them more. But nothing prepared them for the
reality.*

*There was no homeland. Only a vast crater, as far as
the eye could see, dug many, many man-heights into the
ravaged earth. So intense had been the heat of the blast
that had caused it, that the earth at the bottom had been
fused into a lumpy sheet of glassy rock.*

*Ravenwing took her hand from her eyes and looked
again. It was no better at second viewing, and Ravenwing
reached out blindly for the two Clansfolk standing beside
her. She stood with her arms about their shoulders, theirs
about hers; and her eyes streamed tears as she forced
herself to face the death of all she had ever known.*

*She sat inside the hastily-pitched Clan Council tent,
erected to provide shade—and to block the sight of the
destruction. With her sat the shamans, the Clan Elders,*

*every leader of every Clan of the Kaled'a'in. They were
here to make decisions—and possibly, to settle a rift that
was threatening to split the People in twain.*

The dispute centered about magic. Five of the Clans
used it, four did not. Traditionally, the four who tended
and bred the horse herds were the Clans which avoided
the use of magery; Hawk, Wolf, Grasscat, and Deer. The
five Clans which—among other things—actually manipulated the breeding of the horses, as well as other creatures, did so by means of magic. These five had fielded
many mages and Healers to their overlord, Mage Urtho.
Falcon, Owl, and Raven Clans were protesting that they
were not going to give up their powers, as the previous
four were insisting. Two more Clans, Eagle and Fox, were
ambivalent, but were disturbed by the idea of sacrificing
something so integral to their lives.

Ravenwing's own Clan, Taylesederin, was foremost in
demanding that magic be eliminated from their lives.

"Our warsteeds are everything anyone could wish;
there have been no changes made to them for generations. The bondbirds are not entirely all one could wish,
but is it worth holding such a dangerous, double-edged
power simply to improve them a little more?"

That was Ravenwing's Clan Chief, Silverhorse, the
foremost opponent of magic in all its shapes and colors.

Firemare Valavyska, Elder for the Owls, widened her
eyes with contempt. "What, you think that is all magic
does? Precisely what do you intend to do about those who
do not share your scruples, our enemies who would use
any weapon they have against us? Who will protect you
from the attacks of mages if you banish magic from our
lives?"

"Who protected us this time?" Silverhorse shouted,
gesturing wildly at the desolation beyond the tent flap.
"Is it worth a repetition of that simply to have a little
more power?"

"Magic protected you this time by giving you the means
to escape, little brother," rumbled Suncat Trevavyska, of
Falcons. "Magic has saved you before, and it will again.
Besides, how do you propose to cleanse this land if not
by magic? Only magic can undo what magic has done."

It was but the opening blow of a dispute that was to
continue for days. . . .

* * *

The last member of the Five Clans vanished into the north, and Ravenwing dried her eyes on her sleeve, swallowing the last of her tears. In the end, the dispute could not be healed, not by the softest words of the most reasonable and coolest heads in the Clans nor by any appeals to brotherhood and solidarity.

The Five Clans—now calling themselves "Taylesederas," or "Brothers of the Hawks," for their association with the corvine and raptor bondbirds they had been developing—had determined to split from the Four Clans who wished to banish magic from their lives for all time. The Four Clans had no name for themselves at the moment—and no home, no purpose. Their only plan had been to do away with magery. Now that was done, and they had no idea of what to do next.

But Ravenwing and her fellow shamans—from all of the Nine Clans—had been in separate consultations after they had determined that there would be no compromise. And Ravenwing had been chosen to present their thoughts to the Elder of Hawks.

Silverhorse stared after the departing ones long past when the last of the dust had settled. His face was blank, as if he had not truly expected that the People could be sundered. It seemed as good a time as any to approach him.

"Well?" she asked, jarring him from his entrancement. "You have succeeded in this much; there is no longer magic among the People, other than that She and He give the shamans. Now what is your plan? Where do we go? What do we do? Will we find a homeland? Do we seek a new overlord?"

He turned eyes upon her that were bleak and sad. "I do not know," he confessed. "This land is torn and poisoned by magic turned awry; there is nowhere for us to go that we may claim without displacing someone else. Yet we cannot remain here—"

"We could," she offered. He answered with a short bark of a laugh.

"What? And eat rock? Drink our own tears? Watch our little ones warped and changed by the magic gone wild and twisted in this place?" He laughed again, but the pain in his laughter tore at her heart. "Is that all you can offer me, shaman of the Hawk?'' He continued to laugh, but it was becoming wild and hysterical.

She silenced him with a single, open-handed slap. He stared at her—for in all her life, she had never once raised her hand to anyone, Clansman or not. She had been known as one of the softest and gentlest women in all the Clans—certainly among the shamans.

But the past days had hardened and toughened her; and the days to come would only mean more of the same. This she knew, though she was no Seer.

"You told me when you urged that we forsake magic, that we must trust in the Powers for our protection. Are you telling me now that you no longer believe that?'' She let the acid of her words drip into the raw wound of his soul without mercy. "If that is true, then perhaps I should take my beasts and ride out after my Sundered brothers!''

"I—'' his mouth worked for a moment, before he could produce any words. "I believe that . . . but . . .''

"But what?'' Ravenwing looked down her long nose at him, from beneath half-closed lids. "But you do not believe They would answer if we called on them? Or is it that you are not willing to pay the price They might put on our aiding?''

"Would They answer?'' he asked, hope springing into his eyes. "Have you done a Seeking, shaman of the Hawk?''

She nodded, slowly. "I have done a Seeking and a Calling, and I have been answered. But the price of Their aid will be in blood.''

He took a deep breath. "Whose?''

"The Elders of each Clan that is left,'' she replied with authority. "Yours, and the other three.''

She watched his face change as her words struck him. It was not an easy decision that he was being asked to make. He was a relatively young man; as yet unmated, with all of his life before him. And that was part—and no small part—of the sacrifice. Yet when he had taken the Oath of the Elder, he had pledged just this thing; to lay down his life for his people at need. But he had, no doubt, thought if it came to that, it would be in the heat of battle—not the cold loneliness of self-sacrifice.

His eyes widened in a glazed shock, turned inward,

then focused on hers again. She nodded as she saw his attention return to her.

"It is not an easy question," she said quietly. "Your three brother and sister Elders are being posed the same question even now. We do not expect you to answer at once—but it must be soon. The People, as you pointed out, cannot remain here long."

"And if I decline this—honor?" he asked, with a touch of painful irony.

"Then I spill my blood in place of yours," she replied steadily, having faced this possibility herself, and made her own decision. "It must be one or the other of us."

"Leaving Hawk without a shaman."

She shrugged. "It must be one or the other of us. That is the Price the Calling named. We four chief shaman have spoken, and agreed. All of the apprentices have promise, but none is fit or trained to function on his own. If any of the chiefs must go, that Clan must live without a shaman until an apprentice is ready." She stepped away from him, and turned to go. "I will leave you to think on this. Come to me by moonrise with your decision."

He touched her shoulder as she turned away, stopping her.

"I do not need until moonrise," he said, in a tone that made her heart sore. "It is not all that difficult a choice to make, after all."

He smiled, a smile sweet and without fear, and she held back her tears.

"When will you require me?" he asked.

It had taken a full moon for the Clans to position themselves about the glassy crater that had been their homeland, one to each prime direction. It had been hardest for Cat Clan; they had to make the half-circle around the rim to position themselves in the West.

At sunset—in whatever manner they chose—the four Elders gave themselves for their people. Silverhorse had simply stepped off the top of the ridge, vanishing into the darkness of the crater without even a sigh. Now Ravenwing stood above the place he had fallen, her arms spread to the sky, calling on the Powers with every fiber. Behind her in a rough half-circle stood the rest of the Clan, from the infants in arms to the oldest grandsire, adding their prayers to hers.

And with the moon, She came.

Her face changed, moment to moment, from Maid to Crone, from stern Warrior to nurturing Mother, and back again. She filled the sky, and yet She stood before Ravenwing and stared deeply and directly into the shaman's eyes.

She spoke, and Her voice filled Ravenwing's ears and mind so completely that there was room for nothing but the experience.

"I have heard your prayers," She said, gravely, *"as I have heard the prayers of your Sundered brothers. There was a price to be paid for what they asked, and there is a price to be paid for what you ask."*

"In blood?" asked a quiet voice, which Ravenwing recognized as that of Azurestar, shaman of Cat Clan. A tiny bit of her was left to wonder that she could hear the voice as clearly as if Azurestar stood beside her.

She shook Her head. *"Not in blood—in your lives, all of you. I shall give you back your homeland, but the price is vigilance."*

She held out Her hand, and cupped within it was the crater. In the center of the crater, and scattered about it, beneath the slag and fused stone, were shapeless things that glowed an evil green.

"Three things destroyed the homeland," She said gravely. *"The destructive spell of an enemy, the self-destruction of the Gate that you fled through, and the Final Strike of your master Urtho's death by his Champion, meant to remove his enemy as he himself died. Yet despite all this, there are many weapons of Urtho's making that still remain and could be used, buried beneath the slag and rubble. There are weapons there that are too dangerous even for those with good intentions to hold. But you have forsworn magic for all time—they will be no temptation to you."*

Ravenwing nodded, and felt the agreement of the rest.

"Here, then, is the price. You must guard your new land, which you shall call the Dhorisha Shin'a—the Plains of Sacrifice, and yourselves the Shin'a'in—the People of the Plains. You must keep strangers out at all cost, unless they pledge themselves into the Clans, or are

*allies that you, the shamans, must call on Me to judge.
Those will be marked in ways that you will recognize.
You will never swear to any overlord again, but will remain always sworn only to each other and to the Powers.
You have forsworn magic, and you must keep that vow.
Any of your children that are born with Mage-Gift, you
must either send to your Sundered brothers, bring into
the craft of the shaman, or permit the shaman to block
the Gift for all time."*

*It was a sacrifice indeed; of freedom, and to a small
extent, of free will—and not just for them, but for all
generations. They would swear to an endless service, an
endless guardianship.*

But the gain was their home.

*She felt the assent of her people, and added her own
to it.*

*The Goddess smiled. "It is well," She said, and spread
out Her hands, stepped down into the crater, and began
to walk.*

*Where Her feet touched, a carpet of flowers, grass,
and trees sprang up, and spread, flowing over the ruined
earth like a green flood, as She walked westward. . . .*

Kra'heera blinked, and smiled faintly. He had forgotten how powerful the memories knotted into this weaving
were. Ravenwing had been a formidable, strong-minded
woman, and had managed to weave in not only the memories, but the emotions she had felt at the time.

That, of course, was the secret of the shamanic weavings; they held the memory of every shaman who worked
upon them. This weaving held not only Ravenwing, but
the half dozen who had followed her in those eventful
days. Other weavings held the memories of more shamans than that; often in the Plains these days, there was
little to record for years or even decades.

The most significant weavings were kept here, where
all the Clans could have free access to them. There were
more than four Clans now, and it was part of the training
of a shaman that he come here, to experience the beginning of the Shin'a'in, the People of the Plains, for himself.

Ravenwing was responsible for making a great deal of
the early training of shaman a part of the education of

every Shin'a'in, so that every Shin'a'in could invoke the Powers at need. In the event of a Clan losing their shaman, it would be less of a problem to wait on the training of another than it had been in the old days.

She had also been responsible for insisting that whenever possible, more than one shaman and apprentice be resident with each Clan. And she had been the shaman who created the first of the Kal'enedral, those warriors who served, not any one Clan, but all of the Clans together.

Altogether a remarkable woman, indeed.

Kra'heera turned slowly toward his own apprentice, and waited for the memories the shaman had invoked to release the younger man. Finally Tre'valen blinked, and shook his head slightly.

"All that is left is for you to learn the unlocking of these memories, and the weaving of them yourself," Kra'heera told the apprentice. "But that was not why I brought you here now. Have you guessed why?"

Tre'valen, who had already recovered from the effect of the alien memories on his own mind, nodded. "It is because of the rumors, I think," he said. "There are rumors that the Plains have been disturbed. You wanted me to see for myself why it is the People guard them."

Kra'heera considered moving—but the memory-trance relaxed one rather than leaving one tense, and there was nowhere more secure from listeners than this place.

"The rumors are true," he said. "There have been intruders on the Plains, intruders that only the shaman have been able to detect. The border guards cannot stop them, indeed, they have only recently caught sight of them at a distance. They are some kind of magic-made creatures from past the Tale'edras lands, and they have entered from the northern side of the Plains, where the Plains meet the territory of the Tale'edras Clan k'Sheyna."

"The Falcons?" Tre'valen said, curiously. "I do not know them."

"I know a little, but not a great deal," Kra'heera admitted. "I know this much of the enemy: the things that have been looking about have an incredible ability to vanish and have never been seen clearly. They have been sniffing out magic, I think, and when they find it, I think they will call that which created them.''

''They could find many things,'' Tre'valen said grimly.

''And worst case, they could find the remains of the stronghold of Mage Urtho.'' Kra'heera nodded agreement. ''I do not know if it would be possible for an attack to be mounted against the center of the Plains—but I do not know that it would *not* be possible.''

''What of k'Sheyna?'' Tre'valen asked anxiously. ''Are the Hawkbrothers not pledged to help us when dangers come from out of *their* lands?''

''Yes, but k'Sheyna, from the little I know, is a Clan with troubles of its own,'' Kra'heera responded, after a moment to gather his thoughts. ''I do not think they are capable of repulsing a single Adept just now, and if these creatures are the servants of not one, but an alliance of Adepts—well, I do not think there is much hope of aid from them.''

Tre'valen grimaced. ''So. What is it we need do?''

Kra'heera mentally congratulated his apprentice; the youngster had cut to the heart of the matter, without wasting time on things that might or might not be.

''We need to bring together the shaman of two Clans, at least. Then, we must invoke the Kal'enedral—the *leshya'e*-Kal'enedral, as well as what physical Swordsworn we can muster.''

''The spirits?'' Tre'valen said in surprise. ''We can invoke the spirit Swordsworn?''

''If needs must, yes, we can,'' Kra'heera told him. ''It must be done through the living Swordsworn, but it is not done lightly. I think, however, we have little choice at this moment. The spirits bring with them some of Her power, Her magic, and with these, I think we can withstand these intruders. But to accomplish all this, there is one thing more we must have.''

''Time,'' Tre'valen responded promptly.

''Time,'' Kra'heera agreed. ''And to gain time, we need a distraction for these things.''

''Hmm.'' Tre'valen's face grew thoughtful, and Kra'heera felt a lifting of his heart. He had not been mistaken in this young man. Tre'valen did not simply wait to do what he was told—he looked for answers.

''The young woman that Dira spoke of—'' Tre'valen

said, slowly. "Just what is she? Why would she seek us?"

Kra'heera wondered for a moment why Tre'valen's mind had turned to the strangers, but the younger man was Gifted with the ability to sift through bits of information and extract unusual solutions. So here, in this safest of all places, the elder let his own mind range for a moment, asking for a vision that would sum up what these strangers were.

In a moment, he had that vision; the young woman and her friend—with white uniforms, and *leshya'e* horses.

They were Heralds of Valdemar. He had no trouble recognizing the uniform; his cousin Kerowyn had one—though she seldom wore it willingly.

Only one Herald had ever entered the Plains—the great and good friend of Tarma shena Tale'sedrin, long before Kra'heera had ever been born. Herald Roald was something of a minor legend among Tale'sedrin, with his spirit-horse, and his undeniable charm. Other Clans' children envied Tale'sedrin, who had hosted the *ver'Kal'enedral,* the "White Swordsworn," who brought them presents and took them for rides on his beautiful spirit-horse. Kra'heera's father had been one of those so honored, and for years thereafter he had told the children and grandchildren his tales, of the wind-swift horse that had the understanding of a man.

"They are Heralds, from the Queen in Valdemar," he told his apprentice. "I do not know what brings them, but since our cousin Kerowyn is also one of them, I think that everything Dira told us could be true."

"Hmm." Tre'valen nodded thoughtfully. "That must be tested, of course. As they must be tested."

"But not by us." Kra'heera reminded him. "She must test and mark them. But—what were you thinking?"

"That they might prove worthy allies, perhaps enough to help us with these intruders." Tre'valen blinked, owlishly, in the moonlight. "Did you have any other thoughts?"

"Yes," Kra'heera responded, smiling slowly. "I have in mind that they might become our distraction. They have to be tested in any case; why not make their testing a matter of seeing how they respond to these intruders?"

Tre'valen frowned, which surprised his teacher. "Is

this fair?'' he demanded. ''They do not know what it is they will encounter, nor do they know the Plains. *We* know the girl carries a magic thing, the spirit-sword. If these hunters are seeking out magic, will they not sniff *it* out? And what then?''

''Then they must defend themselves if the hunters come for them,'' Kra'heera said with a shrug. ''They are outsiders, are they not? They must prove their worth, must they not? If She finds them worthy, perhaps She will aid them.''

''But what of us?'' Tre'valen asked. ''Should we not aid them?''

''Why?'' Kra'heera responded. ''I see no reason to aid them. If they survive, very well. If they survive and grant us the time we need, we will aid them. If they do not?'' He shrugged. ''The Plains are *ours* to guard. *She* never told us that we were to take in random strangers who come looking for help from us. In fact, by allowing them to cross the Plains, we are granting them more than any other in all of our history. It is only because they are Heralds, and because they come from our cousin, that I allow this at all.''

Reluctantly, Tre'valen nodded. ''It is in the interest of the Clans,'' he admitted. ''But I cannot like it.''

''That which does not overcome us, strengthens us,'' Kra'heera replied callously. ''This will be good for them. And here is what we shall do. . . .''

Elspeth knew by a sudden change in the air that she was no longer alone in her little room.

Tonight she had demanded another room, separate from Skif's. She was not going to share a room, much less a bed, with him anymore. She had hoped that would make it clear to him that she was not going to put up with his nonsense any more.

Skif had protested, but she had overruled him. Now she was sorry she had.

There was an intruder in her room, and if she was very lucky, it would only prove to be a thief.

She risked a quick mental probe, and met a block as solid as a wall of seamless marble.

Crap. It's not a thief—

She started to reach for the knife under her pillows,

and started to call for Gwena—only started; no more. She was frozen in place by a sudden flare of light.

It was the candle at her bedside, lighting itself. And at the foot of her bed was a sinister shadow, arms folded.

Clad in black from head to toe, veiled—there was no mistaking that costume. Kero had described and sketched it in detail, and no one here in Kata'shin'a'in would dare counterfeit it. Not here, not on the edge of the Plains.

Her intruder was Kal'enedral—one of the Swordsworn. She relaxed marginally. If this one had wanted her dead, she would *be* dead, and there would have been none of this drama with the magically lighted candle.

The Swordsworn flicked his (her?) hand, tossing something at the bed. It glinted as it spun, coppery and metallic on one side, enameled on the other. It landed enamel side up; it bore the image of a gold-feathered hawk.

Tale'sedrin. Children of the Hawk! She recognized it instantly; she had one identical to it in her belt-pouch, given to her by Kero as a way of identifying herself when she finally found the Tale'sedrin.

It seemed that *they* had found *her.*

"What—" she whispered—or started to. But the Swordsworn shook her (his?) head, and threw something else onto the bed. This time it was a piece of rolled vellum. Her eyes, caught by the movement, followed it for just a moment—hardly more than an eyeblink. But that was long enough. When she looked up again, the black-clad stranger was gone. There was no movement at either door or window to say which way he had taken—if, indeed, he had taken either.

:What happened?: Gwena demanded. *:Are you all right?:*

:Yes. Yes, I'm fine.: She told Gwena absently about her visitor as she picked up the vellum gingerly and unrolled it. Her heart, which had all but stopped, leapt and hammered with excitement.

It was a map of the Plains, the first such that she had ever seen. Or rather, the first such that she trusted. There had been plenty of folk who had offered her maps, but their reliability ranged from laughable to pathetic. This, from the hand of a Kal'enedral of Kero's own Clan, was something she thought she could put her trust in.

One thing stood out, on a map crowded with detail and closely written markers; an enigmatic little drawing, perched on the northern rim of the Plains, circled in bright red, very fresh, ink.

The Clans migrated with the season; could that be Tale'sedrin's current location?

Well, what else could it be? They know I'm looking for them; this is their answer. I have to come to them, they won't be coming to me.

She said as much to her Companion.

:I don't like it,: Gwena said, unhappily. *:I don't like it at all. You aren't planning on going out there, are you? Well? Are you?:*

Elspeth ignored her, letting her silence declare her intent. She was not about to argue with her Companion on this, and Gwena should have been able to anticipate just that reaction.

:I'd go for it, girl,: Need chuckled. *:Hell of an opportunity. Probably testing you to see if you've got the guts to go into their stronghold.:*

:You would go for it,: Gwena complained resentfully. *:The worst that could happen to you is that you'd have to find yourself another bearer. Don't listen to her, Elspeth.:*

:You just want her to do what you planned for her,: the sword jeered.

:Both of you, shut up, dammit,: she "shouted"—and was rewarded by blessed silence.

She was going of course; there was nothing that was going to stop her. Not Gwena's disapproval, or Skif's; not the possible risk, or the distance involved. She was finally charting her *own* course and following a path that no one had planned for her.

And that, in itself, was reason enough.

Chapter
Seventeen

DARKWIND

As he passed beneath the trees and away from open sky, Darkwind redoubled his shielding. When he had been fourteen and had been caught up in his friends' mating-spell, it had been an accident, and one that brought all of them a great deal of chagrined amusement. But if he were to "eavesdrop" now, it would be deliberate—and since he had not been invited, he was not going to intrude on this most private of moments for them.

Or at least, he had not intended to intrude—

But he was given no choice, after all.

Everything seemed quiet up by the swamp, and he didn't think there was any particular reason to double back and check the area beside the ruins; the gryphons themselves had made an aerial patrol of the forest before the flight. He doubted that anything large would have gotten in under cover of the trees.

On the other hand, it wouldn't hurt to check the trails for signs of intruders. It wouldn't take all that long.

He had just called to Vree, and was halfway through this particular patch of forest. He was heading in the direction of the path to the swamp and the *hertasi*, when a scream of agony cut the sky. A second scream answered the first. A heartbeat later, the world came apart for an instant.

At least that was what it felt like. He *knew* what it was as he slammed down another kind of shield and fought his senses clear; the resonating effect of a magic-blast, powerful, crude, and close at hand. And the tortured scream that had accompanied it, that echoed across the sky, and pierced all his mental shields, had come from Treyvan!

Vree was already shooting up through the treetops, streaking off in the direction of the shriek of rage and pain, screaming a battle cry of his own. Running all out, Darkwind followed on the ground as best he could.

This was wild land, hard to cross at any speed. He ran through it without any of his usual care—breaking branches, leaving behind tracks an infant could read, crashing through the undergrowth like a clumsy young deer in a panic. But still the terrain itself held him back; bushes clutched at him, roots tripped him up, thickets too thick to be forced blocked his way. Heedless of his own risk, he opened his mind to the gryphons, but heard—nothing.

And that was even worse than the cries had been.

Rage and fear blinded him to pain; rage and fear drove him through plum thickets, across a tumble of razor-sharp stone fragments, and loaned him wind and strength. His heart pounded too loudly for him to have heard danger coming up behind him; his soul was torn with claws of agony for what that silence might mean.

:Ahead!: called Vree, shooting under the tree branches like a winged arrow, turning faster than the eye could follow, and shooting away again. *:Here!:*

The bird was too excited and angry to manage anything more coherent than that. Darkwind plunged after him, his lungs burning, his side pierced with a lance of pure pain. Just when he thought that he could not possibly run any farther, he literally stumbled into a tangle of broken branches, then over a fur-covered leg, and fell into a mass of broken brush before he could regain his balance.

The leg belonged to Hydona, who was sprawled in an unconscious tangle, bleeding from one torn and wounded wing.

* * *

"Come on, Treyvan," Darkwind crooned, cradling the gryphon's head in his hands, and slapping his beak lightly. "Come on, old boy. Wake up. Come on, Hydona needs your help; I can't move her without you." Treyvan lay in the middle of a half-crushed bush. It had obviously saved him worse injury when he hit the ground, but Darkwind couldn't free him from the snarl of broken branches unless he could revive the male gryphon and get some help from him.

The eyelids fluttered, the beak opened a fraction, and closed again. The head stirred in Darkwind's hands and Treyvan protested his treatment wordlessly. "Arrwk—rrrr—Daaa—Daaarrrwk—"

"That's right, it's Darkwind. Come on." Darkwind slapped the beak a little harder, pulled at Treyvan's crest-feathers. "Come on. Say something with some sense in it. Wake up, old friend."

"Rrrrrrr." The eyelids fluttered and stayed open this time; the weight of the gryphon's head left Darkwind's hands as Treyvan raised it a trifle. "Hydona—" the gryphon croaked, whining wordlessly with pain, as he tried to turn his head. "Hydona—"

"She's hurt," Darkwind told him, "but I think she'll be all right. Her wing's hurt, I don't think she's broken anything, and she's kind of half-conscious, but I can't get her out. I need to get you out of this tangle, so you can help me get her out of hers."

"Can't—move—" the gryphon said, starting to thrash weakly in alarm. It was obvious then to Darkwind that Treyvan wasn't really hearing him—that, in fact, he was only half-conscious.

He opened his shields to the gryphon, and touched him directly, mind to mind. :*Don't move till I tell you. You're caught. Hydona is all right, but she's hurt and tangled up in some brush, and I'm going to need your help to move her.*:

He glanced back over his shoulder to the right, where the female gryphon lay, eyes half-closed, one wing folded awkwardly beneath her, the other oozing blood from a wound. Vree sat right beside her head, *his* eyes closed in concentration. He was in complete mental contact with her, helping to keep her calm and unmoving. He'd done this before, with wounded bondbirds, and he was remarkably good at it—in fact, if there were such a thing as a Healer among the bondbirds, Vree might well qualify. He might not have been able to hold Hydona if she had been completely awake and aware enough to fight him, or if she'd been delirious and raving, but like Treyvan, she had been—at best—half-conscious when the two of them arrived.

The mental contact seemed to steady Treyvan; he stopped thrashing, and held still. Satisfied that the gryphon wasn't going to lose control, panic, and disembowel his rescuer (a very real possibility with a predator as large and strong as a gryphon), Darkwind moved over to his side.

:All right, old friend. I'm going to start with your left wing. Lift it just a little—that's it—:

It took them much longer than Darkwind wanted to get Treyvan free; by the time they finished, Hydona had slipped a little farther away from consciousness. It took all three of them, Vree included, to rouse her—and all three of them to get her on her feet.

"What happened?" Darkwind asked, glancing sideways at what appeared to be fresh human remains—shredded—as they finally got Hydona, swaying, into a standing position.

"I—don't rrrremember," Treyvan said unhappily. "We completed the flight—yesss—and—"

"Aahhh," said Hydona. She shook her head, and gave a faint cry of pain. "There wasss—a man. Below. Usss. With a weapon. A crosssbow."

"Yesss, a man—" Treyvan nodded, as he put his shoulder to Hydona's to support her. "He sssshot Hydona—that isss all I rrrrremember—"

"Can you hold her up a moment by yourself?" Darkwind asked. "I think I see something, and I didn't get a chance to look over there."

Treyvan nodded and winced as if his head hurt. That gave Darkwind another little piece of information, confirming one of his suspicions. The male gryphon had been the one receiving the blast of magic that Darkwind had felt smash into his own shields, as if it had been nonspecific, and unfocused. Magic was a poor way to render someone unconscious—rather like taking a boulder to smash a fly. The amount of sheer power required to overwhelm was ridiculous—in fact, it was far easier to shape a bit of energy into a dart and shoot them with it. Better far to use a true mind-blast, if one had the Gift, or a physical weapon like the crossbow. A magic blast to the mind had certain side effects—and a headache was only one. It was not the weapon-of-choice, even against a flighted target.

That meant that the gryphons' attacker had no mental abilities of his own. And might not have had any magical ones, either.

Darkwind made certain that Hydona was balanced well, before leaving her side and walking over to what was left of the human who had attacked them.

He bent over the remains and poked at them with the tip of his dagger where he saw a glint of metal. Sure enough, there was a tarnished amulet of some sort about the neck, and the remains were as much blackened and burned as they were clawed.

He checked back over his shoulder; Hydona seemed to be doing better by the moment, so he spent some little time investigating the state of the corpse. When he stood up and returned to the gryphons, Hydona was standing on her own, and Vree had taken a perch in the tree above them, showing not the slightest interest in Treyvan's crest-feathers.

"Well, it looks like I can piece together what happened," Darkwind said, as he reached out for the leading edge of Hydona's injured wing. "At least I think I can."

"I wisssssh I could," Treyvan fretted. "I do not like thisss, not rrrememberrring."

"Treyvan . . . you may never get the memory back," Darkwind told him, fighting off his own guilty feelings. *I should have stayed nearby. I should have guarded them. It wouldn't have taken that long, just to wait around until they were through and on the ground again.* "Here's what I think happened. This fellow was watching you, and when Hydona got within range, he shot, wounding her. Treyvan, when you dove at him, he hadn't yet had time to reload the crossbow—I think he was counting on you to be very slow, since you're very large. I think your speed took him by surprise. He has an amulet around his neck, the kind that can be used to store very basic magic.

When you dove at him, he blasted you with it as kind of a reflex action.''

"But—we have defensssessss," Treyvan said in surprise. "Magic defensssessss."

"True—but they were partially down because of your mating. I remember noticing that as you took off, then thinking it wouldn't matter." *Now I wish I'd said something.*

Treyvan hissed. "Trrrue. It isss neccesssary. I had forgotten that. Not fully down, but—reduced."

He nodded. "Anyway, they were down enough that the blast knocked you unconscious, but *up* enough that you reflected part of it back to him. Since he didn't have any defenses at all, you got him with the back-blast. I don't know if you killed him, but in the end it didn't matter. If he wasn't, Hydona, you definitely killed him when he fell and was within your reach. See?" He pointed to her foreclaws. "There's blood on your talons, and he's fairly well shredded."

"But why don't *I* remember?" she asked unhappily.

"Because you weren't more than half-conscious at the time," he told her. "It was mostly reflex on your part."

"Ah." She accepted that, carefully putting one foot before the other, while Darkwind walked beside her, holding up the drooping wing so that it wouldn't drag on the ground.

"I . . . will have an aching head for a while, then," Treyvan said ruefully. "And I did not even rescue my mate—"

"Oh, you did, it was just rather indirect," Darkwind soothed him. "I wouldn't worry about the headache; I'm going to get the *hertasi* to send over their Healer as soon as I leave you. She'll put you both right."

He was making light of the incident—because he was afraid it might mean more than a simple trophy-hunter, trying to shoot down the gryphons.

How had he found out about them, whoever he was? How had he traced them here? Where had he gotten a protective amulet powerful enough to have knocked Treyvan out of the sky? Why did he use the crossbow instead of magic, if he'd had access to magic that formidable?

And why had he gone after them in the first place?

There were more questions. What were those faint

traces Darkwind had seen, before he had gotten the two gryphons to their feet—traces of a second person who had been moving about the two of them?

He'd been forced to destroy those traces, much against his will; there was no way to get to the gryphons without doing so. Getting in to disentangle their limbs and move brush away was the only way to help Treyvan and Hydona up and get them moving. He hadn't seen the scuffs and prints anywhere else, not even entering the area—and they had been quite clear around *Treyvan's* body, which meant, whoever it had been, the print-maker had *not* been the same person as the archer. The archer had been stone cold by the time the unknown had meddled with Treyvan's unconscious body.

If I had gotten here sooner, I could have caught him— Yet another lance of guilt, none of which was going to be assuaged until Treyvan and Hydona were safely back at their nest, and both of them were healed enough to take to the skies again.

The gryphlets boiled out of their nest as the quartet approached, hysterical with fear, so completely incoherent that not even their parents could get any sense out of them. They simply crowded under the adults' wings, pressing as closely to their bodies as they could, whimpering and trying to hide.

This, of course, did not help at all, but the little ones were too terrified to be reasoned with.

Darkwind couldn't tell if something had frightened them directly, or if they had linked in with their parents and experienced what had happened to the adult gryphons indirectly.

Whatever had happened, it rendered them completely irrational, and also turned them into complete nuisances.

He wanted to comfort them—and Hydona was nearly frantic with maternal worry—but they were in the way, underfoot, and demanding the total attention and protection of their parents, neither of whom were in any shape to give it.

Finally, in desperation, he tried the only one of them who wasn't already fully occupied. *:Vree!:* he called, hoping the bird might be able to at least chase the little ones out of the way.

The gyre came down from his protective circle above them in a steep dive, braking to a claws-out landing on the top of one of the stones. He looked sharply at the shivering, meeping gryphlets, and opened his beak to give a peculiar, piercing call.

The little ones looked straight at him, suddenly silent. Then they resumed their cries, but ran away from their parents and straight for Vree.

Vree, for his part, hopped down to a rock that stood just shoulder-height to the youngsters; he spread his wings and the little ones huddled up to the rock, one on either side, trying to cower under his wings, the tone of their cries changing from frantic to merely distressed. Vree replied to them with reassuring chirps of his own, "protecting" them with his wings.

It would have been funny, if the little ones hadn't been in such distress.

Whatever the cause of their fear, it could be dealt with later, once Treyvan and Hydona were settled into their nest, and the *hertasi* Healer brought to help them.

He left Treyvan leaning up against the stones with Vree and the little ones, while he helped Hydona into the nest-area to clean her wing wound. The bolt had passed completely through the wing, leaving a ragged, round hole. It needed a Healer; there was no way for him to bandage it properly, and it continued to ooze blood, despite the primitive pressure-bandage he put on it. She clamped her beak shut and obviously tried not to complain, but moaned softly despite her best efforts as he bound the cloth in place. Darkwind found himself sweating and apologized clumsily for her pain. He returned to help Treyvan into the nest, keeping the little ones back until the still-unsteady gryphon had settled himself.

"I'm going to get the Healer," he said. "Do you want me to leave Vree with you?"

"Yesss," Treyvan sighed, as the forestgyre herded the youngsters in with all the skill of an expert nursemaid. "If it would not leave you in danger. He issss much help. And after thisss," he concluded, with a hint of his old sense of humor, "I may even *give* him my cresst feath-erssss."

One thing at a time, he told himself. *First the gryph-*

ons, then the little ones—and then I find out who and why—and what this attack on them really means.

One thing is certain. The quiet we've been enjoying was just a momentary lull. We're in for more and worse trouble; I can feel it.

He had felt trouble ahead, like the ache before a storm in once-broken bones. Like a storm, that trouble would strike—and with no warning where or when. He little thought that this time the fury would strike straight at his heart.

He gave Nera and the rest of the *hertasi* a brief explanation of what had happened, while Nyara listened unobtrusively in the background. The Healer, Gesta, left halfway through without waiting for permission—so like the Healers of the Tayledras that Darkwind had to smile. No one gave *them* orders either, and they were not much inclined to wait for permission when they thought their services were needed. Vree came winging in over the swamp just after he answered the last of the lizard people's questions—mostly concerned with their own safety, and what, if anything, they could do to safeguard it.

With Vree back, there was no reason to postpone his regular patrol—and every reason to complete it. There might be traces of those invaders—they might even still be within Tayledras territory, though Darkwind doubted it. In the past, those who had invaded to strike at the Hawkbrothers generally moved in, made whatever action they had come to take, and moved out again.

And there was still no telling if this was a danger to the Tayledras, or simply the foolishness of a trophy-hunter.

But when in doubt—assume the worst. The Hawk-brothers stayed alive by that rule, and it had always been the precept Darkwind operated on. He went over his ground with eyes sharpened by anxiety, looking for traces of the interlopers.

He found only vague tracks, places where something had passed through, but the ground was too dry to hold marks, and it was impossible to tell what had made those traces. It could have been the marksman and his (presumed) companion; a thread caught on a thorn showed it was not simply an animal, despite the trace of lynx hair below it.

At sunset he completed the last of his circuits, being replaced by Starsong, Wintermoon's current lover. He thought she looked at him strangely when she passed him—a pitying glance as she vanished into the underbrush. He puzzled over that odd expression as he headed back toward his *ekele*, thinking only of changing, getting food for himself and Vree, and going back to the gryphons.

But as he hurried up the path, Vree suddenly swooped down in front of him, crying a warning. He froze, one hand on his dagger, as a man-shaped shadow separated itself from the rest of the shadows beneath the trees.

Then Vree swerved away, his cry changing from warning to welcome, as a huge, cloud-white owl rose on silent wings to meet him. Darkwind's hand fell from the hilt of his dagger, as he recognized Wintermoon's bird K'Tathi.

"Brother—" he called softly. "What brings you out here? I thought you were on hunt-duty for a while."

Wintermoon said nothing; only came forward, slowly, worriedly searching Darkwind's face with his eyes. "Then—you have not heard?"

Darkwind shook his head, alarmed by his brother's expression, and his words. "Heard? No—nothing from the Vale, anyway. Why? What—"

Wintermoon clasped Darkwind in his arms, in a rare display of emotion and affection. "Little brother—oh, little brother, I wish it were not so . . . I grieve for you, *sheyna*. Dawnfire . . . is dead."

He searched his brother's face . . . and saw only regret. Darkwind was prepared for almost anything but that. He stood within the protection of his older brother's arms, and tried to make sense of what he had just heard.

"Dawnfire? But—this was her rest day! She wasn't even going to leave her *ekele*, she told me so! Surely you must be mistaken."

"No," Wintermoon said, his voice soft with seldom-heard compassion. "No, there is no mistake. She was found in her *ekele*—"

Then it hit him, with all the force of a blow to the gut.

"No!" he shouted, pulling away and staring at Wintermoon wildly. "*No!* It can't be! I don't believe you!"

But Wintermoon's pitying expression—exactly like Starsong's—told him the truth that he did not want to hear.

He was too well-trained and disciplined to break down—and too overcome with shock to move. His knees trembled, and threatened to give way beneath him. Wintermoon took his shoulders and gently steered him over to a fallen tree at the side of the trail. He urged Darkwind to sit as Vree dove in under the tree branches and landed, making soft whistling noises in the back of his throat.

Darkwind felt blindly behind his back and got himself down on the log before his legs collapsed. "What—happened?" he asked hoarsely, his throat choked, his eyes burning. He blinked, and two silent tears scorched down his cheeks.

"No one knows," Wintermoon replied quietly. "Thundersnow came to see if she wanted to go hunting for game birds, and found her this afternoon. She was—" he hesitated. "Little brother, did she full-bond with her bird often?"

"Sometimes," Darkwind croaked, leaning on his left side. He stared out at nothing, more tears following the first. "She—could not full-bond without trance, but Kyrr was so bright, she didn't need full trance often."

How can she be dead? Who could have touched her in her own home?

His fists knotted, and his stomach. More tears welled up and flowed unnoticed down his face.

"Little brother, it appeared that she was in full trance; that at least is how Thundersnow found her. There were no signs of violence or sickness upon her." Wintermoon paused again. "I would say . . . she must have undergone full-bond with her bird, and that some ill befell the two of them." He paused. "She was not known for caution. It may be that she sent Kyrr into the Outlands, and met something she could not escape from." He rested his hand on Darkwind's shoulder. "I am very sorry, little brother. I—am not known for words. But if I can help you—"

Darkwind seized the comfort he had thrust away earlier, and clasped Wintermoon to him, sobbing silently into his older brother's shoulder. Wintermoon simply held him, in an embrace of comfort and protection, while Vree whistled mourning beside them.

Nyara twisted on the sleeping mat in her little cave, a ball of misery and confusion. When Darkwind came to the *hertasi* with his story of attack on the gryphons, she had been as confused and alarmed as any of them. But now she'd had some time to think about what he had said—and to think back to that last confrontation with her father.

Mornelithe Falconsbane had always hated gryphons, just as a general rule, although *she* was not aware that he had ever had contact with the species. Not directly, at least. But he had been very interested in Treyvan and Hydona, to the extent of pulling every detail she knew about them out of her. She had the horrible feeling, fast growing into certainty, that *he* and no other was behind this attack.

And yet a direct attack was so unlike him. Mornelithe *never* did anything directly; he always layered everything he did in secrecy, weaving plots and counterplots into a net not even a spider could untangle. Why *would* he send someone to shoot at them? And why would he send someone armed with the crudest of amulets, a protection that was bound to fail? It made no sense at all. . . .

The *hertasi* Healer passed the mouth of her cave. Gesta paused a moment, peering shortsightedly into the doorway. "Nyara?" she said, softly. "Are you there? Are you awake?"

Nyara blinked in surprise. "Yes," she responded. "Yes . . . I could not get to sleep. Is there something you need from me?"

Gesta coughed politely. "A favor, perhaps. The winged ones are better, but they need a full night's sleep. Yet they are fearful to sleep, fearing another hunter, this time in the dark. You, I think, can see well in the dark, no?"

"Yes, I can," Nyara responded, and in spite of her worries, a pleased little smile curled the corners of her mouth. *They trust me—or Gesta does, anyway—and they're willing to give me something to do.* "I think I see where you're tending. You want me to guard them, do you not? So that the winged ones may have some sleep."

"Yes," Gesta breathed, in what sounded like relief. "You need not defend them; you need only stand watch and pledge to rouse them if danger comes. You can do that, I think, without harm to yourself. And they asked after you, saying you were a friend. *We* would, but—"

The thin little figure silhouetted against the twilight sky shrugged, and leaned against its walking stick.

"But you do not see or move well by darkness, I know," Nyara responded. "I should be happy to attend them." She uncoiled from her mat and glided silently out to the *hertasi,* who blinked at her sudden appearance.

"Do you go across the swamp?" Gesta asked, taking an involuntary step backward and looking up at her. Nyara realized then that this was the first time the *hertasi* Healer had seen her on her feet. Her slight build might have deceived the little lizard into thinking she was shorter than she actually was. In reality, she was perhaps a thumb-length shorter than Darkwind, but certainly no more than that.

"No," she replied, wrinkling her nose in distaste at the thought of slogging through all that mud and water— and in the dark, no less. "No—if I go around about the edge, I shall find the ruins, no?"

"It will be longer that way," Gesta warned.

"But swifter if I need not feel my way through water in the dark," Nyara chuckled. "I go, good Healer. Thank you for giving me the task."

She slipped down to the path that led to the edge of the marsh before the *hertasi* could reply. And once out of sight of the *hertasi* village, she slipped into the easy run she had been bred and altered for, a ground-devouring lope that would have surprised anyone except those who were familiar with the Plains grass-cats on which she had been modeled.

While she ran, she had a chance to think; it was odd, but running always freed her thoughts, as if putting her body to work could make her mind work as well.

She thought mostly upon the notion that her father might have been involved in this attack upon the gryphons. If he was, what was she to do about it?

Treyvan and Hydona are my friends, she thought, unhappily. *They are, perhaps, the only true friends I have ever had. And Darkwind—oh, I wish that Father had not ordered me to seduce him! He makes my blood hot, my skin tingle. Never have I desired anyone as I desire him— not even Father. Father I hate and need—Darkwind I only need—*

The very thought of Darkwind, of his strong, gentle hands, of his melancholy eyes, of his graceful body, made her both want to melt into his arms, and to pounce on him and wrestle him to the ground, preparatory to another kind of wrestling altogether.

But Mornelithe has ordered me to take him—and therefore—I will not. She set her chin stubbornly, tucked her head down, and picked up her pace a bit.

But what if Mornelithe were behind this; what then?

I think it may depend upon if he sends more creatures against them tonight. Or if he has left a taint of himself that I can read. If I find nothing, I shall be silent. But if I find traces—then if I can—I must speak.

The decision seemed easy until she realized that she had actually made it. The realization took her by surprise.

I—why have I thought that? What are they to me, besides creatures who have been friendly—kindly—

No one had ever been friendly or kindly to her, not since Mornelithe had eviscerated her nurses, and given her sibs and playmates, failures by his reckoning, to his underlings to use as they would.

As he would give me to his underlings, if he judged me a failure. As he would kill me, if he knew of my rebellion.

Therefore he must not learn of it. . . .

She reached the border of the ruins before she expected; she slowed to a walk, and sharpened her eyes to catch the glow of body heat. She knew in general where the gryphons' nest was, but not precisely. She also freed her ears from her hair, and extended them to catch any stray sound.

It didn't take her long to determine where the nest was; she heard the murmur of voices echoing among the stones of the ruins, and traced them back to their source. She froze just behind the shelter of a broken-down wall, hearing not only the gryphons, but Darkwind as well.

"There was a red-shouldered hawk circling around you when I left," he was saying. His voice sounded odd, thick with emotion, and hoarse. "Dawnfire's Kyrr was a red-shouldered—you know, I made her promise me that she *wouldn't* come around here today—''

"Which may have been a missstake," Treyvan interrupted wearily. Nyara peeked around the end of the wall. "Sssshe wasss curiousss. Very curiousss. It isss entirely posssible ssshe did full-bond with her birrrd. And whoeverrr it wasss that attacked usss, may have attacked and killed herrr asss well. If the birrrd diesss, the bond-mate diesss, no?''

"Yes," Darkwind replied, but he sounded uncertain. "If they are in full-bond at the time. But I didn't see any dead—'' he faltered, "—birds—''

"You might not," Hydona said, emerging slowly from the entrance of the nest, the little ones trailing after her. "It might not have ssstruck the grround. Perrrhapsss it wassss caught in a tree. . . .''

She went on to say more, but Nyara didn't hear her. All of her attention had been caught by the female gryphon and the nestlings.

They bore the unmistakable stamp of her father's taint.

Hydona wore the contamination only lightly, a glaring red tracery like burst veins . . . and it was fading, as if Mornelithe had attempted something against her, and had failed. But the gryphlets— She moaned silently, to herself, as she had learned only too well to do.

Now she knew that it *had* been her father who had masterminded the attack on the gryphons. And how, and why.

The physical attack had never been intended to succeed. It had been intended to bring the gryphons down out of action, and only incidentally into his reach. He had attempted to subvert Hydona, to insert his own will and mind into hers. He surely found her too tough for him to take, at least, given the short amount of time he had to work in. She knew he had never really meant to do more than make a cursory attempt to take them, on the off chance that he would succeed by sheer accident.

Because what he had really wanted was the opportunity to get at the little ones and work with them, undisturbed. She knew from bitter experience that it would not take him long at all, with a young thing, to subvert it to his will. The gryphlets would not be as useful, as quickly, as the adults—but they were more malleable, and far less able to defend themselves against them.

And they had one thing the adults did not; a direct tie into the power-node beneath their birthplace.

Mornelithe wanted that; he could pull power away from nodes, by diverting some of the power-flows into them, but he had no direct access to any nodes. The only nodes anywhere near this area were the one beneath k'Treva, and the one beneath the gryphons' nest. Both were within k'Treva territory, and out of Mornelithe's reach.

The power-node here was very deep, but very strong, and its ley-lines ran into k'Treva Vale. Through the young, tainted gryphons, Mornelithe would have direct access to the node, the line, and very possibly, could drain the node beneath k'Treva.

Or move it to his own stronghold.

It was entirely possible he would also have access to lines and nodes in the Plains; she had no idea if the node here was connected there, or not.

And these ruins themselves could conceal artifacts from the ancient Mage Wars. Mornelithe had been trying to collect those for as long as she had been aware of his activities; he had only been marginally successful in his quests, gathering in creatures and devices either flawed, broken, or only marginally useful. His ambition was to acquire something of great power; one of the legendary permanent Master Gates, for instance. One of those would give him access to the old Citadels of the Lord Adepts; and *those,* however ruined, wherever they were hidden, would undoubtedly contain things he would find useful.

But having access to this node is going to be bad enough! She shuddered at the idea of Mornelithe with that much power in his hands. This nexus was far more important, far more powerful than the Birdkin guessed. If they had known, they would have either drained it or built their Vale here. Nyara closed her eyes and saw her father's face, slit eyes gleaming down at her, gloating with power beyond her weak imagination as she trembled.

With that much power, she would never be free of him.

She straightened and walked into the circle of stones before the nest. Her foot stirred a tiny stone as she moved, and the human and gryphons sprang up, gryphons with talons bared, Darkwind with his dagger drawn. They relaxed when they saw her; Treyvan sitting back down with a sigh.

"Gesssta sssaid that ssshe would assk Nyarrra to come ssstand watch thisss night for usss," Treyvan told Darkwind. "Ssshe sssseesss well by night, and we trussst herrrr—"

"You shouldn't," Nyara replied, stifling a sob. "Oh, you should not have trusted me."

Darkwind seized her by the arm, and pulled her into the stone circle. "Just what do you mean by *that?*" he snarled.

And slowly, holding back tears, she told them.

Chapter Eighteen

ELSPETH

This was, possibly, the strangest land Elspeth had ever crossed. There were no roads and no obvious landmarks; just furlong after furlong of undulating grass plains. There were clumps of brush, and even tree-lines following watercourses, but grassland was the rule down on the Dhorisha Plains. It was truly a "trackless wilderness," and one without many ways of figuring out where you were once you were in the middle of it.

Right now, the Plains were in the middle of high summer; not the best time to travel across them. Nights were short, days were scorching and long; the grass was bleached to a pale gold, insects sang night and day, down near the roots. Otherwise there wasn't much sign of life, no animals running through the grass, no birds in the air. Or rather, there was nothing *they* could spot; the Plains might well teem with life, as hidden in the grass as the insects, but silent. Here, where the tall, waving weeds made excellent cover, there was no reason for an animal to break and run, and every reason for it to stay quietly hidden where it was.

A constant hot breeze blew from the south every day, dying down at sunset and dawn, and picking up again at night. And not just hot, but dry, parchingly dry. Thirst was always with them; it seemed that no sooner had they drunk from their water skins than they were thirsty again. Elspeth was very glad of the map; since they had descended into the Plains near a spring, she'd puzzled out the Shin'a'in glyph for "water"—the water that was very precious out here in the summer. This was *not* a desert, but there wasn't a trace of humidity, day or night, and there would be no relief until the rains came in the fall. The mouth and nose dehydrated, skin was flaking and tight, and eyes sore and gritty, most of the time. Many of the water sources shown on the map were not springs or streams, which would have been visible by the belt of green vegetation along their banks, but were wells. There was no outward sign of these wells anywhere; in fact, they were frequently hidden from casual searching and could only be found by triangulating on objects like rocks, a mark on the cliff wall, a clump of ancient thorn-bushes. There were detailed, incredibly tiny drawings of the pertinent markers beside each water-glyph. Elspeth marveled again and again at the ingenuity of the Shin'a'in and their mapmakers. And she was very glad that she did not have to travel the Plains by winter. A bitter winter wind, howling unchecked across those vast expanses of flat land, would chill an unprotected horse and rider to the bone in no time. And there was little fuel out here, except the dried droppings of animals and the ever-present grass. Would it be somehow possible to compact the grass into logs? There were no natural shelters from the winter winds either, at least that she had seen. Small wonder the Shin'a'in were a hardy breed.

Since their goal was the northern rim of the Plains, they had chosen to follow the edge, keeping it always on their right as they rode. But Elspeth wondered aloud on their third day out just how the Shin'a'in managed to find their way across the vast Plains, once they were out of sight of the cliffs. And soon or late, they must be out of sight of those natural walls. How could they tell where they were?

Skif shrugged when she voiced her question. "Homing instinct, like birds?" he hazarded. "Landmarks we can't see?" He didn't seem particularly interested in the puzzle.

The sword snorted—mentally, of course. *:They use the*

*stars, of course. Like seafarers. With the stars and a
compass, you can judge pretty accurately where you are.
I expect some of those little scribbles on your map are
notes, readings, based on the compass and the stars. And
I know the lines they have cross-hatching it are some way
of reckoning locations they have that you don't.:*

Elspeth nodded; she'd heard of such a thing, but no
one in landlocked Valdemar had ever seen the sea, much
less met those who plied it. They both had compasses,
bought in Kata'shin'a'in, though Skif had complained that
he couldn't see what difference knowing where north was
would make if they got lost. She'd bought them anyway,
mostly because she saw them in places where the
Shin'a'in often bought made-goods. She reckoned that if
the Clansmen needed and used them, she should have
one, too. She bit her tongue when he complained, and
somehow kept herself from pointing out that on a fea-
tureless plain, if he knew which way north was, he would
at least be able to prevent himself from wandering around
in a circle.

The cliff wall loomed over their heads, so high above
them that the enormous trees on the top seemed little
more than twigs, and one couldn't hope to see a human
without the aid of a distance-viewer. Elspeth had one of
those, too, purchased, again, in Kata'shin'a'in. Skif
hadn't complained about that, but he had coughed when
he'd learned the price. It was expensive, yes, but not
more than the same instrument would have been in Valdemar—if you could find one that the Guard hadn't com-
mandeered. Here they were common, and every caravan
leader had one. The lenses came from farther south, carried between layers of bright silk, and were installed in
their tubes by jewelsmiths in Kata'shin'a'in. The workmanship was the equal of or superior to anything she had
seen in Valdemar.

Elspeth ignored Skif's silent protest over the purchase
of the distance-viewer, as she'd ignored the vocal one
over the compasses. She had saved a goodly amount of
their money on the road by augmenting their rations with
hunting; she also had a certain amount of discretionary
money, and some real profit she had made by shrewd
gem-selling. She had a notion that Quenten had known
these gemstones, amber and turquoise, change-stone and

amethyst, were rarer here, and therefore in high demand, for he had invested quite a bit of their Valdemaren gold in them. She was very glad the mage had. It enabled her to make those purchases without feeling guilty about the expense.

She'd done very well with her first attempt at jewel trading, so she didn't feel that Skif had any room to complain about how she spent some of that money. There was a curious slant to his complaints—a feeling that it wasn't so much that she had spent the money, but that she hadn't first consulted him. She also had a sneaking suspicion that if she had spent that same money on silks and perfumes, he would not have been making any complaint. And that, plainly and simply, angered her.

Not that she hadn't wanted silks and perfumes, but this was neither the time nor the place for fripperies. Instead of buying those silks and perfumes, she had bought other things altogether; the compasses and distance-viewer, some special hot-weather gear, and a full kit of medicines new to her, but which the Healers here seemed to depend on. If she could get them home intact, she would let Healer's Collegium see what they could do with these new remedies. She had bought two sets of throwing knives, in case she had to use and leave the set she now wore. She had purchased an enveloping cloak, and had gotten one for Skif as well—because as they left Kata'shin'a'in at the break of dawn, they had been wearing their Whites again, and she had wanted to disguise the fact until they were well down onto the Plains.

Wearing their Whites again was not something she'd insisted on just for the sake of being contrary, though Skif seemed to think so. It had seemed to her that, since the Shin'a'in already knew what Heralds were, it would be a good thing to travel the Plains in the uniform of their calling.

Skif argued that they'd been in disguise to avoid spies. She pointed out that it would make no difference one way or another insofar as possible spies were concerned. If Ancar could *get* spies near enough the Plains for them to be seen, he was more powerful than any of them had ever dreamed, and whether or not they wore their Whites would make no difference.

But if he were not that powerful, then wearing their

uniforms could provide them with a modicum of protection from the Shin'a'in. The Plainsfolk had a reputation for shooting first, and questioning the wounded. Being able to identify themselves as "nonhostile" at a distance was no bad idea.

Except that even with all the best reasons in the world, Skif didn't like *that* idea, either.

She was just about ready to kill him in his saddle. Now that he had her "alone," he seemed determined to prove how devoted he was to her safety. But he was going about it by looking black every time she did something that was "unfeminine" (or rather, something that asserted her authority) by disagreeing with her decisions, and by repeating, whenever possible, his assertion that this was a mistake, and they should go back to the original plan. If that was devotion, she was beginning to wish for detestation.

Tonight they camped beside a spring; easy enough to spot from leagues away as a patch of green against the golden-brown of the waving sea of grass. Because of that, she had decided to bypass the well they encountered earlier in the afternoon and journey on into darkness to reach the spring. After all, they were supposed to be making as much time as possible, right? They couldn't possibly bypass the place; it was the *only* spot ahead of them with trees. They couldn't even miss in the dark; they'd *smell* the difference when they reached water and the vegetation that wasn't scorched brown. And even if, against all odds, they did miss it, the Companions would not.

Skif, predictably, had not cared for that either. He only voiced one complaint, that he didn't think it was a good idea to push themselves that hard in unknown territory. But he did brood—she was tempted to think "sulked" but did not give in to the temptation—right up until the moment they made camp. She couldn't think why he should have any objections, not when they'd already agreed to make as much time as possible. All she could think was that it was more of the same—he didn't want her to make the decisions.

Once there, they had chores, mutually agreed on. She avoided him with a fair amount of success. While he set up camp, she collected water and fuel. Not too much of the latter; they didn't need much more than to brew a little tea. Elspeth was nervous about grass fires; one spark could set the entire area ablaze, as dry as this vegetation was. In her view, Skif was simply not careful enough. When she returned with her double handful of twigs and fallen branches, she discovered he had etched a shallow little pocket in the turf, just big enough to hold the fire she intended to build. Plainly that was not good enough; but Skif was a child of cities, and likely had never seen a grass fire. It was hard for someone like Skif to imagine the fury or the danger of a grass fire. A *city* fire, now, that was something they could comprehend—but grass? Grass was tinder, it wasn't serious, it burned up in the blink of an eye and was gone with no damage.

Right.

Elspeth knew better. It *was* tinder; it caught fire that easily and burned with incredible heat. But there was a lot of it out here—acres and acres—and that was what Skif couldn't comprehend. She had never, ever forgotten the description Kero had given her of a patrol caught in the path of a grass fire during her days as merc Captain of the Skybolts. Kero had described it so vividly it still lived in her memory.

"It was a wall of flame, as tall as a man, driving everything before it. Herds of wild cattle were followed by a stampede of sheep. That was followed by a sea of rabbits, frightened so witless they'd charge straight up to a man and run into his legs. That was followed by the little birds that lived in the grass, and a river of mice— and then the wall was on top of you. You could hear it roaring a league away, and nearby it was deafening. It moved as fast as a man can run, and it sent up a great black pall of smoke, a regular curtain that went straight up into the sky. The burning area was farther than I could jump—at the leading edge the ends of the grasses were afire, in the middle, all of this year's growth—but on the trailing edge, all the previous years' growth that was packed down was burning as fiercely as wood, and hotter—"

Kero paused and passed her hand over her eyes.

"Everyone let go their beasts; you couldn't hold 'em, not even Shin'a'in-breds. A couple of the youngsters, I'm told, tried to run across the fire. It was unbelievably hot; their clothing, anything that was cloth and not leather or

metal, caught fire. Not that it mattered. The hot air stole the breath from them; they fell down in the middle of the flames, trying to scream, and with no breath to do it, burning alive. The rest, the ones that survived, wet their shields and cloaks down with their water skins, put their shields over their backs and their wet cloaks over that, and hunkered down under both. 'Like turtles under tablecloths' is what one lad told me. They stuck their faces right down into the dirt, and did their best to breathe as little as possible. That was how they made it. And even some of those got scorched lungs from the burning air.'' She shook her head. *"Don't ever let anyone tell you a grass fire is 'nothing,' girl. I lost half that patrol to one, and the rest spent days with the Healers, for burns inside and out. It's not 'nothing,' it's hell on earth. My cousins fear fire the way they fear no living thing.''*

No, a grass fire was nothing to take lightly. On the other hand, there was no purpose to be served in giving Skif a lecture, especially not the way she felt right now. Anything she told him would come out shrewish; anything she said would be discounted. Not that it wouldn't anyway.

Rather than risk sounding like a fishwife, she simply took out her knife and cut a larger circle in the turf, removing blocks of it and setting them aside to replace when they were finished. She made a clear space about half as wide as she was tall. Skif sat and seethed when he saw her kindling a tiny fire in the middle of this comparatively vast expanse of clear earth, but he didn't comment. Then again, he didn't have to; she didn't even have to see his face, his posture said it all.

Even without her saying a word, he took what she did as criticism. Was it? She couldn't help it. Better to do without a little tea than risk a fire. She decided that he was going to seethe no matter what she did, whether or not she said anything.

And when the tea was boiled and their trail rations had been toasted over the fire, she put the fire out and replaced the blocks of turf—enjoying, in a masochistic kind of way, the filthy mess she was making of her hands—again to the accompaniment of odd looks from Skif.

:He thinks you're doing this just to avoid him,: the sword observed cheerfully.

:I don't particularly care what he thinks,: she retorted. *:I do care about making sure any watchers know that we're being careful with their land. It seems to me that since we're here on their sufferance, we'd better think first about how they're judging us. And I know they're out there.:*

:Watchers?: the sword responded.

:They're there,: she replied.

:There're at least four,: Need said, after a moment. *:I didn't know you could See through shields. You must be much better than I thought.:*

She came very close to laughing out loud. *:I can't. I simply guessed. The Shin'a'in are notorious for not allowing strangers on their land; and that they not only allowed us, they gave us a map, says that they are bending rules they prefer to leave intact. That didn't mean that they were going to leave us on our own, they don't trust us that much; if we didn't actually see anyone watching us, it followed that they were hiding. They aren't going to stop us, but I'll bet that if we did something wrong, we'd be dis-invited, and if we strayed from the path, we'd be herded back.:* She thought about it for a moment; it was the first thing that had offered her any amusement all day. *:Might be fun to do it and see how they'd get us back on track. I bet it wouldn't be as straightforward as riding up and helping us back to the "right" way. I bet they'd start a stampede or something.:*

The sword was silent for a moment. *:Convoluted reasoning, that; 'if we can't see them, they must be there.':*

:Merc reasoning,: Elspeth replied, and let it go at that.

When she finished replacing the turfs, she looked up to see Skif still sitting there, watching her. There was no moon tonight, only starlight, but his Whites stood out easily enough against the high grass and the night sky, and seemed to shimmer a little with a light of their own. He looked like something out of a tale.

Or a maiden's dream, she thought scornfully. *A hero, a stalwart man to depend on for everything. Perfect, strong, handsome—and ready to take the entire burden of responsibility on* his *shoulders.*

She stood up; so did he. She moved off a little, experimentally. He followed.

More than followed; he came closer and put his arms around her, and she stiffened. She couldn't help herself; it just happened automatically, without thinking. She didn't want him to touch her—not like that. Not with the touch of a lover.

"Don't!" he said, sharply.

"Don't what?" she asked, just as sharply, trying to pull away without being obvious about it.

"Don't be like that, don't be so cold, Elspeth," he replied, softening his tone a little. "You never used to be like this around me."

"You never used to follow me like a lovesick puppy," she retorted, getting free of him, walking away a little to get some distance, and turning to face him. "You used to be my 'big brother' until all this started."

"That was before I paid any attention to—how much you'd grown up," he responded. "All right, so I was a fool before, I wasn't paying any attention to what was in front of my nose, but I've—"

Oh, gods, it's a bad romantic play! She didn't know whether to laugh or cry. Both would have been so full of anger that they would have made her incoherent.

"You've been paying too much attention to idiot balladeers," she interrupted, rudely. "All of which say that the young hero is supposed to finally notice the beauty of the young princess, fall madly in love, rescue her and carry her off to some ivy-wreathed tower to spend the rest of her days in sheltered worship." She took a deep breath, but the anger didn't fade. "I've heard all of that horse manure before, I didn't believe in it then, and I don't now. You're not a hero and neither am I. I'm not a beauty, I just happen to be the only woman who's a Herald around here. I don't need rescuing, and I *don't* want to be sheltered!"

"But—" he said weakly, taking a step back, and overwhelmed with her vehemence.

"Stop it, Skif!" she snapped. "I've been nice, I've hinted, I've tolerated this, and I am not going to take any more! *Leave me alone!* If you can't treat me as your partner, *go home.* Nothing is going to happen to me in the middle of the Dhorisha Plains, for Haven's sake!" She waved her arm out at the expanse of trackless grass to the south of them. "There're half a dozen Shin'a'in out there right now, and I doubt any of them is going to let something get past them."

"That's not the point, Elspeth," he said, pleadingly. "The point is that I—"

"Don't you *dare* say it," she snarled. "Don't you *dare* say that you love me! You don't love *me*, you love what you *think* I am. If you loved me, you wouldn't keep trying to prove you were better than me, that I should follow your lead, let you take over, permit you to make all the decisions."

"But I'm not—"

"But you are," she retorted. "Every decision I make, you find a reason not to like. Every job I try to do, you try to do better. Every idea I have, you oppose, *Except* in those times when I'm acting, thinking, like a good little girl, who shouldn't bother her pretty head about warfare, and should go where she's been told and learn the pretty little magics she's been told to learn."

"I'm not like that!" he bristled, "Some of my best friends are female!"

She very nearly strangled him.

"So—any female you're not interested in can be a human being, is that it?" she said, her voice dripping scorn. "But any female you *want* had better keep her proper place? Or is it just that every female who outranks you can have her position and be whatever she needs to be, and anyone who's your peer had better let *you* be the leader? Oh that's noble, that truly is. How nice for you, how terribly broad-minded."

"Just who do you think you are?" he shouted.

"*Myself*, that's who!" she shouted back. "Not your inferior, not your underling, not your child to take care of! Not your doll, not your toy, not your princess, and not your property!"

And with that, she turned and stalked off into the grass, knowing she could lose him in a scant heartbeat—and knowing that Gwena could find her immediately if Elspeth needed her.

She ducked around a hillock, and dropped down into the dusty smelling grass. She held her breath, and listened for his footsteps, waited for him to blunder by in pursuit of her, but there was nothing.

:Gwena?: she Mindcalled, tentatively.

:He's just sitting here on his bedroll,: she said, and the disapproval in her mind-voice was thick enough to cut. *:That was cruel.:*

Elspeth slammed her shields shut before Gwena could reproach her any further. She didn't want to hear any more from that quarter. Gwena was on Skif's side in this, like some kind of matchmaking mama. She'd escaped her real mother's reach, and she wasn't about to let someone else take over the position.

She lay back into the fragrant grass; it was surprisingly comfortable, actually—and looked up at the night sky. The night was absolutely clear, and the stars seemed larger than they were at home.

Her back and neck ached with tension; her hands had knotted themselves into tight fists. Her stomach was in an uproar, and her throat tight.

This was no way to handle a problem.

She tried to empty her mind, just empty it of all the anger and frustration, the need that was driving her out into the unknown, and the heavy burden of responsibility she was bearing. Gradually the tension drained out of her. Her stomach calmed, her hands relaxed. She concentrated on the muscles in her back and neck until they unknotted. She stopped thinking altogether. She simply—was. Watching the stars, letting the warm, ever-present breeze blow over her, inhaling the dry, dusty scent of the grasses she lay in, feeling the earth press up against her back.

This place felt very much alive, as if the warm earth itself was a living being. It calmed her; she found her tension all drained out of her, down into the earth, which accepted it into a tranquillity that her unhappiness could not disturb.

Gwena's right. I was cruel. She felt her ears flushing hotly, and yet if she had the chance to do it over, there was nothing she would not have repeated. *What happened to us? There was a time I would have gladly heard him say he loved me. There was even a time when I might have been able to fall in love with him. Gwena was right; I could do so much worse.*

Tears filled her eyes; they stung and burned. Not from what she had done to Skif—he was resilient, he'd survive. But from what she was going to face in the years ahead. *If we all survive this, I probably* will *do worse. I'll probably have to marry some awful old man, or a scrawny little boy, just to cement an alliance. We'll need all the help we can get, and that may be the only way to buy it. If I took Skif, I'd at least have someone who loves me for a little while. . . .*

But that wasn't fair to him; it was wrong, absolutely wrong. She'd be using him and the affection he was offering, and giving him nothing in return. She *didn't* love him, and there was no use pretending she did. Furthermore, he was a Mindspeaker; he'd know.

Besides, when she married that awful old man, whoever he was, she'd have to break with Skif anyway, so what was the point?

What was the point of all of this, at all? When it all came down to it, she was just another commodity to be traded away for Valdemar's safety. And intellectually, she could accept that. But emotionally—

Why? she asked the stars fiercely as tears ran down into her hair. *Why do I have to give up everything? Why can't I have a little* something *for myself? That's not being selfish, that's just being human! Talia has Dirk, Kero has Eldan, even Mother has Daren. . . . Why isn't there anyone for me?*

There was no answer; she held back fierce sobs until her chest ached. Maybe she wasn't as sophisticated as she had thought, after all. Maybe all her life she *had* believed in the Bardic ballads, where, after long struggle, the Great True Love comes riding out of the shadows.

All right, maybe it's childish and stupid, but I've seen it happen—

Happen for other people. That fact was, the notion *was* childish and stupid—and worse, if she spent all her time waiting for that One True Love, she'd never get anything done for herself.

But, oh, it hurt to renounce the dream. . . .

Chapter
Nineteen

INTERLUDE

Dawnfire woke all at once; her heart racing with fear, but her body held in a strange kind of paralysis. She couldn't see anything. All she could feel was that she was so hungry she was almost sick, and that she was standing; her position seemed to be oddly hunched over, but—

No, it wasn't hunched over, it was a perfectly normal position—for *Kyrr's* body. She was still in the body of her bondbird. Only—Kyrr was gone. She was alone.

She opened her beak to cry out, and couldn't—and then the paralysis lifted, and a hazy golden light came up about her, gradually, so that her eyes weren't dazzled.

She was on a perch.

As she teetered on the perch, clutching it desperately, trying to find her balance without Kyrr to help her, she saw that there were bracelets on her legs, and jesses attached to them, and that the jesses were fastened to a ring on the perch.

The light came up further; she moved her head cautiously at the sound of a deep-throated chuckle to discover that now she could see the entire room. An empty, windowless room—except for a bit of furniture, one couch, and its occupant.

She couldn't help herself; panic made her bate, and she flapped uncontrolled right off the perch. She couldn't fly even if she hadn't been jessed; she hadn't Kyrr's control—and she hung at the end of the leather straps, upside-down, swinging and twisting as she beat at the air and the perch with her wings.

I can't get back up!

That sent her into a further panic, and she flailed wildly in every direction but the right one, with no result whatsoever. She twisted and turned, tangled herself up, and banged her beak against the perch support, and never once got a claw on the perch itself.

Finally she exhausted herself; she hung in her jesses with her heart beating so hard she could scarcely breathe, listening to it thunder in her ears, growing sicker and weaker with every moment she stayed inverted. She had gone, as any raptor would, from a state of uncontrolled panic to a state of benumbed shock.

She was hanging facing the wall, not the room beyond, and its bizarre occupant; she didn't even hear the footsteps coming toward her because of the sound of her own heart.

Suddenly there was a hand behind her back, and another under her feet. She clutched convulsively as she was lifted back up onto the perch. She released the hand as soon as she was erect, transferring her grip to the sturdy wood, as the Changechild took his gloved hand away, and smiled enigmatically down on her.

"Having trouble, dear child?" he purred, stepping back a pace or two to observe her. The glove was the only article of clothing he was wearing, and now he pulled it off, and tossed it on a shelf next to her perch. He really didn't need much in the way of clothing—long, silky, tawny-gold hair covered him from head to toe—except for certain strategic areas.

If she could have blushed, she would have. It wasn't as if she hadn't seen nude males before, certainly there was no nudity taboo among the Tayledras, but he seemed to flaunt his sexuality like some kind of weapon. It was somehow obscene, even though he wasn't doing anything overtly to make it so. It was all in posture, unspoken body-language.

He seemed to sense her embarrassment and take amusement from it—and that made it even more obscene.

He looked like a cat—a lynx—and he moved like a cat as he padded back to his couch. That was where she had seen him when the light came up; reclining with indolent grace on a wide couch piled high with silken pillows, in black and golden tones that matched his hair. He resumed his position with studied care, and a fluidity not even a real cat could have matched, then rested his head on one hand to watch her with unwinking, slitted eyes.

Her feet twitched a little and she teetered on the perch.

That was when she realized just how helpless she truly was. He didn't *need* the jesses, except to keep her from falling to the floor every time she bated. Without Kyrr, she was as helpless in this body as a newborn chick. She could do simple things that were largely a matter of reflex—like perching—but anything more complicated than that was out of the question. She could no more fly now than she could in her own body.

She stared at him in despair; he smiled, and slowly, sensuously, licked his lips.

"I," he said, in a deep, echoing voice, "am Mornelithe Falconsbane. You made the fundamental mistake of attacking me. And I am afraid that you, dear child, are my prisoner. To do with as I will."

Fear chilled her, and made all her feathers slick tight to her body, as he said that. *Mornelithe Falconsbane*—this must be the Adept that Darkwind's Changechild had fled from; the Adept that had trapped and tormented her *dyheli* herd—his name did not invoke a feeling of comfort in a Tayledras.

"It's a pity that you managed to have yourself trapped in that bird's body," he continued. "The ways that I may derive pleasure from it are so limited, but I'm sure you can be flexible."

He mock-sighed and lowered his lids over his slitted, green-golden eyes, looking at her through thick lashes. She clutched the perch nervously, swaying back and forth, her mouth dry with fear as she waited for him to do something.

He raised a single finger. The door beside his couch opened, and a human in golden-brown leather that clung to his body as if it had been sewn around him entered

the room, carrying a deep pannier. He went straight to
her perch, as she flapped in alarm, and put the basket
down underneath it. Then he untied her jesses from the
ring, tied a leather leash to it instead, and attached the
leash to her jesses.

Then he turned his back on her and left her, all without
saying so much as a single word.

She looked down into the basket. Cowering in fear,
and looking up at her, were three live mice.

Now her stomach growled with hunger, even while her
mind rolled with nausea. She stared down at the mice,
ravenous, and feeling just as trapped as they were.

She was starving—this was food. And she didn't have
the slightest idea of how to kill and eat it.

Kyrr would, but Kyrr was gone.

Then it hit her. Kyrr was *gone*. Not waiting patiently
in the back of the bird's mind, but gone completely.
Dead. Part of her soul, her heart, her life—gone without
a trace. She was completely alone, in a way she had not
been since she was ten.

The grief that descended over her was so total that she
forgot everything, including her hunger.

Oh, Kyrr—

Her beak gaped, but nothing happened. Not even a
single sob.

She couldn't cry, she wasn't even human anymore.
How could she mourn as a hawk? She didn't know, and
the inability to cry out her pain and loss redoubled it.
They were both lost, she and Kyrr—and they would never
come home again.

She closed her eyes and rocked from foot to foot,
trapped in a sea of black grief, drowning in it.

A satisfied chuckle made her snap her head up and
open her eyes wide. Mornelithe was watching her with
amusement.

Her grief turned to rage in the blink of an eye; she
mantled and screamed at him, her cry piercing the silence and shattering it—though she was careful to keep
a tight grip on the rough wood of her perch as she
shrieked her defiance at him.

He found that even more amusing; his smile broad-
ened, and his chuckle turned into a hearty laugh.

"Perhaps you won't be a disappointment after all,

clever bird-child.'' He caressed her with his eyes, and her rage spilled away, leaving her weak and frightened again.

He returned his gaze to something in his lap, and as he shifted a little, she could see that it was a dark crystal scrying-stone. He stared at it, his gaze suddenly going from casual to penetrating—and what he saw in it made him frown.

Starblade

Chapter
Twenty

DARKWIND

Starblade turned away from the little knot of Tayledras Adepts and Healers surrounding Dawnfire's *ekele* in despair, and sought the sanctuary of his own *ekele*. The fools were trying to thrash out what could have killed Dawnfire, and why—when it was obvious, as obvious a taint on the girl's body as the taint on his own soul, and the contamination that had cracked the Heartstone.

He knew it the moment he saw it. And he could not say a single word.

He felt old, old—burdened with secrets too terrible to hide that he *could not* confess to anyone, weary with the weight of them, sick to his bones of what he had done. As he had so many times, he climbed the stairs to his *ekele*, then sought the chamber at the top, and stood looking down on the Vale, wondering if *this* time he could find the strength to open the window and hurl himself to the ground.

But the crow on his shoulder flapped to its perch as soon as he entered the room, and sat there watching him with cold, derisive eyes. And he knew, even as he fought the compulsion to turn away from the window and suicide, that Mornelithe Falconsbane still had his soul in a fist of steel, and there was nothing he had that he could call his own. Not his thoughts, not his will, not his mind.

He flung himself down on the sleeping pad, hoping to lose himself in that dark oblivion—but sleep eluded him, and Falconsbane evidently decided to remind him of what he was.

The memory-spell seized him—

Smoke wreathed through the trees as he paused in an area he had thought safe, and the acrid fumes made him cough. The fire was spreading, far faster than it should have. For a moment, Starblade wondered if perhaps he should go back for help. But other emergencies had emptied the Vale of all but apprentices and children, and he had a reputation to maintain. He was an Adept, after all, and a simple thing like a forest fire shouldn't prove too hard to handle. He sought shelter from the smoke down in a little hollow, a cup among some hills, and closed his eyes to concentrate on his first task.

No, you fool, Starblade cried at his younger self. *Go back! Get help! Nothing trivial would frighten that many firebirds!*

But this was a vision of the past, and his younger self did not heed the silent screaming in his own mind.

He reached out with his mind, seeking the panic-stricken firebirds first of all. Until he could get them calmed and sent away, he would never be able to put the flames out. One by one he touched their minds; turned their helpless panic into a need for escape instead of defense, and sent them winging back to the Vale. One of the beast-tenders, the Tayledras who spoke easily to the minds of animals, would take care of them. He had a fire to quench.

There were more firebirds than he had expected, and they were in a complete state of mindlessness. It took time to calm them.

But while he had stood there like a fool, the fire had jumped the tiny pocket of greenery where he worked, and ringed him. He opened his eyes, weary with the effort of controlling the birds, to find himself surrounded by a wall of flame and heat. The leaves were withering even as he watched, the vegetation wilting beneath the heat of the hungry flames. Fear chilled him, even as the heat

made him break into a sweat. That was when he realized,
when he reached for the power to quench it, that he had
exhausted himself in calming the birds—

—and that he was cut off from the node and the nearest
ley-lines. Something had sprung up while he worked;
something had arisen to fence him away from the power
he needed, not only to quell the fire, but even to save
himself. He was enveloped in a wall of shielding as dan-
gerous as the wall of flame.

Smoke poured into the hollow; something brushed
against his leg, and he glanced down to see that a rabbit,
blind with panic, had taken shelter behind his ankle. The
heat increased with every passing moment; it wouldn't be
long before this little valley was afire, like the rest of the
forest here. He was not clothed for a fire; he had run out
in his ordinary gear, a light vest and breeches. He had
nothing to protect him from the flames, nothing to breathe
through. There was only one thing he could do—wrap
the remains of his power about him in as strong a shield
as he could muster, and run—

As the nearest flames licked toward him, he sent his
bird up into the safety of the skies, and sprinted for what
he hoped was the easiest way out. Straight into hell.

On the sleeping pad, his body writhed in remembered
agony, his mouth shaping screams of pain he was not
permitted to voice.

Flames licked his body, hungry tongues reaching out
from burning scrub, a tree trunk. There was no pain at
first—just a kind of warm pressure, a caress as he ran
past. Then came the pain, after the flame had touched—
red heat that blossomed into agony. Sparks fell on him as
he dashed under a falling, blazing branch. He wrapped
his hair around his mouth, and still the air he breathed
scorched his lungs. Within moments, there was nothing
but pain—and the fear of a horrible death that drove his
legs.

Then—cool, smokeless air. He burst out past the fire-
line, into the unburned forest. Freedom.

But not from pain. He fell into a stream, moaning,
extinguishing his smoldering leather clothing and hair.
The stream cooled him but did nothing for the pain, for
the horrible burns where the skin was blackened and
crisped on his arms. How long he lay there, he did not

know. Smoke wreathed over him, but the flames did not grow nearer. He could not tell if it was the smoke that darkened his sight—or his pain. Only that, after a dark, breathless time of agony, salvation loomed out of the smoke, a spirit of mercy—vague and ghostlike.

NO! he screamed. NO! Don't believe him! Kill yourself, draw your knife, kill yourself while you have the chance!

He reached out toward the mist-wreathed shape, who seemed to be someone he knew, yet could not identify. Hazy with an intimation of power, the stranger's white hair was a beacon that drew his eyes. White hair—a Tayledras Adept, surely. Yes, he knew this one; he must. Rainwing? Frostfire? Both were recluses. No matter—he managed a croak, and the other started and turned his steps in Starblade's direction.

No— he moaned. No—

"I thought I heard someone Call," said the other, stooping over him in concern. "I see I was right."

His lips shaped words he could not speak for lack of breath. "Help me—"

Silver hair wove a web of light that dazzled his eyes. The Adept's own eyes, gilded-silver, held his. "I will have to take you to my home," the other said worriedly. "The fire has cut us off from Tayledras Vale. But I can tend you there, never fear. Will that be all right?"

Starblade nodded, giving consent, and as a consequence of that consent, relaxed all of his defenses. And as the other bent closer over him, to lift him in amazingly strong arms, he thought he saw a peculiar gleam in the other's eyes. . . .

He awoke again, resting on something soft, his arms thrown over his head, with a tawny silken coverlet swathing him from chest to feet. He still hurt, but he was no longer covered with angry, blackened burns, and he took a deep, experimental breath to find his lungs clear again.

Then he tried to move his arms—and couldn't.

He tried harder, struggling against silk rope that bound him hand and foot—with no better success. A deep chuckle answered his efforts.

He twisted his head to face the source of the sound.

"So eager to take leave of my hospitality?" said the tall, catlike Changechild, smiling as he paced toward the couch on which Starblade lay tethered. The creature had modeled himself on a lynx; was clothed mostly in his own tawny-silk hair, but wearing a supple, elaborately tooled and beaded leather loincloth. "How—uncivilized of you."

It—he—smiled, with sensuously parted lips. Starblade wrestled furiously against his bonds. "My Clan will know where I am," he warned. "Even if you kill me, they will know where I am, and they will—"

"They will do nothing," the Changechild yawned, examining the flex of his own fingers for a moment, admiring his needle-sharp talons. "You accepted my offer of help, consented to come away with me. You will leave no trail of distress for them to follow—and you are behind my walls and shields now. Call all you like, they will not hear you."

Starblade snarled his defiance. "You forget, Misborn—I am Tayledras. My bird will bring them here!"

He sought for Karry's mind with his own, even as the Changechild moved slightly aside and gestured. "If you mean that—it tried foolishly to attack me."

Starblade followed the gesture to a shadow-shrouded corner, where something thin and almost-human looked up with wild, unfocused eyes, its hands and mouth full of feathers.

Perlin falcon feathers.

Karry's feathers.

Silent tears ran into his hair; silent sobs shook his body. None of it brought Karry back.

The crow cawed; it sounded like scornful laughter.

The Changechild sat on the edge of the couch, and flicked away the covering, leaving him naked and unprotected, even by a thin layer of silk. He shrank away, involuntarily. "I am called Mornelithe, rash birdman," the creature said, idly gliding a talon along Starblade's side. "I think I shall take another name, now. Falconsbane." He glanced sharply at Starblade, who continued to fight his bonds, though his eyes blurred with the tears for Karry he would not—yet—shed. "And believe me, my captive. In a shorter time than you dream possible, you will have another name for me." He paused, and a slow, lascivious smile curled the corners of his mouth. "Master," he said, savoring the word.

Then he bent over his captive and transfixed him with a pair of green, slit-pupiled eyes, that grew and grew until they filled Starblade's entire field of vision.

"I think we shall begin the lessoning now."

Mercifully, he could no longer remember that lessoning, not even under the goad of Mornelithe's spell. It involved pain; it also involved pleasure. Both hovered at the edge of endurance. Mornelithe was a past master at the manipulation of either, of combining the two. When it was over, Mornelithe had the keys to his soul.

He knelt before the Changechild, abasing himself as fully as he could; worshiping his Master, and detesting himself for doing so. All that was in his line-of-sight at the moment was the golden marble of the floor, and Mornelithe's clawed feet. Thankfully, he had not yet been required to kiss them this time.

"Ah, birdman," Mornelithe chuckled. *"You grovel so charmingly, so gracefully. It is almost a pity to let you up."*

Starblade felt himself flush with shame, then chill with fear. Too many times in the past, such seemingly casual words had led to another "lesson."

"You have learned your place in the scheme of things quite thoroughly, I think," Mornelithe continued. *"It is time to let you return to your lovely home."*

Instead of elation, the words brought a rush of sickness. Bad enough, what he had become—but to return to the Vale, bringing this contamination with him—

He wanted to refuse. He wanted to rise, take the dagger at his belt, and slay his tormentor. He wanted to take that same dagger and slay himself.

He tried to assert his will; he closed his eyes and concentrated on placing his hand on the hilt of that dagger. He was an Adept—he had training, experience, his own personal powers. His will had been honed to an instrument like the Starblade of his use-name. Surely he could reclaim himself again. Yes . . . yes, he could. He could feel his will stirring, and opened his mouth to denounce his captor.

"Yes, Master," he heard himself say softly. *"If it is your will."*

He felt his lips stretching in an adoring smile; his head

lifted to meet Mornelithe's unwinking eyes. His hand did not move from the floor.

There were two Starblades inside his mind. One worshiped Mornelithe and looked to his Master for all direction. That was the one that was in control, and there was no unseating it. But buried deep inside, away from all control, bound and gagged and able only to feel, was the real Starblade.

Mornelithe could have destroyed even this remnant; he had not, only because it amused him to see his victim continue to suffer, long after the contest of wills had ended.

"I do not entirely trust you, dear friend," Mornelithe said, softly, as he reached down and touched Starblade's cheek. "You were a stubborn creature, and I do not entirely trust you away from my sight. So, I shall send you a watcher, also—one that the rest will take for your new bondbird. Here—"

He snapped his fingers, and held out his hand—and a huge crow, identical in every way to those the Tayledras bonded with, flapped out of the shadows beside Mornelithe's chair to land on the outstretched arm. The Changechild gestured with a lifted finger that Starblade should rise from his crouch to a simple kneeling position; the Tayledras' body obeyed instantly, even while his helpless mind screamed a protest.

The crow lifted silently from Mornelithe's wrist, and dropped down onto his shoulder.

And what little remained of Starblade's will was frozen with paralysis.

"There," Mornelithe said with satisfaction. "That should take care of any little problems we may have, hmm?"

The crow cawed mockingly, joining Mornelithe's laughter. . . .

The memory-spell released him, leaving him limp and shaking, with the echo of that laughter in his ears.

From the moment he had left Mornelithe's stronghold—which leavetaking he did not remember—he had been completely under the Adept's control. And Mornelithe was an Adept; there was no doubt of that. All that he lacked to make him a major power was control of a node. The only two for any distance around lay in the hands of the Tayledras.

Mornelithe intended to change that. And at the time of his release, that was all that Starblade had known; he had no idea what Mornelithe planned.

Nor, when he was found wandering in the heart of the burned area, did he even remember that he had been taken.

Instead, he had false memories of being overcome with smoke, of losing Karry somewhere in the heart of the fire—of taking a blow to the head from a falling tree. Then vague and confused recollections of crawling off and hiding in a wolverine's hole until the fire passed, of smoke-sickness that pinned him in the area for several days, of bonding to a huge crow who brought him fruit to feed him and supply his fevered body with liquids, and his final desperate attempt to get back to the Vale.

And the false memories passed muster. The crow was unremarked-upon. He had only an unusually touchy temper that caused his friends and son to give him some distance until he should regain his normal calm. Any changes in him, they—and he—ascribed to the trauma he had endured, and they all felt that those changes would pass in time.

All else seemed well, until the ritual to move the Heartstone.

Only then, *after* the disaster, did his true memories return. And it was then that the rest of his hidden memories emerged—

Memories of going to the Heartstone every night, and creating a flaw in it, leeching the power away from a place deep inside, and creating an instability that would not be revealed until the entire power of the Vale had been loaded into it, preparatory to bridging the distance between the old Heartstone and the new.

That was the first night he had tried to fling himself from the top of his *ekele*.

Once again, Mornelithe exerted his power over him, through the compulsions planted as deeply within him as he had planted the flaw in the stone. The crow was the intermediary of those compulsions, and since it never left his side, Mornelithe's hand was always upon him.

And when he tried to confess his pollution, he found

his tongue uttering simple pleasantries. When he tried to open his mind to let others see the traitor within their ranks, he found himself completely unable to lower his own shields. As he had been in Mornelithe's stronghold, he was bound, gagged, and paralyzed, a prisoner within his own mind, still toyed with and controlled for Falconsbane's pleasures and purposes. At least half of the time, that tiny portion of himself that was still free was buried so deeply that it was not even aware of what passed, what Mornelithe made him do, and say.

All he could do, in the moments he was free to speak and act, however, circumspectly, was to alienate his son, in the barren hope that, once made into an enemy, anything Starblade supported, Darkwind would work against. It looked as if the ploy was working.

At least, it had until the death—no, murder—of Dawnfire. Once again the hand of Mornelithe Falconsbane had reached out to take what he wanted, and again Starblade had been helpless to prevent it.

There was only one further hope. Darkwind had withdrawn from the company of mages after the disaster. Darkwind lived outside the influence of the flawed and shattered Heartstone. So Darkwind's powers *should* be uncontaminated by Mornelithe's covert influence. If he could just get Darkwind to take up his powers again— Darkwind would call for help from the nearest Clan. The deceptions that had held for so long would shatter under close examination, and Mornelithe would find himself locked out, once again.

But how to get Darkwind to resume his powers, after all that Starblade had done to keep him from doing just that?

Starblade groaned, and threw his arm over his eyes. There seemed no way out; not for him, nor for anyone else.

K'Sheyna was doomed, and his was the hand that had doomed it. The only way out was death, and even that had been denied him.

Damn you, Falconsbane! he shrieked inside his own mind. And it seemed to him that he caught a far-off echo of derisive laughter.

* * *

Darkwind felt torn in a hundred pieces, divided within himself by conflicting emotions, responsibilities, and loyalties. Treyvan had kindled a mage-light; a dim orange glow in the center of the ceiling of the lair. Yet another surprise to Darkwind; he hadn't known the gryphon could do *that*, either.

He slumped in one corner of the gryphons' lair with his head buried in his hands and his mind going in circles. Hydona curled protectively around her youngsters, trying to minimize whatever harm Falconsbane had already done them. *Her* shields were up at full strength, with Treyvan's augmenting them. Darkwind's shields augmented *both* of theirs; he had never renounced that part of his magecraft, and he squandered his own energies recklessly to stave off any more disaster that might befall his friends.

Nyara sat curled into a ball in the opposite corner of the lair, with as much distance between herself and the rest of them as she could manage.

After his initial outburst of rage—during which he had come very close to breaking her neck with his bare hands—Darkwind's anger toward the Changechild faded. After all, none of this was of Nyara's plotting. He should have known better than to leave her with the *hertasi*, who were mostly creatures of daylight, to keep her watched at a distance by *tervardi* and *dyheli* who also moved mostly by day.

I should have found a night-scout willing to watch her, he thought distractedly. *Hindsight is always perfect.*

"All right," he said, breaking the silence, and making everyone jump. He turned to Nyara, who shrank farther back into her corner, her eyes wide and frightened. "Stop that," he snapped, his tightly-strung nerves making him lash out at her as the only available target. "I'm not going to kill you."

"Yet," Treyvan rumbled. He had taken Nyara's news much worse than Hydona. His mate tended to ignore the past as beyond change, and was interested only in what she could do to fix what had been done to her younglings. Treyvan felt doubly guilty; because he had failed to protect Hydona, and because he had failed to protect his offspring.

Darkwind knew exactly how he felt.

Nyara tried to melt into the rock behind her, her eyes now wide and focused on Treyvan.

Darkwind recaptured her attention. "I want to know everything that *you* know about us, and what *he* knows that you're sure of. I mean not only what you've told your f—Falconsbane, but what he knew before this."

Nyara shivered but looked as if she didn't quite understand his question.

He stood up, walked over to her, and towered over her. "What does he know about the Vale?" he asked, speaking every word carefully. "Begin from the very first thing you knew."

Nyara began, stuttering, to tell them fairly simple bits of intelligence that anyone could have figured out for himself. That the only nodes Falconsbane could possibly access were in Tayledras hands. That he had made several attempts to get at one or the other of the nodes. She identified each attempt that she knew of, going back to long before the arrival of the gryphons. Most of these trials had been low-key, tentative feints. And as she spoke, she gained confidence, until she was no longer stuttering with fear, and no longer speaking in short, choppy sentences.

Most of the feints she described, Darkwind had already been aware of. But then she took him by surprise.

"Then F—father decided to take the Vale from within, I think," she said, her hands crooking into claws, as her eyes glazed a little. "This was when he was angry with me, and he was—he was—he was angry with me." Her expressive face was as still as stone, and Darkwind sensed that this had been one of those periods when Falconsbane had "trained" her, using methods it made him ill even to contemplate.

But this was important. She had said that Falconsbane meant to "take the Vale from within." He had to know what that meant, and what had happened.

"What did he mean by that?" he prompted. She gave him a frightened, startled look, as if she had forgotten he was there.

"He set a trap," she replied tightly. "He set a very clever trap. He sent many of his servants to create diversions—emptying the Vale of all but one of the Adepts."

This was beginning to sound chillingly familiar—but she was continuing.

"When that one was alone—he knew that there was but one Adept still present by the level of power within the Vale—he created a disturbance that required an Adept." She licked her lips nervously and gave him a pleading glance. "I truly do not know what that was," she said, "I was not in favor. He did not grant me information."

"I understand that," he said quickly. "Go on."

"When the Adept came to deal with the disturbance, Mornelithe sprung the trap and closed him off from the Vale. He was hurt—and that was when Mornelithe cast illusions to make him appear to be of the Birdkin, so that the Adept would accept him as rescuer. The bird, Father slew. It was not deceived, and attacked him. But by then the Adept's hurts were such that he was unconscious, and did not know. Father took him to the stronghold and imprisoned him to break him to Father's will."

"And you know who this Adept is?" Darkwind felt himself trembling on the brink of a chasm. If it *was* his father—it would explain so much. And yet he dreaded the truth—

She looked directly up at Darkwind, and said, clearly and forcefully, "I did not know until Father called me on the night of moon-dark who that man was. It was your father, Darkwind. It was he that is called Starblade." She licked her lips, and raised one hand in a pleading gesture. "He wanted you, as well, the son as well as the father—he wanted me to—entice you. I told him 'yes,' but I told myself 'no,' and I kept myself from working his will, as he worked it upon your father."

There it was, the blow had fallen. He surprised himself with his steady, cold calm. "So Falconsbane succeeded?"

She nodded, dropping her eyes, her voice full of quiet misery. "When he sets out to break one to his will, he does not fail. I was—present—for much of it. It was part of my t-t-training. That this could be happening to me. Both the pleasuring, and the punishment. I can tell you some of what he did, what he ordered Starblade to do when he returned to the Vale. You do not want to know . . . what was done to control him."

Darkwind tried to speak and could not. Treyvan spoke for him, in a booming, angry rumble. "Continue! All that you know."

"He was, firstly, to forget what had happened to him. Mornelithe gave him false memories to replace what had truly occurred—until Mornelithe chose otherwise. Then he was to creep in secret to the heart of the Vale." She gave Darkwind a look of entreaty. "I have not the words—"

"The Heartstone," Darkwind supplied, at her prompting, feeling sick.

"The Heartstone," she said. "Yes. He was to go to it in secret, and change it—he was one who created it, so he would know best its secrets. Father did not *know* that his trap would ensnare someone of that quality, but he was so pleased that he had, he forgot, often, to mete out punishment to me."

"Return to the subject, Changechild," Treyvan growled. She wilted, losing some of the confidence she had regained.

"What was it Starblade was supposed to do to the Heartstone?" Darkwind prompted her, with a bit more gentleness. She turned gratefully to him.

"He was to make a flaw in it, a weakness, one that would not appear until the Birdkin prepared to move. *Then* he called back all his creatures, to make it appear that all was made safe here. He even sent *his* creatures to guard beyond *your* borders, so that you would be prepared to shift your power elsewhere."

Darkwind held up his hand. "How much does he know—how can he continue to control Starblade, and does he know our strength?"

She shrugged. "I do not know what he knows, but he has long patience and is willing to move slowly, so that each move he makes is sure. But as to how he controls Starblade, it is with a crow."

"His bondbird." Somehow that was simply the crowning obscenity. To take the closest tie possible to a Tayledras other than a lifebond, and pervert it into an instrument of manipulation—

"He cannot speak, move, or let his thoughts be known. All that is under Father's control, from compulsions planted when he was broken, and held in place by the crow." She hesitated a moment. "There is little, I think, that he can learn unless Starblade goes to him, and that, he has not done. The barriers still in place about the Vale prevent that. But there is much that he can do with the compulsions already in place."

"Not for long," Darkwind said, with grim certainty, heading for the door of the lair. "Hydona, forgive me— I can't do anything about the younglings yet. But I *can* do something about this.

"Go," she replied. "Frrree thisss placsse of the viperrr, then perrrhapsss we can frrree the little onesss asss well."

"*I* will guard the Changechild," Treyvan said, before Darkwind even thought of it.

And before Darkwind could think to ask "how?" the gryphon turned to face Nyara, his eyes flashing. She looked surprised—

And then she slumped over, unconscious.

Darkwind returned to Nyara's side. She was asleep, deeply asleep, but otherwise unharmed.

Treyvan sighed. "I have not hurrrt herrr, Darrrkwind. But it isss better to have the enemy underrr yourrr eye."

"She isn't exactly the enemy," Darkwind said, uncertainly.

"She isss not exactly a frrriend," Treyvan replied. "Ssshe isss at besssst, a weaknesss. I will watch herrr, for my magic isss ssstronger than hersss. Go."

Darkwind did not have to be told twice. He was out the door of the lair and running for the Vale before the last sibilant "s" had left Treyvan's beak. Dawn's first light flushed the eastern horizon, and Vree shot into the sky from his perch on a stone beside the lair crying greeting to his bondmate, projecting an inquiry. While running, Darkwind tried, as best he could, to give Vree an idea of what he had learned, in simple terms the bird could understand.

He conveyed enough of it that Vree screamed defiance as he swooped among the forest branches, preceding Darkwind and making sure the way ahead was clear of hazard. The bird was angered, but he had not lost his head or his sense of responsibility.

:Where?: Vree demanded, his thoughts hot with rage.
:The Vale,: Darkwind replied, as he leapt a bush, and

took to the game trail that led most directly to the k'Sheyna stronghold.

:I go,: the bird said. *:I go* in, *with you.:*

Once again, Darkwind was surprised, but this time pleasantly. *:I go,:* Vree repeated firmly.

That took one worry off his mind. It would be a great deal easier to handle that thrice-damned crow with Vree around.

Now he concentrated on running; as hard and as fast as he could, keeping his attention fixed on the ground ahead and leaving his safety in Vree's capable talons.

Where would Starblade be at this moment? He was an early riser, as a rule. By the time the sun was but a sliver above the horizon, he was generally in conference with one or more of the Adepts. There was a kind of informal ceremony there, as the memorial fire at the foot of the Heartstone was fed with fragrant hardwoods and resinous cedar. Those Adepts remaining—even the most reclusive—generally attended at least one of these meetings; they remembered those who had been lost, and monitored the Heartstone very carefully, looking for changes in it morning and night.

With Father carefully making sure they accomplish nothing, he thought with nausea. *Now I know why he never misses a meeting.*

Now he was on safer ground; he passed his own *ekele,* and that of his brother; passed night-scouts coming in and day-scouts going out, both of whom stared at him in equal surprise. He ignored the ache of his lungs and his legs; dredged up extra reserves of energy and ran on, long hair streaming out behind him. He caught sight of other bondbirds flying beside him, peering down at him curiously, and guessed that their bondmates were somewhere behind. He ignored them; he would take no chances that a carelessly shielded thought would warn Starblade—or more importantly, the thing that controlled him in the guise of a black bird.

Up hills, and down again; he took the easiest way, not the scouts' way—using game trails when he could find them. Finally he came out onto a real path, one that led to the border with the Dhorisha Plains, and had, in better days, been used by visitors from both peoples. It terminated at the entrance to the Vale, and Darkwind took deeper breaths, forcing air into his sobbing lungs. It would not be long now. . . .

The shimmer marking the shields that guarded the entrance flickered between the hills. This was where Vree usually left him.

A cry from above alerted him, and Vree swept in from behind in a stoop that ended with the forestgyre hitting him hard enough to stagger him, and sinking his talons into the padded shoulder of Darkwind's jerkin. A fraction of a heartbeat later, he was through the shields, a tingle of pure power passing through him as the shields recognized him and let him by.

He was inside the Vale, but this was no time to slow down. He flung himself down a side path, bursting through the overgrown vegetation, and leaving broken branches and a flurry of torn leaves in his wake.

He was nearing the Heartstone; he heard voices ahead, and he felt its broken rhythms and discordant song shrilling nauseatingly along his nerves. Vree tightened his talons in protest but voiced no other complaint.

He staggered, winded, into the clearing holding the Heartstone, taking the occupants by complete surprise.

Vree did not wait for orders; he had an agenda of his own. Before Darkwind could say a word, the forestgyre launched himself from Darkwind's shoulder, straight at the crow that sat like an evil black shadow on his father's shoulder, as if it was whispering into Starblade's ear.

The crow squawked in panic and surprise, and leapt into the air—heading for the shelter of the undergrowth, no doubt counting on the fact that falcons never followed their prey into cover. But the evil creature did not know Vree; his speed, or his spirit. The gyre hit the crow just as he penetrated the cover of the lower branches; hit him with an impact audible all over the clearing. Rather than taking a chance that his stunned victim might escape, instead of letting it fall, Vree bound on with both sets of talons, and screamed his victory as he brought his prey to the ground. And Starblade collapsed.

The action of Darkwind's bird stunned the Adepts, all but Stormcloud, who shouted something unintelligible, and flung out his hand in Darkwind's direction. The scout found himself unable to move *or* speak, and fell hard on his side—

Vree bent and bit through the thrashing crow's spine, ending its struggles.

Darkwind fought against his invisible bonds as the outraged Adepts converged on him—but as they started to move, an entirely unexpected sound made them freeze where they stood.

"Free—" Starblade moaned, the relief so plain in his voice that it cut to the heart. "Oh, gods, at last, at last—"

The Adepts turned to stare at their leader, and Darkwind took the momentary distraction to snap his invisible bonds.

He stumbled to his father's side and reached for his hands. Starblade took them; his mouth trembled, but he was unable to say anything. It seemed as if he was struggling himself, fighting against a horrible control that even now held him in thrall.

"He's been under compulsion! Put a damn *shield* on him!" Darkwind shouted, throwing his own around his father, and startling the others so much they followed suit. And just in time; Darkwind felt a furious blow shuddering against his protections as the others added their strength to his. Another followed—then another. A half dozen, in all, before the enemy outside gave up, at least for the time being.

And now I know your name and face, Darkwind thought with grim satisfaction. *I know who you are. Now it's just a matter of hunting you down.*

Starblade groaned, still fighting the binding that kept him silent. "I know, Father," Darkwind said, urgently, as the other Adepts gathered around them. "I know at least some of it. That's why Vree killed that damn crow. We'll help you, Father. I swear it, we'll help you."

Starblade nodded slightly, and closed his eyes, silent, painful tears forming slowly at the corner of his eyes and trickling down his ghost-pale cheeks as Darkwind explained what he had learned from Nyara as succinctly as possible. The others wasted no time in argument; Starblade's own reactions told the truth of Darkwind's words.

"Let me tend to him," Iceshadow said, when Darkwind had finished. The scout moved over enough for the older Adept to take a place cradling Starblade's head in both his hands. Iceshadow stared intently into Starblade's eyes, but spoke to the son, not the father. "Tell me in detail everything you know."

Darkwind obeyed, detailing Nyara's explanations of how Falconsbane had caught Starblade, and how he had broken the Adept and set the compulsions. Iceshadow nodded through all of it.

"I think I have enough," he said, then looked down into Starblade's eyes. "But first, old friend, I must bring down your shields. *He* has trained you to respond only to pleasure, or pain. And since I do not have time for pleasure—forgive me, but it must be pain."

As Starblade nodded understanding, Iceshadow caught Darkwind's attention. "Take his left hand," the Adept said. "Spread it flat upon the ground."

As Darkwind obeyed, mystified, Starblade closed his eyes and visibly braced himself.

"Take your dagger and pierce his hand," Iceshadow ordered. And when Darkwind stared at him, aghast, the older Tayledras frowned fiercely. "Do it *now,* young one," he snarled. "That evil beast has tied his obedience to pain, and I cannot *break* his shields to free his mind without driving him insane. Now do what I tell you if you wish to help him!"

Darkwind did not even allow himself to think; he simply obeyed.

Starblade's scream of agony sent him lurching to his feet and away, tears of his own burning his eyes and blurring his sight.

When he could see again, he found Vree standing an angry and silent guardian over *his* victim, the crow that Mornelithe Falconsbane had used to control Starblade and shatter the lives of everyone in k'Sheyna. Showing a sophistication that Darkwind had not expected of him, Vree had neither eaten his victim, nor abandoned it. The first might have left him open to Falconsbane's contamination—the second might have given Falconsbane a chance to recover his servant, perhaps even to revive it. Almost anything was possible to an Adept of Falconsbane's power. It only depended on whether or not he was willing to expend that power.

Even if they buried the crow, it was possible that Falconsbane could work through it, to a limited extent. There was only one way to end such a linkage.

Destroy it completely.

There was always a fire burning beside the Heartstone; that memorial flame to the lives of those who had died in its explosion. Darkwind picked up the bird carefully by one wing, and took it to the stone basin containing the fire of cedar and other fragrant woods long considered sacred by both the Shin'a'in and the Tayledras.

He raised his eyes to the shattered Heartstone, truly facing it for the first time since the disaster.

The surface of the great pillar of stone was cracked and crazed, reflecting the damage beneath. The invisible damage was much, much worse.

And none of it—*none*—was his fault. The personal burden he had carried for so long, the ghost of guilt that had haunted his days, was gone.

Darkwind bent over the basin's edge and closed his eyes in a prayer to the spirits of the woods and an apology to the spirits of the Tayledras that had died when the Heartstone sundered.

Mornelithe Falconsbane, you have a great deal to answer for.

He drew back and hurled the body of the crow into the fire pit—so hard that something shattered with a splintering *crunch* as it hit—perhaps the bird's bones, perhaps the branches of the fire. . . .

The Adepts were so intent on Starblade that they didn't even look up, but a sudden heavy weight on his shoulder, and the soft trill in his ear, told him that Vree approved.

The feathers caught fire quickly; the rest took longer to burn—but the flames from the resin-laden branches were hot, and eventually the flesh crisped and blackened, then burst into flame. He watched until the last vestige of the bird was ash and glowing coals, and only then turned back to the rest.

Iceshadow still cradled Starblade's head in both his hands. A pool of blood had seeped out around Starblade's hand, with Darkwind's knife laid to the side. The expression on Iceshadow's face was just as intent, but Starblade's expression had changed entirely.

Darkwind wondered now how he could ever have mistaken the changes in his father for anything other than a terrible alteration in his personality. *Here* was the father he had loved as a child—despite the pain, the grief, and the suffering etched into his face.

Starblade opened his eyes for a moment and saw him; he smiled, and tried to speak.

And couldn't. Once again, he came up against a terrible compulsion. His face twisted as he strove to shape words that would not come.

"Keep trying," Iceshadow urged, in a low, compelling voice. "Keep trying, I'm tracking it down."

Iceshadow was seeking the root of the compulsion, and reversing it; since Falconsbane had changed his father's will rather than placing a simpler block, it was not a matter of removing a wall. Instead, Starblade's mind had to be altered, set back to normal bit by bit as each compulsion was found and changed, so he could regain the use of all of his mind.

The internal struggle, mirrored in Starblade's face, ceased as Iceshadow found the series of problems, and corrected them one by one.

Darkwind dropped to his knees beside his father, and took the poor, wounded hand in his own. Blood leaked through an improvised bandage, but Starblade managed a faint ghost of a smile, fleeting, and full of pain.

"I made you my enemy," he whispered. "I made you hate me, so that anything I told you to do, you would do the opposite. Then, when M–M–" his face twisted with effort.

'Mornelithe," Darkwind supplied.

Starblade sighed. "When *he* twisted my thoughts, so that they were no longer my own, I knew that *he* would want you to take up magic again. If you did, eventually *he* would find a way to take you, too, through me. And blood of my blood, you would have been vulnerable."

'He almost had what he wanted," Darkwind replied grimly, thinking of all Nyara had told him.

Starblade nodded. "The only way I could think of to protect you was to drive you away from me. So that the more I tried, beneath his compulsion, to bring you back to magic, the more you would fight it. Then . . . when my mind was not my own . . . you were safe." He looked up tearfully, entreatingly, at his son. "Can you . . . ever forgive me?"

Darkwind blinked away tears. "Of course I can forgive

you,'' he said quickly, and took a deep breath to calm himself. He looked up at Ice-Shadow. ''How clear is he?'' he asked.

Iceshadow shook his head. ''I've only begun,'' the Adept replied, exhaustion blurring his words a little. ''It's going to be a long process. The bastard set the compulsions in a few days, but they've had all this time to work and develop. We'll have to keep him under shield the whole time.''

''Put him in the work area,'' Darkwind suggested. ''It has strong shields, and there aren't any apprentices who need it right now. Those shields are the best we have.''

''Which is why I was not—permitted—to go there,'' Starblade whispered. ''The bird would not let me.''

''Then that is a good indicator that the shields will hold, don't you think?'' Darkwind responded. He started to let go of Starblade's hand, but his father clutched it despite the pain that must have caused.

''Wait,'' he coughed. ''Dawnfire—''

Darkwind froze. Iceshadow asked the question he could not manage to get out.

''What about Dawnfire?'' the Adept asked. ''She's dead.''

''No,'' Starblade said urgently. ''The bird was never found, but M–M—*his* sign was on her body. I think he has her—trapped in her bird. Still alive, but helpless. A—another toy.'' Starblade's face was twisted, but this time with what he remembered. ''It would—please him— very much.''

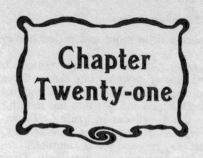

Chapter
Twenty-one

ELSPETH

The sky burned blue, but eight hooves pounded their own frantic thunder on the earth of the Plains; grass stems lashed their legs and the barrels of the Companions as they fled. Elspeth risked a look back, her hair whipping into her face and making her eyes water. The pack of fluid brown shapes streaming through the grasses behind them seemed a little closer. It was hard to tell for certain; they were visible only as a flowing darkness in the grasses, and the movement of the vegetation as they disturbed it. Then the lead beast leapt up, showing its head, and she was sure of it.

"They're gaining on us!" she shouted at Skif. He looked back, then bent farther down over Cymry's neck like a jockey. She did the same, trying to cut her wind resistance.

The Companions were running as fast as they could—which was very fast, indeed. The ground flowed beneath their hooves at such a rate that after one look that made her dizzy, she kept her eyes fixed ahead. She could not imagine how any creature could be capable of keeping up with them. It seemed impossible that *they* could be moving this fast.

:What are these things?: she asked Gwena who flat-

tened her ears a little more and rolled her eyes back at her rider.

:I don't know,: the Companion replied, bewildered. *:I've never heard of anything like them.:* Sweat streamed down her outstretched neck, and the ends of her mane lashed Elspeth's face and got into her mouth.

:I have,: the sword cut in gruffly. *:Damn things are magical constructs; beasts put together by an Adept. Probably all they're good for is running.:*

Elspeth looked back again, nervously. The pack leader gave another of those jumps, that took it briefly above the level of the grass stalks; this time showing its head clearly. Its mouth was open, its tongue out like a dog's. All she really *saw* were the jaws, a mouth full of thumb-length fangs.

:Well—running and killing,: Need amended. *:Whatever, they're not of a type I've seen before. That makes them twice as dangerous; I can't tell you what they're capable of.:*

"Thanks," Elspeth muttered under her breath. She peered ahead, wishing there was any way she could use her distance-viewer. Somewhere on the cliff ahead of them—hopefully somewhere near—was a path like the one they had descended. This trail was next to a water-fall, and she strained her eyes for a glimpse of water streaming down the side of the cliff into the Plains. If they could reach that path, they could probably hold the things off. They might be able to climb it faster than the beasts could; certainly they would be able to hold the narrow trail against their pursuers if they turned to stand at bay.

At the top of that path lay the place circled on the map. Whether or not there was any help for them there—

The Companions were getting tired. How long could they keep this pace up?

Her nose caught the scent of water as they topped a rise, just as she saw the line of green, a line of verdant trees and bushes, at the edge of a long slope, down below them. There was a glint of reflected light from the cliff; she assumed that was the promised waterfall.

She closed her eyes for a moment, and set loose her FarSight; looking for a place to make a stand. There wasn't much else she could do at the moment, other than make certain she was in no danger of being tossed off if Gwena had to make a sudden move.

Nothing at the bottom of the cliff; no, that was definitely no place to make a stand. The waterfall splashed down onto rocks right beside the beginning of the trail; the rocks were wet and slippery, marginal for booted feet, treacherous for hooves. In fact, the entire path was like that, winding beneath the waterfall at times, skirting the edge of it at others. This was not a straight fall; the water dropped through a series of basins and down many tumbles of rocks, keeping spray to a minimum. It might almost have been sculpted that way, and the path appeared to be an afterthought, cut into the stone around the fall as best as could be.

The path was narrow, too narrow to allow more than one rider at a time. She scanned the entire length of it, and found no place wide enough for the four of them to hold off their followers. If they made a stand, it would have to be at the top.

So she turned her FarSight to the top—and there, at last, was the shelter she had been searching for.

There were ruins up there; tumbles of massive rocks, identifiable only as ruins because of the regular size and shape of the stones, and the general shapes of what might once have been walls. Right where the path reached the top, there was a good place to hole up.

:*There's magic there,*: Need said suddenly, looking through Elspeth's "eyes." :*Do you see that kind of shimmer? That's magic energy. With luck I can use it to help with defense.*:

:*I don't intend to get close enough to those things to have to use a blade,*: Elspeth retorted.

:*Dunce. I didn't mean for you to fight. I mean to channel my magic through you. I was a fairly good mage. You may even learn something.*:

Elspeth felt stunned. :*I thought you only protected—*:

:*That was when I was asleep,*: the sword said shortly. :*Why don't you see what you can do about picking off some of those beasts? Maybe if you kill one, the others will stop to eat it.*:

Well, it was worth trying. The long slope gave the Companions some relief; though tiring, they were running with a bit less strain. Gwena's coat was still sweat-foamed, but her breathing beneath Elspeth's legs was easier.

Elspeth pulled her bow from the saddle sheath; freed an arrow from the quiver at her knee. She clamped her legs tight around Gwena's barrel, and turned, sitting up a little higher in her saddle as she did so.

The leader of the pack had a peculiar bounding rhythm to his chase; it was, she discovered, rather like sighting on a leaping hare. And she had done that so many times she had lost count; hunting had been one of the few ways she could escape the Palace and her rank and position.

Although I wish I had a hawk right now to set on them. A big hawk. With long, long talons. . . .

The leader's bound carried him below the grass; she nocked and loosed—and he leapt right into the arrow's path.

Soundless they were on the chase; soundlessly he fell, and he fell right under the feet of his pack. Whether or not they would—as Need had so gruesomely suggested—stop to eat him, it didn't matter. At least not at the moment, not while at least half the pack tumbled over the body of the leader, and the rest stopped their headlong chase to mill aimlessly around the dead and the fallen.

She nocked and loosed another arrow, and a third, both finding targets, before Gwena carried her out of range. Never once did any of those she hit utter a single sound.

:Good work,: the Companion said, without slowing. *That should buy us some time.:*

:Assuming something else doesn't take their place, or join them,: the sword pointed out grimly. *:I hate to say this, but I do sense things stirring; energies being disturbed, and some kind of communication going on that I can't read. I'm afraid we're going to have something else on our trail before long.:*

She didn't say what she was thinking; it wasn't as if Need had willfully called these things up. *:Will we have a chance to get up on that path first?:*

:I think we'll make it up to the top. But there's more trouble up there. It's at the border of a bad area, and it has its own energies that are reacting to the changes elsewhere. I think you should know that disturbance brings predators and scavengers alike.:

Well, that was no more than the law of nature. She sheathed the bow again and looked back down their trail. There was nothing immediately in sight.

But there *was* a dark golden clot of something on the horizon, something tall enough to be visible above the grass, and it was coming closer. She rather doubted it was a herd of Shin'a'in goats.

The scent of water was stronger; she turned to face forward. The belt of greenery was near enough now to make out individual trees and bushes, and the waterfall dashed down the side of the cliff with a careless gaiety she wished *she* shared.

She knew what awaited them and held Gwena back a little to let Skif shoot ahead of her. Cymry's headlong pace slowed as she met the slippery rocks of the trail. Gwena's shoulders bunched beneath Elspeth's knees as she prepared to make the climb.

The scramble up the trail was purest nightmare. If it had not been that the Companions were far more sure-footed than the Heralds were, and far, far faster even on footing this treacherous, she would have stopped to dismount. As it was, she clung to the saddle with legs and both hands, drenched with water spray and her own sweat of fear. If she dared, she would have closed her eyes. Gwena skidded and slipped on the spray-slick rocks; she went to her knees at last once for every switchback, and there seemed to be hundreds of those. Every time Gwena lurched sideways, Elspeth lurched with her—further unbalancing the Companion and hindering her recovery. The only good thing was that the slower pace enabled Gwena to catch her breath again.

Ahead, Cymry and Skif were in no better shape. That presented a second danger, that they might lose their balance and careen into Gwena and Elspeth, sending all four of them to their deaths.

Gwena might have read her mind; the Companion stopped for a moment, sides heaving, to let Cymry put a little more distance between them. She stood with her head hanging, breathing deeply, extracting everything she could from the brief rest.

Elspeth used the respite to peer through the spray, down to the foot of the trail.

The entire trail was visible from this vantage point,

and there was nothing on it except them. Yet. But peering up at her—at least, she presumed they were peering up at her—were several creatures of a dark-gold color that would have blended imperceptibly into the grasslands. They stood out now, only because of the brilliant green of the vegetation below the waterfall. Milling around them were some dark-brown slender beasts, whose fluid movements told her that the pack that had pursued them had recovered from the loss of its leader. In fact, there seemed to be more of them.

I think I know what that blot on the horizon was now. I wonder where the other "hounds" came from, though. . . .

And mingling with those creatures was something else; black, small animals that hopped rather than walked.

She guessed from their behavior that there was some kind of consultation going on. The black creatures seemed to be the ones in charge, or conveying some kind of orders. As she watched, the thin creatures arrayed themselves below the cliff, providing a kind of rear guard. The golden-brown forms lined up in an orderly fashion, and started up the path with a sinister purposefulness. And the black dots sprouted wings and rose into the air.

Crows— she realized. Then, as they drew nearer— *Dearest gods—they're so big!*

They were heading straight for the Heralds. And they could do a great deal of damage with those long, sharp bills, those fierce claws.

Without being prompted by the sword, she pulled her bow again, hoping that dampness hadn't gotten to the string. She nocked and sighted, and released; and repeated the action, filling the air below her with half a dozen arrows.

Only three reached their mark, and one of those was by accident, as a crow flew into the path of one of the arrows while trying to avoid another. Of those three, one was only a wound; it passed through the nearest crow's wing, and the bird spiraled down to the earth, cawing its pain, and keeping itself aloft with frantic flaps of its good wing.

Poor as the marksmanship had been, it was enough to deter the rest of the birds. They kited off sideways, out of her arrow range; caught a thermal, and rowed through the air as fast as their wings could flap to vanish over the top of the cliff.

Gwena lurched back into motion, and Elspeth was forced to put her bow away and resume her two-handed clutch on the saddle pommel. They were barely a third of the way to the top of the cliff and the shelter of the ruins.

She hoped they would see that shelter—and that what awaited them at the top was not a further nest of foes.

Wherever the crows had gone, they had not managed to herd another clutch of magically-constructed creatures to the ruins to meet them. And they didn't return to harass the Heralds themselves.

Elspeth heaved a sigh of relief that was echoed by Gwena as they approached the edge of the cliff without seeing any further opposition to their progress. They reached the end of the path without meeting any other dangers than the treacherous path itself—though the last third, so high above the floor of the Plains, had put Elspeth's heart in her throat for the entire journey. She tried to use her FarSight to spy out the land ahead, but either her fear or something outside of herself interfered with her ability to See. She *thought* the way was clear, but she drew her bow—again—just in case it wasn't.

They scrambled up the final switchback, with Elspeth praying that there wasn't anything lying in ambush, and found themselves on a smooth apron of masonry, uneven and weathered, with weeds growing through the cracks.

But there was no time to marvel. A new threat climbed the trail behind them—a threat that was surefooted enough to have closed the gap between them. Elspeth had not had any chance to shoot at these new followers, but they were much bigger than the first creatures that had pursued them across the Plain as well as being armored with horny plates, and she was not terribly confident that their arrows would make much of an impression on these beasts. And they were barely two switchbacks behind the Heralds.

She and Gwena pushed past Skif and scrambled for the shelter of that ruined towerlike edifice she had Seen. He followed right on Gwena's crupper; the Companions' hooves rang on the stone in perfect rhythm, sounding like one single horse.

They reached the shelter of the stones just barely ahead of their pursuers; the first of the creatures came over the edge of the cliff as they whisked into a narrow cleft between two standing walls, a cleft just wide enough for the two of them, or one of them and a Companion, but deep enough for several to work unhindered behind whoever held the front.

Skif and Cymry reached the cleft last, which put them in the position of initial defenders. As Elspeth threw herself from the saddle, she reached for bow-case and quiver. As she fumbled with the straps that held both in place on the saddle-skirt, the sword at her side uncoiled its power, and struck.

At her.

Her hand closed on the hilt of the blade before she was quite aware of what was happening. But as Need moved to take over the rest of her body, she fought back.

It was a brief, sharp struggle; it ended in the blade's surprised capitulation.

:*What in hell is wrong with you, girl?*: Need shrilled in her mental "ear." :*I thought you were going to let me work magic against those things!*:

:*Through me, not using me,*: she snarled back. :*That's my body you're trying to take over. You didn't ask, you just tried to take.*:

Need seemed very much taken aback. While the blade pondered, Elspeth retrieved her bow and quiver, and counted out her shots. There were depressingly few arrows left; what she had, she would have to use carefully.

:*You've got a mothering-strong Mage-Gift,*: the blade said, as Elspeth positioned herself behind Skif, with one arrow nocked to her bowstring. :*I think if I guide you through it, we ought to be able to fend these things off long enough to give us a breathing space. Relax a little, will you?*:

Elspeth let down her guard, reluctantly. :*That's all I need,*: Need said. :*This will be like learning how to shoot. My hands on yours, guiding. That's all. Now look, with your FarSight, below us.*:

Elspeth obeyed, wondering if this was a waste of time. But to her amazement, there *was* something down there.

A kind of web of light, with a bright glow where the lines all met.

:Those are ley-lines; the thing in the middle is a node. Reach out and touch it. I'll help you.:

There *was* an odd sensation that was similar to that of having hands on hers; she followed the guidance of those invisible "hands," reaching out to touch—just barely touch—that bright glow.

Although her physical hands merely pointed off into the heart of the ruins, those other "hands" penetrated deeply beneath the ground—deeper, she sensed, than the Plains below them. It was *not* effortless. She was sweating and trembling by the time she made contact; weak-kneed with the effort, as if she had run up a second cliff trail as long as the one they had just traversed.

Then she touched this "node"—and was hit with a blast of power, as if she stood in the path of an onrushing torrent. If she could have cried out, she would have. She had never felt so entirely helpless in her life.

:Dammit—: Those invisible hands caught her; steadied her. She saw how they were holding her against the power, and altered her "stance," opening to it instead of resisting it. Opening what, she didn't know; in point of fact it "felt" like opening a door that she hadn't been aware existed.

Now instead of being swept away by the flood of power, she had become a conduit for it. It filled her, rather than overwhelming her.

:Good,: the sword said, with grudging admiration. *:I wasn't that quick even when I was your age. And I never could handle nodes, only local energy, shallow lines, and power-pools. I think I'm jealous.:*

Elspeth opened her eyes to discover that the creatures that had followed them were only now lining up in front of their shelter. Amazingly, hardly any time at all had passed.

:Well, child,: Need said, with grim satisfaction. *:Let's show these beasts that the mice they thought they trapped have fangs.:*

Elspeth followed the blade's direction, raising her hands above her head and clasping them together for a moment while the power built within her, flooding channels she discovered as they were being filled, then letting it loose with a gesture of throwing.

:You won't need to do that forever,: Need told her, as a lance of energy, like a lightning bolt, leapt from her hand to impact squarely in the chest of one of the creatures. *:Eventually, you'll be able to send power without making those stupid gestures. And you'll be able to use it less—crudely. But this will do for now.:*

Even as the blade spoke, she guided Elspeth through another three such displays. Skif and the Companions had been taken entirely by surprise; they stood looking at Elspeth as if she had suddenly grown an extra head, staring despite the danger outside the cleft, as if they did not recognize her.

For that matter, she wasn't entirely sure she recognized herself. Here she was, flinging *lightning bolts* about as if they were children's balls—Elspeth, protected Heir, who had never been outside of Valdemar. Elspeth, otherwise very ordinary Herald, who had never been thought to have a particularly strong Gift, much less something like this. The power sang through her mind, light coalescing at her fingers and striking out in showers of sparks.

Unfortunately, when the dazzle cleared from her eyes, it was apparent that her fiery attacks had not impressed the hunters that much.

:Damn,: the sword swore. *:They've been given some protection against magic attack. I didn't know that could be done with constructs.:* And, as if to herself, *:I wonder what else has changed. . . . :*

As the exhilaration of power and the impetus of fear both faded, Elspeth leaned against the rock wall and blinked to clear her eyes. For the first time Elspeth got a good look at their foes, as they huddled at a respectful distance from the opening of the cleft, their heads together as if they were discussing something. Perhaps they were. . . .

They were shaped rather like cattle, with horny plates instead of hair, and all of that uniform golden-brown that resembled the color of the parched grasslands of the Plains. They were not as clumsy, however, and were as tall at the shoulder as any of the Ashkevron warhorses. Nor were their heads or legs at all bovine; they bore resemblance to no animal that Elspeth recognized. From sharp, backswept horns, to wide, slitted eyes, to fanged mouths, their heads were alien and as purposeful as the pack of beasts that had chased the Heralds across the Plains. And there were odd feet on those legs, a kind of claw-hoof; the front legs more like a dog's than a cow's.

The consultation ended, and half of the beasts trotted out of sight. Elspeth had no fear that they would come in from behind; those hooves were never made for climbing rock, and the tumble of stones behind them was beyond the capability of anything lacking humanlike hands and feet. What they were undoubtedly doing was making sure that the *Heralds* did not escape by climbing the rocks and slipping away.

The remainder of the creatures settled down, as if perfectly prepared for a long wait.

:I hate to tell you this,: Need said gloomily, *:but if these things have defenses to magical attacks, they have probably been constructed very well. They might not need to eat, drink, or even sleep.:*

She sighed, and pulled her damp hair behind her ears. "Well, that was just what I needed to hear," she muttered.

"What was?" Skif asked, and she realized that the blade had left him out of the conversation again. Probably deliberately.

Elspeth explained, as she and Cymry traded places.

"Oh, hell," he groaned. "We're safe for now, I guess, but how are we going to get out of here? Poison the damn things?"

"They *have* to have a weakness somewhere," she replied absently, studying the beasts with narrowed eyes. "If they're protected in one area, that probably means they've given up protection somewhere else."

Suddenly, one of the beasts, which had been utterly silent up until then, let out a bloodcurdling shriek. The one nearest the opening reared up to its full height, pawing at something in its throat, its head and neck extended as far as they could reach while it shrieked again. As it reared, they saw what had hit it.

An arrow, buried to the fletchings in its throat.

The underbody was covered with soft skin, unlike the horny hide-plates. The area of weakness Elspeth had been hoping for. Her heart surged with elation, and her energy returned redoubled.

A second arrow whirred past and thudded into the creature's chest as it teetered on its hind legs. It bellowed again, then collapsed, and did not move.

While its fellows began to look about confusedly, Skif darted out of cover before Elspeth could stop him. As a third arrow skimmed past him, just beyond his shoulder, and bounced off the hide of the nearest beast, distracting it, he flung one of his throwing knives at the beast's eye. It hit squarely; the tiny knives were razor-sharp and heavy for their tiny size. The second beast threw up its head and collapsed like its brother.

Skif darted back into cover.

Before he had done more than reach the shelter of the cleft, a huge shadow passed overhead.

They both looked up, as a second shadow followed the first, and a cry, like that of an eagle, but a hundred times louder, rang out.

Dear gods—

Elspeth gasped, and for one moment she could not even think.

:What—the hell—are those?: the sword asked.

Elspeth shook with nerves and fear, as the huge gryphons stooped on their pursuers. She had known, intellectually, that gryphons existed; Heralds had seen them in the sky north of Valdemar, but no one she knew had ever seen one this close.

Or at least, if they had, they'd not lived to report the fact.

For one panicked moment, she thought they had come to join the other beasts against them—and *these* creatures would not have the limitations of the hooved ones in prying the Heralds out of their shelter.

But they attacked the strange creatures with talons and beaks, knocking one of them entirely off the cliff, and killing another before Elspeth could react, shrieking defiance as they shredded flesh and flew off again.

Well, whatever they are, even if they aren't on our *side, they aren't on* their *side either.*

The rest of the beasts turned to defend themselves, forming a heads-out circle, and it was clear that there would be no more easy kills.

It was also clear that the gryphons were not going to give up. Nor, from the carefully placed arrows, was their still-unseen ally.

And damn if I'm going to let them do this alone. Maybe they've heard the old saying about how "the enemy of my enemy is my friend."

She ran out, nocking another arrow to her bow, before Skif could grab her and haul her back to safety.

"Come on!" she shouted back at him, allowing a hint of mockery to enter her voice. "What are you waiting for? Winter?"

Elspeth rested her back against a rock, and slid down it. Skif slumped nearby, with his head hanging, his forearms propped on his bent knees, and his hands dangling limply. There was a long shallow gash in her leg that she didn't remember getting, and another wound (a bite) on her arm that she only recalled vaguely. It was a good thing she had more clothing with her; all Whites, though, the merc outfits were filthy. She'd taken both hits after she'd run out of arrows and knives, and the damned sword had insisted on getting in close to fight hand-to—tooth, horn, whatever.

Neither wound was bleeding, and neither one hurt. . . .

:I told you. That's my doing.: That was Need, still unsheathed and in her hand. It was covered in dark, sticky blood, and she had not yet regained the energy to clean it. She had the feeling that the sword wouldn't care—but if she ever put any blade in its sheath without cleaning it, she knew in her soul that Kero *and* Alberich would walk on air to beat her black and blue. The smug satisfaction in the sword's tone would have been annoying if she hadn't been so tired. *:I let 'em bleed enough to clean 'em out, then I took care of 'em.:*

:Well, you were the one that was responsible for my getting hurt in the first place,: she retorted, watching the gash and bitemarks Heal before her eyes. *:I should* think you'd take care of them!:*

The sword muttered something about ingratitude; Elspeth ignored it. The gryphons—and presumably the archer—had gone in pursuit of the enemy creatures once their combined attack had broken the beasts' circle and forced them into flight. Neither the Heralds nor their Companions had been in any shape to join the chase.

Gwena plodded over to Elspeth's side and nosed her arm. :*At least that piece of tin is useful as a Healer,*: the Companion observed. :*Are we going to find somewhere safe to rest, do you think? Someplace secure? I'd really like to go sleep for a week or so.*:

"Unless those gryphons saved us just to eat us themselves, I think we are," Elspeth responded, unable to muster much concern over the prospect of becoming gryphon-fodder. She had just learned the truth of something Quenten had warned her about. It took energy to use energy—and hers was spent, and overspent. Right now she was just about ready to pass out, safe or not.

But the sound of a falcon's cry made her look up; there was an enormous raptor skimming along, barely clearing the tops of the stones, winging his way out of the forest. An omen? That would be all they needed now; something more to wonder about.

For a moment, she thought it was her weary, blurring eyes that made the vegetation behind him seem to move, as if part of the forest had separated and was walking toward her. But then, the "vegetation" stepped a little farther out into the open and became a man.

Her hiss of warning brought Skif's head up, and they both struggled to their feet to meet the stranger standing, their Companions moving a little into the shadows out of immediate sight as they rose. She stood so that Need was not so obviously still in her hand; no point in looking belligerent.

He was a somber-looking young man, tall, taller than Skif, and slender. And handsome, strikingly handsome, with a sculptured face and tough, graceful body. He'd already slung his bow across his back; a longbow, much more finely-crafted than anything Elspeth had ever seen in use before. His green, gray, and brown clothing blended so well with the forest that he faded into the background every time he paused. His long hair was an odd, mottled brown that helped with the camouflage-effect considerably. As he neared, Elspeth saw that he had the same piercing, ice-blue eyes and bone structure of the Shin'a'in she had seen, though his complexion was a paler gold than theirs.

As the man drew nearer, the falcon wheeled and returned. Without looking, the stranger held out his gauntleted wrist, and the falcon—*much* larger, she realized, than any bird she had ever seen, other than, say, an eagle—dropped down gracefully to his fist, and settled itself with a flip of its wings.

That was when she finally made the connection. *Dear gods—he must be one of the Hawkbrothers.* She felt as if she really *had* stepped into the pages of a legend; first she was visited by a Shin'a'in Kal'enedral, then chased by monsters, then rescued by gryphons—and now here was a Hawkbrother, a creature out of legends so remote that she had only found references to them in Vanyel's chronicles. *Moondance and Starwind, Vanyel's friends— Mages, Adepts in fact, from the Clan of k'Treva.*

The man paused at a polite distance from the Heralds, and frowned, as if he wasn't certain how to address them, or which of them to speak to first. She wondered if she should solve his quandary.

But before she could speak, he made up his mind. "Who are you?" he demanded arrogantly in tradetongue. "What are you doing in Tayledras lands? Why are you here?"

And who are you to ask? I didn't see any boundary markers! She drew herself up, answering his arrogance with pride of her own. "Herald Elspeth and Herald Skif, out of Valdemar. And we were chased here by monsters, as you likely noticed," she replied stiffly, in the same language. "We didn't exactly plan on it, and we didn't stop to ask directions. Any more questions?"

To her surprise, he actually started to smile, at least a little. But that was when Gwena poked her nose from behind her Chosen, and looked at him with a combination of inquiry and tentative approval. His eyes widened and, to Elspeth's amazement, he paled.

She took an involuntary step backward, and that brought Need into view. He glanced down, took a second, very surprised look, and went a little whiter.

He mumbled something under his breath that sounded like Shin'a'in, but was different enough that she couldn't make out what he was saying. It seemed to have something to do with bodily functions.

Well, as long as he'd seen the damned sword and hadn't

interpreted it as hostility, she might as well put it away properly. She turned a little, fished a cleaning rag out of Gwena's saddlebag as he watched her warily, and began wiping the blade clean.

It practically cleaned itself. Then again, maybe that wasn't surprising, all things considered. The Hawk-brother mumbled something again, and she looked up as she sheathed her sword properly, and wiped off her filthy hand. "What did you say?" she asked politely, but with a touch of the same arrogance he had been showing them.

He shook his head, but he did seem to be unbending just a little. "Never mind," he said, "It matters not. It would seem that I am to add you to the colony of Out-landers I am collecting."

"And what if we don't want to go?" she retorted, taken aback by his assumption that she would obey him without a second thought. "There are four of us and only one of you."

"This is our land you trespass on. There are four of us," he corrected mildly, as the gryphons swooped in from behind her to land at his side, the wind created by their wings as they landed making a tiny tempest that blew dust into her face and made her squint. "And I think two of us are bigger than all of you."

She tightened her jaw, refusing to be intimidated. "Is that a threat?" she snapped. "I think we might surprise you, if it is."

He sighed. "No, it is not a threat; if you wish to de-scend to the Plains, you are free to do so. But I must tell you, there *are* four of us that stand guard here, I will not permit you to pass through Tayledras lands, and your escort still awaits you below the cliff. Our Shin'a'in brethren have not chosen to disperse them, and we above do not trespass upon the Plains without invitation."

"Oh," she said, deflated. :*What do you know about these people?*: she asked the sword.

:*Not a damn thing,*: Need replied. :*Never heard of them, and I don't recognize the language. They're either something I never ran into, or they sprang up after my time.*:

The young man cleared his throat, delicately, recalling her attention. "I feel as if I must point out that you would not be safe from *anything* with *that* at your side."

He pointed to the sword with his chin.

She raised an eyebrow and looked back at Skif. He shrugged. "I don't think we have much choice," he said quietly.

"Your friend speaks wisely," the Hawkbrother put in. "It may be your escort was attracted by you, or by the weapon you carry. It is magic, and such things are drawn by magic. I think that you would be safer in the company of two mages."

"*Two* mages?" boomed out a new voice. Elspeth's heart leapt right out of her body, and only Gwena's shoulder behind her kept her on her feet as her knees dissolved from a combination of startlement and fear.

"*Two* mages?" repeated the smaller of the gryphons. "Darrrkwind, do my earrrsssss decsssseive me?"

It talks, Elspeth thought, faintly.

The Hawkbrother—Darkwind, if the gryphon had called him by his correct name—shrugged again. "This is neither the time nor place to speak of my decisions," he replied, and turned to the Heralds. "I phrased myself poorly. I think that you have no real choice. I think you must accept my hospitality, for your own safety and the safekeeping of that which you carry. Though what the Council will say of this," he added, looking at the gryphon who had spoken, and shaking his head ruefully, "I do not care to contemplate."

The arrogance was back, an imperious quality more suited to a prince of some exotic realm than this—whatever he was. She wanted to angrily deny the fact that they needed protection of any kind, much less *his*. But much as she hated to admit it, she *didn't* want to have to face any more bizarre monsters. Not right away, anyway.

:*I think we'd better go along with him, Elspeth,*: Skif Mindspoke tentatively, as if he expected her to turn on him and lash him with her anger for such a suggestion. :*I don't know about you, but we can't face any more without some rest. And I really would like to know a little more about what's going on around here before we go charging off on our own.*:

He's some kind of Border Guard, she thought, though not without some resentment. *It is his land. I could do with a little less of an attitude, though. . . .*

She would have preferred to tell him exactly what he

could do with his so-called "protection"—to tell him
that she would be perfectly fine—to inform him in no
uncertain terms, that whatever he *thought*, she had been
sent here, to this very place, by those "Shin'a'in brethren" of his, and that she intended to wait here for them.

On the other hand, she had no idea *why* the Shin'a'in
had sent her here, nor if they themselves intended to meet
her. Maybe all they had meant was to put her in the hands
of these Hawkbrothers. . . .

:What do you think?: she asked Gwena.

:That he is right, we have no choice,: came the Companion's prompt reply. *:It is not necessarily a bad thing;
you were in search of mages. He is a mage, so is the
gryphon. And according to the chronicles, many of the
Hawkbrothers are mages. They taught Vanyel, did they
not, when the Herald-Mages could not?:*

*:Let's see if someone's willing to come with us, or teach
me, first,:* she replied sourly. So, it was fairly well unan-
imous.

"He's right," she told Skif shortly, in their tongue,
much to the older Herald's relief. "And so are you. We're
all tired, and as long as this isn't an imprisonment—"

"I don't think it is," Skif replied. "I think he'd let us
go if we really wanted to. I've got the feeling that we're
kind of an annoyance to him, not something he'd keep
around if he had the choice."

That didn't make her feel any better. "All right," she
told the Hawkbrother, trying to conceal her annoyance.
"Where is it you want us to go?"

Instead of replying, he gestured curtly for them to follow; she seethed a little at the implied discourtesy. As
the gryphons lofted themselves into the air, she stood
aside for Skif and Cymry to get by her. She did not want
to follow him too closely just now; she was afraid she
would lose what was left of her temper.

She had gotten used to being the one making the decisions. Now she was again following someone else's orders. That galled her as much as this Darkwind fellow's
arrogance.

In fact, she decided somewhat guiltily as she led
Gwena in Cymry's wake, it probably galled her
more. . . .

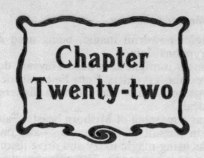

Chapter Twenty-two

Darkwind led the way for this strange parade of Outlanders, winding through the piles of stone on the weed-grown path that led from this end of the ruins to the gryphons' lair. It was a good thing that they had enlarged it; between two Outlanders, their spirit-horses, and Nyara, it would have been crowded otherwise. He wished strongly for something to ease his aching head, or to make him able to forget everything that had happened for the past several days. Or both.

Well, perhaps not everything.

I have my father back again. That was no small gain, even when weighed against all the grief and pain.

He concentrated on staying on his feet; glad beyond telling that this incursion would likely mean there would be nothing more today. If only he were in his *ekele*—he had begun this day wearied and emptied of all strength, or so he thought. He had not found anyone able to take his patrol for him, so he had taken to the border, resigned to another stretch without rest. It had been two days without sleep, now.

But it had been quiet, amazingly so—until, when (of course) he was at the very opposite end of his patrol, he sensed magic, powerful magic, being used somewhere near the gryphons' lair.

He'd thought it might have been Treyvan, doing something to free the gryphlets from Falconsbane's control. But any hope he'd had of that had been shattered by Treyvan's Mindcall.

There was a massing of Misborn beasts, Falconsbane's creatures, in pursuit of two humans—and one of those humans was using magic to try and drive them off. Without success, as it happened. The gryphons were going to their aid. It was his territory; so must he.

He, and they, had arrived on the spot simultaneously, to play rescuer to Outlanders. That had irritated him beyond reason; he was tired, and he saw no reason to save ignorant fools from the consequences of their own folly. He had intended to send them back where they came from, whether they were still in danger or not—until he actually *saw* who, or rather, *what*, he had rescued.

He glanced back over his shoulder at them, trying not to look as if he was doing so. "Unsettled" was the mildest term for the way he felt right now. "Shaken" probably came closer; profoundly shaken.

Well, it is not every day that a pair of Guardian Spirits and a pre-Mage-War Artifact fold wings on your doorstep. . . .

And when one added the fact that the person bearing the Artifact—and in the charge of the more potent of the Guardian Spirits—was a completely untutored mage of Adept potential—

If this is a trial of my abilities—the gods have no sense of proportion.

He was exhausted, bewildered, and one step short of collapsing. All he could think of was to take these Outlanders to the gryphons' lair, where they had left Nyara. Treyvan agreed; and concurred with his judgment that they did not dare let these two—four—*five*—wander about with things as unsettled as they were. If Falconsbane got his hands on them, as he was so obviously trying to do, Darkwind was not willing to think about what uses he might make of them.

With any luck, the Elders were so concerned with Starblade that they would not find out about these "visitors" until they were long gone.

And meanwhile, perhaps he could find somewhere safe to send them. To the Shin'a'in? No, they had forsworn magic. . . .

Could these two have *stolen* that sword from the soil of the Plains? That horrifying thought nearly stopped him in his tracks, until he remembered that the blade did *not* have the air of disuse about it that something of that nature would—and that it *did* have the air of something that was alien to the kind of magics that lay buried in the Plains. *Woman's magic;* that was it. No, this was nothing that had been created by the thoroughly masculine Mage of Silence—and it did not have the look or feel of anything forged by the Shin'a'in. Weapons made for the servants of the Star-Eyed were as sexless as the Kal'enedral; this artifact was as female in its way as—as Nyara.

He staggered a little as he neared the lair; recovered himself before the Outlanders noticed. Above all, he *had* to present a strong front to them. There was no telling what kind of unwitting havoc they could cause if they thought he was less than vigilant, ineffectual—he was certain now that they meant no harm, not with Guardian Spirits hanging about them, but they could cause a great deal of trouble if they chose to meddle without knowing what they were about.

I could wish they were Shin'a'in; then we would have two more useful allies at this moment. . . .

Hydona was already in the lair when they reached it; Treyvan waited outside. "In there," he said, shortly, wishing he dared shake his head to clear his eyes. "If you have gear, Hydona will tell you the chamber you may use."

When the young man looked from him to the spirit-horse doubtfully, he added, "The white ones, too. We will find them food if you do not have it." He bowed a little to the mare. *"Zhai'helleva,* lady. You honor k'Sheyna with your presence."

The spirit-mare looked flattered and surprised—so did the young man.

:You do not look well,: Treyvan noted.

:I do not feel well, but I shall survive,: he replied. He gave Vree a toss to send him to a perch above the lair "doorway" and stood, leaning (he hoped) casually, against the doorpost. The young man entered with his

spirit-horse. The young woman's spirit-horse started to follow, and he averted his eyes with discomfort—

Then he found himself sliding dizzily toward the ground, clinging not-so-casually to the rock as his knees buckled.

Quickly, the young woman knelt beside him and unsheathed her sword.

:Peace, brother, she means no harm,: Treyvan said calmly.

Darkwind wasn't so sure. He tried to get up a hand to fend her off—but instead, she put the hilt of the thing *in* his hand.

And he heard a strange, gravelly voice in his mind—

:She says if I don't Heal you she's going to drop me down the nearest well,: the sword told him, annoyance warring with amusement in the overtones of its—her— Mind-voice. *:I think she must have been taking lessons in rudeness from her predecessor. And knowing Her Highness, she probably would.:*

He nearly dropped the thing in shock, and only long training—never, never, *never* drop a blade—kept his numb fingers clutched to the hilt.

:Huh. Nothing too bad—overwork, under-rest. And—: He Felt the thing probing him and his memory, then suddenly pulling back. *:Oh, youngling,:* the sword said, dropping all cynicism. *:You've had more heartbreak than anyone should ever face in a lifetime, and that much I can't Heal. But I'll do my best for you. Open your shields to me.:*

She sounded so much like one of his teachers, an old, old Adept who had ordered him about as if she had been his mother, that he obeyed without thinking twice. She took instant action; in the next moment a gentle warmth stole over him, making him relax still further. He closed his eyes gratefully and let it in. Healers had worked on him before, but that had been for a major injury, not for general exhaustion.

First came the warmth and relaxation; then came new energy, new strength. It rose in him like a tide, rather than a flood; a rising tide of warmth and golden-green light that touched him within and without, folding him in great wings of brilliance, sheltering him as he had not been protected since he was a child. But the blade not only filled him with renewed physical energy, she also reopened his long-unused mage-channels, replenishing him with magical power as well.

He was vaguely offended at first, but then practicality took hold. He *had* said he was a mage. Any reasons for renouncing powers were gone. There was, in fact, every reason why he *should* take up magecraft again.

:Thank you,: he told the blade.

:Thank the girl,: Need responded. *:Oh, I was an Adept, but never with the ability she has. She and her teacher were the first in I don't know how long that fought me and won. And all this power—it's coming through her. So save your thanks for her. I'll be done soon.:*

The blade was as good as its word; the dizziness and weakness were gone, and shortly after that, he felt as refreshed as if he had never endured the stresses of the past five days.

He stood up and gingerly passed the sword back to its bearer. "That was kindly done," he said, with all the courtesy he could muster, embarrassed by the awareness that his dealings with her had been woefully short of courtesy up until this moment. "Thanks is not adequate, but it is all I can offer."

She seemed first surprised, then pleased, then blushed, averting her eyes. "That's all right," she said, "I mean, you looked like you needed help. *She* doesn't like men much, but I figured I could convince her to do something for you."

He looked to the young lady and spirit-mare, nodding gravely. "There have been troubles here," he told her. "There still *are* troubles—evil ones—and you have tumbled unwitting into the midst of them. My time is short, my powers are strained, and my patience, alas, never was particularly good. Please, even if I offend you, never hesitate to follow my orders or Treyvan's. It may well mean not only your life but ours."

She looked back up at him, resentment warring with respect in her eyes. Respect won.

"I will," she said, a little grudgingly, and he sensed that she was not often minded to follow anyone's orders, much less a stranger's. "You're right, I suppose. We're not from around here; we can't possibly know what's going on."

Imperious, he noted thoughtfully. *Used to giving the orders, not taking them. The sword called her "Highness." That may well be truth, rather than sarcasm.*

"I am Darkwind k'Sheyna," he told her. "This ruin is nominally part of k'Sheyna territory; Treyvan and Hydona are the actual guardians here. There are few who would care to dispute boundaries with them."

He meant that as a subtle warning, but she cocked her head to one side, looked from him to Treyvan and back again, and said accusingly, "There is something very wrong here. You said we've walked into a situation we don't understand—but everything, absolutely everything I've seen tells me that it's worse than that. You people are in trouble."

He narrowed his eyes speculatively. "Why do you say this?" he asked before he thought.

"Well, I'm thinking of you, for one thing," she said. "Need says you were exhausted, that you'd gone days without rest. You don't do that unless you're in some kind of trouble. Everything around here seems—well, it feels like being on the edge of a battlefield, on the eve of a war. And if that's what we've walked into, I'd like to know." She gulped. "I think, on the whole, I'd just as soon take my chances with those things you chased off. I'd rather not get caught in another all-out war. Especially not a war involving magic."

Again, he spoke before he thought, with a little more scorn than he had intended to show. "And what do *you* know of warfare?"

She scowled. "I've fought in a few battles," she snapped. "Have you? And you still haven't answered my question."

"Why should I?" he retorted. He raised his head proudly, planting his fists on his hips. "I know nothing of you, other than that you came across the Plains—and *that* you likely did without the knowledge of the Shin'a'in—"

"What, you want my credentials?" she scoffed, now obviously very angry, but keeping a firm grip on herself. She turned quickly to her saddlebag and turned round again with a roll of vellum and something else. "All right, I'll give you what you'll recognize. My teacher's teacher was Tarma shena Tale'sedrin. My teacher is Captain Kerowyn of the Skybolts, cousin to most of the Tale'sedrin. She no longer rides a warsteed, but when she did, it was *always* called Hellsbane. I came to Kata'shin'a'in looking for Tale'sedrin. One found me; a Kal'enedral. He, she, or it gave me these.''

She thrust the roll and an enameled copper disk at him. The latter, he recognized. It was one of the Clan tokens customarily used to identify Clansfolk passing through Tayledras lands. And it was, indeed, a genuine Tale'sedrin token. He even recognized the maker's glyph on the back. That they had given this Outlander one meant that they expected her to be passing through both the Plains and Tayledras territory, and had granted her as much safe passage as they could.

But the other thing, the roll of vellum, proved to be as great a shock as the spirit-horse.

It was a map of the Plains. Darkwind had heard of such things, but the normally secretive Shin'a'in had never before let one out of their hands, to his knowledge, not even to their cousin, Captain Kerowyn. And it *was* a genuine map, not a fake. It showed every well and spring in the Plains, used the correct reckonings, and showed the correct landmarks—at least as far as he could verify. For that much it was priceless. It showed more than that; it showed, if you knew what to look for, the locations of common camp-sites of the four seed-Clans and the off-shoot Clans. Anyone who had that information would know who held which territories, and where to find them. . . .

And it also showed the ruins here on the rim, circled in red ink, fresher than anything else on the map.

''That was where I was supposed to go, at least that's what I guessed,'' she said assertively, stabbing her finger at the red mark. ''I don't know what it was I was intended to find, but it certainly looks to *me* as if I was to come here. If you know better, I'd be pleased to hear where I'm supposed to be.''

''No,'' he replied vaguely, still staring at the solid evidence of Shin'a'in cooperation in his hands. ''No, I would say that you are correct.''

This incident was rapidly turning into something he was not ready to deal with. It had looked like a simple case of Outlanders wandering where they didn't belong.

Then it became a case of keeping these people out of Falconsbane's hands. But now it looked as if the *Shin'a'in* had sent these Outlanders here. And what that could mean, he did not know.

"Please," he said, rolling up the map and handing it back to her. "Please, if you would only rejoin your friend, the young man, I need to speak with Treyvan."

She set her chin stubbornly, but he could be just as stubborn. He crossed his arms over his chest and stood between her and the pathway out, silent, and unmoving except for his hair blowing in the breeze. Finally she stuffed the map back in her belt with an audible sniff and turned to enter the lair.

She went inside—but the white spirit-horse did not.

The mare stared at Darkwind for so long he began to feel very uncomfortable. It was very much as if she was measuring him against some arcane standard only she knew. In fact, she probably was, given the little he knew about manifesting spirits; Starblade had once seen a *lesh-ya'e* Kal'enedral, but he never had, and he had been perfectly content to have it remain that way.

Evidently the gods had other ideas.

:*A word with you,*: the spirit-mare said. Then she looked up at Treyvan and included him in the conversation. :*Both of you,*: she amended.

Treyvan looked down at the little mare from his resting place atop the lair, and rumbled deep in his throat. :*We have many problems and little leisure, my lady,*: he replied in Mindspeech. :*I do not mean to belittle your troubles, but we have no time for yours.*:

She tossed her head and stamped one hoof with an imperiousness that matched her rider's. :*That is exactly what I wish to speak with you about, your troubles! You are being very foolish to dismiss us so lightly. I tell you, you need us, and I swear to you that you may trust us!*:

With every word, she glowed a little brighter to his Mage-Sight, until he finally had to shield against her.

:*Lady, I know you think I can trust you,*: he replied, stubbornly, :*but you and she are not of my people; your ways are not ours, and what you think important may mean nothing to us.*:

:*And please to dim yourself,*: Treyvan added. :*You do not need to set the forest afire to prove what you are.*:

Her glow faded, and she pondered for a moment. :*It is true that we are not of the same peoples, but I will tell you what brings us here. The child needs tutoring in magecraft. That is the most important of our tasks. Other than that, we have no agenda to pursue. And we are four more to stand at your side in your troubles.*: She snorted delicately. :*We have departed from the road that had been planned for her. At this point, I do not see how further deviation from that plan can matter.*:

The road that had been planned for her? Interesting words, and ones that explained a great deal about the girl's temperament. *I doubt I would care for being blown about by the winds of fate. In fact—I just might become as belligerent as she has.* He began to feel a bit more in sympathy with the girl. And quite a bit more inclined to trust her.

:*Lady, we may not agree on what is to be done here,*: he warned. :*This is Tayledras land; we follow the task given to us by our Lady, and nothing is permitted to interfere with that.*:

She shook her mane impatiently. :*Does it matter in whose name good is done? Evil done in the name of a Power of good is still evil. And good done in the name of a Power of evil is still good. It is the actions which matter, not the Name it is done for. You stand against evil here; we will help if you will have us. And then— perhaps—you may help us.*:

Well, that seemed reasonable enough. He raised an eyebrow at Treyvan; the gryphon, adroit at reading human faces, cocked his head to one side. :*She seems sincere. She is—something that cannot speak falsely. And—Darkwind, we and k'Sheyna are not strong enough that we can afford to neglect any form of aid. Especially if we are to free Dawnfire and my children.*:

He nodded. :*If that's the way you feel, then I agree.*: He turned to the mare. :*Lady, we accept your offer with thanks.*:

The spirit nodded emphatically. :*Good. Shall we confer on what needs to be done?*:

Things to be done—the rescue of Dawnfire, for one thing. After Starblade's revelations, he was certain that she *was* in Falconsbane's hands. He *could* not leave her there—he told himself it was for k'Sheyna's sake, that the Clan could not afford another like Starblade—but it was as much for his sake as the Clan's. Over and over the thought had plagued him, intruding into everything, that if he had only been more vigilant, if he had only taken the time to explain why he had wanted her to stay clear of the gryphons that day, none of this would have happened to her. He knew now that he was not to blame for the shattering of the Heartstone—but this he *was* guilty of. He had allowed Falconsbane to lure him into relaxing his guard. And this was the result.

:*Bring your people out,*: he told the spirit. :*As soon as they are ready to talk. And I will see if I can explain this before night falls. And explain,*: he added grimly, :*just what it is that we mean to do.*:

To his surprise—although he should not have *been* surprised—the Outlanders had a very good grasp of the situation once he sketched it. As the young man said, "It's not much different from our position at home. Except that the scale is a lot smaller."

The girl sat with her chin resting on both her hands as she listened, then offered a question. "Why is it that this Falconsbane hasn't made a frontal assault on k'Sheyna? He has to know that you're in trouble, and this would be the perfect time to take you."

This Elspeth seemed much easier and more relaxed, now that her blade was out of its sheath and away from her. The spirit penned within the sword—"Need" was its name—had stated that there was very little it could contribute. It had never been a tactician or a leader and did not care to begin learning the craft now. Furthermore, there *was* a great deal she could do to shield the gryphlets from further tampering; so that was what she had been left to do.

Elspeth *had* been a leader and a tactician—at least in small skirmishes—and she had studied her craft under one of the legendary mercenary Captains of the modern times. Word of the Shin'a'in "cousin" had penetrated even into Tayledras lands, via the few Bards that had congress with Tayledras and Shin'a'in. And her pupil's question had merit.

"I do not know," he replied frankly. "I am fairly certain that he has the power to pursue a frontal assault. It may be that he has not simply because he does not think in those terms; because he prefers to weaken from within, and gnaw away from without, until little by little he has wrought such damage that he can overcome his target with little effort or losses.''

''That only works if you don't know what he's doing,'' she pointed out. ''Once his victim knows—''

''It may be too late,'' Treyvan rumbled. ''I sssussspect hisss tacticsss have done verrry well in the passst.''

''He probably *enjoys* working that way,'' the young man—Skif, a very odd sort of name, to Darkwind's mind—put in. ''I mean, it's obvious from what the cat-lady said that he positively revels in making people suffer. Seems to me he wouldn't get half the pleasure out of being straightforward.''

Elspeth bit off an exclamation. ''That's it!'' she exulted. ''That's his weakness! That's what makes him vulnerable! He's so busy with his convoluted plans that if he sees us trying one thing, he might not expect a second attack that was perfectly straightforward. Look, Darkwind, if I were you, that's what I'd do; I'd pretend to try to negotiate with him, and while he thought he was tying me in knots, I'd make a straight assault to get Dawnfire free. I'd also try and do as much damage as I could on the way out,'' she added thoughtfully, ''but then, I'm well known to be a vindictive bitch.''

She glanced sideways at Skif as she said that, and the young man looked sour. Evidently she was using words he had thrown at her at some point, and he was not enjoying hearing them now, tossed back in his face.

For his part, Darkwind was a little surprised by this interchange. He had been under the impression that these two were lovers, but evidently this was not so. He tucked the information into the back of his mind for later use in dealing with them. There were niceties needed with a pair of lovers that could be disposed of when working with a pair of friends or colleagues.

Such as splitting them up, for instance, sending one on one mission, and the second on another.

''It is a good notion,'' he told the girl. ''Except that we are not supposed to know that Falconsbane even exists, much less that he holds Dawnfire.''

''Damn,'' she said, with a frown. ''I'd forgotten that.

Well, what about that daughter of his, Nyara? Can she be useful?"

Now that was a thought. Treyvan rose, anticipating his next words.

"I sssshall wake herrr," the gryphon said, folding his wings to fit more easily through the door of the lair. "We ssshall sssee if ssshe isss rrready to be morrre frrriend than enemy, asss ssshe claimsss."

Darkwind nodded, grimly. Now was the time for Nyara to show her true allegiances. There was a great deal about her father and her father's stronghold and abilities that she could tell them, if she chose. And—just perhaps— some of his weaknesses.

And if she did not choose to help them—well, she would see the Vale after all, as she had often wished. From inside, as he turned her over to the Adepts to be judged. He wondered what they would think of the crea- ture that had eaten Starblade's bondbird before his eyes. No matter how extenuating the circumstances, he did not think they would be inclined to kindness.

Dawnfire stood on her squeaking mouse, killed it messily, and leaned down to pick it up head-first. She started swallowing it whole, trying her best not to think about what she was doing.

At least I'm not like a poor, stupid eyas that doesn't know which end to start on, she thought unhappily. *At least I know enough to kill the things before I try to eat them. And I knew how to kill them in theory, if not in practice.*

In fact, she had learned a lot more than she was dis- playing. She blessed the many times she'd spent in full- bond with Kyrr, and blessed Kyrr's memory for the way the hawk had shared every experience with her. No, she was *not* a bird—but she had the memories of what it had been like to be a raptor, and once she had overcome her initial despair, those memories had helped her learn the ways of her new body.

They did not help her overcome her fear.

Fear of Falconsbane was only part of it. There was another fear, a constant fear that never left her, waking or sleeping. She knew what would happen as she re- mained in Kyrr's body—the longer she remained, the more of herself she would lose, until there was nothing left but the hawk. The fact that she had adapted to the body so quickly was both bad as well as good. The more comfortable she felt, the easier it would be to lose herself.

She tried to hold onto herself, with utter desperation. She tried to remember everything about the scouts, the Vale, Darkwind—and she panicked when she found herself in the midst of a memory and could not remember a face, a name, a setting. Was it just that these things had slipped her mind—or was it that her mind was slipping? There was no way to know.

And what had happened to her body, back in the Vale? What if Falconsbane had killed that along with Kyrr's soul? What would she do then?

The past two days had felt like two months. Time stretched out unbearably—and there was nothing to distract her from fear and brooding.

When those thoughts drove her into a state of frenzy, there was only one way to break the cycle. She plotted her escape. She had been taken outside enough times on a creance to know all the places where escape might be possible. If she could get away—no, *when* she got away, she would *not* think "if"—she would head straight up, as high as a red-shouldered could go. From there, she would have an unparalleled view of the countryside; her scouting experience would tell her where she was. If she didn't recognize anything, she would circle until she did see a landmark she knew. And Falconsbane shouldn't be able to touch her.

Planning kept her sane; planning and practice.

When Falconsbane was not in the room, she practiced, as she had seen the fledglings practice; flapping until she lifted herself just above the perch; hopping down the length of her jesses and flying back to her perch. When she had to kill her food, she did so with a clumsiness that was feigned more and more often. She took out her anger on the hapless mice, ripping them with talons and beak after she had killed them.

Though it was still all she could do to force herself to eat the mice afterward.

Falconsbane was not paying a great deal of attention to her, but she continued the charade, lurching clumsily up to the perch and taking a long time to get settled. She watched him carefully as she cleaned her talons and beak. He'd been very preoccupied today; and he had evidently forgotten, if he had ever known, just how wide a field of vision a raptor had. She could watch him easily without ever seeming to pay attention to him.

He had been staring at the scrying stone; no longer relaxed, and no longer so infernally pleased with himself. She had finally decided that the scrying stone wouldn't work anywhere except this room; certainly he never took it with him, and there was nothing else here but her perch, his couch, the cabinets he kept his toys of pain and pleasure in, and the stone. For the past two days he had spent more and more time here; watching the stone, and getting very intent about something. She overheard him muttering to himself; evidently he had also forgotten how sharp a raptor's hearing was.

There was something about "heralds," though what that would have to do with anything, she had no notion. There was more about "Valdemar" and a "queen;" "Hardorn," and "Ancar." He seemed very preoccupied with two quite different sets of people. One set seemed to be traveling, and they had something he wanted.

"Wanted?" That was like saying that she "wanted" her freedom. He lusted over this object, whatever it was, with an intensity she had never seen him display before.

The other people were connected with this "Ancar," who seemed to be the enemy of the first group of people. From the pacing and muttering that went on after he had watched this person, she gathered that he was toying with the notion of contracting with this "Ancar" and proposing an alliance.

That was something new for him, or so she gathered. He wanted to—and yet he did not want to chance losing the slightest bit of his own power.

Then, this afternoon, something had changed. The people he had been watching escaped what he had thought was a perfect trap. And they had taken the thing that he wanted with them.

Falconsbane flew into a rage and flung the stone against the opposite wall with such force that he splintered the rock of the wall and reduced the stone to fragments, and she shrank back onto her perch, doing her best not to attract him to her by moving or making a sound. He paid no attention to her whatsoever; he roared for one of his servants to come and clean up the mess, and stood over the trembling boy, looking murderously at him as the terrified child carefully gathered the sharp shards in his shaking, bare hands.

Dawnfire trembled herself, expecting at any moment that he would take out his temper on the boy as he had on the stone. There would be true murder then—

With a sick feeling, she watched him reach down, slowly, clawed hands spread wide—

But before he touched the boy, the door flew open, and two men in some kind of ornate uniform flung themselves into the room to abase themselves at his feet, babbling of "failure" and "mercy." Falconsbane started, then grabbed the child to cover his surprise. He pulled the boy up to his feet by his hair, and threw him bodily toward the door, showering the shards around him. This time the boy did not try to pick them up; he simply made good the chance to flee. The guards blanched and immediately went back to groveling with more heartfelt sincerity than before.

He listened to them a while, then cut them short with a single gesture. "Enough!" he growled, the fingers of his right hand crooked into claws, with the talons fully extended.

The two men fell absolutely silent.

"You failed to capture the artifact," he said, his voice rumbling dangerously. "You failed to corner the quarry, you failed to keep them from finding aid, and you failed to acquire the artifact when you had the opportunity. I should take your lives; I should—remake you."

The men whitened to the color of fresh snow.

"There is nothing you can say that will redeem your complete stupidity," Falconsbane continued. "You will report to Drakan for your punishment. I have not the time to waste upon you."

The two men started to get up; a single snarl from Falconsbane sent them back to their faces.

"I *do* have time to retrieve from your worthless bodies a modicum of the power you *wasted* in this effort." He stretched out his right hand and spread it over the two prone men.

Dawnfire was not certain what exactly he did—but she saw the result clearly. The two men sat back on their heels suddenly, jerked erect like a pair of puppets. Their white faces were frozen in masks of pain, and their limbs trembled and jerked uncontrollably. Their mouths were open, but they uttered not so much as a single sound.

What was truly horrible about the entire tableau was the expression on Falconsbane's face.

He looked like a creature in the throes of sexual ecstasy. He had tossed his long, flowing hair back over his shoulders, and he stared off into nothingness with his eyes half-closed in pure pleasure. His fingers flexed; every time they did, the two men's bodies jerked, and their faces took on new lines of agony. Falconsbane's eyes closed completely, and he lifted his face to the light in obscene bliss.

Finally, he knotted his hand into a fist; the men shuddered, then collapsed.

He opened his eyes, slowly, and gazed down on his victims with a slow, sated smile. "You may go," he purred. *"Now."*

Limbs stirred feebly; heads raised, and the two men began to move. Too weak to do anything else, they crawled toward the door, slowly and painfully.

And that wasn't even their "punishment." That was just Falconsbane's way of reminding them that he was their master in all things.

The first man reached the door and crawled out. All of Dawnfire's feathers slicked down flat to her body in fright. She couldn't have moved now if she had wanted to.

"Greden," Falconsbane said, as the second man started out the door.

The guard stopped, frozen; in a macabre way, he looked funny, like someone caught pretending to be a dog.

"Greden, send Daelon to me on your way out." Falconsbane turned, ignoring the man's whispered acknowledgment, and began pacing beside his couch.

In a few moments, another man entered; an older man, lean and fit, with elaborate, flowing garments and dark gray hair and beard. "My lord?" he said, waiting prudently out of reach. Falconsbane ignored him for a moment, his face creased with a frown of concentration. The man waited patiently; patience was a necessity with Mornelithe Falconsbane, it seemed. Patience, and extreme care.

Finally Falconsbane stopped pacing and flung himself down on the couch. "Daelon, I am going to propose an alliance, to King Ancar of Hardorn."

"Very good, my lord," Daelon responded, bowing deeply. "Alliances are always preferable to conflict."

Falconsbane smiled, as if he found the man's opinions amusing. "I've been in contact with him for some time, as you know; with him, and some other rulers of the East. He agreed to meet with me in person, but he would not set a time." Falconsbane's smile faded. "When he would not specify a date, I insisted that he must come here, and that it was to be within three months of the initial agreement."

"I assume that he has set a date, my lord?" Daelon asked smoothly.

"Finally." Falconsbane scowled. "He told me just before that disaster Greden was in charge of that he will be arriving in three days' time."

"Very good, my lord. By Gate, my lord?" Daelon asked, with one eyebrow raised.

Falconsbane snorted with contempt. "No. The fool calls himself a mage, yet he cannot even master a Gate. That, it seems, was the reason he would not set a date. He had to travel overland, if you will, and he did not wish anyone to know that he was en route."

Daelon produced a superior, smug smile. "Then you wish me to ready the guest quarters, my lord?"

"Exactly," Falconsbane nodded. "I expect I will be able to persuade him to accept my hospitality after several weeks of primitive inns and the like."

Daelon raised one eyebrow. "Do I take it he will not be coming directly here?"

Once again, Falconsbane snorted. "He prefers, he says, to remain in 'neutral' lands. I directed him to the valley I flooded with death-smoke a while ago. It is secure enough, the horned vermin will not be using it again soon, and if he proves unreliable, well—" the Adept shrugged, rippling his hair and mane. "I flooded it once and can do so again."

"Very good, my lord," Daelon bowed, and smiled. "Better to eliminate a menace than deal with a conflict."

Falconsbane chuckled; the deep, rumbling laugh that Dawnfire knew only too well. She crouched a little smaller on her perch. "Ah, Daelon, your philosophy is so—unique."

Daelon bowed again, smiled, but said nothing. Falconsbane waved negligently at him. "Go," he said. Then as Daelon started for the door, he changed his mind. "Wait," he called, and scooped something up from beside his couch. As Daelon turned, he tossed something at him; and as the servant caught it, Dawnfire saw it was the falconer's glove.

"Take that bird with you," he yawned. "I am fatigued, and she no longer amuses me. Take her to the mews; it is time for her to learn her place in life."

"Very good, my lord," Daelon repeated. When the servant approached Dawnfire, she tensed, expecting trouble, but evidently he was so unfamiliar with falconry that he did not even attempt to hood her. He merely took the ends of her jesses, clumsily, in his free hand, and stuck his gloved hand in her general direction.

If he didn't know enough about falconry to hold her jesses properly, he might not know enough to hold them tightly.

She hopped onto his hand as obediently as a tamed cage-bird, and remained quiet and well-behaved. And as he carried her out of the room, and away from Falconsbane's sight, she saw with elation that he was barely holding the tips of her jesses. Of course, she had fouled them; she couldn't have helped that. He evidently found that very distasteful, and he was avoiding as much contact with the chalked leather as possible.

And he was holding the arm she rested on stiffly, far away from his body, lest (she supposed) she also drop on his fine robes. And if that particular function had been within her control, she would have considered doing just that.

He could not find a servant anywhere as they passed through silent stone corridors on the way to the outside door; that elated her even further, even as it visibly annoyed him. He was going to have to take her outside himself. . . .

He dropped the jesses, leaving them loose, as he wrestled with the massive brass-bound, wooden door, trusting in her apparent docility. She rewarded that trust as he got the door open; a real hawk would have bolted the moment a scrap of sky showed, but she was not sure enough of her flying ability to try for an escape. The man was so fussy she was hoping he would take the time to make sure the door was closed before reaching for her jesses again.

Please, Lady of Stars, please don't let him see a servant out here. . . .

He looked about him, squinting in the light, as he emerged from behind the bulky door into the flagstoned courtyard, frowning when he found the courtyard as empty as the corridors. He held her with his arm completely extended, away from his body, as he started to shove the door closed.

YES!

She crouched and launched herself into the air, wings beating with all her might, just as she had practiced. With a cry of despair, Daelon made a grab for her dangling jesses—

But it was too late. She flung herself into the freedom of the blue sky, putting every bit of her strength into each wingbeat, exaltation giving her an extra burst of power, as Daelon dwindled beneath her, waving in wild despair.

Mornelithe Falconsbane

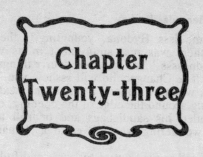

Chapter
Twenty-three

Skif sat very quietly in his corner of the gryphons' lair and made up his bedroll with meticulous care. Elspeth had complained a few days ago that she felt as if she were being written into a tale of some kind. Now he knew how she felt. Strange enough to see gryphons this close—but to be rescued by them, hear them talk—

No one at home is ever going to believe this.

The fighting had been real enough, and he'd seen plenty of misshapen things in the ranks of Ancar's forces. Too many to be surprised by the creatures that had been sent against them. But talking gryphons, Hawkbrothers—

No, they're going to think we made this up.

He tried not to show his fear of the gryphons, but one of his friends was an enthusiastic falconer, and he *knew* what a beak that size, and talons that long, could do.

The bigger of the two gryphons was already inside the roofed-over ruin when he entered it. The place was ten times larger than his room at Haven, but it seemed terribly crowded with the gryphon in it.

"Excuse me, my lady," he'd said humbly, hoping his voice wouldn't break, "but where would you like me?"

"Hydona," said the gryphon.

He coughed, to cover his nervousness. "Excuse me?"

"My name isss Hydona, youngling," the gryphon said, and there was real amusement in its voice. "It means 'kindnessss.' You may put yourrr thingsss in that chamberrr. The Changechild will ssshow you."

That was when he noticed a girl in the next chamber over, peering around the edge of the opening; obediently he had hauled his saddlebags and bedroll across the threshold, wondering what on earth a "Changechild" was.

Then the girl moved out of his way, and fully into the light from the outer door, and his eyes nearly popped out of his head.

She didn't have fur, and she didn't walk on four legs—but she had sharply feline features, slit-pupiled eyes, and the same boneless, liquid grace of any pampered house-cat he'd ever seen.

He managed to stammer out a question about where he was to put his things. She answered by helping him; and that was when he noticed that once the initial shock of her strangeness wore off, she was very attractive. Quite pretty, really.

He smoothed his bedroll and watched her out of the corner of his eye as she brought armfuls of nest-material to put between it and the hard rock. She was more than pretty, she was beautiful, especially when she smiled.

"Thank you," he said, just to see her smile again. Which she did, a smile that reached and warmed those big golden eyes. There hadn't been a lot of smiles out of Elspeth lately . . . it was nice to see one.

"Let me aid you," she said softly, and knelt beside him to help him arrange a more comfortable bed without waiting to hear his answer.

There hasn't been a lot of help out of Elspeth either, lately, he thought sourly. In fact, this girl was Elspeth's utter opposite in a lot of ways. Quiet, soft-spoken, where Elspeth was more inclined to snap at the most innocent of questions.

"What's your name?" he asked her, as they took the opposite ends of the bedroll, and laid it over the bedding prepared for it.

"Nyara," she said and looked shyly away.

That was when Elspeth came in and put her own gear away, efficiently and without a fuss, but it broke the tentative conversation between himself and Nyara, and the girl retreated to her corner.

She's so—mechanical. She's like a well-oiled, perfectly-running clockwork mechanism. She's just not human anymore.

In fact, for all of her exotic strangeness, Nyara seemed more human than Elspeth did.

He stripped off his tunic and changed his filthy, sweat-sodden shirt for a new one, with sidelong glances at Elspeth.

She changed torn shirt and breeches, both cut and stained with blood, although there was no sign of a wound on her. She took no more notice of him and Nyara than if they had been stones.

No heart, no feelings, no emotion. No patience with anyone who isn't perfect. As cold as . . . Nyara is warm.

A sound at the door made him start, as he laced the cuffs of his shirt. The man who had rescued them—Darkwind—stood shadowing the door. Skif had not heard him until he had deliberately made that sound. *He* spoke with gryphons, moved like a thought, hid in the shadows—he was far more alien than Nyara, and colder than Elspeth.

He looked slowly and deliberately into Skif's eyes, then Elspeth's, then Nyara's. "Come," he said, "it is time to talk."

"Why does it seem as if a whole week has passed since this morning, and a year since we first entered the Plains?" Elspeth asked, her dark brown eyes fixed on the horizon as the last rays of the sun turned the western clouds to gold and red streaks against an incredibly blue sky. The young man called "Skif" was contemplating Nyara, as he had been since she had been awakened.

Darkwind was watching Elspeth and her friend—though mostly Elspeth—rather than the sunset. She had washed and changed into another of those blindingly white uniforms, and he found himself wondering, idly, how she would look in one of the elaborate robes Tayledras Adepts favored. In better days, he'd had time to design clothing for his friends; Tayledras art had to be portable because they moved so often, and clothing was as much art as it was covering. His designs had been very popular back then; not as popular as Ravenwing's feather masks, but she had been practicing her art for longer than he'd been alive.

In fact, he had been proud, terribly proud, that his father had worn some of his designs. One of the things that had hurt him had been finding those outfits discarded soon after he had joined the scouts, in the pile of material available to be remade into scout-camouflage. Now he knew why his father had done that; discarded the clothing where he would be certain to find it. He'd meant to drive Darkwind farther away, to save him. The knowledge turned what had been a bitter memory into something more palatable.

As he contemplated Elspeth, he imagined what he would design for her. Something hugging the body to the hips, perhaps, showing that magnificently muscled torso, then with a flaring skirt, slit to properly display those long, athletic legs—definitely in a brilliant emerald green. Or maybe something that would enable her to move and fight with complete freedom; tight wine-red leather trews laced up the side, an intricately cut black tunic, a soft red silk shirt with an embroidered collar and sleeves. . . .

What in hell am I doing? How can I be thinking of clothing right now?

Maybe it was that she cried out for proper display. White was not her color. The stark uniform only made her look severe, like a purposeful, unornamented blade. After talking with her at length, there was no doubt in his mind that she was a completely competent fighter— that this was an important part of her life. But there was more to her than that; much more. Her outer self should mirror her complicated inner self.

She needed that kind of setting, with her spare, hard-edged beauty. Unlike Nyara, who would never look anything other than lush and exotic, sleek and sensuous, no matter what she wore.

Nyara sat on the opposite side of Skif, glancing sideways at him; Skif couldn't take his eyes off her. She had proved, once revived, not only cooperative but grateful that all Treyvan had done was put her to sleep. Her reaction—completely genuine, so far as Darkwind was able to determine—had shamed him a little for behaving with such suspicion and cold calculation toward her.

On the other hand, she herself had confirmed what Darkwind and Treyvan had suspected; that she was a danger. She confessed that she could be summoned by her father at any point, and if unfettered, she would probably go to him, awake or asleep. She did not know if he could read her thoughts at a distance, but was not willing to say that he couldn't.

"If you have any doubt, you must send me to sleep again, and tie me," she had said humbly. "Do not waste shields upon me that you may give to the little gryphons."

That last had won Treyvan; Darkwind was still not so sure, but his own misgivings were fading. She had given them an amazing amount of information about Mornelithe's stronghold; the problem was, the place was a miracle of defensive capability. Nyara bitterly attributed her easy escape now to the fact that her father had wanted her to get away. Extracting Dawnfire from that warren was looking more and more difficult. Active discussion had died before the sun sank into the west.

But Elspeth was still thinking about the problem and not simply admiring the sunset. "Darkwind, she's a bird, right? What about getting in, turning her loose, and making some other bird look like her?" Elspeth turned toward Darkwind as the last sliver of sun vanished. "One person, maybe two, could get away with that."

:*Now that is the kind of sortie I know how to run,*: the sword put in.

Darkwind looked pointedly at Nyara.

She coughed politely. "This would be a good time for me to absent myself. Could I take a walk, perhaps?" she asked. "Could someone go with me?" And she glanced significantly at Skif, who flushed but did not look as if he would turn down the invitation.

Darkwind found himself torn by conflicting emotions. He knew very well what was likely to happen as soon as those two found themselves alone, and while on the one hand, he was relieved that Nyara had found herself a safer outlet for her needs than himself, he also was unreasoningly jealous.

He didn't trust himself with her. He didn't trust *her;* she had already told them that Falconsbane had ordered her to seduce and subvert him. Doing anything except exchanging pleasantries with her was the worst possible idea at the moment.

That didn't stop his loins from tightening every time she looked at him.

And it didn't stop him from being envious of anyone else she cast those golden eyes upon.

"I've done my share of breaking into buildings in my misspent youth," Skif said hesitantly, with one eye on Nyara. "But I have the feeling you're thinking of using magic, and that's where you lose me. I suppose we could go take that walk, out of earshot. If only one person goes in, I guess it wouldn't be one of us Heralds—so what I know is pretty superfluous."

Darkwind glanced at Elspeth; he thought he saw a little smile playing at the corners of her mouth, but the light was fading, and he couldn't be sure. He wondered if she would be so amused if she knew what *he* knew about Nyara.

But there didn't seem to be any reason to object. "Stay within the ruins," he said, curtly. "Skif, I hold you responsible for this woman. Remember what she's told us; she can't even trust herself."

Skif nodded, but he also rose to his feet and courteously offered Nyara his hand to help her rise as well. Nyara took it, though she didn't need it any more than Darkwind would have. And she held it a moment longer than she needed to.

I don't think he has any idea of what he's in for. She just may eat him alive.

He stopped himself before he could say anything. *She isn't my property. She's too dangerous right now for me to touch. It doesn't matter what I want. Acting on what you want is something only children think is an adult prerogative.*

So he held his tongue and watched the two of them walk slowly into the shadows of the ruins, side-by-side, but carefully not-touching.

The sexual tension between them was so obvious that they might just as well have been bound together by ropes.

"I know I'm being incredibly obnoxious to ask this," Elspeth said behind him. "But were you two lovers?"

"No, lady," he said absently, as he struggled to get

his jealousy under control. "No, we weren't. She has that much control of herself; her father ordered her to seduce me, therefore she would not. Otherwise—" he paused, then continued, sensing that this particular young woman would not misinterpret what he was saying. And sensing that he could somehow reveal anything to her, without fear of coming under judgment. "Otherwise we might well have been. She was created for pleasure, I think you know that, or have guessed. It drives her before hunger or pain. She is probably quite—adept at it. She has had most of her life to learn it, and practice."

Elspeth considered his words for a moment, as he turned back to face her. "You aren't angry at Skif, I hope."

He uttered a short, humorless laugh. "Angry, no. She cannot help what she is. Envious—yes. Much as I hate to admit it. Envy is not a pretty trait. And you?"

Her soft laugh was genuine. "I am so relieved that he has finally found someone to—well—"

"Drag off into the ruins?" Darkwind suggested delicately.

"Exactly. I can't tell you how relieved I am. He has been a very good friend for many years," she said, tilting her head to one side as she sat silhouetted against the indigo sky. "And he has been under a great deal of strain lately."

"And were *you* lovers?" Darkwind asked sharply, in a tone that surprised even him. *Why should I care?* he wondered. *They're Outlanders. They'll get what they need and leave, like the breath of wind on a still pond. The only impression they can make is a fleeting one.*

She didn't seem to notice. "I haven't been entirely candid with you, Darkwind—though mostly it was because I didn't think rank was going to impress you any, and might have made you reject us out of hand."

Ah, so my surmise was right.

She took a deep breath. "I'm next in line for the throne. Not that I particularly want it," she added, and there was a kind of chagrined surprise in her voice, "Which is odd, because when I was little, I thought that being made Heir was the highest possible pinnacle of success. But there it is; now I have it, and I rather wish

I didn't. Skif has always been a kind of big brother to me, and there were always rumors about the two of us."

"But were they true?" he persisted. He shifted a little; not because he was uncomfortable outside, but because he was acutely uncomfortable inside. Jealousy again, and this time for *no* damned reason!

It must be overflow from Nyara, he decided. *Gods of my fathers; this is embarrassing . . . have I no self-control?*

"No," she said calmly, relieving his jealousy by her answer. "No, he always thought of me as a little sister. Until we went out on this trip together. *Then* he suddenly decided that he was in love with me." She sounded annoyed, to his great satisfaction. "I cannot for the life of me imagine why, but that's what he decided, and I've been trying to discourage him. Maybe once I would have been happy for that, but—it's not possible, Darkwind. I have duties as the Heir, if I ever get back in one piece. If I were to make any kind of alliance, I have to consider my duties first. And anything permanent would be weighed against them. Love—even if genuine—could only be secondary. Mother married for what she *thought* was love the first time, and it was a total disaster. Skif is so blinded by his own feelings that he won't even consider anything else."

"Ah," he replied, "I take it that you are far from convinced that what your friend feels is love."

She snorted. "Infatuation, more like it. I've been trying to emulate my teacher—Kerowyn—since we left Valdemar, and he worships her. That may have been the problem."

So she feels no tie beyond friendship for this Skif, he thought, with a feeling of satisfaction. *Well, if she is going to learn magic, that's just as well. She'll have a great deal to learn, coming to it this late, and she'll have no time for anything but study.* "That may have been the situation," he responded, sensing she was waiting for some kind of a reply. "But—you sounded very annoyed just now with him. May I ask why? If there is friction other than what you have told me, I need to know."

"Nothing other than that once he became infatuated, he wanted to wrap me in silk and stick me in a jewel box," she replied, the annoyance back in her voice. "I think I have him cured of that, but in case I haven't, the problem may come up again.''

He nodded, forgetting that it was dark enough that she wouldn't see the nod, then coughed politely. ''Thank you, Elspeth. That could cause some problems. I hope I have not caused you distress by asking you these questions.''

''No, not at all,'' she replied, surprise in her voice. ''You are a very easy person to confide in, Darkwind. Thank you for giving me the chance to unburden myself. My Companion thinks Skif is perfect for me, and Need thinks he's an utter loss, so any time I say anything to either of them, all I get is lectures.''

Companion? Oh, that must be the spirit-mare. But she said it as if it were a name. . . .

''Companion?'' he asked, as the first breath of the evening wind flowed through the stones and breathed the hair away from his face.

''My not-horse,'' she replied, and there was a smile there that he felt across the darkness between them. ''The one you have very graciously been treating not like a horse. We call them 'Companions'; every Herald in Valdemar has one—they Choose us to be Heralds.''

''They—'' he hesitated in confusion. ''Could you please explain?''

''Certainly, if you don't mind my coming closer,'' she replied. He peered through the darkness at her to see if she was being flirtatious—but she appeared to be swatting at her legs. ''There seem to be some kind of nocturnal insects on this rock, and they like the taste of Herald.''

''By all means, come sit beside me,'' he replied, grateful to the night-ants. ''There are no night-ant nests here.''

She rose, brushing off her legs, as he moved over on his rock to give her room.

''Now,'' he continued, ''About these 'Companions' of yours—''

''Shouldn't we be discussing how to get Dawnfire free?'' she replied as she seated herself, her tone one of concern. ''It's easy to get distracted.''

''We are discussing Dawnfire,'' he told her, a little grimly. ''You and this 'Companion' of yours may be better suited to the task than I. I need to know as much as possible about you.''

''But Skif—''

''Won't be back for some time,'' he assured her. ''And I have but two concerns regarding him. The first—that her father not attempt to contact or call her while he is with her.''

''And the second?'' she asked.

He sighed, and leaned back on his hands. ''That she leave enough left of him to be useful.''

She chuckled, and he felt the corners of his mouth turning up in a smile. ''Now,'' he continued. ''About this 'Companion'. . . .''

Nyara could have shouted her joy aloud, as Darkwind gave them tacit permission to go off alone. Skif could have been ugly, foul-breathed, pot-bellied, bow-legged, bald and obnoxious, and she would not at this moment have cared. He was *safe*, that was what mattered. Mornelithe had not ordered her to seduce him; did not even know that he existed, so far as she knew. She could ease the urges that had been driving her to distraction since her body began to heal, and do so without the guilt of knowing she would be corrupting him—do so only to pleasure herself and him, and not with any other motive of any sort.

That he was cleanly handsome, well-spoken, well-mannered—that turned the expedition from a simple need to a real desire.

She wanted him, in the same way she wanted Darkwind, but without the guilt. Likewise, he wanted her. She guessed, however, that he was shy, else he would have proposed dalliance when they were first alone, in the gryphons' lair. So, it would be up to her.

She had a cat's hearing, to be able to discern a mouse squeak in the high grass a furlong away; and a cat's eyes, so that this light of a near-full moon was as useful to her as the sun at full day.

So when he had just begun to turn to her, to tentatively reach for her hand, she already knew that they were well out of earshot, and that there was a little corner amidst the pile of rocks to their left that would suit his sense of modesty very well. No ears but those equal to hers would hear them; and no eyes but an owl's would spy them out.

Thank the gods—not Mornelithe—that she had learned trade-tongue, and that these strangers spoke it well.

"Nyara," Skif said shyly (oh, she had been right!), taking heart when she did not pull her hand away, "I'm sure this sounds pretty stupid, but I've never met anyone like you."

"You have no Changechildren in your lands?" she asked, stopping, turning to his voice, and standing calculatedly near him. Near enough that her breast brushed his arm.

He did not (oh, joy!) step away. "No," he replied, his voice rising just a little. "No Ch-changechildren, no magic."

"Ah," she purred. And swayed closer. "You know what my father made me for? Darkwind has told you?"

A slight increase in the heat of his body told her he blushed. "Y–yes," he stammered.

"Good," she replied, and fastened her mouth on his.

He only struggled for a moment, mostly out of surprise, and the anticipation that this was part of a ruse, that she meant to escape. Since that was the last thing on her mind, she told him so, with every fiber of her body.

He stopped struggling, believing her unspoken message. She molded herself to him, each and every separate nerve alive and athrill. Then, as he finally began responding instead of reacting, she led him back into the little alcove, step by slow, careful step.

She was on fire with need, and so was he; she felt it, and, for the first time in her life, Felt it as well, a flood of emotion and urgency that washed over her and mingled with her own.

That was such a surprise that she came near to forgetting her own desire. She melted in his need, pulling him down into the shadows, marveling at this precious gift from out of nowhere. To Feel his pleasure, his desire— it heightened her own beyond any past experience.

I am an Empath? I had never dreamed—my own hatred and fear must have shielded me.

But that didn't matter at the moment. All that was truly important was getting him out of his clothing. Or part of it, anyway.

He pulled away, and she clutched him, ripping his shirt with her talons. Why was he trying to evade her? She could Feel his overwhelming need so clearly.

"—rocks!" he gasped, as she tried to fasten her mouth on his again. "You'll hurt your—"

She proceeded to prove to him that the setting didn't matter, and neither did the rocks. Soon they were writhing together, joined in body and mind, and she bit her hand to keep from screaming her pleasure aloud. Mornelithe knew her body as no one else; he knew every way possible to elicit reactions of all sorts from her. But *this* was pleasure unmixed with anger, hate, self-hatred. She had never been so happy in all of her short life.

He reached the pinnacle; she followed, and they fell together.

They lay entwined, panting, sweat-soaked and exhausted. He stroked her hair, with a gentle hand, murmuring wonderful things that she only half heard. How amazing she was; astonishing, a dream come to life. These things were never to be believed if a would-be lover whispered them before the bedding—but after?

She probed his feelings delicately, taking care with this new sense. And there was some truth there, a little something more than mere infatuation. Yes, he was infatuated, but he thought her brave for even trying to resist her father, he thought her admirable for giving them the aid that she had.

And he thought her lovely, desirable, beyond any dream. Nor did he despise her for using her body as she had, or even (and she held her breath in wonder) for being used by her own father.

But there was a bitterness to the joy; he imagined her to have been forced into submitting.

He could never understand the forces that had been bred and formed in her; that her father would call, and she would come, willingly, abjectly, desiring him as fervently as she desired anyone. . . .

She resolved not to think about it. The chances were, she would never see him again after the next few days. If they freed Dawnfire, she would use the Tayledras' gratitude to enable her to put as much distance between herself and her father as her feet would permit.

If they did not—

She would not think of it. Not now. And there was a most excellent distraction near at hand.

She reached for Skif again; he pulled her closer, pillowing her head on his shoulder, thinking she only wished comfort.

She was going to give him such a lovely surprise. . . .

In speaking to Elspeth, Darkwind found himself baffled and dazzled by turns. By the time Skif and Nyara returned, disheveled and sated, smelling of sweat and sex, Darkwind had begun to realize that there was even more to this complicated princess than he had thought.

She had her flaws, certainly. An over-hasty tongue; not in saying what she should not, but in doing so too sharply, too scathingly. A habit of speech, of speaking the truth too clearly and too often that could earn her enemies—and probably had. A hot temper, which, when kindled, was slow to cool. The tendency to hold a grudge—

Hold a grudge? Dear gods, she treasures *a grudge, long past when it should have been dead and buried.*

She would, without doubt, pursue an enemy into his grave, then make a dancing-floor of it. Then return from time to time for a jig, just to keep the triumph alive.

She flung herself into the midst of disagreements before she entirely understood them, basing her response on what had just happened, rather than seeing what had led to the situation. She was impatient with fools and scornful of those who were ruled by emotions rather than logic. And she took no care to hide either the scorn or the impatience; without a doubt, that had earned her enemies as well.

But to balance all that, she was loyal, faithful, and truly cared for people; so blindingly intelligent that it amazed him, and not afraid of her intellect as so many were. She tried, to the best of her ability, to consider others as often as she considered herself. Her sense of responsibility frightened him, it was so like his own. So, too, her sense of justice.

Dawnfire had been—*was*, he told himself, fiercely—a paragon of simplicity compared to her. Of course, Dawnfire was ten years her junior, or thereabouts, but he wondered if Elspeth had ever been uncomplicated, even as a child.

Probably not; not with all the considerations the child of a royal couple had to grow up with. Every friend must be weighed against what he might be wanting; every smile must be assumed to be a mask, hiding other motives. Such upbringing had made for bitter, friendless rulers in the Outlands.

It was a very good thing that these people had their Heralds; a very good thing that the monarch was a Herald, and could know with certainty that she would always have a few trustworthy friends.

He didn't entirely understand what the Heralds did, but he certainly understood what they were about. They embodied much the same spirit as the Kal'enedral of the Shin'a'in; like them, it appeared that they were god-chosen, for if the Companions were not the embodiment of the hand of the gods, then he would never recognize such a thing in his lifetime. Like them, they were guided, but subtly—for the most part, left free to exercise their free will, and only gently reminded from time to time if they were about to err. It seemed that the unsubtle attempt to steer Elspeth down a particular course was the exception, and not the rule—and it appeared to him to have failed quite dismally. And as a result, Elspeth's Companion Gwena was now, grudgingly, going to admit her defeat and permit Elspeth to chart her own way from this moment on.

The Heralds were very like the Kal'enedral in another way; for as each had his Companion, so each Kal'enedral had his *leshya'e* Kal'enedral, the spirit-teacher that drilled him in weaponry and guided his steps on the Star-Eyed's road.

And the Heralds themselves were blissfully unaware of the fact.

If they didn't know—and the Companions chose not to tell them—he was not inclined to let the secret slip. *"It is not wise to dispute the decisions of the Powers,"* he thought, wryly quoting a Shin'a'in proverb. *"They have more ways of enforcement than you have of escape."* The decision to set Elspeth on a predetermined path was probably less a "decision" than a "plan." Another Shin'a'in proverb: *"Plans are always subject to change."*

He found himself making a decision of his own; when all this was settled, he would teach her himself. He would find a teaching-Adept, perhaps in another Clan, like k'Treva, and as he relearned, he would teach her. He had the feeling that she respected what he had done, and she would continue to respect him for going back to pick up where he had left off.

Besides, as Tayledras had learned in the past, those who were in the process of learning often discovered new ways and skills, just by being unaware that it "couldn't be done." Perhaps they would discover something together.

But that was for the future; now there was a rescue to be staged.

"We have decided," he said, as Skif reclaimed his boulder, and Nyara seated herself near it. Not quite at his feet, but very close. Darkwind suppressed a last fading twinge of jealousy. "We think we have a plan that will work."

"It's going to need a lot of coordination, though," Elspeth added. "It's going to involve more than just us. Skif, can you get Cymry listening in on this? I just called Gwena."

"Cymry?" he responded, sounding confused. "Uh—sure—"

"They don't need to be with us to be in on conferences," Elspeth said in an undertone to Darkwind. "The Herald-Companion link is even closer than a lifebond in many ways; no matter how weak your Gift of Mindspeech is, your Companion can always hear you, and, if you choose, listen to what you hear."

"And right now they need very badly to be eating," he supplied. "Indeed, the *dyheli* are so, after a long, hard run".

He felt her smile, though he could not see it. "Why don't you start, Darkwind, since this was your idea."

"What of me?" Nyara asked in a small voice. "Should I—"

"You are going to be *inside* the Vale by midmorning," Darkwind told her. "I am going to tell Iceshadow something of your past, and put you in his custody, asking him to keep you always within the shields of the apprentice's working place, where my father is. If your father can break the Vale shields *and* the working-shields, he is merely toying with us, and anything we do is trivial against him. I am going to ask you to answer all of Iceshadow's questions about my father's captivity, no matter how painful they are to you."

"Why?" she asked, huddling a little smaller.

"Because you will be helping Iceshadow determine what was done to him, and so break the bonds Falconsbane placed upon him," Darkwind told her, letting the tone of his voice inform her that he would grant her no more mercy than he granted himself. "That much, at the least, you owe him."

Skif made a little movement, as if he wanted to leap up and challenge Darkwind, but wisely kept himself under control.

"I will then summon the nonhumans that Dawnfire worked with," he continued. "They will help be our diversion; *tervardi* and *dyheli,* they will concentrate on a place where you, Heralds, will be. In the neutral area, as if you had passed across Tayledras lands and were going westward. It will look to Falconsbane as if you have summoned them, and he will assume it is through your sword, Elspeth."

Elspeth took up the explanation where he paused. "All he can tell is that it's magic, Skif. That's probably why those things were chasing us across the Plains. He wants it, and he hasn't got a clue that he can't use it."

:*Oh, he could* try, *I suppose,*: the sword said dryly. :*But he doesn't know I'm in here. It's quite likely that it would be impossible for him to make any real use of me without destroying me.*:

"I suspect he will decide that it is one of the ancient devices used to control the nonhumans in warfare." Darkwind rubbed the bridge of his nose. "I can tell you that if he thinks *that,* he will be mad to have it. And he will be equally determined after his last failure that he will not leave the task in the hands of others."

"So he'll come in person," Skif stated, and he was plainly not pleased with the idea. "Where does that leave us?"

"Standing inside the Vale," Darkwind chuckled, wishing he could see Skif's face. "It will be your images and your auras in the neutral area, and no more. It is a spell that is not often cast, for it is broken as soon as one moves more than five paces in any direction. Need re-

minded us of it. In fact, Need intends to be the mage
casting it." He made a little bow in Elspeth's direction.

*:Thank you for the confidence, but save your applause
for if it works. And it'll be Elspeth casting it; I'll just be
showing her how.:*

"That leaves me outside," he continued, "And I shall
be the one making the attempt to free Dawnfire. If I have
the time, I shall place the illusion of the proper hawk on
some other bird in his mews, and blank the beast's mind.
He will assume that Dawnfire's personality has at last
faded. Or so I hope."

He hated to subject an innocent bird to that, but with
luck, it would be one of Falconsbane's own evil creations.

"If I do not have the time," he continue, "I shall
simply free her and attempt to escape. I do not think he
will return before I am away again."

Skif whistled softly. "That's going to take some good
timing," he observed. "And you're the one taking the
packleader's share of the risks."

"But it could not be done without all of you," he
responded. "I cannot ask you to take the kinds of risks
that I will—but I cannot make this succeed without you."

"And afterward?" Elspeth asked softly. "When you
have Dawnfire free, but still trapped in a hawk's body,
her true self fading with every day—what then? You didn't
speak of that."

He remained silent because he didn't know—and he
didn't want to contemplate it, having to watch her struggle against the inevitable, and lose.

A long, unhappy silence descended, which the sword
finally broke.

:Oh, worry about it when she's free,: the blade replied
irritably. *:For one thing, I know a bit about transfer
spells. Maybe I can get her into something with a big
enough brain that she can stay herself. Or maybe I can
get her into something like a sword.:*

"Would that not be just as bad?" Nyara asked doubtfully, voicing exactly what Darkwind was thinking. He
suppressed a groan.

:At least she'd stay herself, girl,: the sword retorted
with annoyance. *:There're worse fates than being hard
to break, heart included.:*

Darkwind decided to end the discussion right there. "Enough; we have a great deal ahead of us—

"And not much time," Elspeth said firmly. "And best to work on it in the morning."

They returned to the lair, and gave Treyvan and Hydona the basics of what they had decided. Treyvan did not ask about the fate of his own young, but Darkwind could tell that he was gravely worried and weary; evidently Falconsbane had tried something while they were talking and had been beaten back, but at a cost. They were all too tired for anything more, and put off further discussion. Nyara bedded down in the same chamber as Skif and Elspeth, with Darkwind across the door and Treyvan blocking the entrance for added security.

But Darkwind could not fall asleep as easily as the rest. He lay staring at the silhouette of the sleeping gryphon, watching the shadow climb up the wall as the moon set. And over and over, the question repeated in his mind.

What do I do once she is free?

She would never again wear the body of the girl he had traded feathers and favors with. At worst case, he would watch her fade, slowly, into the hawk. If Falconsbane had slain the spirit of her bird with Dawnfire's body, she might well hold on longer, but the end would be the same. And whether she stayed in the hawk, or Need managed to find a way to put her in another form, the result was the same. She would never again be "Dawnfire," she would be something else, something he could no longer touch.

What, in the gods' names, do I do when she is free?

Chapter
Twenty-four

The alarm cry of a falcon woke him at dawn—and the answering, deeper scream of a hawk.

He started awake, all at once, and knew he was not at home. The rock floor, the lack of movement, and the darkness told him that much before he even opened his eyes. His hand was on his knife-hilt as he blinked the haze of sleep away, running rapidly through all the possibilities of where he was and what had become of his *ekele*—

Treyvan's lair— That was all he had a chance to remember as the falcon cried alarm again. He cast about for the door, still disoriented by the strange surroundings.

That's Vree—but whose was the hawk?

:Out!: Vree demanded, his mental cry as shrill and penetrating as his physical scream. *:Out now! Hurry! Help!:*

That wasn't the "Help me," version, it was "I need your help." He scrambled over Treyvan's prone body as the gryphon struggled up out of sleep. "Grrrruh?" Treyvan responded, as Darkwind slid down his haunches and into the sunlight. "Wrrrrhat?"

There were two birds up above, one flapping as clumsily as a just-fledged crow, the other unmistakably Vree. The gyre circled in guard-fashion above the first, protecting it as it tried to come in to land.

It was a red-shouldered hawk—

It was—

Dawnfire!

:Help me,: came the faint and faltering mental cry. *:Help me—:*

She doesn't know how to land— he realized, just as Treyvan shouldered him aside, leapt into the sky, rose to meet her, and scooped her from the air with his outstretched talons. He wheeled and dropped, cradling her safely in his foreclaws, coming to rest delicately on his hind feet only, in a thunder of wing-claps, before Darkwind realized what he was doing.

Treyvan balanced precariously as he had alighted, keeping himself from falling with his outstretched wings. The bird lay exhausted in Treyvan's claws, every last bit of energy long since spent. Darkwind took her from the gryphon, and held her in his arms, like an injured, shocked fledgling. She lay panting, eyes closed, as he folded her wings over her back, and stroked her head.

Another hand joined his; a hard, but feminine hand. It was Elspeth, wearing only a thin undershift and hose, but carrying her blade unsheathed in her other hand. Her eyes were closed; a slight frown was her only expression—but the moment her fingers touched Dawnfire's back, the bird began to revive.

Her head lifted, and she craned it around to stare up at him. *:Darkwind?:* she Mindspoke, softly. *:Is this real, or some illusion* he *created to torment me? Am I truly free? And home?:*

"You're free, *ke'chara,*" he replied, anger and grief combined rising to choke off his words. It was one thing to know intellectually that she might have been trapped in her bird's body; it was another to see it, Sense it.

:I saw Vree, or he saw me, I forget,: she said, closing her eyes again, and bending her head, as if she did not want to see him through the hawk's eyes. *:He brought me here, but I was so tired—:*

"The sword will work better through direct contact," Elspeth said quietly. "If you can put her down on my bed, and I can lay Need next to her—"

No sooner spoken than done; and with the blade touching her, Dawnfire gained strength quickly, asking for water and food. The latter, Darkwind fed her as he would an eyas: little morsels cut from a fresh rabbit that Vree brought back within moments of her asking for something to eat. She took each tidbit daintily, and it was plain from her condition that she had not been feeding well in Mornelithe's hands.

Outwardly he was calm. Inwardly he was in turmoil. How to tell her that her body was dead—that she was still as trapped now as she was in Falconsbane's hands? There was no hint of Kyrr in her thoughts—so the blade's guess, that Mornelithe had killed the bird's spirit with her body was probably right. That gave them a little more time than if she'd had to share Kyrr's mind—but it would only postpone the end a little longer.

Joy at her recovery, anguish at her condition, rage at the one who had brought her to this—guilt because he was partly to blame. Warring emotions kept him silent as he fed her, wondering what to say and how to say it.

"Dawn—" he began, hesitantly.

:*Darkwind, you're in danger,:* she interrupted urgently. She twisted her head to look at the strangers. :*You're* all *in danger, terrible danger!:*

Quickly she told them of all she had heard; and most importantly, Outland, of Falconsbane's new plan, his decision to make Outland alliances.

Alliances? Oh, blessed gods— He forgot his other worries in the face of this new threat, for Falconsbane alone was bad enough. Falconsbane with allies was a prospect too awful to contemplate. Allies with mage-powers, allies with armies—either would spell disaster for the precarious hold k'Sheyna maintained on power here, but this Ancar evidently had mages *and* armies, according to Elspeth. K'Sheyna would be obliterated, and every other Vale faced with a formidable threat.

If he gets help like that, there won't be anything beyond him—

The Heralds—and their Companions—questioned Dawnfire closely as he closed his eyes and tried to think of all the possibilities. Their reaction was identical to his—not too surprising, given that he thought this "Ancar" that Dawnfire said Falconsbane was meeting was undoubtedly the same man who had been doing his best to level *their* land. It was not a common name; it was beyond likely that there were two of them.

And although it seemed a terribly long way to travel just for a meeting with a possible ally, Mornelithe *was* a powerful Adept, and a desirable acquisition, so far as Ancar's position was concerned. The King of Hardorn *needed* mages; he'd been actively recruiting them. He might not yet have any Adept-class; it might be well worth it to him to come this far.

And a similar search had already brought Elspeth and Skif just as far.

:He said he was meeting the man in three days,: Dawnfire was saying when he opened his eyes again to pay attention to what was going on around him. Now there were seven sets of eyes fixed on the exhausted hawk; the two Heralds, the two gryphons, the pair of Companions, and Nyara, who seemed as upset as any of them.

He thought he knew the reason why. *Perhaps she sees herself in Dawnfire's entrapment. . . .*

:That was two days ago,: Dawnfire continued. *:I escaped that afternoon, and I've been flying in circles ever since, trying to find my way home. So today, or the day after, they will meet.:*

"Ancar wouldn't have come all this way just to turn around," Elspeth said grimly. "He wants this alliance, wants it badly. He's got no other reason to leave his own realm, and I don't care how much Hulda taught him, he wouldn't leave the place even in *her* hands if there was any other way out. Gods—with Falconsbane's power and Ancar's armies—and his recklessness—we won't have a chance. We've got to stop this before it happens."

"We have an opportunity to put paid to both our enemies," Darkwind growled, his hands clenched into fists. "Not only to stop this alliance, but take both our enemies at one stroke. I must talk to the Elders."

He started to get up; Skif caught his elbow and his attention. "You'd better include Elspeth in your plans, no matter what else you do," he whispered, "or she's likely to march right in there on her own."

She, who holds a grudge like an eyas binds to a kill. He nodded curtly, annoyed, but knowing Skif was right.

The gryphons had a grudge of their own to settle. They probably wouldn't try to stop her.

:Settle down, you lot!: Need growled suddenly, startling all of them. *:I don't know what's set the burr under your tails so you aren't thinking, children, but I stopped falling for tricks like this one a millennium ago and I'm not going to let you cart me into a trap now. I said he likely wouldn't be able to use me; I'd prefer not to put that to the test, if you don't mind.:*

They stared at each other in shock, Dawnfire included.

"What?" Darkwind asked.

:Let me spell it out for you. Dawnfire was allowed to escape, so that she could bring you this trumped-up story. So that you lot would go charging off straight into his loving arms.:

Nyara was the first to recover. "Oh, no," she whispered. "It is too, too like my own escape—an escape that was not. This sword is right!"

Elspeth set her chin stubbornly, her eyes flashing for a moment, then sighed, and threw up her hands. "Bright Havens, I *want* to believe it, I really do, because it's such a good chance to get the bastard now, while he's away from his support and his army—but you're right, you're both right. It's too damned pat, too coincidental. Mother's intelligence web had Ancar safe in his own palace when we left. We made much better time than he could have because we're riding Companions. The only way he could possibly have matched our time would be to ride in relays, and how would he manage that off his own lands? He has farther to come than we did on top of all that. So how could he *possibly* be arriving here just at the same moment we did?"

"And why sssshould he perrrmit Dawnfirrre to overhearrrr hisss planssss?" Treyvan rumbled. "Mossst essspecially, why ssshould he have given herrr to one who wasss not competent with hawksss to take to the mewsss? He wanted herrr to fly to usss with thisss."

"And then wanted us to—what?" Elspeth asked. "Falconsbane never does anything for just one reason. He wants us not only to try and break up this nonexistent meeting, he wants us moved. Why? What's so special about this neutral area where the supposed 'meeting' is?

Is it a particularly good place to stage a double ambush?''

"There's nothing special about it that I know of," Darkwind replied, frowning with concentration.

:He can't have meant to catch you as he caught the dyheli, *can he?:* Dawnfire asked, drooping a little, as she, too, acknowledged the fact that her escape had been too easy. *:He deliberately reminded me of what he had done to them there—:*

"Which probably means he wanted us to concentrate on that as well," Skif mused aloud. "We know he wants the sword. From what Quenten told me, he probably wants Elspeth as well."

"Oh, yes," Nyara agreed, nodding her head vigorously. "Yes, an untrained mage? He uses such as tools. He would be pleased to have you in his hands, lady."

"So, is there anything else he wants? Something we'd leave unprotected—something even the whole Clan might leave unprotected, if we went to them and got more help for this?" Skif continued.

Elspeth glanced sideways at Darkwind. "The Vale itself?" she hazarded. "Or your father?"

He shook his head. "No, the static protections are too much for him to crack easily. We could return and entrap him before he had even begun to break the outermost shields."

"The Heartsssstone?" asked Treyvan, then answered himself. "No, it isss the sssame as for the Vale—"

The squall of a hungry young gryphon cut across their speculations, and sent all eyes in the direction of the inner lair.

"No," Treyvan whispered, his eyes widening.

"Yes!" Nyara cried, in mingled pain and triumph. "Yes—that is what he wants—as much as sword and mage, and Starblade and Starblade's son! Revenge, and the souls of your younglings!"

"And I . . ." Treyvan whispered, his eyes wide with horror, "nearrrly gave it all away to him . . . again."

It had taken Darkwind no time at all to create a scale-model of the area around the lair, using rocks, twigs, and the flat expanse of sand near the entrance. It was the only place big enough for all of them. Elspeth shook off

the many memories of time spent bending over a sand-
table with Kero, and paid close attention to Darkwind.
She wondered now how she could have mistaken simple
stress for arrogance.

Not thinking clearly lately, are we? she asked herself.
*Not observing at all well. When this is over, it might be
a good idea to take a few days to rest and think. About
a lot of things.*

"You'll be here," Darkwind said to Skif, placing a
pinecone on the bits of rock representing the ruins to the
left of the lair.

"And I'll be moving around if I can't get a good knife
or bow-shot from there," Skif added.

The Hawkbrother nodded. "Exactly so. You are best
as mobile as possible. Now, the little ones, Dawnfire,
and the sword will be *here*, in front of the lair." He
placed a cluster of weed-stripped seed-heads and a sliver
of wood before the large stone representing the lair, and
gave Elspeth a penetrating glance. "You are certain you
are willing to give up the use of the blade? It seems
unfair."

Elspeth shrugged. "It was Need's choice, remember,"
she pointed out. "We've got to protect the bait somehow,
and two of the three of them are female."

:Crap, I'll take care of the little male, too,: the blade
said gruffly. *:What do you think I am, some kind of baby-
killer? Besides, the bastard would twist him up as badly
as he has Nyara, if he got his claws on the lad.:*

"You are not such poor bait yourself, blade-lady,"
Darkwind replied. "He wants you as well, as I recall."

:Just make sure he doesn't get me.:

"No help coming frrrom the Vale?" asked Hydona,
leaning over Skif's shoulder to look at the setup.

Darkwind shook his head. "Not since the message I
sent them by bondbird-relay. They are rightly fearful that
this may be a double ruse—a feint at the little ones, a
pretense that draws us into ambush, and a real strike at
the Vale. They have been badly shaken by what they have
seen done to my father and do not share my confidence
in their own shields. They have called in all the scouts
but myself, and are bracing for attack."

"Firrrsssst ssssmarrrt thing they've decided in agesss,"
Treyvan growled, "Even if it doesss leave usss to bearrr

the burrrden of ourrrr own defenssssessss. I take it we are herrre, and herrrre?''

The gryphon pointed a talon at two feathers stuck in the sand on the opposite side of the lair from Skif's initial position, behind a line of rocks representing the wall the lair had been built into.

''Precisely,'' Darkwind agreed, ''And here are Elspeth and myself.'' He dropped two rough quartz-crystals opposite the gryphons and nearer to the lair than Skif. ''Then the Companions, watching for his creatures coming at us from behind.'' Two large white flowers, one beside Skif's pinecone, one beside Elspeth's crystal. ''Treyvan, we will try to bracket him with magic; once that occurs I do not think he will be looking for a physical attack. That is where you come in—'' he nodded at Skif. ''And you, because of that, are the pivotal point of the defense. You look for your opening and take it. The man is as mortal as any to a well-placed knife or arrow. You are our hidden token, our wild piece.''

''What about me?'' Nyara asked, in a small voice. ''Is there nothing I can do?''

Elspeth bit her lip to keep from saying what she was thinking; that there was no way they could trust the Changechild enough to give her a part to play. They certainly couldn't make her part of the bait; neither the gryphons nor Darkwind wanted her near enough to be in range for an attack on *them* if her father regained control of her.

''Falconsbane does not know you are still with us,'' Darkwind said, after an uncomfortable silence. ''The longer this remains so, the better.''

''Stick with me,'' Skif suggested. ''I'm staying out of sight.''

:*Is this wise?*: Darkwind asked Elspeth worriedly. She shook her head just enough to make her hair stir imperceptibly.

:*He's assassin-trained,*: she replied wishing there were somewhere safe they could leave Nyara until this was all over. :*And Cymry will be with him, watching his back, the way Gwena will be watching ours. She won't be able to catch him with an unexpected attack. I just hope he doesn't find himself in the position of being forced to let Cymry kill her.*:

:Or killing her himself,: Darkwind added.

Anything more he might have intended to say was lost, for at that moment, Vree sounded the alert from overhead.

:He comes!: the bird shrieked, with mind and voice. *:He comes now!:*

They scattered for their posts.

Falconsbane prowled the woods that the Birdmen thought were theirs with an ease they would have found appalling, noting the increased levels of shielding about the Vale with a mixture of contempt and anger. There was no doubt of it; they had poured more power into their old shields, added new, and every Adept within the Vale was undoubtedly on alert. The tentative plan he'd formed to extract Starblade from his protectors and retrain him for further use was obviously out of the question now.

He paused in the shelter of a wild tangle of briars and searched for a weak point. There was nothing of the sort. Since there was no one to see him, he permitted himself a savage snarl. All that work, all the patience, the careful planning, the investment of power in Starblade's transformation to puppet, and in the construct that controlled him—all wasted!

He wished he had been able to see through the simulacrum's eyes, but the protections about the Vale had made that impossible. He still had no real idea what had happened when he'd lost his contact with the simulacrum. Starblade had been near the Heartstone; he knew that much. Since it had been near dawn, Falconsbane assumed that he must have been conducting his usual nonproductive assessment of the state of the Heartstone. Then, out of nowhere, a flash of panic from the crow—

And then, the backlash of power as the bird was destroyed. Why, or by whom, he'd had no clue.

He had immediately diverted the wild, uncontrolled power, killing one of his servants—the toady of a secretary, Daelon, who had the misfortune to be nearest.

That wasn't too much of a loss; Daelon had been useless as a mage, and only moderately useful as a secretary. But any loss at all angered him. He had lashed back immediately, flinging spells intended to resnare Starblade before anyone could protect him. It might have been an accident; it might have been the foolish simulacrum venturing into someone's protected area, or even bumbling into something—doing something as stupid as frightening a pet firebird. Any of those things could have killed it.

But as his spells battered against a new and powerful set of shields, it became obvious that it had not been accident that killed the simulacrum. It had been deliberate; his plots had been discovered.

And later tries against Starblade had proven just as fruitless. The Birdman had been well protected within shields that predated Falconsbane's interference with the Heartstone; strong, unflawed shields that he could find no way past.

Now he passed within easy striking distance of the Vale—"striking" distance, only if he'd had that alliance with Ancar of Hardorn that he had feigned, if he'd had a dedicated corps of mages, Masters and Adepts—and as he saw the shimmer of power above the Vale he could only curse at his own impotence. Somehow, some way, someone within k'Sheyna had learned what he had done to Starblade, had surmised how he controlled the handsome fool. Perhaps it had been one of the Adept's former lovers; in retrospect it had been a mistake to force Starblade to retreat into hermitlike isolation. But he had been afraid that the new persona he had laid over the old would not withstand the scrutiny of close examination.

I should have let him keep his lovers; should have had him employ some of the pleasuring techniques he learned at my hands. That would have kept them quiet enough. Nothing stops questionings like unbridled lust and the exhaustion afterward.

It was too late now; he'd not only lost Starblade, he'd lost the Vale. The Birdmen were alert now; there would be no subterfuge clever enough to bypass their protections, and though weakened, they were too formidable for him to take alone.

With luck, the two Outlanders and Starblade's son were on their way to the trap he'd laid for them. Camped within the valley even now were a host of human servants, garbed in the livery of Ancar of Hardorn, led by one who was like enough to that monarch to be his twin. And no illusion had been involved; the conscript was already similar in height, build, and coloring—the same spells that sculpted changes into Falconsbane's flesh had been used at a subtler level to reform this human's face. There would be lingering traces of magic; but that was what the Outlanders would expect. Ancar was a mage, after all.

Once the Outlanders were in place, watching, the rest of his army would take them from behind.

If I cannot have Starblade, I will have Starblade's son. If I cannot take my vengeance upon the Vale, I can take it upon his sweet, young flesh.

There would be that other young man—malleable, possibly of some use as well. Certainly an entertaining bit of amusement. Likely to be a bargaining chip in some way.

And then there was the girl. Her potential as a mage was high. She was curiously naive in some areas; and that left her a wide range of vulnerable points for Falconsbane to exploit. It had been a very long time since he'd broken a female Adept to his will. He was going to take his time with this one; there would be no mistakes that way—and it would, not incidentally, prolong the pleasure as well.

He slid from shadow to shadow beneath the trees, as surefooted and quiet as the lynx he had modeled himself for. As keen of ear, swift of eye, and cunning—

Not even the Birdmen, the scouts and their so-clever birds had ever caught him. He had been wandering freely amid their woodlands since k'Sheyna first settled here. And they never once guessed at his silent presence.

My fighters will take Starblade and the Outlanders, and kill or catch the gryphons. I hope they can catch them. I want the satisfaction of killing them myself.

The deep hatred that always rose in him at the thought of *gryphons* choked his throat and made him grind his teeth in frustration. No matter how remote the memories of his other lives were, *that* one was clear, balefully clear.

Gryphons. They had foiled his bid for supremacy in the Mage-Wars, they had defied his power, ruined his plans, destroyed his kingdom—

Gryphons. Wretched beasts, they were no more than jumped-up constructs. How *dared* they think of themselves as sentients, equal to human, independent and proud of their independence? How dared they use magic, as if they had a right to do so? How dared they *breed* at all?

Animals they were, and one day he would reduce them to the position of brute animals again. And in so doing, he would achieve the sweetest revenge of all, for he would undo everything that the wretched beast who had brought him down had lived and worked for. Only then would he be able to face the memory of Skandranon, the Black Gryphon, with satisfaction.

I will have the parents, he thought, snarling, as he slipped through the underbrush without leaving so much as a footprint behind. *But most importantly, I will have the children. And through them I will not only control the node, but have the downfall of the entire race in my hands. Through them I can spread a plague and a poison that will destroy the minds of any gryphon they meet, and turn them into mere carnivorous cattle. My cattle. To use as I wish. And it is time and more than time that I have that pleasure.*

He entered the area of the ruins, skirting the edge just within the cover of the forest. The lair lay beneath the shadows of the trees in the morning, though it enjoyed full sunlight in the afternoon. This was the nearest he had been, save for that one quick foray to place his hand and seal on the youngsters, binding them to himself.

They can't have left the young ones alone, without some form of protection. There may be shields, or some of the beast-guardians. He paused for a moment, one deeper shadow within the shadows, his spotted pelt blending with the dappled sunlight on the dead leaves beneath the trees, with the mottled bark of the trunk beside him. He wore scouting leathers very similar to what the Birdmen wore; that was one subterfuge that had stood him in good stead in the past. If he *was* seen, he had only to create a fleeting illusion of Birdman features, and other scouts would assume he was one of their number.

A quick glance upward showed him nothing was aloft—nothing but what he expected. Two tiny specks, hardly large enough to be seen, circling overhead. Waiting. That would do.

He set out a questing finger of Mage-Sight, looking for

what might have been left behind with the gryphon young.

A shimmering aura flickered about the lair in a delicate rainbow of protection. But beneath the shimmer—a brighter glow of power. *The shields I knew of—yes—and something more—*

He paused; Looked, and Looked again, hardly able to believe his luck.

They had left the artifact behind to guard the young ones! Its protections were unmistakable, and just the touch of them awoke avarice in his heart. *The age—the power—woman's power, but there is little I cannot overcome and turn to my own use—I must have this thing. I must! And they have left it for my taking!*

Elation faded, replaced by cold caution. Perhaps the Outlanders would be that foolish, and even the gryphons—but would Darkwind? The boy was a canny player; surely he had left more protections behind than that, for all that he had renounced magic.

Falconsbane Looked farther, deeper into the ruins than he had ever bothered before; looking for traps, for any hint of magic, even old, or apparently inactive magic. It was always possible that some ancient ward or guardian still existed here that Darkwind had left armed against him.

But there were no signs of any such protections.

He Looked farther still. He had assumed that they knew by now what he had done to the young ones. Was it possible, barely possible, that they did not *know* of his hand on the gryphlets? Had he overestimated their intelligence, their caution? Was it possible after all that they had been so caught up in what he had done to Starblade and Dawnfire that they had missed his sign and seal on their own young? Or could it be that the advent of the Outlanders had distracted them?

No. No, that is why they left the artifact, I am sure of it. To protect the young against me. The shields are too obviously set against my power; even the shields of the artifact itself.

Then, just when he thought perhaps he was searching in vain for further traps, he caught a hint of magic-energy, a tremor of power. Old magic.

Very old magic.

It was not active, but the presence of magic that ancient attracted his curiosity anyway. He had time to spare; such potentials were worth investigating. It was probably nothing; perhaps some long-abandoned shrine, or an ancient talisman, buried beneath a mound of rubble. It might be worth retrieving at some point, if only as a curiosity.

He moved in for a closer Look, half-closing his eyes, his talons digging into the bark of the tree beside him as he concentrated.

And he tore an entire section of bark from the tree trunk as his hand closed convulsively.

A Gate!

No. Yes. It couldn't be. Not the site of a temporary Gate, but one of the rare, powerful, *permanent* Gates—

No more than a handful of Adepts at the time of the Mage-Wars had ever constructed permanent Master Gates; they required endless patience, vast expenditures of energy that could have gone into constructing armies and weapons. Those few who had done so had made a network of such Gates, all tied into one another, crisscrossing their little kingdoms. Urtho had been one of those; that was how the Kaled'a'in had survived the downfall of his kingdom to become the Shin'a'in and Tayledras—they had fled through the Gate at the heart of his citadel to one on the edge of the area. Possibly even this one. Falconsbane had never built one—not in any of his lifetimes. He'd known of the network Urtho had built, of course, but he had never once entertained the idea that even part of that network could still exist.

A Gate, even a Master Gate, couldn't have survived the Wars, or the years, could it? It simply wasn't possible—

Falconsbane could not ignore the proof of his own senses. It was possible. And the Gate had survived.

The touch of it drove him wild with the desire to have it under his control. The node, the gryphons, the artifact, and now this—

He had to have it. He *would* have it. Then he would excavate it, study it, learn how to set it—and *use* it, use it to penetrate to the remains of Urtho's stronghold at the heart of the Plains. With a Gate like this one, he could bypass all the protections of the damned horse-lovers, get in, get what he wanted, and get out with no interference. He could go anywhere there was another permanent Gate, whether or not he knew the territory. He could construct temporary Gates no matter where he was and link into this one at any distance, once he keyed it into himself. Working that way would drain only a fraction of the energy of an ordinary Gate-spell from him. That was the deadly burden of Gating; the energy for the Gate came from the mage.

Or from someone tied to the mage with the kind of bond as deep as a lifebond. Not many knew that a mage tied by a lifebond to another mage could feed his beloved with the energies needed to fuel the Gate-spell.

Fewer knew what Falconsbane knew, that there was another bond as deep as a lifebond; the bond he built between himself and his victim when he made that victim an extension of himself.

As deep as a lifebond; it had to be, to survive the endless struggle of his victims to be free. Built out of both pleasure and pain at the most primitive, instinctive levels, it made his servants need him more than they needed food, drink, sleep—

That opened all their resources to him; to the point, if needed, that he could drain them to their death. He could use those resources to open the Gate and make it his in a way that no other Adept ever had.

But first—he had to make the area his. And that meant retrieving and subverting the young gryphons, to open up the node to his use. Right now there didn't appear to be anything in the way of that.

He released the trunk of the tree, dropping bits of wood and bark as he shook his tingling hand, and stepped cautiously out into the sunlight.

He kept to the shadows, still. There was no point in walking about in the open and alerting a perfectly ordinary guard. It was entirely possible that one or more of those tiresome scouts had been posted here, and Falconsbane had no intention of walking into one of them.

Still, there seemed to be nothing at all blocking his way as he approached the site of the nest. Finally he straightened, and moved into the open, taking a deliberate pace or two forward before the young ones noticed him.

They looked at him curiously, with their heads cocked to one side, as if they had never seen him before. He smiled with satisfaction.

Good. The spell I cast before I left them, to cloud their memories, worked. They do not fear me, so they will not call for help until it is too late.

"Hello, little ones," he purred, and moved into the open. But then something fluttering on the ground caught his eye, and he stopped, suddenly wary.

Flowers. Feathers. Rocks laid in deliberate patterns that teased his memory; he paused for a moment, frowning, as he tried to match pattern with memory.

Then he recognized it for what it was.

So that's the plan, is it? He noted the position of the lone brown pinecone. *I think not.*

He stood very still, listening for movement behind him. There—the scrape of leather on stone; the whisper of wood on wood, sliding.

Oh, I think not, young fool.

He whirled, both hands spread before him, and caught the white-clad young man full in the chest with the bolt of magic, before the Outlander could loose the arrow he had nocked to his bowstring.

A second power-blast left Falconsbane's hands before the first reached its target; this one aimed, not at the man, but at the horse behind him. The "horse" that radiated the same kind of power as some of those damned nomad shamans.

The bow snapped, the arrow shattered, and the young man was blasted off his feet to land in an unconscious heap some distance away.

The "horse" toppled like a fallen tree.

Mornelithe smiled with great satisfaction. He had deliberately held back his strength when he recognized the Outlander clothing. He wanted to—discuss a few things with this young man.

But a feline shriek of pure rage tore through the air, startling him, and he turned again as Nyara—*Nyara?*—leapt upon him, teeth and talons bared, prepared to rip his throat out.

He had no time for other than a purely instinctive reaction; he backhanded her with all his strength, catching her in mid-leap, and sending her flying across the clearing and into the two young gryphons. There was a squeal of outrage from the largest as Nyara landed atop it, and a squawl of fear from the smallest.

But there was another attack coming—

He drew his arms up in a defensive gesture, his powers massing around him in his shields as bolts of mage-energies blasted him from either side.

"What's he doing?" Elspeth whispered to Darkwind, as the Adept calling himself "Mornelithe Falconsbane" paused just outside the ambush zone. He was certainly everything that Darkwind and Nyara's stories had painted him.

Her very first sight of him had terrified her, despite having seen his daughter Nyara and fought his monsters, the things Darkwind called "Misborn," and she had no idea why. Perhaps it was the fact that Falconsbane was so obviously once human, but had given up that humanity. Perhaps it was the cold and focused quality of his gaze. Perhaps it was simply what she knew of him. Darkwind had confided to her—and her only, perhaps because he trusted her, perhaps he thought these were things she in particular needed to hear—some of the horrors that Iceshadow had extracted from Starblade. Nyara wore a haunted look that made her certain—horrible as the idea was—that Falconsbane had visited some of those same torments on his own daughter.

Yet what she knew of him was no worse than some of what she had learned concerning Ancar. Neither made for easy dreams . . . but Falconsbane was nearer right now than Ancar.

I might feel the same way about Ancar, if I ever see him.

Falconsbane was surely the stuff of which nightmares were made; there was very little of the human left after all the changes he had wrought upon himself, but the effect he had created was of something warped, and not for the better. If one took a lynx, sculpted a perfect human body with a half-human face, then granted it an aura of power that was nothing like anything she had ever experienced before—it still would not be Mornelithe Falconsbane. He was sinister and beautiful, all at the same time, and Elspeth found herself shivering at the mere sight of him.

He had simply appeared, some time after Vree's cry of warning. She had not seen him approach; he was simply *there,* standing amid the rocks, looking down at the earth. "What is he looking at?" she repeated, as Darkwind frowned.

"I don't—*shaeka!*" he spat.

She had no chance to ask him what was wrong; even as he rose to a half-crouch, Falconsbane whirled and dropped to one knee, arms outstretched, hands palm out. Elspeth's stomach knotted with fear.

Darkwind uttered a strangled cry and rose to his feet, flinging one hand protectively toward Skif.

Too late. Elspeth choked on a cry of horror as Falconsbane's bolt of magic struck Skif and threw him into the stones of a ruined wall.

And too late for Cymry, as well; a second bolt struck her, dropping her where she stood like a stricken deer.

Elspeth's horrified *"No!"* was lost in the scream of pure hatred that tore the air like a jagged blade as Skif's limp body dropped to the stones beyond Cymry's.

It was Nyara, leaping in defense of Skif, who attacked her father with the only weapons at her disposal; her claws and teeth, her face a snarling animal-mask of pain, anguish, and hatred.

He intercepted her in mid-leap, and with a single blow of his powerful arm, flung her across the open space to land stunned atop the largest of the young gryphons.

There was no time to wonder if Skif and Cymry survived; no time even to think. She bottled her fear, her anger, though they made her want to run to her old friend's side—or run and hide. The Hawkbrother had joined in combat with the Changechild Adept, and there was no turning back now. Elspeth joined her power to Darkwind's, feeding him with the raw energy she drew up from the node. He knew how to use it; she could only watch and learn—for when he tired, it would be her turn to strike. From the other side, lances of fire rained down on Falconsbane, power pouring from the outstretched claws of Treyvan, with his mate backing him as she backed Darkwind.

For a moment, it was impossible to see the Adept beneath the double attack—and during that moment she dared to hope.

But then, a shadow appeared amid the glare of power—then more than a shadow—then—

Pain.

She thought she cried out; she certainly fell back a pace or two and covered her eyes with her upraised arm, as Darkwind's blast of power reflected back into their faces.

When she blinked her tearing eyes clear, Falconsbane stood untouched, within a circle of scorched earth.

Darkwind had taken the brunt of the blast on their side, as had Treyvan on the gryphons'. Treyvan crouched with head hanging, panting; Darkwind was on his knees beside her, shaking his own head, dazed and unable to speak.

Falconsbane ignored the rest and concentrated his cold gaze on her. Her stomach turned into a cold ball of ice. He smiled, and she stepped back another pace, her hand reaching for a sword she no longer wore, palms sweating, feeling the blood drain from her face.

"Well," he said, his voice full of amusement. "So you have some fight still. I will enjoy breaking you, Outlander." His eyes narrowed, and his voice lowered to a seductive purr. "I will enjoy taking both your mind and your body—"

"Not this day," called a high voice, in pure Shin'a'in, from the ruins behind Falconsbane.

Falconsbane's head snapped around; Elspeth gathered her primitive, clumsy power just in case this was nothing more than a ruse.

But there were people behind the Adept; perched atop rocks, peering from behind walls, an entire line of people. Black-clad, one and all, some veiled, some not, but all with the same cold, implacable purpose in their ice-blue eyes. And one and all with drawn bows pointed at Falconsbane's heart.

"Not this day, nor any other," Darkwind coughed, struggling to his feet. Elspeth gave him a hand, and stood beside him, helping him balance. He did not look to be in any shape to enforce those brave words; he swayed as he stood, even with Elspeth's unobtrusive support, and his face was drawn with pain.

But there were all those arrows pointed at Falconsbane; surely they had him now—didn't they?

Or did they?

After the first flash of surprise, Falconsbane straightened again and laughed, sending a chill down Elspeth's back. "Do you think me so poor a player, then, to show all my counters before the game is over?"

Elspeth did not even have a chance to wonder what he meant.

She had *no* idea of where the thing came from, but suddenly it was dropping down out of the clouds—a huge, black, bat-winged creature that seemed big enough to swallow her whole and have room for Gwena afterward. It buffeted her with its wings, knocking her off her feet with a single blow, then slammed her into a rock—all the breath was driven out of her by the impact; her head snapped back against the stone, and she slid down it, seeing stars.

She blacked out for a moment, but fought back from the dark abyss that threatened to swallow her consciousness. As she struggled back, shaking her head and swallowing the bile of nausea, Falconsbane laughed again.

Her eyes cleared. That was when she saw that there were two of the things. One of them had Hydona trapped beneath it, its talons on her throat, ready to rip it out if she struggled. She looked out helplessly as the creature drew blood and looked expectantly at its master. Then Elspeth could only stare in horror—

The other had Gwena in the same position.

Darkwind lay in a heap just beyond her; eyes closed, unmoving. Treyvan faced the beast that had his mate with every feather and hair standing on end, kill-lust making him tremble. Muscles rippled as he restrained himself from attacking, and the stone beneath his talons flaked away in little chips from the pressure of his claws.

:Gwena—: she Sent.

:Don't!: the Companion shot back. :Don't move, don't anger it!: Her mind-voice died to a whisper as the beast tightened its grip on her, and little beads of blood stained her white coat under its talons. :Don't do anything. Please.:

"Stalemate, I think?" Falconsbane said genially. The

arrows of the Shin'a'in did not waver, but neither did the archers loose them.

"Well, then. In that case, I think I shall fetch what I came for."

Hydona uttered a wail that was choked off by the brutal grip of the beast prisoning her. Treyvan seethed with rage, eyes burning with fury.

"*It is not yours, Changechild,*" said one of the Shin'a'in, in a hollow voice that sounded as if it came up from the depths of a well. "*It was not made by you, it does not obey you; it is not yours.*"

Falconsbane lifted an eyebrow. And half-turned to lash out with yet another bolt of power; this one aimed at the young gryphons, a flood of poisonous red.

"*NO!*"

The cry was torn from Elspeth's throat—but from others as well. One of those others was free to act.

Nyara leapt to her feet, her hands full of Need's hilt, holding it between herself and her father. The bolt of power struck the blade instead of the young gryphons, and built with an ear-shattering wail as Need collected the blast—

And changed it; from sickly red to burnished gold. Elspeth's heart stopped as she watched, not fully understanding what was happening but fearing the worst. She heard Darkwind mutter something about "transmuting," and then he trailed off into a stream of what she guessed to be incredulous Tayledras curses.

Need split the sphere of power in two, one half enveloping each young gryphon, filling them with light. Falconsbane's scream of rage drowned Elspeth's gasp of joy, but it could not stop what was happening. The golden light burned away at a kind of shadow within the two youngsters—the shadows melted even as she watched, melted and evaporated, leaving them clean of its taint.

Distracted by the light and their master's cry of outrage, Mornelithe's dark beasts loosed their grip a little.

Darkwind moved.

Faster than a striking viper, he whipped the climbing-stick that never left him from the sheath on his back, and hooked it into the beast's throat. He never gave the creature a chance to realize what had happened; he yanked the hook toward himself, giving Gwena the opening to kick and buck herself free of it as the creature tried to both right itself and disengage the hook that was tearing its flesh from inside. The Companion scrambled out of the way, sides heaving, legs trembling, blood pouring from a dozen puncture wounds, to collapse at Elspeth's feet.

The creature paid her no heed; all of its attention was taken up with Darkwind.

Elspeth hovered protectively over Gwena; the Companion was shaking like an aspen leaf in the wind, but her wounds were already closing. She leapt up to stand between Gwena and the beast, but there was no need for her protection. She had wondered about Darkwind's peculiar weapontool; now she saw how an expert used it.

Darkwind's face was contorted into a snarl of rage as he attacked the creature, forcing it to go on the defensive; the spiked end of the tool drove into an eye, blinding the beast, as Darkwind backed it into a rock and it staggered. He slashed in a broad flat stroke, laying the beast's belly open, and it fell forward to protect itself. It screamed, and Darkwind reversed the stick, hooking the beast's mouth and tearing at the tongue and lips. It tried to buffet him with its wings, screaming as its eye and mouth dripped thick, brownish blood; he simply hooked the membrane of the wings and tore them, while he ducked under claw-strikes, or fended them off with the spike. Every time there was an opening, he darted in and stabbed again with the spike; he wasn't yet doing the beast lethal damage, but he had to be causing it a lot of pain. It bled from a dozen wounds now, and Darkwind showed no signs of tiring.

Screams of bestial pain from across the court made her dare a glance in that direction. Hydona, bleeding, but still full of fight, stood defiantly between Falconsbane and her children. Her wings were at full spread, mantling over her young, every feather on end. Treyvan clung to the back of the other beast, trying to sever its spine, each strike succeeding in removing a foot-long strip of meat from its neck. The creature screamed and tried in vain to throw him off, leathery wings flailing. No matter the gryphon was half this beast's size; he was going to win. Treyvan was astride the beast's back even if it tried to roll, his claws gouging deep and holding fast with its every swift move, then moving upward as if he was walking up the thing's back like it was a rock, driving deep holes in with every step, and taking a clump of meat with him at every opportunity. Elspeth swallowed in surprise; she had imagined what the gryphons' fearsome natural weaponry could do, but actually seeing it was another matter.

Falconsbane seemed to be ignoring both the beasts, his attention fixed on the Shin'a'in. A moment later she knew why, as a flight of arrows sang toward him, only to be incinerated a few arm's lengths away.

Another scream in her ear reminded her that there was equal danger, nearer at hand. Darkwind's beast was holding its own against him now, and even regaining a little ground, its one good eye mad with rage and fixed on its target. Even if Treyvan won his contest, he could still lose if this beast killed Darkwind.

She had to help him, somehow—

One good eye—

She acted with the thought; dropped one of her knives into her hand from its arm-sheath, aimed, and threw, as one of the beast's lunges brought that good eye into range.

It missed, bouncing off the eye-ridge. The creature didn't even notice.

She swore, and dropped her second knife, as Darkwind slipped on blood-slick rock and fell.

Crap!

The beast lunged with snapping jaws, managing to catch his leg in its teeth. He screamed and beat at the beast's head with his stick, trying to pry the jaws apart, stabbing at the eye.

Suddenly calm, Elspeth waited dispassionately for her target to hold still a moment—and threw.

The creature let Darkwind go, throwing its head up and howling in agony—and instead of scrambling out of the way as Elspeth expected, Darkwind lunged upward with the pointed end of his staff, plunging it into newly-revealed soft skin at the base of the thing's throat, and leaning on it as hard as he could.

The creature clawed at the stick, at him, falling over sideways and emitting gurgling cries as he continued to lean into the point, thrashing and trying to dislodge it from its throat, all with no success. Darkwind's eyes streamed tears of pain, and he sobbed under his breath, but he continued to drive the point deeper and deeper.

It died, breathing out bubbles of blood, still trying to free itself.

Across the stretch of scorched earth, Treyvan had clawed his way up his enemy's back to the join of neck and spine. As Elspeth looked briefly away from Darkwind's beast, Treyvan buried his beak in his foe's neck, and jerked his head once. The beast collapsed beneath him.

Treyvan's battle shriek of triumph was drowned in Falconsbane's roar of rage.

Before anyone could move, the Adept howled again, his eyes black with hate, his hands rending the air as he clawed at it. Elspeth did not realize he was making a magical gesture until an oily green-brown smoke billowed up from the ground at his feet, filling the space between the ruined walls in an instant, completely obscuring everything that it rolled over.

Poison! That was her first, panic-stricken thought, as the cloud washed over her before she could scramble out of its path. There was a hum of dozens of bowstrings as the Shin'a'in loosed their arrows.

But though the thick, fetid smoke made her cough uncontrollably and brought tears to her eyes, it didn't seem to be hurting her any. She reached out a tentative Mindtouch for Gwena.

:I'll be all right,: came the weak reply. *:Don't move; the nomads are still shooting.:*

And indeed, she heard bowstrings sing and the hiss of arrows nearby. But not a great deal else.

"Darkwind?" she called. "Are you all right?"

"As well as may be, lady," he replied promptly, pain filling his voice. He coughed. "Stand fast, I am going to disperse this. I have enough power for that, at least."

A moment later, a fresh wind cut through the fog, thinning it in heartbeats, blowing it away altogether as Elspeth took in deep, grateful breaths of clean air and knuckled her eyes until they stopped tearing.

She looked first for Falconsbane; he was no longer there, but where he had stood were dozens of arrows stuck point-first into the earth—and leading away from the place was a trail of blood.

That was all she had time to recognize; in the next moment, a surge of powerful energy somewhere nearby disoriented her for a moment. She might have written it off as a spasm of dizziness, had she not seen Darkwind's face.

He stared off into the ruins, his mouth set in a grim line.

"He used the last of his energies to set a Gate-spell back to his stronghold," the Hawkbrother said, bitterly. "*Shaeka*. He has escaped us."

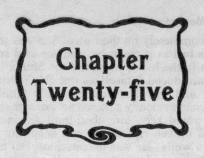

Chapter
Twenty-five

This isn't finished yet.

Tension still in the air knotted her guts like tangled yarn. And it wasn't just Falconsbane, either. Something was going to happen. There was unfinished business here—but whose it was—she couldn't tell.

The trail of blood ended in a little pool of sticky scarlet, directly in front of an archway in a ruined wall, or so said the Shin'a'in who had followed it to its end. There wasn't any reason for them to lie, and although they did seem a bit too calm and detached for Elspeth's liking, she assumed she could trust them. Darkwind apparently did. He made no effort to see for himself, but simply allowed the Vale Healer to continue working on him, although his lips moved with what Elspeth suspected were curses.

Elspeth swore under her breath herself as she tested Cymry's legs for any more damage than simple bruises and sprains. Skif's Companion was suffering mostly from shock; somehow between them, the Companion and Darkwind had managed to shield Skif and herself from the worst of Falconsbane's blows. That was nothing short of a miracle.

Gwena's talon-punctures had been treated, and would

soon heal completely on their own. She was in pain, but it wasn't as bad as it could be, and she said so.

Skif was in the hands of one of the Shin'a'in, the one who had introduced himself as the Tale'sedrin shaman, Kra'heera, and who had seemed oddly familiar to Elspeth. Skif had evidently suffered no worse than a cracked skull that would keep him abed until dizziness passed, and several broken ribs that would keep him out of the saddle for a while. He was unconscious, but not dangerously so. Nyara had satisfied herself on that score even before Elspeth and had taken a place by his side with Need in her hands. Since the blade's Healing power was working on the cat-woman's hurts, and might well aid Kra'heera's efforts with Skif if Nyara managed to persuade the blade, Elspeth saw no reason to take it away from her.

She herself had gotten off lightly, with scratches and cuts; but Darkwind and Treyvan looked like badly-butchered meat. When Hydona had flown limpingly into the Vale to fetch help, the Vale's own Healer had timidly come out of protection to treat them and bandage them, then had scuttled back to safety like a frightened mouse. Elspeth didn't think much of him; oh, his skills were quite excellent—but she didn't think highly of any Healer who wouldn't stay with his patients until he knew they were well. Darkwind saw her thinly-veiled scorn, though, and he'd promised an explanation.

It better be a good one.

The Shin'a'in were still searching the ruins for Falconsbane, though Darkwind was certain that he was long gone out of reach, and Elspeth agreed with him

Of them all, only the gryphons were happy, despite wounds and pain. Somehow Need had transmuted the power of Falconsbane's magic into something that burned the little ones clean of his taint. Need might not think much of her own abilities, compared with Elspeth's potential, but Darkwind was impressed. Transmuting was evidently a very rare ability. The adults had taken the young ones to the lair and curled up in there, refusing to budge unless it were direst emergency.

Beside her, Darkwind leaned back against the rock supporting him, and stared at the red-shouldered hawk perched above the door of the lair, her head up and into the wind, her wings slightly mantled. He looked haunted, somehow. As she studied his face, Elspeth thought she read pain and anxiety there, though it was hard to tell what the Hawkbrother was truly feeling.

But when he looked at Dawnfire, *that* was when the feeling of tension solidified.

It's her. That's what isn't finished. She can't stay the way she is—

She wrapped Cymry's foreleg to add support, and looked over at the bird herself.

Dawnfire—what were they going to do about *her*? She was still trapped in the body of a bird.

Even the Shin'a'in seem to feel sorry for her—or something.

The Shin'a'in were returning from their hunt by ones and twos, all of them gathering as if by prearrangement on the area below Dawnfire's perch, all of them silent. They seemed in no hurry to leave, and Elspeth mostly ignored them in favor of the task at hand despite the growing tension in the air. Even if something was about to happen, there wasn't much she could do about it.

Then Cymry's nervous snort made her look up.

As far as she could tell, all of the Shin'a'in had returned and now they were standing in a rough circle below Dawnfire. All but the shaman, that is; he had left Skif and now knelt beside Darkwind, with an odd expression as if he were waiting. . . .

This is it. This is what I've been feeling—this is the cause of all the tension and pressure—

Were they glowing slightly, or was that only her imagination? There seemed to be a hazy dome of light covering them all.

One of the Shin'a'in, a woman by the build, finally moved.

Kra'heera grabbed Darkwind's shoulders and physically restrained him from standing up, as the woman put up a hand to Dawnfire. The bird stared measuringly at her for a moment, then stepped down from her perch onto the proffered hand, and the woman turned to face the rest.

Like all the others, this one was clad entirely in black, from her long black hair to her black armor, to her tall black boots. But there was something wrong with her eyes . . . something odd.

Darkwind struggled in earnest against the shaman, but he was too weak to squirm out of Kra'heera's hands. "Be silent, boy!" the shaman hissed at him as he continued to fight. "Have *you* any life to offer her? Would you watch her fade before your eyes until there is nothing left of her?"

Elspeth paid scant attention to them, concentrating instead on the black-clad woman who had taken Dawnfire. There was something very unusual about her—a feeling of contained power. Elspeth Felt the stirring of a kind of deeply-running energy she had never experienced before, and found herself holding her breath.

The woman raised Dawnfire high above her head and held her there, a position that must have been a torment after a few moments, and as she did so, the entire group started to hum.

Softly, then increasing slowly in volume, until the ruins rang with the harmonics—and Dawnfire began to glow.

At first Elspeth thought it was just a trick of the setting sun, touching the bird's feathers and making them seem to give off their own light. But then, the light grew brighter instead of darker, and Dawnfire straightened and spread her wings—and began to grow larger as well as brighter.

Within heartbeats, Elspeth couldn't even look at her directly. In a few moments more, she was averting her face, though Darkwind continued to stare, squinting, into the light, a look of desperation on his face. The light from the bird's outstretched wings was bright enough to cast shadows; the black-clad Shin'a'in seeming to be shadows themselves, until the bird appeared to be ruling over a host of shades.

The Shin'a'in shaman caught her staring at him. He met her eyes, then returned to gaze fearlessly into the light, and seemed to sense her questions. "Dawnfire has been chosen by the Warrior," he said, as if that explained everything.

Oh, thanks. Now of course I understand. I understand why a hawk is flaming brighter than any firebird; I un-

*derstand why Darkwind looks as if he's at an execution.
What in Havens is going on?*

Gwena looked at her as if the Companion had read those
thoughts. *:It's business,:* she said shortly, *:And not ours.:*

And I suppose that's going to tell me everything.

Darkwind's eyes streamed tears, and she longed to
comfort him, but she sensed she dared not; not at this
moment, anyway.

The light was dying now, along with the humming, as
she looked back toward the circle of Shin'a'in.

The bird on the female fighter's fist was no longer a
red-shouldered hawk; it was a vorcel-hawk, the emblem
of the Shin'a'in Clan Tale'sedrin, and the largest such
bird Elspeth had ever seen. The light had dimmed in the
bird's feathers, but it had not entirely died, and there was
an other-worldly quality about the hawk's eyes that made
her start with surprise.

Then she recognized it; the same look as the female
fighter's. There were neither whites nor pupils to the
woman's eyes, nor to the bird's—only a darkness, sprin-
kled with sparks of light, as if, rather than eyes, Elspeth
looked upon fields of stars.

That was when she remembered where she had heard
of such a thing. The Chronicles—Roald's description of
the Shin'a'in Goddess.

Her mouth dried in an instant, and her heart pounded.
If she was right—this was a Goddess—

And Dawnfire was now Her chosen avatar.

And at that moment, she found she couldn't move. She
was frozen in place, as a string of bridleless black horses
filed into the clear area, led by no one, each going to a
Shin'a'in and waiting.

The Shin'a'in mounted up, quite literally as one, and
rode out in single file; the woman and the hawk last,
heading for the path that wound around the ruins and led
down into the Plains. Those two paused for just a moment, black silhouettes against the red-gold sky, sunlight
streaming around them, as they looked back.

Darkwind uttered an inarticulate moan. It might have
been Dawnfire's name; it might not.

Then they were gone.

* * *

Sunset did not bring darkness; Darkwind and Treyvan used their magecraft to kindle a couple of mage-lights apiece, and they all crowded into the lair. Right now, no one wanted to face the night shadows.

Darkwind looks as if he's lost. Not that I blame him. He and Dawnfire were . . . were close. Whatever happened to her, I have the feeling she's pretty well gone from his life.

"Where's Nyara?" Skif said, struggling to sit up, the bandage around his head obscuring one eye.

"Right there." Elspeth glanced at the niche among the stones by the door that Nyara had been occupying since the fight, Need on her lap, only to find her gone. And she didn't recall seeing the girl move.

Darkwind glanced up at the same time, on hearing Skif's voice; their eyes met across Nyara's now-empty resting place.

"I didn't see her leave," Darkwind began.

"Nor did I," Elspeth replied grimly. "And she's got my sword."

:What do you mean, your sword?: Need's Mind-voice asked testily, the quality hollow and thin, as if crossing a bit of distance. Elspeth had started to get to her feet; she froze at the touch of the Mind-voice, and a glance at Darkwind showed he had heard it, too.

:I'm not your sword, Elspeth, I'm not anybody's sword. I go to whom I choose. And frankly, child, you don't require my services anymore. You're a fine fighter; a natural, in fact. You're going to be a better mage than I am. And you are ridiculously healthy in mind and body. Nyara, on the other hand. . . . : A feeling of pity crept into the sword's tone. *:Let's just say she's a challenge to any Healer. And if she's not going to fall back into her father's hands, I figured I'd better take an interest in her. she needs me more than you ever would.:*

The mind-voice began to fade. *:Fare well, child. We'll see you again, I think.:*

Then it was gone.

Elspeth stared at Darkwind with a mingled feeling of relief and annoyance. At least this meant there was one less thing to fight, but she'd gotten used to having the blade around to depend on.

I'd gotten used to it—well, maybe she was right. If

what she told us was the truth, she never let anyone depend *on her powers. . . .*

"Do you think the artifact will be strong enough to keep Nyara out of *his* hands?" Darkwind asked, worriedly.

Elspeth shrugged. "I don't know. She was strong enough to turn Falconsbane's spell against him."

Darkwind nodded, slowly; his face was in shadow so that Elspeth could not read it, but she had the feeling he was somehow at war within himself. As if he was both relieved that Nyara was gone, and regretting the fact.

Then he moved a little, and the cold light showed a look of such naked loss and loneliness that Elspeth looked away, unable to bear it.

She turned to Skif instead, who was still trying to sit up. "Nyara," he said fretfully, squinting at her. He was doubtless experiencing double vision, and a headache bad enough to wish he were dead. "Where's Nyara? Is she all right?"

"Need's taking care of her," Elspeth told him, giving him the bare truth. "She's fine."

Satisfied, he stopped trying to fight his way into a sitting position, and permitted her to feed him one of the herbal painkillers she had picked up in Kata'shin'a'in. Shortly after that, he was snoring; and she looked up to find Darkwind gone as well, taking his thoughts and his pain into the night.

She hugged her knees to her chest and waited for a while, but he did not return. Finally she went to bed, where she lay for a long time, listening to Skif's drug-induced snores and the young gryphlets making baby noises in the next room.

It was a long night.

Darkwind returned to the gryphon's lair late the next morning; it had been a long night for him, as well, and it had ended with a morning session of the Council of Elders.

He had found himself in the odd position of Council Leader; he was not certain he liked it. Virtually anything he thought to be a good idea would be adopted at this point, when his credit was so high with the rest of the

Elders, but how was he to know whether what he wanted was going to be good for the rest of the Vale?

Especially where these Outlanders were concerned.

But he wanted them to stay. Although he was tired, heartsore, and uncertain of many things, of that much he was sure.

He found the young woman outside the Lair, taking advantage of a cool breeze and a chance, at last, to rest in the open without fear of attack. She rose on seeing him, and he made idle talk for a moment before finally coming to the subject.

"Falconsbane is gone; perhaps for good. Your sword is no longer with you. I can and will direct you to a teacher among the Vales, and k'Sheyna is not likely to be a comfortable place to live for a while. So what is it you would do now?" he asked, refusing to meet Elspeth's eyes. "There is no need for you to stay."

She set her chin stubbornly. "You promised to teach me magic; are you going back on that promise?"

"No," he replied slowly. *Is this wise? Perhaps not— but I am weary of being wise.* "But—"

"Does the Council want us to leave?" She looked very unhappy at that idea; he rubbed his hand across his tired eyes. Was it only she thought there would be opposition that she would have to fight without an advocate if she went to another Vale?

"No, not at all," he said wearily. "No—it is—I thought perhaps you and Skif—"

"Skif isn't going to leave here unless you force him to," she told him bluntly. "It's that simple. He can't travel any time soon, and after that—" She shrugged. "He may go home, he may decide to stay, that's up to him. Nyara's out there somewhere; he may decide to try to find her, and personally, I think he will. But *I* plan on staying, if you're still willing to teach me."

"I am," he replied soberly, "But I must warn you that I have never taught before. And you are a dangerous kind of pupil; you come late to this, and you wield a great deal of power, very clumsily."

She bristled a little. "I haven't exactly had a chance to practice," she retorted. "I don't think you'll find me unwilling to work, or too inflexible to learn."

"I, too, will be a kind of pupil," he reminded her. "I

have not used my powers in a long time; I shall have to relearn them before I can teach you."

But it is easier for two than one. And my friends are few enough. Elspeth has become one.

She shrugged. "If you don't care, I don't. What I do care about is that you can teach me as quickly as I can learn. I don't have a lot of time to spend here."

Dark thoughts shadowed her face; he guessed they were thoughts of home, and all that could be taking place there. He softened a little, understanding those worries only too well. "If you will give me your best, I will give you mine," he replied.

She met his eyes at last. "I never give less than my best," she said.

He glanced at the slumbering Skif out of the corner of his eye. "Not even to him?" he asked, a little cruelly, but unable to help himself. *You must know yourself, strengths and weaknesses, before you dare magic.*

"I gave Skif my best," she replied instantly, without a wince. "It just wasn't what he thought he wanted. He's still my friend."

He nodded, satisfied, and rose, holding out his hand to her. "In that case, lady, gather your things again."

This time she did wince. "Why? Did you change your mind just now about throwing us out?" She sounded a little desperate.

"No." He stared at the forest for a moment, wondering again if he was doing the right thing.

But he was doing something, and his heart told him it was right. And that was infinitely better than doing nothing.

"No . . . no, Elspeth," he replied after a moment, tasting the flavor of the strange name, and finding he liked it. "I have not changed my mind. As soon as you are ready, I will have Skif brought to the Vale, and conduct you there myself." He turned toward her and found himself smiling at the look of complete surprise she wore. "You have succeeded in winning a place where no Outlander has been for generations."

He clasped her forearm in his hand, searching in her eyes for a moment . . . then speaking to her softly.

"As Council Leader of Vale k'Sheyna, I offer you the sanctuary and peace of the Vale; I offer you the honor

and responsibility of the Clan. If you will take it, I give
you the name Elspeth k'Sheyna k'Valdemar. . . ."

Somewhere overhead, a forestgyre called his approval
as he rode the winds, watching over the forest; for Vree's
bondmate had begun his healing at last.

Author's Note:

Just as the Companions are *not* horses as we know them, so the Tayledras bondbirds are *not* hawks and falcons. They have been genetically altered to make them larger, more intelligent, telepathic, and *far* more social than any terrestrial bird of prey. The "real thing" bears the same resemblance to a bondbird as a German Shepherd does to a jackal.

The ancient art of falconry can be thrilling and enjoyable, but the falconer must be prepared to devote as much or more time to it as he would his job. The birds must be fed, trained, and exercised every day without fail, and frequently will not permit anyone but their handler to feed them. For the most part, the falconer must make all his own equipment. And in order to obtain the licenses for his sport, he must pass a lengthy Federal examination, and the facilities for his bird must pass a Federal inspection. The licenses themselves must be obtained from both the Federal and State governments. All native birds are protected species, and possession without a permit is subject to a Federal fine as well as confiscation of the bird. The Apprentice falconer is only permitted to train and fly the red-tailed hawk or the kestrel (North American sparrowhawk), and must do so under the auspices of a Master. This is not a hobby to be taken on lightly, nor is it one that can be put in a closet on a rainy day, or if the falconer doesn't feel well that day. For the most part, birds of prey are not capable of "affection" for their handler, and the best one can expect is tolerance and acceptance. Falconers speak of "serving" their bird, and that is very much the case, for this is a partnership in which the bird has the upper hand, and can choose at any moment to dissolve the relationship and fly away. And frequently, she does just that.

Falconers are single-handedly responsible for keeping the population of North American peregrine falcons alive. They were the first to notice the declining numbers, the first to make the connection between DDT and too-fragile eggshells, and the first to begin captive breeding programs to save the breed from extinction. They are intensely involved in conservation at all levels, and are vitally interested in preserving the wilderness for all future generations.

Mercedes Lackey

The Novels of Valdemar

DAW

A note from the publishers concerning:

QUEEN'S OWN

You are invited to join "Queen's Own," an organization of readers and fans of the works of Mercedes (Misty) Lackey. This appreciation society has a worldwide membership of all ages. Nominal dues are charged.

"Queen's Own" publishes a newsletter 9 times a year, providing information about Mercedes Lackey's upcoming books, tapes, convention appearances, and more. A network of pen friends is also available for those who wish to share their enjoyment of her work.

For more information, please send a business-size SASE (self-addressed stamped envelope) to:

"Queen's Own"
P.O. Box 132
Shiloh, NJ 08353

(This notice is inserted gratis as a service to readers. DAW Books is in no way connected with this organization professionally or commercially.)

MARION ZIMMER BRADLEY

THE DARKOVER NOVELS

☐ DARKOVER LANDFALL UE2234—$3.99

☐ HAWKMISTRESS! UE2239—$4.99
☐ STORMQUEEN! UE2310—$4.99

☐ TWO TO CONQUER UE2174—$4.99
☐ THE HEIRS OF HAMMERFELL UE2451—$4.99

☐ THE SHATTERED CHAIN UE2308—$4.50
☐ THENDARA HOUSE UE2240—$4.99
☐ CITY OF SORCERY UE2332—$4.99

☐ REDISCOVERY* UE2529—$4.99
☐ REDISCOVERY (hardcover)* UE2561—$18.00
☐ THE SPELL SWORD UE2237—$3.99
☐ THE FORBIDDEN TOWER UE2373—$4.99
☐ STAR OF DANGER UE2607—$4.99
☐ THE WINDS OF DARKOVER
& THE PLANET SAVERS UE2630—$4.99

☐ THE BLOODY SUN UE2603—$4.99
☐ THE HERITAGE OF HASTUR UE2413—$4.99
☐ SHARRA'S EXILE UE2309—$4.99
☐ THE WORLD WRECKERS UE2629—$4.99

*with Mercedes Lackey

Tad Williams

Memory, Sorrow and Thorn

THE DRAGONBONE CHAIR: Book 1
☐ **Hardcover Edition**   0-8099-003-3—$19.50
☐ **Paperback Edition**   UE2384—$6.99

A war fueled by the dark powers of sorcery is about to engulf the long-peaceful land of Osten Ard—as the Storm King, undead ruler of the elvishlike Sithi, seeks to regain his lost realm through a pact with one of human royal blood. And to Simon, a former castle scullion, will go the task of spearheading the quest that offers the only hope of salvation . . . a quest that will see him fleeing and facing enemies straight out of a legend-maker's worst nightmares!

STONE OF FAREWELL: Book 2
☐ **Hardcover Edition**   UE2435—$21.95
☐ **Paperback Edition**   UE2480—$6.99

As the dark magic and dread minions of the undead Sithi ruler spread their seemingly undefeatable evil across the land, the tattered remnants of a once-proud human army flee in search of a last sanctuary and rallying point, and the last survivors of the League of the Scroll seek to fulfill missions which will take them from the fallen citadels of humans to the secret heartland of the Sithi.

TO GREEN ANGEL TOWER: Book 3
☐ **Hardcover Edition**   UE2521—$25.00
☐ **Paperback Edition, Part I**   UE2598—$5.99
☐ **Paperback Edition, Part II**   UE2606—$5.99

In this concluding volume of the best-selling trilogy, the forces of Prince Josua march toward their final confrontation with the dread minions of the undead Storm King, while Simon, Miriamele, and Binabek embark on a desperate mission into evil's stronghold.
